Too Lucky
To Live

Books by Annie Hogsett

Somebody's Bound to Wind Up Dead Mysteries
Too Lucky to Live

Too Lucky to Live

A Somebody's Bound to
Wind Up Dead Mystery

Annie Hogsett

Poisoned Pen Press

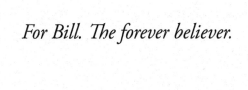

For Bill. The forever believer.

Gratitude

To my family, Bill and John, who didn't laugh when I sat down to write, even when I was inclined to doubt myself. Extra kudos to Bill who always encouraged me to take risks and honor my ambition. For Vicky and Chet—a sister and brother for me. And to Cujo the cat, my warmest, furriest friend. You were always there for me. Biting my ankles. Begging for food.

To my family of origin. Mark and Margaret. My father's legacy came via the memories of people who witnessed his love for me in a time I don't remember. Obviously, love is one kind of immortality. My mother's confidence that I was destined for wondrous things ferried me over my own doubts about a million times. Momma, after you died I found a book in which you'd underlined the author's counsel to: "Write something every day." And in the margin you'd penciled, "Ann."

To Tina Whittle for solid advice, cheerleading, better ideas, empathy, networking, and Left Coast

Crime. You helped me find my voice and my tribe. And to Lynn Lilly, for helping me feel good about my work, teaching me the power of revision, and, of course, for introducing me to Tina Whittle.

To Rip Ruhlman for taking my manuscript to read when you had no time to spare. And for always making me feel confident and appreciated. Rip, we were robbed when we lost you.

To Thrity Umrigar, amazing author, stalwart friend. When you said I was good, I was pretty sure you knew what good is. I owe you for that. And for Victoria.

To my agent Victoria Skurnick for sound advice, steadfast efforts on my behalf, and a speed-of-light response rate that dazzles every time. So grateful for your wisdom and kindness.

To Poisoned Pen Press. Everybody. My editor, Annette Rogers, who believed in my story and gave me courage to make it better. To Barbara Peters, who provided polish and fresh inspiration. To all the rest of the team, especially Rob Rosenwald, Diane DiBiase, and Beth Deveny, and the "Posse" of authors who made me feel welcome in their midst, even before I was one of them.

To Melissa Woods for help with permissions.

To Tony DeRoss and Adam Tully for advice about hospitals and libraries, respectively.

To the Northeast Ohio Sisters In Crime and The Persistent Fictioneers, for solidarity.

To my book groups. Reading with you all reminds me of why I love to write.

Group #1: Anne, Cathy, Elaine, Fran, Ida, Jane, Karen, Susan, Terry, Traci. You encouraged me from the beginning, read the earliest version, never gave up, and honored me with your friendship.

Group #2: Bernice, James, Janice, Juanita, Linda, Louise, Mary, Pat, Peggy, Rick, Vivian. You cheered me home. And never let me drown.

To my host of friends. You make the fun and bring the love. As far as I'm concerned, without fun and love there's nothing worth writing about.

Elaine Martone, who has always been there with courage for the work, support for the disappointments, and champagne for the celebrations. And friendship forever.

Laura Starnik, who's walking the same path with different goals. Some things are worth waiting for.

Joe and Mary Lucille (and Pat, behind the scenes), you have been my writer's group and more. Support. Sustenance. The taste of home.

Bob Robinson, for those things, too.

The Usual Suspects: Bob. Doug. Thom. Dan. Kathy. The Ripley Yippees. And all the Shore Acres neighbors and readers.

"Comes a time when the blind-man takes
   your hand, says,
'Don't you see? Gotta make it somehow on
   the dreams you still believe.'
Don't give it up, you got an empty cup only
   love can fill,
Only love can fill."
                    —*Robert Hunter and Jerry Garcia*

"Winning the lottery is the worst thing
that ever happened to me."
                    —*Billy Bob Harrell Jr.*

Chapter One

Tuesday, August 18

You know you live in a rough neighborhood when somebody honks at a blind man in the crosswalk. The blonde in the Hummer laid on her horn, and the guy with the cane lost control of his flimsy plastic grocery bag. It ripped open and cans of tomatoes went bouncing and rolling all over the street. In about ten seconds, traffic in both directions ground to a big honking standstill, and the blind man stood frozen in the middle of it all.

Tough town, Cleveland.

I was sitting in the bus stop on Lake Shore across from Joe's Super Market, waiting for the Number 30, so I ran out in front of the Hummer and pitched the driver a carefully calibrated look of outrage while I helped the guy gather up his tomatoes, his pound of ground chuck, some chipotle peppers in adobo sauce, a packet of McCormick's

Tex-Mex Chili Seasoning, and his MondoMega-Jackpot ticket.

"Thanks!" he shouted. "I thought I was a dead man."

"Happy to help!" I tried to sound as reassuring as I could over the din. "It's going to be okay in about a minute. I'll take your stuff. Grab onto my arm."

By the time I got us sitting down in the RTA shelter, more traffic had piled up behind Little Ms. Hummer. Drivers everywhere were honking their brains out at her, and the light had turned red. Twice. I had plenty of time to catch her reluctant eye and read her lips. She was muttering "BITCH" at me as she drove off. Boiling. Ha!

All in all, it was a gratifying experience. I was enjoying the buzz of doing good while I sat there with the guy, his name being, as it turned out, Thomas Bennington III, so I let the Number 30 go by. For one thing, on closer inspection, he was cute.

After our brief exchange in the middle of the road, Thomas Bennington III had been silent. He was looking pretty composed, though, for a man who'd just escaped from the Valley of the Shadow of Joe's. Since he was blind, I could take the opportunity to stare, and I seized it. *Carpe* stare, I say.

Right off the bat, I had to admit that he was way more than cute. Handsome was more like it.

And young—early-thirty-ish, by my calculation—a bonus. Plus tall, tan, lean, and fit. He was clean, too, which I appreciated, given the general quality of grooming one often encounters at the bus stop. He smelled like good soap.

I nudged myself. *Say something to this guy, Allie. Go on. Talk.*

"Well, that sure was scary, Thomas. Are you okay? Was it okay for me to grab you like that? I didn't want to alarm you. Everything was so loud. You must have been terribly disoriented—"

Oh, no. Shut up!

When I encouraged myself to speak, I should have warned myself not to babble. I took a deep breath and closed my mouth.

He smiled. There was a dimple. Oh, yeah.

"No, no. And it's Tom. You were great. Seriously. That was—no kidding, I am happy to be alive." Those were the first words beyond mere pleasantries he ever spoke to me. His voice was deep and chocolaty, with a dollop of Southern drawl. About eighty proof.

"Let's just sit here," he continued in that intoxicating voice, "and savor the moment. I need to count my arms and legs, okay?"

"Okay, Tom." I was hoping he couldn't hear my state of mind. "Let's."

It was a moment worth savoring. A cool breeze

was flowing off the Very Great Lake Erie, located behind the subsidized housing across the street from Joe's. On its way to our bus stop, this breeze had passed over the roof of a McDonald's, adding the slightest watery tang of lake and algae to the rich bouquet of grilled meat and French fries. Top that off with Tom's soapy goodness and I judged it to be about the most perfect smell ever. I inhaled, trying to be present whilst also trying to ignore a certain, almost unfamiliar, tingle.

"Mmm, Mmm."

"Oh, yeah," Tom agreed. "The world is smelling both good and interesting. You, especially. What's that fragrance?"

"Jo Malone, Wild Fig & Cassis. I got it in the divorce settlement."

"Good deal. But…" He paused, considering… "the cologne, not the car? This is the bus shelter you've rescued me into."

I zoomed away from the car question. "Yes. The bus shelter. I thought you might need a minute to regroup. And I do have a car. It's…ah…being worked on right now."

This was kind of a lie. Well, technically, a total lie. My salsa red VW bug convertible, which was one of the handful of things I had salvaged from my sojourn among the affluent, needed a big, fancy, upscale repair job. I was saving to get it worked on.

I figured this was going to take about two years of bus time.

I'm not sure why I was embarrassed enough to lie, since at that moment I still believed this Tom the Third was living in public housing and wouldn't be shocked by my car-deprived situation. I felt off-kilter, like he was somebody I didn't want to disappoint with my ordinary self. I mean, anyhow, who was I these days? Plus again, he was way above average in the hot department.

But he saw right through me.

"Could be it's you working on it? Saving up for repairs, maybe?" There was that dimple again. In his wonderful, smooth-shaven cheek. *God.*

"Yeah. You got me." I felt my ears warming. "You're rather insightful—" I stopped myself.

"For a blind man? Oh, let's not worry about the sight metaphors. There are about a billion. And I don't want all the apologies and awkwardness to get in the way of our being friends. You can't hurt my feelings about this, I swear. Okay?"

"Sure." I added another *Mmm Mmm* to myself on the "our being friends." He was handsome. He used impeccable grammar. He thought we could be friends. The trifecta.

What was I doing? I'd known him for maybe ten minutes. Two of which I'd spent rescuing cans and getting badmouthed via lip-synch. Where had

my five years of total monogamy and the two ensu-
ing years of absolute celibacy gone, that I could so
easily start scoping out this guy's dazzling white
tee-shirt, his nice, tanned, well-defined arms? The
way his dark glasses made him look stealthy like a
sexy spy. How nice he smelled…?

What the heck?

I made up my mind not to go overboard with
the brakes. First of all, how many blind serial killers
did I think there were in Cleveland? And, second,
wasn't it non-monogamous behavior on the part
of Mr. Tall, Dark & Unfaithful, Esquire that had
landed me here at this bus stop in the first place?
Six flavors of Jo Malone, a small but lovable red
car, and a ridiculously insignificant amount of
cash wasn't much compensation for half a decade
of Big Mistake. The universe owed me something,
for goodness sake. How much could it hurt to ask?

"You were going to make chili?"

He shifted the torn bag he was now cradling
on his knees. His hands played over the contents
and he frowned. "I was. But apparently some
tomatoes got away."

I glanced out onto Lake Shore. Sure enough,
there was a flattened Red Pack can, bleeding onto
the pavement. "Oh, there's a can out there that can't
be saved, I'm afraid. But listen…" I focused myself
on sounding casual. "…why don't you ride the bus

with me to my house? I'll throw in some of my tomatoes and you can share your chili stuff. I have Coronas and limes, too. If that works. And I can borrow a car from a friend to drive you home—"

I was struck by the audaciousness of inviting this man to come home with a voice he'd never heard before. I knew me, and I could see him, but what did he have to go on besides the odds against meeting a female serial killer at the bus stop? I backpedaled. "Or I could run into Joe's and get you another can."

He needed to decide. The next Number 30 was an ugly gray square in the distance.

"I'll go with the bus, the tomatoes, and the sharing." He operated the dimple again. "But I can't go home with you unless you tell me your name."

"Oh, sorry. Of course not. How did I skip over that? " I hesitated a beat. "Al…exis. Alexis Harper."

He turned his handsome face to me. Quizzical. "You don't sound like an Alexis to me. You sound more like an…Alice."

So he reads minds? This could be a big complication.

"I hate Alice. Don't I deserve a fresh name after living under the cloud of Alice all these years? My friends call me Allie. Is that better? Are you psychic? Or what?"

He grinned. "I may be blind, but I've got an

excellent fib detector. Also my blind-guy spidey sense. Which…hmm…tells me you might not be too dangerous. I will go with you, Allie-not-Alice, and commingle my chili with your tomatoes and beer. It's a much better plan than the one I had when I started across the street. I believe I hear the bus."

Hallelujah. This day was turning out so great. *Be cool, Alice.*

"Don't get too thrilled with yourself," I answered him. "I can hear it, too. It's only half a block away."

Chapter Two

I'm going to go on record here that this particular evening—of this unadorned, shaping-up-to-be-predictably-ordinary Tuesday in August—was the best evening of my life. Not the best midnight nor the best wee hours of the morning, but for the part between, oh, say, 4 p.m. and 11:05? This is the evening that rules them all.

And what did we do? Nothing much. I showed him my house. Which is to say I told him some things about it. How it was vulnerable, perched as it was on the brink of the big lake. How it was run-down, and not at all posh, but deliciously all mine. Except for the part about being rented, of course.

Then he told me how it was for him. The fragrance of my scrubby little garden, the murmuring voices of the water, the way the sound and feel of a room could describe its size and shape to him. His words made it flower for me, as though I'd overlooked half the things there were to love about it.

I guided Tom and his battered Joe's Super Market bag into my kitchen and cleared off a bar stool so he could sit. He took off his dark glasses, planted his elbows on my ugly ocher counter, and settled in, listening to me make chili while enjoying his beer.

I was adding his seasoning packet and two of the chipotles when Margo, my landlady and best friend in the current world, stuck her head around the door and called "Al? You here?" and then, "Oops. Sorry. I'll come back later."

She was using her moment of retreat to scope out poor, unsuspecting Tom. She shot me an approving glance and kept backing out. I stopped her. "Come on in, Margo. Say hello. I met this guy on my way home from work. And stop fussing with your hair. He's blind. Pay me ten bucks and I'll tell him you're blond, five-six, and a hundred and ten pounds."

Margo Gallucci would be more accurately described as none of the above. Black hair, dark eyes, a complexion rosy enough to inspire a Tintoretto. She's a short, round Italian Buddha. A woman of indeterminate, but ample, age. Her temperament is a fascinating and sometimes appalling swing from Zen serenity to Italian pyrotechnics. And back. Margo's Alternating Current, I call it.

Margo was now giving Tom her full signature onceover. I could see her checking off the long leanness, ravishing tee-shirt, brown, unfocused, eyes. Check. Check. Check.

He passed.

"I'd like to shake your hand, but the way I see it—oops, sorry. I bet that's a never-ending problem. Let's agree to bulldoze over that one—you're going to have to lead off. Otherwise it's awkward."

He crinkled his eyes in his irresistible smile and presented her with the dimple as he offered his hand. "Thomas Bennington."

"The Third," I added.

"The-pleasure-is-all-mine-Thomas-Bennington-the-Third-may-I-call-you-Tom?" She turned to me and added the word "babe" with almost silent lips.

Margo. My own little matchmaker.

"Margo, his hearing is acute. You might as well tell him straight up you think I might have somehow missed that he is a babe."

He was nodding in time to my words. "Tom is plenty, Margo. I use the rest of it to put women at ease after they save my life at the bus stop. She's right. Sound is my secret weapon. Thanks for putting in the babe recommendation with—did you call her Al?"

"I did. She doesn't like the name her mom and dad gave her which is—" She shot me her evilest glint. "Al...exis."

"He's also got a fine-tuned lie detector, Margo. Get over yourself. We've agreed on Allie."

"Well," Margo shrugged, "it certainly beats Alice Jane. Now, I'd love to stay and hear all about how our Al saved your life at the bus stop, Tom, but I truly was passing by. We'll talk later." She gave me a meaningful, but soundless glance. "Day after tomorrow maybe? Wonderful to meet you, Thomas Bennington the Third. I hope I see you—oh, sorry. Oh, screw that—again soon."

Margo. Over and out.

• • ● • •

I pulled some odds and ends from the fridge and converted them into a simple salad. While the chili simmered, we ate that. He knew how to be quiet and enjoy his food. I like that in a man.

"Your Margo is good. Tell me what she really looks like. To me she sounds fifty-ish, about five two and a hundred-seventy. Do not tell her I said that. She'd never forgive me if it's not true and she'd kill me if it is."

I was staring at him, stunned silent by the accuracy of his guesses. After a second, I ventured, "What about me? Do you have one of those magic mental pictures for me?"

He winced. "That's so tricky. Okay, I'll try. Remember I took your arm when you helped me across the street? I estimate you're five-ten, a couple inches shorter than me, and…hmmm…one-thirty-five?"

He paused.

I waited for the rest of me.

He shook his head and mumbled, "Don't be a dope, Tom…." But he sighed and forged on. "You sound maybe late twenties. Brown hair. Brown eyes—that's a dead guess. And pretty," he added, hastily. "Very pretty."

His eyes were a fantastic brown, that was for sure. They followed the sounds he was listening to, though not the way vision tracks sight. When he smiled, the smiling warmed them even warmer. He seemed comfortable with his face. I like that in a man.

All in all, he was close to right on, although I chalked those "pretties" up to self-defense. I could see his blindness was not going to give me the glamour boost I'd been counting on and, what with the human lie detector thing, I wasn't going to press my luck. I went ahead and signed off on the whole package. And added, "Very-early-thirties." For honesty's sake.

"Early-mid-thirties, for me," he returned. "As long as we're telling the truth here."

"You haven't been blind forever."

"No. I had a stroke. The doctors called it a

'bizarre anomaly.' When I was twenty-five. Almost done with grad school. All ready to get married and start my life. For a long time they thought I'd be able to see again. The other effects wore off. But my sight never came back."

"That must have been—"

"Yes. It was. All that. I was angry. Bitter. Hard to be around. The girl dumped me. Not because I was blind but because I was a terminal pain in the ass. And then, oddly enough, I started to cheer up. She was beautiful, this girl, but not a lot of fun. I think I maybe drove her away on purpose because I'd realized, down deep, she wasn't the woman for a blind man."

"You're from somewhere in the South. Even I can hear that."

"Atlanta."

"How did you end up here? In this neighborhood, of all places? And what do you do? You went to grad school? Do you have a PhD? I could call you Dr. Bennington, III? I went to grad school, too. You can call me Allie Harper, M.A. Or maybe Master Allie…."

He exhaled a chuckle. "Stop with the 'Doctor,' Master Allie. Let me answer your questions—which are numerous, I'd like to point out—in order."

"Sorry. I'm interested, is all."

"And I'm looking forward to grilling you when

it's my turn. Let's see." He ticked off a question on one finger. "I ended up here because my family wouldn't let me be independent."

Something about the shape of his hand compelled me to stare at it, and I was glad that he couldn't see me watching. It was slender and sinewy, his fingers tapered and graceful. I closed my eyes, breathed in the soapy guy smell of him, and listened to his voice, telling himself to me.

"I needed to be someplace people would let me fall down and not pick me up."

My eyes popped back open. "Well, you sure chose the right place for that."

"True. You'd have to say it's a pretty tough neighborhood when someone would honk at a blind man with a cane in a crosswalk."

"I had the same thought. Go on."

"But you picked me up."

"In a manner of speaking."

"Don't get all weird about it. I was grateful. That was a bad moment. All those horns. I had no idea what was happening."

"A lot of them were honking at the woman in the Hummer. Because of what she'd done to you."

"God. It was a Hummer? I'm lucky to be alive. And a woman. That's cold."

"We're currently at the question about what do you do?"

"I had always planned to teach. Even before the stroke. And us blind associate professors?" The dimple flashed. "We're everywhere. A campus can be a contained, manageable space. And now there's incredible technology for reading and writing. Apps for everything…I love teaching. My students are great."

"What do you teach?"

"English Lit. At CWRU." He named the university maybe more famous for its science and engineering than its liberal arts.

"Isn't literature a stepchild there?"

"Not anymore. And anyway, those smart, ambitious young scientists need to get their heads in contact with their hearts. That's my specialty." He paused, listening, I knew, to the sound of me breathing. Maybe he could even hear the thud of my own disconnected little heart.

We were sitting at the counter with our salad plates pushed back and the beers empty. I could smell the chili cooking down. I should jump up and fill our bowls and get us new beers. But I sat still, looking at him, meeting his gentle unseeing eyes with my own. It felt unnervingly intimate, how he opened his face to me, a woman he'd never seen. My heart thudded faster. What was this? Hadn't he been a stranger in a crosswalk? Hadn't we barely met?

"I'm not all head. That's for sure—" I faltered,

trying to ease the moment back to solid ground. But he leaned toward me and with one, unerring motion, captured my face in those beautiful hands. Now he knew exactly where my mouth was. I closed my eyes.

Chapter Three

But he didn't kiss me. He ran his beautiful fingers over my face in a way that set every inch of me on fire. "You're lovely, Alice Jane," he murmured after a moment. "I'm so looking forward to getting to know you. If I'd had any idea you were going to rescue me today, I'd have laid myself and my chili mix right down in the road. Hummer and all."

He took his hands away and I opened my eyes, trying to gain control over my disappointed mouth. For a long moment, I couldn't say anything. And then I blurted, "Oh. Chili. Speaking of chili. It's ready. We should eat."

Way to go, Allie.

So we had the chili. After a couple seconds of awkwardness, we segued back to the getting-acquainted talk. When the rubberiness had purged itself from my arms and legs and the flames had died down in some other parts, I got interested in the conversation again. Soon we were chattering like zoo monkeys.

He loved books. I loved books. He loved poetry. I loved poetry. I liked to write. He liked to read. He liked indie, classical and jazz. I liked those, plus bossa and country. He enjoyed teaching. I enjoyed my part-time, pathetic-paycheck job at the Memorial-Nottingham branch of The Cleveland Public Library. He had accepted living in a dicey part of town so he could hear the sound of water.

Well, me too.

As the evening cooled, we moved ourselves out to the backyard to sit side-by-side in a couple of rickety Adirondack chairs. The sunset was one of those that linger over the water on August nights, long after dark. Tom recited to me a sunset poem about a man lying in a hammock by a field in summer. It might seem to be about horse manure, this poem.

The poet says,

The droppings of last year's horses
Blaze up into golden stones.

But then he says,

I lean back, as the evening darkens and comes on.
A chicken hawk floats over, looking for home.
I have wasted my life.

Bam. Just like that, it pierced my heart, the way truth and poetry does. The poet, this James Wright, had nailed me and my question. Would I ever make anything of myself? Had I let my prison sentence of a marriage and my wrecked finances derail me from whatever I was supposed to be doing? Should I stop trying so hard? Let myself breathe and enjoy the sunset? Not waste all this? This unearned, precious, fragile gift. My human lifetime?

Tears surprised me and I said, "Ah." With a catch in my throat I couldn't suppress. He reached out and found my hand.

After a moment, I swallowed a couple of times and got my voice back on track to ask him another question. "What's the lake like for you? It's so visual for me. Watching the sky change and the water. It's different every day. Maybe every moment of every day. Should I apologize for reminding you?"

"No. Of course not. I'm mostly over losing my sight. It's been a long time. I went straight through the stages—denial, anger, bargaining, getting your girl to dump you—the whole thing.

"Now I have my sixth sense. It's a kind of fusion. Of sound, of course. And smell, which is almost touch because of the way it comes inside you, down into your lungs, all the way into your blood. And touch, which is a blend of everything it means to have a body. What's inside, what's outside, how the inside and the outside commune."

Commune. After forever sitting here alone, here I was with a man who used words like "commune." *God bless you, HummerWoman.*

Unaware of my silent prayer of thanksgiving, he continued. "It also explains why I live here. I can afford a small house like yours, one good for me like this one is for you. And since I don't see that the neighborhood is rundown, it doesn't make me uneasy the way it might others. Having all sorts of beautiful, expensive things, living in a fancy zip code, would be more important if you could see, don't you think?"

Yeah, maybe. But I didn't want to admit that. I'd spent too many years uptown. I didn't want to confess I'd squandered them on the accumulation and management of shiny objects. Especially since I didn't have most of the objects anymore.

"Tell me what you hear right now that maybe I'm missing."

"Well, for starters, I hear the waves rushing in and crashing around, because of the wind, which is picking up. The wind sound is layered over the water noise. But there's also a hole of some kind in the rocks at the bottom of your cliff, and the water glugs in and out of there every once in a while. There are a couple of gulls circling high up, crying.

Somebody behind us, up the street, is playing an excellent recording of the Goldberg Variations, maybe Glenn Gould, but I can't be sure yet. And your neighbor on our left is watching some sitcom, turned up loud."

He tugged on my hand. "Take me over to the top of your cliff so I can hear that glug sound up closer."

I put some suspicious eye-squinting into my voice. "Is that a ploy?"

"Are you kidding? Standing on the brink of oblivion, in the night, with a pretty woman who picked me up at Joe's? That's no ploy. That's living dangerously. C'mon. How about it?"

The end of my lawn is about six long strides from the chairs. There's a steep, scary flight of steps leading down to the lake, but I almost never go down there. I don't swim or sail. Most of the time, I sit and look. Most of the time, I'm alone. As noted. Alone and lost in the morass of my own head. Perhaps, after tonight, I thought, I'll breathe more deeply and use my ears better. And appreciate my eyes more, of course. Even if, after tonight, I'm all alone here again.

Shut up, Allie. Carpe *tonight.*

We'd reached the edge. Tom had a firm grip on my arm. It was hard for me to fathom what it would be like to walk and not know there was a twenty-foot drop in your path. "If I weren't here, would you know how close you are?

"If you weren't here, I'd have my cane and it would keep me from falling off. I'd be a lot more cautious, though." He paused. "And if you weren't here, I'd wish you were."

He reached out toward my face again. This time when he found me, he ran his fingers along the line of my jaw and then up into my hair, until he was cradling my head in both his hands.

I was having one of those sixth-sense moments myself. I imagined I could feel the blood circulating in my veins and the oxygen from the heavy night air feeding my blood. Fueling my galloping heart. The night was full of sound, the most intrusive at the moment being an amped up commercial on Ralph's annoying TV. I tried to block that out and only hear gulls and water as Tom bent down and put his lips on mine.

I closed my eyes and summoned the lush darkness he had described to me.

His mouth was warm and sweet. We both tasted like chili and beer. Not a bad thing. I moved in closer, figuring out for this first time how our bodies could fit against each other. He was taller. I was rounder. As a kiss, this was working fine. Our lips parted. He was a talented and committed kisser. I like that in a man.

My fingers went to the delicious smoothness of his neck, exploring the supple curve of his spine and the prickle of his hairline as he bent down to me. He slid his hands from my face over my shoulders and on down until they met at the small of my back, gathering me into him, pulling me close, close. And then—

Everything stopped.

He dropped his arms, pulled away, and stood there, frozen, with his head cocked to one side. Frowning. Listening. In the moonlight, he looked like a handsome animal alerted by an almost inaudible threat. My lips were tingling and my body still yearned toward the heat that had been building between us. This felt like being thrown into cold water. Again.

Damn.

At my back I could hear a woman's voice. Loud. Saying numbers. "Thirty-four, fifty-seven…"

In the darkness, she sounded chill, impatient. Almost angry. What the hell? And then she droned, "Mondo Ball: Eight." Ah ha. The lottery drawing on Ralph's TV. This guy was checking his number?

Tom's frown had deepened and his expression was worried. He refocused on me. "Sorry, Allie. Sorry. That was unforgivable. I'm so sorry. But—I—do you know what happened to the lottery ticket I had in my bag?

Chapter Four

We were back in the kitchen. I had tossed the torn grocery bag into the recycling can, and when I fished it out, the piece of paper was crumpled. Tiny, electrical sparks zinged down my fingers as I extricated it, and my heart rocked as I laid it down on the counter, smoothing it as best I could.

For some reason I heard my mother's voice. "Alice Jane Harper, only you could throw five hundred million dollars into the trash."

Now the ticket lay—small and stupefying—between us on the counter. There should have been a full-choir singing sound, like from the monolith in that Space Odyssey movie, but it was quiet as a mouse. I'd carried it to my computer and confirmed on the lottery's website that this was indeed the winning number. And that there'd only been the one.

7-9-16-34-57-8. Bingo.

I had never imagined knowing—let alone kissing—someone who'd won the Mondo. Especially a gigantic one. Especially someone who didn't seem happy about it. Not at all.

He was sitting with his elbows on the counter and his chin in his hands. His expression could only be classified as morose.

"How much is the pot?"

His voice was…grim?

"Somewhere around five hundred million, last I heard. Maybe more now. Do you play a lot?"

"First time."

"You bought one ticket in your entire life? And you won? That's not even lucky. That is an act of God."

"That's exactly what it is. Big and terrible. Like an earthquake or a tsunami."

"Aren't you glad? Aren't you excited? I mean, five hundred million dollars. That's going to be something like two hundred million after taxes. Wouldn't you rather have that much money than not?"

"God. Allie. I don't have a clue. You seem to know a lot about the lottery but this is all new to me. I had no intention of winning. I never even thought about that. Just the opposite. There's this kid…."

The story came out.

Tom's house was next door to the high-rise subsidized housing project, but it had a small beach. There was a kid who liked to come down and play on Tom's beach. "Runako Davis."

"Runako?"

"African name. He told me it means 'handsome.' I don't know whether he is handsome or not. But I know he's smart and full of life. Funny, too.

"He prefers to be called Rune. What is it with my friends? Never happy with their given names." He brightened in my direction for a second and then his face fell again.

"Rune's mother has a lot of what people love to call 'challenges.'" Mostly she has the challenge of getting involved with rotten men and—here's where all this started—with gambling.

"Rune tells me she spends probably fifty bucks a week on Mondo tickets. I guess she believes it's the only way she'll ever have anything, for Rune, for herself. For a better life. But it's a vicious cycle. Two hundred dollars a month would buy—" His voice trailed away and I followed his thoughts onto what five hundred million could buy. I didn't have to be blind or psychic to read his mind on that one. But I still didn't understand what the big problem was.

"So, how—?"

"So Rune and I were talking yesterday and he tells me he wished he had a dollar for a Mondo ticket. Big alarm goes off for me. So I said, 'Rune, you're way too young to play the lottery. It would be against the law. Besides, you've seen your mother play over and over again. Has she ever won anything?'

"And he says, 'Maybe a hundred dollars once or twice. But she doesn't play the good numbers.'

"I fell into his trap and asked him what makes a number good? And he says, 'It has to be a special number you pick. She gets the auto ones.' This is the point at which I made the big mistake."

"And won five hundred million dollars?"

"I'm afraid I've sowed havoc like you would not believe."

"Say more."

"Well, then I said to him, 'You think if you picked the numbers yourself, you'd have a better chance of winning? What numbers would you pick?' I was just talking, you know. Making conversation.

"He says, 'It's not me picking that matters. It's that they're picked. They have to be numbers that mean something to you. That's what makes a number good. Lucky. If you bought a ticket and you picked numbers that are special to you, like your birthday or your mom's birthday, and maybe I picked the Mondo Ball number—I'd pick my age, which is eight—then I think we'd have a chance.'

"All I wanted, Allie, was to talk with him about *not* gambling. Buy a ticket with our special numbers and then show him how we wouldn't even get one number right. I wanted him to know there are good, sound ways to make money.

"I told him I'd get the ticket and we'd plan

out the numbers and if—when—we didn't win, maybe we could talk about some better ideas. How he could save for college. I could help him with that. I'd like to. And of course he answered, 'What if we do win?'

"And I told him, 'It isn't legal for you to gamble. You have to be eighteen and you've got a whole decade to go. So I'd deposit any money in the bank and I'd pay you a hundred dollars for helping me choose the numbers.'

"Because, again, I didn't think it would even be healthy for him to think about how much money it could be if you actually won. Because I knew we wouldn't win. How could we possibly win, Allie? The odds are...."

"One hundred seventy-five million to one. I looked it up once. They're probably worse by now."

Tom shook his head and sighed, "We picked my birthday and my mother's birthday and his age. The Mondo Draw number is Rune's 8."

"You have to scramble the numbers around to make it work." He smiled. "It took us about forever to figure out how to get it so we had no more than five picks besides the Mondo Ball. Rune made a little chart to keep it straight. He was so proud when we got done. And I promised him..." The smile died.

"Oh, no. Oh, shit."

"What? You promised him what? Tom?"

He'd started running his hands through his hair, frantic. "I promised him we could go to the drawing together. There's a TV in the common room at the complex, and people hang out in there on Tuesday nights when the drawing is. I told him I'd come over and we'd watch together. Then the thing on Lake Shore happened and I came home with you. I'm not sorry, Allie, it's that—"

"He waited and thought you stood him up. And after you won, that you ditched him and kept his hundred dollars. But you can explain it to him, Tom—"

He was off the stool, moving with his hands stretched out in front of him, lost as he'd been in the midst of the cacophony of horns. He stopped himself then and stood still, his face gripped by emotion. "No, it's not that. That's the least of it. Think about it, Allie.

"He's there alone in a roomful of people. He's a kid. They're adults. Most of them are perfectly nice. Some not so nice. Some just plain bad. Ruthless. Stupid. Drunk. Stoned, maybe. God. And he's told them what his numbers are. He would do that.

"Then, when the number is called, he's bouncing off the walls. And the bad ones, they'll want the ticket. They'll think maybe he has it and try to get it from him, and when they can't, they'll figure they can use him to get it from whoever does have it. From me. He'll be in the middle. That room may be the absolute worst, most dangerous, place to find out you won an obscene amount of money. I have to go, Allie. I have to go. Right now."

"I'll borrow Margo's car and drive you. But, Tom, you need to put this ticket in a safe place. Even if you only want to use it to help Rune. You go down there with this in your pocket, anything could happen. And he still might not be okay. The money could be his education, a better place for him and his mom to live."

"You're right. I'm not thinking straight. Will you hide it for me? Nobody knows I'm here. Nobody knows I'm with you. I don't blame you if you don't want to have anything to do with it. With me. But I don't know what else to do."

"Sure. I'll hide it. But let's go quick."

Hide it where? I let my eyes drift around the room. Every place I looked seemed ridiculously obvious. I envisioned a bunch of scary men rampaging through my precious house, overturning furniture, ripping stuff off the walls, stabbing giant holes into my couch cushions. Stuffing flying everywhere—

I stopped myself from envisioning anything else and after a long moment, a promising spot captured my attention. One of the metal doors of the cabinets below my kitchen sink was ajar and in the corner of its upper edge I could see a rubber stopper. It was supposed to keep the door from slamming. I knew this because a lot of those doors were missing their stoppers and they slammed all the time. Each stopper fit into a small hole—a tiny, almost invisible chink through which I could slip a piece of paper, down inside the door. But how to get it in—and still get it back out when we wanted it?

Think, Allie.

I rummaged in my overpopulated junk drawer and came up with a spool of thread. I rolled the ticket into a tiny cylinder and tied the thread around it. Tight. My fingers were shaking. I used a kitchen knife to pry out the stopper and slipped the ticket into the hole, leaving a tiny tag of string hanging out. Then I stuck the stopper back in and closed the door. As I went, I described it all, step by step to Tom.

"Do you trust me, Tom?" I asked, as we grabbed his cane and my purse and hurried, with his hand on my elbow, out the door. "It's a lot of money and you barely know me."

"I trust you with my life, Alice. And I promise to start kissing you again as soon as we get this mess straightened out."

Chapter Five

Margo handed me her keys without the slightest hesitation. No explanation required. No questions asked. I repaid her trust by driving her battered Volvo faster and way more recklessly than the law allows, up to the fateful stretch of road where this whole lively new chapter of my life had begun mere hours before. The bus stop was empty. Joe's Super Market was closed. The McDonald's, too. It was 11:45 on a hot, muggy August night, and this darkened world was cashing it in for the evening.

We parked in the lot at the high-rise and I rushed us straight in through a dismal lobby and down a dim hall to the common room. Two old black guys and one old white guy—all three in wheelchairs—were watching Jimmy Fallon's show and not laughing. No sign at all of an eight-year-old kid.

I was filling Tom in on the visuals as we went. Him with his cane, but with his hand on my arm.

Walking into this place, I was glad to feel him there. I could see that there'd been some confusion. A couple of chairs and a table were overturned, but I had no way of knowing if maybe that was the way it always was.

I led Tom to where the men were sitting and knelt down next to one of the black guys. I took in his tired, wrinkled-up face, his old man smell. It cost me a few seconds to coax his eyes away from the screen, but when I did, his gaze rolled on by and up to Tom, standing silent behind me. What he said to me then chilled me but good.

"Is that the blind guy 'ut won the Mondo?"

I didn't answer. I didn't need to. I could see he was computing one degree of separation from five hundred million dollars. I put my hand on his shoulder and gave it a gentle shake. He slid his focus back down but my hold on it was tenuous. I needed him to talk to me and stop glancing up at Tom. Maybe if we exchanged names…

"Mister." I began. Mister—?"

He regarded me with fresh interest, due to my having shown up in the company of the Mondo blind guy, no doubt. "Grant," he answered, "Ulysses A. Grant. That A is a switcheroo, ain't it? For Aeneas. My dad was a jokester. And a reader. Ever read *The Iliad* and *The Odyssey*, Miss…?

"Harper. Al—Alice Harper. Yes. Yes. I read

them. Please. Mr. Grant. There's a problem. Do you know Runako Davis? The boy who was here?"

He nodded. "Yeah, but don't nobody 'round here call him Runako. It's Rune. Nice kid. He's gone now. Ran out yelling like a house afire. Don't know where he went."

His expression deepened into concern.

"People followed him out, though. People always follow the big easy money. It's a dam' curse y'know. Prob'ly worse than being poor and crippled and having to live here. Although I wouldn't mind havin' the chance to find out. For a change of scenery, y'know?" He stole a hopeful glance up at Tom but Tom appeared oblivious, so he continued.

"You might try his mom's place. She's up on fourteen. One floor down from the top. On the lake side. 1415 mebbe?" He gave me a knowing wink and his mouth worked around into the parody of a smile, exposing an ill-fitting set of yellowed false teeth. "I'm good with numbers, y'know. Like 7-9-16-34-57-8."

Damn.

The first elevator we got to was broken and the second one was scary slow. It reeked of urine and not very appetizing food. I wondered how Tom was enjoying his enhanced senses now. He hadn't said a word since we left the common room. His whole being was concentrated on finding the boy and there was nothing for us to say. We just needed to get up to fourteen.

The elevator jerked to a stop on the tenth floor and a guy got on. Rail thin. Faded Hawaiian shirt. Tight black pants, white shoes, large dark glasses, even more incongruous in the dead of night than the ones Tom was wearing. He offered me a smarmy smile.

I don't know what he intended by this smile, but the impression it made on me was predatory. I wanted not to be in a slow, smelly elevator in public housing in the middle of the night with this man. I saw how he was looking at Tom. Like Tom might be the blind, white LeBron James. Five hundred million is instant celebrity.

Hawaiian Shirt Guy's grin widened. *Yeesh.* I scanned his outfit for a gun, but it didn't look like there was room to hide anything substantial anywhere. Except maybe in the back waistband of his pants. Where I couldn't see. I fervently hoped to keep it that way.

He licked his lips and cleared his throat. "Hey, man? Like. Show me the money? You got that ticket on you? I'd sure love to see me a winner ticket. Just once."

Tom shook his head. I would have bet it was the headshake he used when one of his students asked if she could turn a paper in three weeks late.

And although his grip on my arm tightened, his voice was steady as stone.

"No. Of course not. Sorry. I don't have it here."

Tom's "here" clearly communicated how inappropriate "here" would be as a place for such a ticket. I gave him a lot of points for that.

Shirt was a man who'd learned to take no for an answer. He paused, perhaps considering his options, and then shrugged. "Too bad. Well, have a nice evening folks. You all enjoy being rich, now."

The bell dinged. The elevator heaved to a stop. We got off on fourteen and the guy didn't follow. An unexpected blessing.

The hall was poorly lit which was maybe also something to be thankful for. It was tidy enough. No actual debris anywhere. But the beige-y carpet and the beige-y walls were stained with something I didn't need a better look at. I guided us along as quickly as I could and stopped outside 1415.

I looked up at Tom, searching his pale, worried face for reassurance. "Do you think the old guy was right about 1415 being Rune's mom's place?"

"Well, we know he's 'good with numbers.'" Sardonic. "And it's all we've got. Go ahead. Knock."

So I took a deep breath and rapped smartly on the door. Like all those times I'd seen on TV, it moved under my knuckles. Not good. I'd have assumed everybody in this joint locked their door.

Deadbolt. Chain. Metal bar. And much, much more.

I muttered to Tom, "It's not locked. I'm going to push it open."

"Go for it."

I pushed, and the door sagged inward with the sickening screech of ripping wood. What I hadn't seen, due to the stress-induced fuzziness of my head, was that it was damaged. There were a couple of ugly black scuff marks in the center, and it had broken away from its hinges. That's one way to bypass a lot of locks. Someone had set it back into place so that in the half-light it had looked okay.

Every individual brain cell I had was telling me not to go in. How many times had I made fun of people on TV for going in? Hundreds? Thousands. But the look on Tom's face was now so strained and terrible I shoved the door out of the way and pulled him in behind me.

A lamp with no shade was lying on the floor. From what I could see by its weak, stuttering light, the room was a torn-up mess. This was bad.

Even worse was the body of the plump, young-ish black woman sprawled on the floor. What if whoever had done this was in here with us? The place was so dark and wrecked—who could tell? No doubt there were closets, too, and at least one other room for someone to hide in. No sign of Rune.

"Tom." I tried not to let my voice tremble. "I don't see Rune, but there's a—There's an unconscious woman here. I'll find out if she's…if she's okay."

I paused, waiting for my guts to kick in.

I have always felt that with some training, I'd make an excellent P.I. A cross between V.I. Warshawski and Kinsey Millhone, with a dash of Stephanie Plum, Bounty Hunter, thrown in for insouciance. In the real world—before I started working for The Cleveland Public Library and disqualified myself from further entries—I'd won a "Behind the Scenes" contest the library threw to encourage people to read. My first-prize choice was "Behind the Scenes at the Medical Examiner's Office." Not good. I'd wanted to run, scream, cry, and throw up all at the same time.

So now I was supposed to ignore the fact that I was in an apartment with a kicked-in door, fourteen floors up in public housing, in the middle of the night? And walk over and touch a dead woman?

But there was Tom, waiting with his face set like cement. And his Rune kid, God knew where. And I believed this woman was Rune's gambling-addicted, crappy-man-picking, almost-certainly-dead mom.

His one and only mother.

I had to do it.

So I did. I took a deep breath.

"Stay here."

I left Tom standing like a statue by the door while I made my way over and around the stuff that was scattered all over the place. I knelt down and put my fingers on the dead woman's neck. Her skin was cold. Now that I was closer, I could see dark smudges that sure looked like blood on her face and blouse. I swallowed hard and felt around for a pulse. No success. Right then, however, she groaned.

Sweet Jesus. A miracle! A scary miracle. I almost peed myself.

"Tom!" I yelped. "She's alive! I'm going to call 9-1-1."

A voice from outside the busted door, calm and professional, announced, "No need for that, ma'am. Somebody already did. I'm going to ask you to come stand by the gentleman here. And please keep your hands where I can see them."

Chapter Six

We didn't get arrested. Or shot. Those were the two good things that happened to us during that portion of the night, and they were a welcome surprise. The pair of cops—one tall and young, the other shorter, older, and tireder—summoned an EMS unit for Renata Davis, and after they'd done what little they could for her, they questioned us closely. I could tell, though, that somewhere along their way to 1415 on this night they'd heard about the blind Mondo winner.

They must have found it improbable that this blind guy would have, upon winning five hundred million dollars, proceeded to public housing to beat some unknown woman senseless. It couldn't be totally dismissed, of course, but for the most part it didn't compute.

After a couple of edgy minutes they started treating us more politely. And even as they secured the scene, wrote down our information, and looked at our picture IDs, they zeroed in on another major cause for concern. An eight-year-old boy had announced his lottery numbers to a room spilling over with a bunch of nice, not very well-to-do people and with some probable ruthless felons. Now that his numbers had come in, he was missing.

Tom explained to them in shorthand form why he'd bought the ticket, ending with, "I wanted to show him that gambling is no way to make money."

The older of the two cops, whose last name was Valerio and who was not quite paunchy enough to be Donut Cop but cynical enough to play one on TV, snorted. "And how's that workin' for you, Mr. Bennington? The Third."

The EMTs labored over Renata, pronounced her ready to be transported, and then transported her. After the groan that had taken at least fifteen years off my life, she hadn't been responsive, so no one could ask her who had beaten her or what had happened to her son.

"Tom? Did Renata—*does* she—have family around here?"

"I have no idea. I only talked with her a couple of times. I assumed she was making sure I wasn't a pervert. Seemed like a reasonable thing for a responsible mother to do. She told me she was glad

Rune had somewhere safe to go sometimes. Safe." His voice cracked. It broke my heart.

We were waiting in the hall outside Renata's apartment for the police to tell us we could leave. They'd searched for Rune inside, even the smallest niches, but he wasn't anywhere. Given the shape his mom had been left in, I couldn't tell whether that was good news or bad, but I didn't feel relieved.

The cuter of the two policemen, who'd introduced himself as Officer Clark, came out to tell us we could go. He lingered for a minute, deciding what to say, how much to get involved, how much trouble to ask for. He looked both of us over and then addressed himself to me. "You guys have a winning Mondo ticket, correct?"

Tom answered. Maybe he couldn't tell who the cop was talking to. Maybe he'd gotten used to being talked over and around because of his disability. "Yes. We do."

The cop refocused himself toward Tom. "Not on you, I trust."

"No. It's—it's in a safe place."

"Buddy, there isn't a safe place on the planet for a piece of paper worth 524 million dollars."

"Five-hundred-twenty-four?" I squeaked. "I thought it was five hundred." Not that I meant to quibble. After 450 million or so, who's counting?

"That was awhile ago. And when the pot gets

big, it always jumps up right before the drawing. People rushing to get in. That's the last number I heard."

"Great," Tom mumbled. "That is just fantastic."

The cop glared at him in disbelief and shook his head. "You really didn't want to win, did you?"

I watched him assess the fundamental unfairness of this situation.

Tom heard it in his voice and tried on about half a grin. "It never even occurred to me that I might. It was the last thing—I think I'll be glad I won, once I see Rune is safe."

That seemed to mollify the cop, who nodded. "You live around here."

"Yes. Over on Waterview."

"You been home all evening?"

"No. I was at—No. I haven't been home since maybe three o'clock this afternoon."

"Well, you're free to go—"

Grouchy Cop glanced up from his note-taking.

"You people may want to hang out here a couple of minutes and let us go down there with you. If people know where you live…." He let the sentence die out, but his meaning was clear. Who knew what we'd find at Tom's.

Tom waited, thinking it over, and then nodded. "Okay, yes. Please. I'd like you to go." He sighed. "No need to be stupider than I've already been."

Cute Cop gave him a sympathetic smile, which, of course, was lost on Tom, but won the guy a few points with me. He was maybe twenty-five or so. Tall, blond, and muscular. Bold blue eyes, a bronzed complexion, and an earnest manner. On a different day in a different decade, I'd have thought he was a candidate for one of those Officer Stud-Muffin calendars.

He cleared his throat. "Here's some advice. When you have your ticket in your possession again, sir, sign it. It's a bearer instrument. Anyone who has possession of it can cash it in. Signing it doesn't completely protect you. If you don't have it, you don't have it. So don't lose it. But signing it helps. And someone who took it from you would have to answer a lot of questions. Just be careful."

Tom was listening to him with a interested expression. "You've thought about this a lot, haven't you, Officer—? Sorry. I've forgotten—"

"Clark. Bob Clark. Yeah. I play all the time. Not big. A buck. But regular. It's—I don't know—I'm never going to make much money, but it's entertaining to fantasize what it would be like."

"Would you quit your job? If you won?"

He smiled, and hesitated for a second. Fanta-sizing, I assumed. "Nah. I like my job. Now, you and Ms. Harper stand over there. As soon as a couple of other guys get here to take over, you can ride down to your place with us."

Chapter Seven

Tom's house was small and spare. White Dutch lap siding and green shutters. A deep porch that ran the width of the front and faced the water. Wicker furniture. Flower boxes along the railing. Waves crashing. Tom's beach house. All neat and tidy on the outside.

The inside had reaped the Mondo whirlwind. Furniture overturned. Braille books and regular books strewn around. Cabinets yanked open. A lot of expensive stereo equipment passed over in a wild search for something smaller but substantially more valuable. It was a mini disaster. Earthquake. Tsunami. Tom had been so right. I was looking at it.

Officers Clark and Valerio gave it a quick look-see while I walked around, applying the practiced eye of a messy woman who'd cleaned up a lot of wrecked rooms in her life. "It's not so bad, Tom. Things are only slightly, uh, dislocated. Nothing much damaged that can't be fixed. I'll help you put it back. You can tell me where everything goes."

"It's Rune I'm worried about." He was standing in the center of the room, using his cane to poke at his scattered possessions. His expression was impassive, but the death grip on his cane and a good-sized clench in his jaw gave him away. "I probably shouldn't stay here until I can put it all back. I depend too much on knowing where everything is. This is an obstacle course. I'd break a leg trying to get around. I'll go to a hotel, and tomorrow I'll decide what to do." He gave the clutter of books at his feet an angry kick.

"No. Tom—" I began.

But young Officer Clark cut me off.

"You need to stay completely away for a while, Mr. Bennington. This is a drop in the bucket to what might have happened if you'd been home when they came in. We can circulate a car by here. No guarantee, of course, but that should help. In the meantime, you need to go somewhere, so that nobody knows where you are except the people you totally trust."

He'd taken his policeman hat off, revealing a white-blond crew cut. "This money. I can see it doesn't matter to you. A few folks around here'd kill you for a twenty if the moon was full. As soon as you can, get your ticket, sign it, and cash it in. Then lie low. Until things get better. Until people forget."

Tom sighed. "People will never forget." I watched as he pulled himself together, squaring his shoulders against the despair I could read on his face. "Allie, can you help me get some clothes and things together? Then we'll go. And do whatever comes next about Rune."

We made our way into the bedroom, Tom using his cane to deflect the wreckage of his comfortable home. Me, murmuring little warnings. His hand dragged heavy on my elbow now. We pulled together a few changes of clothes. Odds and ends. He wasn't teaching this summer, he explained, so he didn't need clothes for work. I admired a nice, neat stack of those fabulous white tees.

We found his special laptop undisturbed in a case by the bed. The intruders hadn't made as much of a mess of the bedroom. I could hear Officers Clark and Valerio talking quietly and static bursts from exchanges with a distant dispatcher.

I was folding things and getting ready to start rooting out a suitcase, when Tom went still. Listening. I was reminded of his deer-in-the-headlights freeze when he'd started hearing his numbers. And had stopped kissing me. "What—?"

He put his fingers to his lips and pointed toward the closet. The door was partly open from the cops' earlier walk-through and whatever Tom had heard was coming from in there. I heard it then, too. A rustle, a small scuffling noise like a burrowing animal. Tom turned to me and gestured toward the chatter of the policemen in the living room.

Got it. I stepped to the door and waved to them, motioning them to silence. They came with guns drawn and advanced on the closet, pushing Tom and me back and away from the door. They would have shoved us out of the room but Tom shoved right back. He grabbed onto me and showed me, with his palm flattened and parallel to the floor at waist level, the universal sign for "child."

Clark saw it, too, and he showed his partner. They didn't lower their guard, but they eased up enough. And Clark's voice was gentle. "You. In the closet. It's okay to come out now."

And Tom said, "Rune. It's me. I'm here. Come on out."

The door eased open and a skinny boy about four feet tall, wearing torn jeans and a red-and-white striped shirt, stepped into the light. His hands were empty and the cops disappeared their weapons. Rune's eyes were wide with fright. He'd been crying at some point, but, apart from dusty streaks on his cheeks, there was no evidence of recent tears. He passed between the two policemen as if they weren't there and ignored me, too, as he walked straight to Tom and looked up at him. Mournfully. Accusingly.

"We won. And you didn't come."

Tom squatted down. "Rune. I'm so sorry. I had a little accident this afternoon and this lady, her name is Allie, took me home with her. She made me some good chili and I forgot all about the ticket. Remember, I didn't think we'd win. And then, as soon as I heard the numbers, we came to find you. We went to the common room but you weren't there."

The boy nodded. "That's okay, then. I figured it had to be something like that for you not to show. But did you see my mom? I came over here from the rec room because I thought you'd be here. But they followed me, so I hid. I heard them, looking for me...talking about her. Like they'd gone to see her to make her give them the ticket or tell where it was. But Tom, she didn't know. I don't even know. I'm afraid they hurt her. Did you see her?"

Tom nodded. "Yes. I'm sorry. She's injured, Rune, but she's alive. She's at the hospital. I'll call about her. And you can see her when she's up to it."

The boy accepted that with a resignation that made me sad. "Can I go home?"

Bob Clark squatted down too, and looked Rune in the eye. I was appreciating him more and more. "Rune, I'm Officer Clark. Your home is a mess now. Like Mr. Bennington's house here. It can be fixed fine but it's not ready to be lived in.

And you're not old enough to live anywhere by yourself. I'm going to call a very nice lady I know and she'll come here and you can go with her for tonight. How would that be?"

"Can't he come with us?" I pleaded. "He knows Tom—"

Clark cut me off with a shake of his head. "I have to follow regulations, Ms. Harper. Plus, you've got plenty going on without trying to protect Rune. Besides, this lady is nice. She's my wife. She's a social worker. Helping kids is her job."

He turned back to Rune and smiled encouragement at the boy, who was regarding him without the slightest scrap of trust. "You'll like her, son. She's very pretty. You'll see. You can phone Tom tomorrow and he can come visit you. And of course you'll be able to see your mother, if—when—she's able to have visitors. We'll wait a short while, and Marie—the nice lady—will come."

Having made all our decisions for us, Officer Clark moved to the door, cell phone in hand. He stepped out onto the porch and I heard him say, "Marie?" Then he lowered his voice so, I suspected, we wouldn't be able to listen to a man explain to his wife that she needed to haul out at hellacious a.m. to find a safe place for a little lost boy. The lake sounds rose around him as he walked down the steps and swallowed his no doubt conciliatory words.

We waited. We talked some. The cops asked Rune if he recognized the guys who'd followed him. But he shook his head. He explained that after he'd run to the house and hidden in Tom's closet, they'd come in and started making their way from room to room.

"I was sure they'd find me because I made a mistake and hid in an easy place. I was afraid the closet was where they'd look first thing. But one of the guys' phone rang and they got spooked. The man said *fuh*—the very bad word—and then, 'He's not here. He's there.' And the other guy said it too. They ran away fast. But I told myself, 'Don't come out yet. They might come back.'"

His eyes were still a tad reproachful. "So I waited for you, Tom."

• • ● • •

After a while, Rune and Tom both dozed off, sitting on a couch which Officer Clark and I had hauled up off its face and set back on its legs.

Tom's arm was cradling Rune's shoulders and the boy was resting his head with absolute confidence on Tom's chest. They looked good together. I'd have to tell Tom later, that, yes, Runako with his burnished brown skin and trusting young face was handsome as his name.

I was wide awake, of course, handling the

worrying, the scheming, and the planning about how the three of us could stay alive, cash the ticket, and then, maybe, make a safe place for Rune in the midst of Tom's private tsunami. Now I could see where Tom's grim look had come from while I was doing my Mondo happy dance. Heads up, Allie.

It was well after one when Marie Clark came to get Rune. He went, reluctant but docile with sleep. And she was indeed pretty, as blond and blue-eyed as Bob, with a warm smile that soothed even old skeptical me. They were a matched pair. Him in his dashing navy blue uniform. Her in her trim, tailored navy blue suit. Marie looked insanely buttoned-up and professional for one in the morning. As advertised, she was quite nice. She had that serene demeanor I've always aspired to but had the good sense not to pursue into the land of futility.

She was inspecting Tom, and her eyes were thoughtful. News travels fast. Poor Tom. Poor, *nouveau riche* Tom. He'd been right. People would never forget. Nobody who knew his story would ever look at him again without doing the math. I was glad I'd met him back when he was just another hot blind guy stuck in the crosswalk.

It took us and the cops maybe fifteen more minutes to corral Tom's getaway stuff and close the house up as tight as possible. We left a light on in every room.

We caught a ride in the squad car back to the parking lot and Margo's Volvo. After they helped us transfer Tom's things and said good night, the cops moved back toward the big gloomy high-rise, Officer Valerio leading the way, Officer Clark striding behind. They would keep looking for answers. Making notes. Writing reports. Doing whatever cops do in the dead of night to follow up on break-ins and beatings.

I stole one last glance up to the rows of dead blank windows before I joined Tom in the Volvo, locked the doors, and took off. I was feeling an itchy sensation that could be caused by the laser focus of a hundred pairs of invisible eyes. Tracking our every move.

Chapter Eight

Wednesday, August 19

One less-than-comforting thing about driving down Lake Shore at two in the morning was that anything moving stood out like a sore thumb. The streets were empty. No people. No cars. Not even a stray cat. Nobody but good old us in the Sore Thumbmobile.

The moon had popped out from the clouds and the street was overspread with clear, silvery light. The corners where moonlight couldn't reach were deep in shadow. Plenty of places where someone could lurk, still and watchful, for a little Mondo opportunity to drive by.

I was recalling Bob Clark's warning about the "folks around here who'd kill you for a twenty if the moon was full." Which, in fact, it was. This very night. I didn't worry so much that they'd kill us right off the bat. They'd want the ticket first.

Then they'd kill us. I wished we'd asked the cops to follow us home, and hoped my paranoia would start easing up sometime soon.

News of money travels fast. It felt to me as if all of Greater Cleveland had already heard that the winner of the Mondo was a local blind guy. I was betting this was a regular flash bulletin among the kill-you-for-a-twenty-moon-crowd. I glanced over at Tom, settled back in the passenger seat, gazing at nothing behind his dark glasses and amended my previous thought. The winner of the Mondo was "a local, *hot* blind guy." I may have been in a tricky situation, but I wasn't dead yet. I could still appreciate hotness in my passenger. My now peace-fully sleeping passenger.

Time to call it a night. An interesting night. I was beat. We were both zombies. I headed the Volvo home and parked it in Margo's driveway. I woke Tom and hustled him, his cane, and his suitcase across the street and into my place. No hotel for him tonight. Although Tom was getting more famous by the minute, I figured he was more anonymous with me. No one who had seen me with him tonight should have any idea who I was or where I lived. We hadn't been followed, as far as I could see, and I'd looked behind us as thoroughly as any normal paranoid person would do. All was quiet. Peaceful, even. Bedtime. At last.

My living room couch may have been the best flea market find of all time because, in addition to being pretty, it's double-wide. It's not a sleeper sofa but it makes up into a reasonable bed. I'd spent many a night on it myself after succumbing to the sedative effects of late-night television. I keep a couple of sheets, a comforter, and some pillows in a nearby chest for overnight guests.

I parked Tom, uncomplaining and pliable as a sleepy child, in a chair and made up the couch. Then I led him to the downstairs bath, helped him locate all the fixtures, waited outside until he came out and led him back. He peeled out of his jeans without the slightest hint of embarrassment, got under the covers in his tee-shirt and boxers, and was snoring lightly in less than a minute.

I waited another thirty seconds to be sure he was under before I peeled off my own jeans and crawled in next to him in my panties, bra, and shirt. That seemed circumspect enough. No way I was going upstairs and leaving both of us alone. Who knew what might grab either one of us before dawn? I nudged him with my butt until he surrendered enough room for me to lie beside him. I lay there for ten seconds, listening to us both breathing, savoring my stolen closeness, and followed him down into dreamland.

• • ● • ·

I was wrenched out of a sound sleep into a noise so huge it felt like it was inside my chest. I suppose the storm had been rumbling in, but until lighting struck almost in the yard and the thunder fell upon us like a truckload of rocks, Tom and I had slept in sweet oblivion. Now, though, we were instantly, totally awake.

He sat straight up and in the flare of another lightning flash I saw the stricken confusion on his face.

"Tom." I said his name as calmly and quietly as I could, given how loud my own heart was thundering. "Tom. You're with me. Allie. It's only a storm. We're okay."

"Allie," he whispered. "Thank God, it's you. What are you doing here? I thought you were going upstairs to bed."

I told the mostly truth. "I was scared. I didn't want to leave you alone. I didn't want to be alone myself. I needed to…huddle, you know?" I was ambushed by the echo of tears in my voice.

We were up now for sure. Sitting side by side. On a couch. Like regular people. Both wide awake. Both getting oriented to our new and different reality. He slid his hand over until it contacted mine and then he took it in both of his. "I'm sorry you were scared. I'm glad you stayed. I probably would have jumped up and run into a wall if I'd been by myself. That was loud."

"But we're okay now. We're here. We're together."

He was quiet for a second before he murmured, "Plus, we're awake."

"I am. That's for sure."

"I believe I promised I was going to start kissing you again at the first opportunity."

The tingle was back. "I'm confident you're a man of your word. And if there ever was an opportunity for kissing, this would be it. We're alone as can be. It's storming like a banshee, so no one would want to be after us and your ticket right now."

Plus, I added to myself, neither one of us is actually wearing pants.

He bent down, then, to put his lips in the center of my palm. Mmm. Nice move. I felt reckless. We'd survived it all, up until now. The danger we'd come from. The danger out there somewhere in the rainy dark. I'd lost my sense of—what? Respectability? Protocol? Ah, here was my answer: I'd lost my sense of common sense.

His mouth found mine as if he could feel my lips waiting. The kissing took up where it had left off when we were interrupted by Tsunami Millions. Nothing had changed. I wanted him to keep kissing me until I died from it.

Also, I was becoming aware that while the

kissing was as intoxicating as before, our bodies were now much, much less encumbered by the presence of clothes. He pulled me over to him until our bare thighs were touching too. About then another reckless rule-breaker of an idea presented itself.

I bounced it off him.

"Why don't we go up to my room and slip into something more…roomier. Everything that's happened? I think this should count as at least a third date."

"Definitely. I feel as if we've known each other for weeks. Decades."

"Years. What are we waiting for?" I kissed him again for luck and took his hand.

My house has one real bedroom. It's set on top of the first story like a very large, squared-off cupola or a very small squared-off room. The space is barely big enough to hold my queen-sized bed and one dresser. There's nothing else upstairs but the bath, with its ancient, battered claw-foot tub. The windows push out for the breeze but, with the deep eaves, a straight-down rain can't get in. It was raining buckets, straight down. What with all the celibacy, I had never brought a man up there before tonight.

I held tight to Tom Bennington's hand as we navigated the stairs. Halfway up, I lost my nerve and turned back to him, to try to talk him out of it. To talk me out of it. To talk us both down from the ledge we were standing on. But when I stopped to do that, and began, "Tom. Wait. Maybe we—" he drew me to him and our bodies locked tight together, commanded by the magnet of desire.

Therefore, I let him press me against the stair wall and put his lips on mine, sweet and urgent as before. This time, though, he also slipped his hands up under the front of my shirt. The delicious sensation of his palms on my bare skin, and his fingers, sneaking deftly around to unfasten my bra, and then coming back around to slip up under there, too, erased the whole, sensible-reasoning, frontal part of my brain.

The rudimentary animal cheering section at the back of my brain took over and it was rooting for only three things. More and more touching. Fewer clothes to get in the way of the touching. And the inevitable moment when all of Animal Brain's deepest, most intractable instincts would be addressed. For a very prolonged and rhythmic time.

So the kissing and touching got more intoxicatingly urgent, and I forgot my reluctance, my name, and why I'd ever had a moment's doubt that this hot, wild, utterly uninhibited thing was the only thing to do.

When we got to the top of the stairs, I

whispered, "You'll need to be careful up here, Tom. There's nothing between you and the stairway."

And he replied, "I'll just have to stay close to you, Allie. And never come down."

"That'll work." I stopped talking so he could kiss me again.

Upstairs in the dark room, with the roar of rain and thunder drowning out even the clamor of the waves, we kissed some more and undressed each other the rest of the way. The currents of cool, moist air from the rainy night washed over our skin. We laid our naked bodies across my smooth, white bed and touched some more. Delicate now, exploring, finding all the best spots. And then urgent, everywhere. Kissing and touching.

Heat.

More heat.

Fusion.

Chain reaction.

Multi-megaton explosion.

I like that in a man.

• ● ● ● •

It was better sleeping with him in my bed than on my couch. Understatement. Lying in his arms, still skin to skin, still moderately aroused, more by the delicious idea of him—his warm, muscular belly pressed so pleasantly against my slightly rounded one—than the delicious body of him now, I listened to the rain. It was slowing down at last, the thunder trailing the lightning at longer and longer intervals. Probably worn out by its wild night, just like us.

This right here was the moment when a person—in this case the person being me—might have had some second thoughts. What did I know about this man, really, except that he was blind—I was pretty sure about that—easily spooked by Hummers, and newly rich? Stop. Make that exceedingly newly rich to about the tenth power. Also, that he was very good looking, used excellent grammar, quoted poetry of heart-wrenching beauty, and made first-class love. To about the tenth power.

This could be a recipe for a Lothario, for all I knew. Not a gold digger, though. In this equation I figured the gold digger was me. Nope. I might have second thoughts later. Maybe he would too. But for now, I was fine.

No regrets.

Tom was breathing slowly and deeply. I was drifting away, pondering lightly and without remorse that a mere twelve or so hours ago I'd never met Tom, never had sex with him—twice—never had sex with a multi-millionaire, and, as far as I could tell, never lived at all. The interludes of danger and disaster seemed worth it at the time. I was happy. I didn't care. And then I was asleep.

• • ● • •

When I awoke in the dappled glow of a sunny morning, we were both still in the bed, both still unclothed but not touching anymore. Good. That meant I was able to slip out and brush my teeth before he woke up.

One completely awesome thing about sleeping with a blind man, apart from that fabulous "I will read your whole body like Braille" aspect, is that it doesn't matter how you look when you wake up together. Woo hoo, I say. A touch up with the toothbrush, a splash of water, a comb and I was presentable. As far as I could tell, his looks hadn't deteriorated one whit. So we were even-steven.

As I crawled back in, he stirred, rolled over on his back, stretched out, and ran his hand down over his bare chest, noticing, I assumed, that his tee-shirt and boxers had gone away somewhere. I saw him frown the teeniest bit, and then I lay very still to watch the memory of one completely surreal afternoon and night wash over him.

To his credit, he didn't pull the covers over his head. He reached his hand out until he found me.

"Good morning, Alice Jane. I'll give you ten million dollars if you'll let me do that again."

Chapter Nine

But he didn't. Even though I would definitely have given him one freebie. Or at the very least a five-million-dollar coupon: Buy One, Get One Free. Reality was catching up with us. There was a lot of stuff to take care of that we needed to hop out of bed and get dressed for.

Nonetheless, after we were securely clothed we stood in the kitchen and kissed for a long couple of minutes while the coffee dripped. I had developed a proprietary relationship to his beautiful self and therefore felt quite comfortable running my hands over most of it as he kissed me. But I stayed out of the truly perilous places as best I could. He seemed to be operating by the same guidelines.

"Dr. Bennington," I breathed against his cheek as we came up for air. "Mmm Mmm."

"I concur, Master Allie. You are the epicenter of Mmm Mmm in all of Greater Cleveland. Perhaps the universe."

"Epicenter, huh? I thought you didn't approve of earthquakes."

"That was before we broke the Richter Scale. Now stop kissing me before I forget how much trouble we're in."

Damn.

We had coffee. And OJ. I found some steel-cut oats I'd cooked up earlier in the week and stashed in the fridge. Microwaved, doused with milk, brown sugar, and a handful of dried cranberries, they were good as new.

We ate, making small talk such as recent acquaintances might if they found themselves sharing a cab. Or a bed. Maybe a smidge of "Wait a second. Who is this person?" Companionable but still slightly awkward. I knew both of us were mentally prioritizing the things that needed to happen before we and Rune could be out of danger.

The ticket, squirreled away inside the cabinet door, barely an arm's length away, was weighing heavily, of course. On me, at least. Although it was Tom's ticket, I was all about its well-being. I wanted to hold its crumpled self on the palm of my hand and poke at it repeatedly to make sure that it was still breathing. That it was real. I wanted to check those numbers one more time and feast my eyes upon their accuracy. I wasn't obsessed with all that money—exactly—but the ticket preyed on my mind. How many of my grinding budgetary issues could be rendered insignificant, no, infinitesimal, by this scrap?

Think previously insurmountable car repair, Alice.

Not that I coveted Tom's ticket. Exactly. It was just so small. So…vulnerable.

I noticed that when I stopped talking so I could ponder all this, Tom got a funny, alert expression. As if he could hear me thinking what some people might interpret as greedy and rapacious thoughts.

I decided to think merely practical thoughts. Like wondering what was going to happen next.

"Tom. Do you know how we cash in your ticket?"

"Are you kidding? You're the Mondo expert. Don't you know?"

"Nope. My lottery fantasy always ended in one of those New York restaurants where I could spend a month's salary on an appetizer. I'm shallow that way. There were some instructions on the back of the ticket, but I didn't take time to look at them and it's out of our reach right now."

"I didn't even have a fantasy. Although that New York thing sounds interesting. We need to consult some experts."

"Maybe we need to steer clear of experts just now."

"Good point."

Lovely as it would have been to simply sit quietly in the kitchen together for a while, share our romantic first oatmeal ever like normal people, and after that maybe go back upstairs? Not happening. Our moment galloped by. Sweet, with a splash of jumpy.

"Let's go see Margo. She'll have answers. She has answers for everything. And we'll beg her to lend us the Volvo again."

I was confident we'd be able to get the car away from her because this time of morning was Margo's regular R&M time. Relaxation and Meditation. She'd be there and I was confident she'd be excited to get the Mondo News Flash. I couldn't wait to see the look on her face.

Margo lives directly across the street and her house is bigger and in better repair than mine. Her garden is for sure more wonderful than mine. Her property opens onto the lake too, but instead of a rickety fence, a rustic stone wall shelters Margo's plot of ground. Her view is all secret sanctuary and glorious water.

I kept my voice low as Tom and I stepped, hand in hand, through Margo's gate, figuring to ease her gently out of nirvana.

"Give me some sixth-sense magic on this, Tom," I murmured, leaning toward him until our shoulders did that companionable touch thing. "I'll fill in the blanks."

"It's splendid. All roses, all the time."

Oh, boy. I loved to hear that man talk. About anything. But roses—roses were extra sexy.

I needed to get a grip. "Roses and much, much more. Margo actually gardens. Wears a big straw hat, carries her basketful of tools, gets down on the ground, and digs."

"Commendable. It's so green. Dense and moist. I hear a fountain. Quite big and bubbly. Can you see the lake? Except for the fountain it's so…" he paused, listening, "…so still in here."

"There's no wall on the lake side but it's asleep this morning. The fountain is in the center of everything. Margo's garden has a real design. Little walkways. Special beds. Herbs—"

"Yes," he sniffed the air with his most appreciative dimpled smile. "And it smells like somebody has tromped through her herb bed. Rosemary, tarragon, basil, cilantro. All crushed up. Very fresh."

I sniffed. "Wow. Yes." I leaned down and brushed my fingers over bruised leaves. Some feckless soul had stepped off the path into Margo's herb bed. "Margo is going to murder somebody. We'd better hope she doesn't think it was us. But it smells so heavenly. I wish we had time to sit for a while. This place is loaded up with comfy benches. And there's a hammock, too, all shaded by trees. It's so beautiful—"

And sensual. That old electromagnet of desire was fully charged again.

I had expected to find Margo parked under the wisteria arbor in her favorite wicker chair, cup of tea and open book by her side. But the garden was empty. Quiet, too. Tom was right. Except for the bright music of the fountain, it was dead still. Not even the usual birdsong disturbed the hush.

Tom frowned. "Are you sure she's home? It feels…empty to me."

"I suppose she could have gone out. Or maybe she's in the house. Let's go around and make sure the car's here before we go barging in."

The Volvo was up against the garage where we'd left it. We trudged up the walk and I started to tap gently on the front door. It moved freely at my touch, swinging inward. A chill started at the nape of my neck and trickled down my spine.

Dear Lord. Not again.

I tried to shake it off. Margo was always cavalier about locking up. Not that the thought made me feel much better.

I called out. "Margo? It's Allie. And Tom. Where are you?"

Nothing.

"Margo?" My voice quavered.

"Allie?" I could hear Tom's worry, too. "What's happening? What do you see?"

"Nothing. It's so dark in here. Margo?"

After the brilliance of the morning, the front hall was dim and the living room with its heavy wooden shutters was thick with shadow. For a long moment I couldn't see much of anything, and then I made out a still shape in a chair in front of the fireplace.

Oh no. I was pleading with God, with the Fates, with all the assorted resources I turn to whenever I'm under serious duress.

Please. Oh, please. Not Margo.

Tom hung firmly onto my elbow all the way across the room to the body. "Margo." Her name was a sob, stuck in my throat.

"Margo?"

She had been tied to the chair. There was a patch of duct tape over her mouth and a giant purple bruise spreading over her cheekbone. But she was breathing. A lot. I could see her ample bosoms heaving. Her eyes were open, and the gleam in there was pure fury.

"She's conscious, thank God," I muttered to Tom. "But she's extremely mad. She's got a big piece of tape stuck to her mouth. This is going to get ugly."

He offered a small sound of sympathy and support, but it was clearly my ball game.

I needed to get the tape off, but it was going to be a lot trickier than your simple Band-Aid removal. Margo was watching me, her eyes darting side to side, warily, as if she knew what was going through my mind. I used a fingernail to loosen one corner of the tape, trying to decide if I should go for the clean and jerk or the slow peel.

I took the cowardly route and started gently pulling it away. The skin underneath—Margo's lovely, virtually unlined, Tintoretto-worthy skin—of which she was justifiably proud and protective—was red and irritated. Not as red and irritated as Margo appeared to be, but painful to see.

She made a "Rrrr-rrrr-rrrr" sound in her throat and glowered at me in a meaningful, get-this-over-with way.

Alrighty.

I tightened my grip on my corner and let her rip.

"Ow. *Ow!* Damn it, Allie. Ow. Son of a bitch! Fucking, two-bit, dip-shit moron! Not you, Allie. Thanks so much. Sorry. That dumb, ridiculous, shit-for-brains, motherfu—"

She continued in that vein for some time, and, not feeling suicidal, I let her roll on.

For an enlightened being, Margo has quite the potty mouth. It's that alternating current thing again. So after I removed the tape, I had taken a short step back and brought Tom back with me.

Thus, we were not bowled over by the deluge of invective.

I was impressed, though. And so was he. Even for Margo, this was getting very detailed. I stepped bravely back in, and got her untied. She didn't even seem to notice.

One of the themes she touched on in the grand panoply of her swearing was that Tom appeared to have won the fucking 550 million-dollar Mondo and we'd not told her. It took all my self control to resist squealing a response aimed at the enhanced number. Glancing sideways at Tom, I could see he was mortified all over again.

Tom and I gave Margo the super-condensed version of the backstory of the accidental jackpot and our fear for Rune. Plus an even-more-abbreviated account of the trip to the high-rise and all that had transpired at Tom's house. I did not mention how or where we'd hidden the ticket. Dangerous knowledge. I was somewhat sorry I knew.

Our hasty explanations mollified Margo enough to redirect her wrath back onto the intruder who'd shown up in the early morning hours, slapped her around, and tied her to the chair.

"You're bleeping lucky," she growled, "that I didn't figure out what ticket he was actually talking about until after he'd put the tape over my mouth."

Once Margo has vented all of the obscenities

in her repertoire, she usually regains control of her temper and begins to make a few euphemistic substitutions for her more florid profanities. She actually says "bleeping." A lot.

"That bleeping little weasel," she snarled, her attention blessedly diverted from us. "That ferret-faced, numb-nuts, little dip-shit. Him and his miserable, bleeping ridiculous Hawaiian shirt, for crissake. If he hadn't had that great big gun, I'd have wiped the floor with him and planted his skinny rear-end under the skunk cabbage."

"Wait a sec," I held my hand up. "Stop. Your ferret-faced little dip-shit sounds exactly like our ferret-faced little dip-shit. I think he got on the elevator with us with us last night. Margo. Let's be grateful he didn't shoot you. He must be incredibly stupid not to realize you could identify him."

"I don't think he had the guts to shoot me. I saw him think about it. He put it at the back of his mind and forgot where he left it. He's a lightweight, your ferret. You're going to have a lot more competent criminals than him after you in a heartbeat, girl. You and the blind babe-a-rama here had better get out of Dodge until this blows over. How did your weasel find me, anyway?"

"I can't imagine, Margo. We weren't followed. There was nobody on the street last night."

Margo was regarding me with disbelief. "I don't

suppose," she offered in a tone thick with irony, "that anybody up in the projects would have been able to see the Ohio plates on the front and back of the Volvo you drove off in, honey. Would they?"

"Oh." I devoted a half second to the realization that any confidence about my own anonymity last night had been ill-considered. "Oh. Oh, Margo…"

She sniffed. "'Oh, oh' is right. You need to brain up, sweetie. I can definitely tell neither one of you is what I'd call a lottery aficionado, but surely you know that even if you take the lump sum payout, and even after taxes, 550 million dollars boils down to many, many millions of dollars.

"Right now, people who might be looking for you would maybe—just maybe—not know precisely where you live. But they obviously know you were driving my car. Somebody was already smart enough to do one of those online searches and find me. WhitePages, Google Maps street view, and lookie! Here's your name, address, and a picture of your house." She sucked in a breath.

"You both need to be careful. You need to be extra careful about the boy."

She waved her arms. Her chunky costume jewelry rings caught what little sunlight pierced the shutters and threw tiny sparkles across the ceiling. "Most of the time I buy that line about how 'money is neutral.' In the hands of a kind person—and you both are kind people, I know that—it can do wonderful things. Bad person? Bad things. That's the common wisdom. And it works for common amounts of money. That's anything under a hundred dollars these days.

"But for this situation? That money-is-neutral thing is crap. Your kind of money? The uncommon amount of money we're talking about here? Fucking *Mondo* money? Somebody's bound to wind up dead. I only hope it's Dip-Shit and not you."

She was a sight to see, standing there barefoot in her shadowy foyer, robed in a magnificently large, boldly embroidered, silk dressing gown. Our Roman Goddess of Wrath. Her curly black hair straggling out of its helter-skelter bun, her lips chapped and swollen from the tape, the ugly bruise, dark eyes gleaming, rings flashing. She swept her gaze from Tom to me and back, trying to gauge the level of our acquiescence to her advice. Then the expression on her face underwent a radical shift.

Her eyes narrowed. She appeared to be actually seeing the two of us for the first time that morning. Her chin jutted out. Her lips were pursed. Calculating.

Uh oh.

"Wait a sec," she commanded, squinting even tighter. "Wait. Hold on. I just now figured out where the two of you yahoos were last night while I was getting beaten up on your behalf. You were over there across the street. In bed. Together. Weren't you? *Weren't* you?

"Al, you can tell me. Look at me. Eye contact. This is Margo. Your best-friend-in-your-current-world. Ha! You did it. I know you did. Was it great? Was he fabulous? Was it two years overdue. Or what? C'mon! Give! Or I'll kill you myself."

I was only minimally embarrassed. This was Margo, after all, and I was used to hearing the contents of her mind spill out all over the place with absolutely no editing. But the expression on Tom's face was, like they say, priceless.

"Margo…" I commanded. "Shut. Up." I glanced at Tom, who was looking exceptionally nonplussed but not at all humiliated and not in the least sorry. Right then I fell the rest of the way in love with him.

"No, seriously, Margo, shut up. And, yes. Yes, indeed. He was fabulous."

She clasped her hands over her massive chest and favored me—and Tom, by proxy—with her most beatific smile. "I knew it. I knew it. Go! Get out of here. Figure out how to handle the money and keep yourselves and that little boy safe. And for godsake, be careful. You just found happiness, Al. This is no time to die!"

Chapter Ten

Tom and I took the Volvo and headed off to the Cleveland Fifth District Police Department headquarters to see if they'd put a car on my house and Margo's, too. Which I doubted. They aren't loaded up with extra cop cars in our end of town, but it was a place to start. I hoped we'd have a better chance if we showed up in person and were fifty percent blind and fifty percent feminine and vulnerable. I also hoped they might be able to provide some guidance on how to cash in your Mondo ticket without getting beaten senseless.

But about five minutes down the road, my cell phone played a couple of bars of "One Night in Bangkok" and it was Margo, subdued and worried. "That guy. That ferrety guy, you know, the one you saw and the one at my place, in the loud shirt?"

How could I not know that guy? Last time I remembered, we were speaking of him in a substantially less respectful tone of voice. I recalled that she had even wished him dead instead of us. Things must have taken a turn.

"I remember him. Why?"

"He's dead. And two other guys. A fat black guy with dreads. And a white guy with no distinguishing features except that he was old and in a wheelchair. And dead. They're all dead. Shot. Up at the projects. The cop who came to file my report showed me pictures on his phone because my description of my guy—rest his pathetic, annoying soul and may he do better next time around—matched up with the photos of the scene. With that."

Her voice was trembling now. "Are you being careful? Because even seeing a picture of someone you barely know and don't especially like shot dead is worse than I imagined. I can't imagine what it would be like if…well, what it would be like.

"The cop says the theory they're working is these guys got to arguing about what they were going to do with the money when they got it, and they killed each other. That's the kind of money you and Tom've got going on, Allie. The kind people kill each other for when they don't even have it yet. For only thinking about how they would split it up if they got it."

"Margo," I began in my most placating mode. "Margo—"

She swept right on through. "Allie, listen to me. You have got to get that ticket of yours and turn it in. Then at least you can prove you turned it in already if somebody grabs you for it. And then you need to get your cash and buy some protection. Bodyguards. Security systems. Big toothy dogs. An airplane to Tahiti. Whatever it takes.

"You need to protect yourself the way rich people know how to do. But you need the money to do that. You need to be rich for real. Stop wussing around and get Tom's cash where it can do you some good. It's the only protection you've got right now."

I glanced over at Tom who was lost in his thoughts, unaware that his unvalidated ticket and unclaimed jackpot had recently caused three guys to kill each other. Plane ride to Tahiti sounded perfect at that moment, but there was Rune to think about. And Margo, too. She wasn't home free either.

"Thanks, Margo, I'll tell Tom and we'll decide what to do."

I pulled over to the side of East 152nd, which doesn't have much of a side to pull over to, so I could break this piece of Mondo news to Tom and we could think. One thought I was having was "white guy in a wheelchair?" That could have been the white guy wheelchaired up next to my own

Ulysses A. Grant last night. Was Ulysses okay? Since he wasn't listed in my inventory of the deceased, I decided to park Ulysses and his chair for a minute and worry about him later.

"Tom, there's a problem."

After about three minutes, punctuated by a lot of honking, yelling, and some finger gestures from folks whose progress up the road we were obstructing, Tom calmed down ever so slightly, and we decided to stop thinking, turn around, and head back to my place.

Margo was right. It was time to get the ticket out of hiding, for Tom to sign it, and to let the lottery people take it from there. Surely we could figure out how to do that. We had Google like everybody else. Getting the ticket into Lottery Sanctuary wouldn't solve our global Mondo problem, of course. But it would help with the dilemma of our needing a lot of money to protect us from the complications of winning a lot of money. At least it would be a start.

Before we left our noisy parking spot, though, I brained up in a way that would have made Margo proud. I called the police.

• • ● • •

Understaffed, underfunded, and over-stretched as the police were, I was sure "I'm afraid to go home" was not going to fly as a flat-out 9-1-1 emergency, so I used the information number for the department. I described our lottery-winning/two-related-assaults/one-break-in situation to the person who took my call. I said we were returning to my house which was right across the street from one of the assault locations, and we needed police protection for that visit. I did my best to strike a nice balance between freaked and matter-of-fact.

This person had clearly missed the news about the Mondo and therefore took that part with a grain of salt. On the basis of the beatings, she did, however, get my address and said she'd "send someone around." The drive home took maybe seven minutes, and I knew from common neighborhood wisdom that it would have to be "shots fired" to get somebody that fast.

We'd have to wait for the cops.

I pulled up in front of my gate and glanced over at Tom. His handsome jaw was set, as if he couldn't clench his teeth hard enough to stop bad stuff from happening. My heart stabbed me. "Tom." I put my hand on his arm. "It's going to be okay. We'll be fine. We're…we're…off balance right now."

He snorted. This snort conveyed sarcasm like there was no tomorrow.

"No, listen," I persisted. "Margo's advice was

good. We need to get your ticket to a safe place and be very careful ourselves until we get all this sorted out—Tom?"

His face, if anything, had gotten stormier. I wasn't helping things.

"Allie. You. Don't. Get it." He bit off the words. Small, angry bites. "I have worked so hard, for so long to make my life work. Everything needs to be where it belongs. My house. My job. My students. My nice predictable paycheck. That's where my independence comes from. When any part gets disrupted—like at my place last night—I'm a blind man. Staggering. I'm lost."

"Shhh." I touched my fingers to his beautiful mouth. "Shhh. Don't say that. You are not a blind man staggering, Dr. Tom Bennington. Or lost. For one thing, I'm right here. You have me now."

That hauled me up short. Did he even want me here now? I faltered, "That is if—"

"Allie, don't. Don't be an idiot. How about letting me be the only idiot in this car right now? You can have your turn again in a minute." The dimple sparked like the sun poking out from behind a cloud and then vanished after the second and a half it took to warm me. "You are the only good thing that's happened to me since I left Joe's and walked out in front of that Hummer."

"Well, you do have the 550 million dollars. And change. Probably there'll be some change."

He clenched up again. "That is not a good thing, Allie, in case you haven't noticed."

I shook my head to rattle some sense into it. I had managed to get myself hooked up with a man who thought I was better news than money raining down from the sky. He was going to change his mind about that pretty soon, I was sure, when the money rain started. I needed to think of ways to be very nice to him. I thought of some ways, and leaned over to plant a kiss on the spot where the dimple had last been seen.

"Okay. If I'm your good thing, stop grousing at me and let me help you get us out of your multimillion-dollar mess. The cops are going to take another forty minutes. We'll just open the door and check. If it's all clear, we'll get the ticket out and run."

Home again, home again, jiggety-jig.

The front door was ajar.

Alrighty.

Chapter Eleven

Between our visit with Margo and the short drive to and from nowhere, we'd not been gone all that long. However, there had been ample time for somebody to break in and ransack my house.

Even from well outside the door, I could see plenty of stuff out of place. Flipped over. Tossed around. We scrambled backwards toward the car. I stood on the front walk, heart skittering, ears singing, the taste of metal in my mouth, and clutched on tight to Tom's arm.

I fished in the depths of my purse for my cell phone. "This is ridiculous. I'm calling 9-1-1." My sweaty, shaking fingers scrabbled around, sorting tissues, pens, mints, wallet, hairbrush. Crap. "In a minute."

Then I noticed that he had a cell phone of his very own. In his hand.

"Oh. You have your own, your own—"

"Phone? Honey, this is the twenty-first century.

I may be a blind man, but I've got a phone. And from the sound of things it may be a while before you do."

Cool. The stuff I didn't know about how the world worked had increased exponentially since yesterday. It had been such a busy time.

He called. Impressed a dispatcher with the nature of his emergency. And after a long ten minutes, a siren wove its way to us.

Two cops, a man and a woman, emerged from their car and cautioned us to stay behind our car while they checked things out. The woman warned us that if "anything happened," we should run. She gave the two of us a skeptical look. "Do you think you can do that?"

We thought we could. We were almost running already.

They disappeared into the house. Minutes passed. No yelling. No screaming. No shooting. I heard a small, distant thump and shortly after that the front door opened. The guy cop stuck his head out.

"Ms. Harper, could you and your friend come in?"

He led us into the kitchen which was messed up, but not exponentially more messed up than usual. I was most interested in the cabinet doors which were all hanging open. I could still see the string peeking out from under its rubber stopper. I gave it a hasty, confirming glance, and congratulated myself on being a crafty ticket-hider.

Our policeman did not offer any information. He had a folded piece of paper he was using to make some detailed notes to himself about our crime. The silence was heavy, awkward, and bewildering. Tom and I waited as patiently as we could. And then the other cop appeared in the kitchen door with a prisoner, hands cuffed behind her back. Looking royally pissed off.

Margo.

Margo?

Undeniably Margo.

Still disheveled and bruised from her earlier encounter with the now-dead dip-shit, exhibiting as much dignity as possible under trying circumstances, she appeared to be righteously enjoying herself.

"*Margo?*"

There were at least six or seven questions in my voice.

Here's a thing I was finding out that morning: Large sums of money drive everybody nuts, and furthermore, they breed suspicion like warm pond water breeds tadpoles. Before I could shut off the rush of bioelectricity through the synapses of my brain, I had ever so slightly suspected Margo of ransacking my—or actually her—house. And before I could ridicule my own electric rush with a firm *This is Margo, you dope. Your best friend in your current world*, she had seen the whole scenario unfold on my face.

"Al…" She used her calmest Buddha tone. "You know I didn't break into your house."

Damn you, Margo Intuition.

"Margo." I gave her back calm for calm. "I do. I do. I merely needed a couple of seconds to sort that out for myself. Things have been… but, hey, what *were* you doing here?"

She forgave my unforgivable breach of our friendship with the beatific Margo Smile Of Absolution.

"I was hiding."

This part made some sense to me.

"I came over to wait for you so I could give you more advice."

I knew that part was true. This was my Margo, after all.

"I saw the mess and went upstairs to make sure nobody was still here."

I opened my mouth to comment on how dumb that was and then shut it back. I, myself, had not been Stephen Hawking today.

"And Al, listen, I gotta say, that bed. Those are some good vibrations."

For not the first time during this conversation, I steeled myself to ignore the presence of the officers of the law.

"Margo, knock it off. Look around. Pay attention. Somebody actually broke in here. Keep explaining so these officers will understand you're not a criminal and take the cuffs off you."

"Okay. So I heard the downstairs door open and I thought, 'More robbers and killers.' I guess that must have been the cops. But how was I supposed to know? So I snuck into the bathroom and closed the door. But it stuck. Well, to be honest, I was holding it closed because, if you'll recall, I was expecting robbers and killers. So naturally, these…"

She was clearly reviewing her impressive store of epithets.

I held my breath.

"These…*people* in blue…"

I exhaled.

"They kicked the door in. They must have mistaken me for a breaking-and-entering person holed up in your bathroom. So please, Al, tell them I'm not."

She smiled at me.

I smiled back.

Best friends again.

Chapter Twelve

A phone call back to Fifth District headquarters filled the officers in on a report from the police who'd visited Margo this morning. I vouched for her. Tom vouched for her in a surprisingly heartfelt manner, in spite of the fact they not known each other long. He even mentioned what a devoted gardener she was.

I felt a little jealous.

After the reports and our vouching, the cuffs came off. There were some moderately sincere apologies from the police and a gracious, "No worries. I'm sure I appeared quite dangerous...to *you*" from a vindicated and self-satisfied Margo.

She left.

A few minutes later, reinforcements, in the person of our own Officer Robert Clark—in his civvies—arrived to give us a hand. It was turning out to be a lovely, lovely post-breaking-and-entering-party.

The crime scene investigation was more

perfunctory than I'd been led to expect by prime-time television. Nobody put down those yellow numbered tent thingies. I deduced that maybe it was because there were no shell casings, praise the lord. The officers looked the situation over and were polite. Told us to inventory anything that was missing and to come into the station and file a report about that.

They found the point of entry, which was a window on the west side of the house. They dusted it for prints. That part was quite authentic. And messy. But there weren't any on the window frame or its environs. Things had been wiped down. Like I figured, maybe smarter than your average dead dip-shit.

After the cops had moved on in their cursory inspection, I saw, on the floor by the window, a scrap of fabric which I didn't recognize as ripped anything-belonging-to-me. I presented it, with some pride, to the officers and suggested maybe my intruder had ripped it off himself when he came through the window.

I guess the forensic ability to identify any garment and the owner of that garment from a quarter-size scrap of plaid is not as inevitable as it looks on TV. They shrugged and shook their heads and, in the absence of any high-tech instrumentation of my own, I stuck it up on the kitchen windowsill and walked away.

In due course the regular cops left and Bob stayed. He'd asked us to call him Bob. He was off duty. He'd been headed to the grocery store when he heard the call come in over his personal scanner. He was driving his own car, a beat-up Camaro convertible, and in his jeans and periwinkle blue polo shirt, looked even younger, blonder, and more freshly scrubbed than he had in uniform.

"It was nice of you to stop by, Officer…Bob." We were sitting in the kitchen drinking some lemonade I'd made from concentrate after moving a few things back into place and hunting down three unbroken glasses. The intruder hadn't been intentionally destructive, but he/she/they hadn't been scrupulously careful either.

I wasn't freaking out the way I would have expected. I didn't even feel violated like you're supposed to. Maybe the reason was that there hadn't been much damage to my house and nothing was missing as far as I could see. But mostly it was that my freak-out threshold was up about ninety percent over yesterday's reading.

"I felt like I had to follow up." Bob drained his glass and then rose from his stool and put it the sink. Thoughtful guy. Or maybe he'd been trained by a very buttoned-up woman. I was never able to teach my former spouse to pick up a towel.

"After you left, I realized we should have

followed you home. You shouldn't have been out on your own with everything that was going on. We went too much by the book. Not enough common sense."

"No, no. That's okay. We were fine." All things being equal, I was pleased they hadn't come home with Tom and me. We did great on our own. I checked Tom's expression, saw his thoughts overlapping with mine, and darted my eyes away so Bob wouldn't catch both of us looking like that. "And don't worry," I added, "the ticket's safe."

Bob brightened up. "Is it? That's good. I went online and researched what you need to do. There's a regional office over on Snowdon Road. You call them, sign the ticket, take it there, and fill out a form. I wrote down the phone number and address.

"You should get rid of the ticket, Tom. Only stupid people would be after it now that everybody knows the winner is not just some unidentified black kid. But trust me, stupidity can be godawful dangerous. I've seen it myself. If you want to go right now, I'll follow you in my car, make sure you get there safely. Then at least, you'll get the money."

Tom had been listening intently to everything Bob was saying. I wondered if his blind spidey sense had been activated by Bob's keen interest in the ticket, but he was nodding and looking grateful. Good. I felt pretty positive that Bob was on our side. I was thrilled that someone had given us the very information we'd been trying to get a handle on when assorted crimes had intervened. In fact, I felt happier than I had since the kissing-in-the-kitchen-before-breakfast episode, which seemed like a long time ago.

After the lemonade, Bob and I walked around, checking to make sure things were locked up as tight as we could make them. We switched on some lights even though it was daylight, because by then we knew for sure Tom and I wouldn't be coming back that night.

I went upstairs and took one last long look at the bed in which I'd been so happy the night before as I changed into a freshly laundered version of the jeans I'd been wearing. Then I tossed some odds and ends into a gym bag.

Hurray. And done. I pride myself on my extreme portability.

My last official act before we left the house was to pry off the rubber plug and reel in the ticket from the inside of the door. The ticket roll wasn't as easy coming out as going in. The round edge balked at the opening several times and I was afraid the thread was going to break and we'd have to take the door apart. Or, worse, the whole thing might rip into shreds too small to be reassembled.

It didn't help that Officer Bob was observing

my efforts with a look on his face that could have been either consternation or hysterical laugh-suppression. His lips were compressed so that no clue of whatever emotion it was could slip out. I appreciated that.

In the end the ticket slipped free. I pinched it with my fingers, pulled it through, untied and unrolled it.

Here's the deal. It is impossible to unroll an insignificant, beat up, nothing piece of paper and, like, get that it represents 550 million dollars. I read the numbers to Tom so we could reassure ourselves. The way things were going it would be worse now not to have won. We needed the money to get the vultures off our backs.

But that was one thing that hadn't changed since last night. 7-9-16-34-57-8. All in a row.

I found Tom a pen and showed him where to sign. Then we called the number Bob had found for us and they were all, "Come on in." So we went.

Chapter Thirteen

The lottery's regional location on Snowdon Road was not the glittering pleasure palace one might have envisioned. The office occupied an unassuming, two-level building with the standard commercial entryway. Our off-duty police escort got out of his convertible, followed us all the way to the door and watched us go in before he left us.

His parting words were, "Rent a car, Allie. Figure out how to get your friend Margo her Volvo without you going back there. Drive around for a while. Make sure you're not followed. Stay in a hotel. Don't tell anyone where you are. Not even me. I have your cell numbers. And you know how to reach me."

His stolid expression opened a crack, and a grin sneaked through. "Dial 9-1-1."

He put the top down and drove away, his blond brush cut gleaming in the sun. I imagined him announcing for his own benefit, "My work here is done."

We went in. No fanfare. No pearly gates. One of those security airlock things you buzz in and out of. That was it. Inside, the office exuded the atmosphere of a business where paperwork rules. The afternoon light was dusty yellow, filtered by Venetian blinds. Phones rang. Printers hissed. Keyboards clucked. No music played. It smelled like cleaning products and slow time.

The lottery people were nice enough. Mostly they were middle-aged women. The glamour of working for an organization responsible for the disbursement of incredible amounts of money didn't appear to have turned their heads.

There was more than one form to fill out, of course, and scrupulous attention to correct forms of ID. All this reminded me that the lottery, in spite of the dazzle of its advertising, is government-regulated out the wazoo. Showing up to file for your millions had quite a lot in common with trying to get your driver's license renewed.

But not entirely. Mary, who handed us the forms and offered her congratulations, was visibly nervous. Her hands trembled as she showed us what to do. And I couldn't miss how people were popping up like gophers and passing through in larger numbers than their daily routine might require. They were jockeying to get a glimpse of Tom, and they could feel free to stare as much as they wanted because he wasn't staring back.

I thought the odds were excellent—because the odds of anybody, anywhere, ever winning were so incredibly terrible—that they'd never had a MondoMegaJackpot winner through the door before today. I heard muffled exclamations, laughs, and whispers, and my tadpole pond of suspicion heated up. I speculated about what it would be like to be so close to Mondo money and yet pull down a civil service salary. I bet these folks got paid more than a part-time librarian—but not Mondo more. I pondered how much personal contact information about Tom was going into the forms and how a little careless access to that data might be disseminated rather indiscriminately under the right circumstances. Then I slapped myself—mentally of course—and stopped focusing on the predatory negative.

Clearly, nobody who was sneaking glances in my direction knew what to make of me. "Gold digger" was the obvious conclusion. I wondered what they would say if they knew I'd met Thomas Bennington III, PhD, almost exactly twenty-four hours ago and had fallen into bed with him about five or six hours after he found out he'd won. "Gold digger slut." That would be my guess. I didn't care.

I particularly didn't care since, after the ticket

have been perfectly acceptable for either of us the day before.

We required a hotel with a serious lobby and people paying at least cursory attention to who came and who went. A decent restaurant within its sturdy walls would be a bonus. Moreover, Tom was approaching a moment when money was no longer going to be an object ever, ever again. And I was with Tom. Big time. Those factors in combination made the selection of the fanciest Marriott within a hundred miles our most efficient choice.

I admit I was looking forward to a nice hotel. I liked fancy. I wasn't sorry I'd walked away from all that and the lying rat who went with it, but I still had fond memories of the upscale world.

So why was I feeling so unthrilled, heading downtown to the Marriott at Key Center with Associate Professor Mondo Fabulous? Well, probably because the Number One thing I was feeling was scared. So scared I was choking the steering wheel of our rental car with both my sweaty hands.

I kept hearing Margo saying, "They're all dead." Three actual guys—one of whom I'd more or less met. All dead, and probably at the ME's right now, covered up with sheets in a chilly gray room.

I was checking behind us. And around us. And in front. The more I checked the more sinister vehicles and scary people I found. I could see I'd had minimal training in distinguishing ordinary Clevelanders from axe murderers. I was going to have to get a crash course in that one.

There was a spot in the center of my chest, close to my heart, that was jumping and cringing like it wanted to get out and run some place safer. I freed up a sweaty hand and pressed on it. Hard.

This helped. And it helped, too, when I pointed out to myself that I was alive right now and here with Tom, which at five o'clock yesterday would have seemed like a Christmas miracle. I promised myself I'd stay alert and not let either Tom or me end up in the morgue. After that I told myself to shut up.

We checked in at the Marriott Key with a minimum of fuss, took our negligible luggage with us into the dining room and had lunch/dinner before we headed upstairs to our room on the concierge floor. The extra barrier of keycard exclusivity would give us that much more peace of mind.

All the while we were eating the Marriott's tasty food, electricity had been building—outside the hotel and inside our clothes. The flicker of lightning on the windows was getting more and more frequent. The lights dimmed a couple of times. Dark clouds had spread out like spilled ink until the whole sky was blackened. Streetlights had been duped into turning on.

We rode up to our room on the special concierge-level elevator and let ourselves in. The view was magnificent. Lake and city arrayed in front of and beneath us under the dramatic, black sky. I did the visual interpretation for Tom while he ran his thumbs slowly along both wings of my collarbone and nuzzled my ear.

Too bad the *X-Games* don't have an undressing competition. We would dominate in our division. For style as well as speed.

Lightning struck so close by I could almost feel its heat radiating off the flat brightness on the window. Heat. I put my arms around Tom's neck and we moved in close enough to drive each other wild. Teasing. Tantalizing. Some very sensitive parts ever so slightly brushing. Our personal storm intensifying in the momentary postponement of full body contact.

I touched my lips to the smooth, salty warmth of his shoulder and then worked my way up to kiss the pulse that was throbbing in his neck. Lightning flashed again and the thunder resonated in my bones. "Oh, my, Tom. Listen." I whispered. "They're playing our song."

And then the storm got so out of control we had to lie down and take shelter on our big safe, luxurious bed.

After a considerable while I found myself

resting on his chest. Face to face, skin to skin. Feeling satiated and exhausted but still affectionate in an intellectual way. There was something I wanted to know and this seemed like a promising, if somewhat sweaty, opportunity to ask him.

"So. I've got a question I've been saving for a moment when you're in a good mood and no one is trying to kill us."

He put his hand to my face with the accuracy that so took me off guard, brushed my hair out of my eyes, and secured it behind my ear. Then he started caressing my flushed cheek with his gorgeous, brilliant fingers. Darn. And a mere second ago I didn't desire anything.

"Well," he began, oblivious to the enthusiasm with which my girl parts were responding to his simple gesture of friendship. "I suppose anybody at any time may decide to kill us and take all our fabulous money, but I'm feeling pretty safe right now. And if I were in any better mood, I'd need CPR."

His fingers searched out my mouth and he delivered a very accurate, very warm and cheerful kiss to it. "Go ahead. Ask me anything."

I suppressed all my natural responses and forged ahead. *Focus, girl, focus.*

"Well, if you don't mind, I've been wondering. You told me your fiancée, back in the day, though beautiful, was perhaps not the woman for a blind man. So. Am I? Am I the kind of woman for a blind man? Am I a lot of fun?

Both of our bodies vibrated to rhythm of his laughter. "You're the kind of woman for a lucky man, Alice," he answered, rolling us both over onto our sides, face to face. He touched his forehead to mine. "You're the woman I want. And you're almost too much fun. Now go to sleep before you kill us both."

Chapter Fourteen

But after all that, I was still wired.

I would have liked to talk myself down but my inner part-time librarian was also part-time OCD. At the Memorial-Nottingham Branch we had a cart for returned books and videos. Sometimes I would be the one to push it around the aisles like a stroller for baby books and tuck each one into its own special place. It was…soothing.

Maybe all that sorting and shelving had given me a compulsion to get every single thing handled. I found myself obsessing about whether I should have pocketed that stupid scrap of plaid. Then I traveled back in time and revisited my three dead guys, the beatings of Rune's mom and my Margo, the ransacking of Tom's house. And mine—

Stop it, Allie!

Tom was out cold. I wrestled with the assorted components of the awesome and famous Marri-ott Bed. I moved my Euro pillow and two of the "soft-but-firm" down pillows to the foot of the bed and hung out there until the air conditioner chilled me. Then I migrated back to a more conventional position, pulling the silky, one hundred-gazillion-thread-count sheet and the fluffy comforter over me. For comfort. Time passed. Alas, no luck.

It wasn't the bed's fault. The bed was doing its job flawlessly. I couldn't get settled down. After what felt like eons of positioning and repositioning, I got up. It wasn't midnight yet. Early. I decided to take a shower and calm down. Then, once I was clean, but still not all that much calmer, I decided to get dressed and go downstairs to the bar. Have a drink to knock me out.

My clean, fresh clothes felt lovely on my clean, fresh skin. Everything all over myself felt good. I might not have peace of mind enough to call it a night but my body, at least, had achieved nirvana. So the corporeal part of me was euphoric. And my soul was also pretty darn blissful. It was the barking guard dog chained to the inside of my head who circled and circled and circled some more. But couldn't lie down.

I paused by the bed, watching Tom sleep in the pale light from the bathroom. I couldn't leave him a note, but I'd be back in a half hour. He was out. He'd never miss me. I stuffed the key card into my jeans pocket, grabbed my purse, and headed downstairs.

Jake's Lounge was empty of patrons, but still open. The bartender hovered in front of his pyramids of luminescent bottles, watching late-night ESPN. I waited for a moment out of the light, scanning the surroundings for anything sinister. Except for a lady with a very nice handbag and matching shoes, waiting for the elevator, and a pair of business guys dragging their own rolling luggage, it was just me and the bartender in view at the moment.

I slid onto a stool, thinking that this scene was that line out of the Joni Mitchell song about the girl sketching her lover's face on a bar coaster in the blue light from a TV. That song. It's about irresistible attraction, doomed longing, and sex, of course. I'd always thought "A Case Of You" was maybe the sexiest song ever written.

"Oh you're in my blood like holy wine
You taste so bitter and so sweet
Oh I could drink a case of you darling
Still I'd be on my feet"

Obsession. Clearly I wasn't the only one who let the hunger of holding on and the dread of losing make me abandon common sense. I considered turning around and going back up to the room to lie still in the darkness by this man, who was fast becoming my one all-consuming desire. That would have been good. That would have been so smart. But then my phone rang my any-old-unidentified-caller ringtone—The Who's "Who Are You?"

That jarred the Joni-induced heat out of the pit of my stomach.

"Yes?" I was hoping for a wrong number. No such luck.

"Miz Harper? It's me. Ulysses Grant. Up at the apartments by Lake Shore. We got us a problem."

Damn.

On second thought, I was relieved to hear his voice. He wasn't among the dead.

"Uh, hi, Ulysses. Mr. Grant. What's up?"

"It's about Felix and Muff and Frank. I got somethin' to tell you. Somethin' you need to know. You're involved. You and that blind Mondo guy."

"Involved how? And who's this Felix? And Muff? And Frank?"

"They're dead guys now, Miz Harper. You met Frank. Or at least you saw him th'other night. White guy. He's—he was—in a chair like mine. Mebbe he's got him angel wings now, for all I know, but I seriously doubt it." He paused to laugh, a harsh rumble that ended badly in a dry cough. He picked his story back up.

"Muff. Fat guy with a lot of long dreads in a bundle. Him, I hardly knew, but Felix—Felix

Reposado. Skinny dude, all'a time flashy shirts, shades. He was around a lot. Somethin' of a player."

Oh, come on. Felix Reposado? What kind of name was that? Sounded like cheap tequila in a cat-shaped bottle. Had to be an alias. Still, it seemed pitifully fitting for the dip-shit ferret we'd all come to know and not miss very much.

As if in answer to my unspoken disrespect, Ulysses snorted. "Not like that was Felix's real name. He never told nobody his real name. I b'lieve it was somethin' like Raymond. Raymond Leon Somethin'. Sorry son'a bitch. Loser from birth.

"He knew somethin', though. Ain't no way on God's green Earth he and Muff and Frank shot each other over money they ain't even got yet. I know for sure they didn't. They was none of 'em the brightest bulb in the hall, but they wasn't that dumb. Somebody should check the ballistics on that crime scene."

Is everybody a CSI?

"But, hey. I can't keep puttin' money into this phone forever, girl. You rich. Not me. Come pay me a visit. I'll be waitin' in the rec room where we met before. And don't bring the blind guy. He looks like easy money on a stick down here. More easy money than anybody down here ever seen. Just you. You white, but you could fit in."

Hey, thanks for the vote of confidence with the condo board, Ulysses.

"We need to talk. Ain't nobody safe unless we do. Not you. Not the Mondo guy. Not me. Will you come? Now? Tonight?"

Would I? Hell no. Not if I were smart. Then again, not having a clue about any of this was making my inner guard dog ultra nervous. Seemed like everybody knew everything about Tom and me. Like, for example—"Ulysses? How did you get my cell number?"

"Honey, ev'rybody got your number. His, too. This is the Age of the Internet. Age of In-fo-mation, baby. Didn' anyone tell you that? We poor, but we tec' savvy." He hawked up that laugh again, and then turned serious.

"Another thing. That kid. That Rune boy. His momma's so-called significant other was prowling around tonight, lookin' for him. Says he has rights. Cust'dy rights.

"I may not be smart and rich like you and the blind guy, but I know trouble when I see it. That guy is trouble with the big T. This is one danger-ous situation for your blind guy and for Rune, too. You care about that boy, Miz Harper, you need to hear me…hear what I got to say. What I got to show you.

"An' you think about this, girl. If those guys

didn't kill each other, if somebody else is killin' for money, who'd *you* think would be next?"

Terrific. Old Lady Obsession grabbed me again.

I had to go. Had to find out.

Tom was blind. And fast asleep. Besides, Ulysses was right. Bringing Tom back to the projects would be like waving a major chunk of cash around. And Rune threatened by this big-T trouble-guy? That pushed me right over the edge.

I was scared. I knew this was semi-crazy. But Ulysses would be waiting for me, at least. Crazy or not, here I went.

Be careful," he growled.

"You, too."

Careful?

No bleeping kidding. I could see myself driving out the Shoreway and on into history like Amelia Earhart. Except I wouldn't even make the news. If I vanished, Ulysses would probably just cross me off his list. He hadn't struck me as a man who would go out of his way to find trouble. Tom wouldn't have a clue where I'd gone. Maybe ever, or at least until it was way too late.

I spent a long couple of minutes weighing the consequences between scaring Tom or letting him wonder what had happened to me for the rest of his life. Or until he got over it and forgot all about me. Or until they found my body.

Ah. There was my answer.

I stopped at the front desk. The guy there looked wide awake so I figured him to be the night desk person. I asked him if he had paper and an envelope so I could leave someone a note.

He did.

I wrote a very succinct message to Tom about where I was going. I did not try to explain why I was going there without him. This was a note for life or death, not diplomacy. And I didn't have time or heart for a maybe goodbye. I shoved it into the envelope and wrote down Tom's name and the room number.

The guy was watching me with mild interest.

"Uh," I said. "Will you still be here at two a.m.?"

His eyebrows went up and he grinned. "Does it look like I'm doing that lousy a job?"

"No. Of course not. I just…."

I handed him the envelope.

"Look. If I don't come here and take this back by two a.m., please call this man in this room and read it to him. Okay?"

A well-trained hotel guy, he accepted the envelope without blinking and tucked it neatly into the breast pocket of his suit.

"Of course. I'll take care of it. And I'll hope to see you back with us before then."

Me, too.

Once outside, I scooched up against the wall and made myself as small as I could until the valet brought the car. The rain had all but stopped, but the gutters were swirling muddy water. The smell of hot asphalt tempered in the hiss of cold rain was intoxicating. Tom had opened my third eye onto the world of the senses. In so many ways.

I put that thought out of my head, tipped the valet, and drove off into the steamy darkness, wondering if I could order a vanity plate that read "DAMN."

Chapter Fifteen

I parked in the lot as close to the building as I could. My modest rented Maxima was the nicest, newest vehicle there. It had all its hubcaps. I stood by the car, debating.

Stay? Go?

Run?

I didn't see a soul anywhere, and it was dead silent for such a big, tall place. Was someone in there waiting for me? Watching from behind one of those blank, hovering windows? My neck prickled. My heart hammered. I could hear it all the way up in my ears. If Tom had any idea I was down here, he'd be frantic. And probably livid. And justified.

Breathe, Allie. Get a grip.

I breathed.

The night air was warm and heavy, weighed down by the rain. I could hear my great lake now. Out there heaving away in the darkness. I breathed again, deeper, inhaling its mossy perfume. I wanted to raise my arms and invoke its power to protect me. That's how I feel about Lake Erie. Like it is the earthly deputy of God.

Okay. Better now. Stop with the lake worship, Alice. Get going.

My sandals grated against rough concrete. I picked up the pace. Out of the parking lot. In through the doors. Down the echoing hall. One new addition to the corridor since last night was the yellow crime scene tape stuck across one of the doors.

Chill, chill, double chill. I knew what crime that one marked. Make my chill a triple. Three dead before dawn. Right behind that door. Goose bumps swarmed up my bare arms all the way to my neck.

That did it. I was almost running.

The common room at the end of the bleak passageway hadn't changed. The upended chairs and tables were still down and over. The TV was droning some paid programming thing about a nifty floor steamer/cleaner you could have put to excellent use in this very room.

I kept walking. Ulysses was sitting all by himself. Of his two former companions, one was dead, one off somewhere unknown tonight. Ulysses was waiting for me right where we'd first found him, hardly twenty-four hours ago. His back to the door. His head tilted at a good angle for watching.

Or sleeping. Poor old guy. He should be in bed. I slowed myself way down, letting my sandals slap on the floor so as not to embarrass him for falling asleep.

Now I was right behind him.

He didn't move.

I called his name. "Ulysses?"

Ever read The Iliad and The Odyssey?

"Ulysses? Ulysses!" I was almost shouting now. His head was lolled back more than I'd thought. His eyes were a little bit open, but the pupils were rolled up out of sight. Only the whites, which were not white at all, but yellowish and crosshatched with tiny red vessels, showed…

Wake up, Allie.

Forget the *eyes.* I was getting caught up in the details because I hated the big picture. Ulysses A. Grant was dead.

I put my hand to his neck, still hoping, remembering Renata and that almost-peed-my-pants groan. But Ulysses was silent and although his skin was warm, he wasn't breathing. When I pressed my shaking fingers to his wrist for a pulse, a folded up piece of paper dropped out of his limp hand onto to the floor. That's when I knew for sure.

I didn't scream. People who find bodies on TV scream. Big, echoing, throat-shredding shrieks. Staring down at Ulysses, I could feel my whole body screaming out fear and horror loud enough to shatter glass, but the sound that fought its way out of me was a pitiful croaking moan.

Here was all that was left of this old man, now that his quirky humanity, his hopes and pride had just…gone. My moan for Ulysses—who'd died and left me here all by myself—was truer than any phony actor scream I'd ever heard. It got the job done for me and for him.

Besides, by the time I'd wrenched up enough breath to be loud, I was warning myself, *Shhh! Don't scream, Allie. Screaming is for when you believe someone will come to help you. This isn't the time or the place for that.*

I fumbled around in my purse, shoveling crap out onto the floor, digging for my phone. Once I had it trapped in my stupid, sweaty, trembling hand, I punched in 9-1-1.

"9-1-1. What is your emergency?"

The voice that came out of my mouth sounded nothing like me.

"A man. Ulysses A. Grant," the voice said. It was calm. "He is dead. In the rec room on the first floor of the westernmost high-rise across from Joe's Super Market on Lake Shore. Please send somebody right away," Then I threw my phone and my purse down onto its scattered contents, beat my fists against my knees, and bawled like a baby.

After about a minute, I stopped that. Mostly. I wiped off my face and pulled myself together. A little. I waited there with Ulysses, as quietly as I could, considering how much I was trembling. What was I supposed to be doing? This might be a crime scene. I knew that much from watching the CSIs et al., over the years. Too bad I'd already broken the CSI Don't Bust Out Crying Rule of dead-guy-discovery.

I knew enough to preserve the area around any dead body—around Ulysses Aeneas Grant, a formerly alive human being of my acquaintance, whom I had liked—intact. So I loaded my junk back into my purse and stepped back, but as I did, I spotted the scrap of paper lying on the dirty floor where it had fallen from Ulysses' hand.

Evidence?

The first rule of crime scene television: Leave the evidence undisturbed. I could hear a siren unraveling a thin ribbon of sound. Closing the distance between itself and me.

Leave the evidence undisturbed.

No kidding.

I was just looking….

I glided over, picked up the slip of paper, and stepped further back into the room, sneaking a glance at my reflection in the blackened windows. My heart was trying to hammer its way out of my chest. Had anyone seen? Wouldn't there be a security camera in here somewhere? Was it a felony to disturb a crime scene? What class? How much jail time? Too many questions, with answers I probably wouldn't like.

Camera first. I swiveled around, scanning. *Crap.* Yes. There was one.

Good news. It was dangling by its wire. Any video it had captured would be a close-up of the wall.

So I had disturbed the evidence? Tough. I was willing to bet that this paper had something to do with why Ulysses had lured me down here, had risked his life. And mine. With mixed results. So far.

The siren was still pretty far out, but its fragile whine was rounding into a fuller, deeper wail. Getting closer. Not too late for me to drop my incriminating scrap back onto the floor beneath Ulysses' dead hand. But wait. Wouldn't my prints be stuck to it? Didn't your prints stick to practically anything?

Jesus wept.

Siren. Closer. A throaty howl. I unfolded the paper. It was lined, like a ripped off half page out of a small notebook, stained all over in smudges of reddish brown. My hands shook. I forced them quiet so I could read. Here's what I read:

DIRTY!!!~~

Seriously?

This was evidence? This was a clue? The word and its oversupply of punctuation ended in an unreadable scrawl. Great. I'd risked probably jail time for one word, three screamers, and a squiggle. Served me right.

I clenched my hand around the note to make it smaller. While I'd been staring at it, the siren had blasted up and been choked off. Footsteps clattered toward me down the hall. I faced the door, trying not to look like I'd had my hand in the cookie jar, or that the cookie was still scrunched up in my fist, as Officers Valerio and Clark rushed into the room.

Chapter Sixteen

I didn't get arrested this time either. Not that I didn't deserve it. Valerio and Bob had focused all their attention on Ulysses' lifeless body at first. They handled him in a way that probably would disturb the evidence. Grabbing him out of the chair, laying him on the floor, pulling open his shirt, checking for any sign of life. Then the EMS team arrived and they checked, too.

Don't bother, I could have told them.

The distractions worked fine for me, since I had recently probably become a Class-Something Felon. While everybody was dealing with the body of Ulysses, I slipped my scrap of contraband into my jeans. Tucked in behind the Marriott key card, it wouldn't show up at all.

I brought my self-serving little mind back to Ulysses. By the way they attended to him, I decided neither the police nor the EMTs thought they were looking at a crime. There was no gunshot wound.

Therefore, no gunshot residue, or as I like to call it, "GSR," either. I congratulated myself on my extensive knowledge of police procedure. No wound. No blood. No petechiae that would indicate strangling or asphyxiation.

He was simply an old guy with yellowed, bloodshot eyes. Probably drank too much and ate bad. When they'd rolled him out of his chair I was shocked to realize that one of his legs was missing below the knee. A diabetic, probably. He'd called me and then had himself a heart attack. And died without any help at all. That looked likely. Surely, that was possible. And plenty sad enough.

Except. In my pocket was a piece of paper that might have been Ulysses' dying message to me.

DIRTY!!!

At the very least, someone warned someone else that another someone was dirty. Or maybe some *thing* was. Could be this note was about the floor in the common room. Or some unknown rotten shame? What did I know? The brown stains sure looked like blood to me. I needed some of that magic cop blood-identifier spray.

My brain was back online. All in all, I found it to be an improbable coincidence that Ulysses had called me to share information about a crime and then just…died. But I could only be sure about two things: Ulysses had something to tell me. And he was gone now.

The rest was up for grabs. Dirty could mean anything. As far as that went, Dirty could mean cops.

My no good very long day caught up with me and I swayed, dizzy.

Bob saw me swaying and that put the spotlight of interrogation back onto me. "What the hell?" He caught the look Valerio shot him. "Sorry. Pardon my French. But why are you here, Ms. Harper?"

I would have dearly loved to take Bob aside and spill the whole story. I thought, given our friendship, he'd probably look the other way on my felonious meddling with the note if I handed it over and said, "Here. I picked this up for you." But tough old Valerio was standing right in front of me. Glaring in a disconcertingly by-the-book way. And besides, what if DIRTY did mean cops? I had a couple of those right here, looking grouchy at me.

An icy trickle snuck down my back.

I needed a story to explain my presence but I had nothing plausible prepared. So I dived in with the bare bones of the truth. "I got a call from this man here. Ulysses. We met last night right here in this room. He told me he had something to tell me. That Tom and I were in danger. So I came. But when I got here, he was already dead."

Oh, and I found this cool note, too. And I got my sleazy prints all over the damn thing and now I have to hide it or probably go to jail.

I bit my tongue and arranged my face for innocence and stupidity. "Maybe the strain of calling me brought on the attack?"

Officer Valerio gave me a look which I interpreted as *Thank you so much for providing us with the obvious explanation, Ms. Clueless Civilian.* But then he shrugged.

"You're probably right. I don't see anything particularly suspicious here. We'll look into it. But if you're thinking 'murder,' Ms. Harper, you can probably let that one go."

Murder? Yes, sir. I was. I was, for sure, thinking murder.

My worldview tilted and I got dizzy again.

These guys were all saying, by word and demeanor, "Nope. Nothing homicidal here."

Not me. No way. I could see murder, rolling on, like that giant stone in the Indiana Jones movie, crushing a path that led straight from a woman's voice reciting numbers in the night to this. Twenty-four hours later, murder had found me here, standing over the body of a spunky old man named Ulysses Grant in this scary room.

Overnight, it brushed by Renata on its way to smash the life out of Felix, Muff, and Frank. It bruised my Margo and now it had obliterated poor Ulysses. I couldn't see a rational pattern or plan in any of it.

Yet.

Maybe everything until right now could be chalked up to senseless violence. But this right here? Oh, yeah. Murder. I could feel it right down to the soles of my cold little feet.

The piece of paper in my pocket was burning a nice felonious hole in my leg.

Buck up, Allie. Escape with your Clueless Citizen reputation intact and take your lethal ideas about what's going on to a safer place where you can decide what to do.

And hide.

My lame "natural causes" scenario had at least made me out to be a good citizen. Not at all smart, but not particularly criminal either. After a few minutes the cops released me on my own recognizance and gave me an EMS man to escort me to my car.

The return drive downtown, with a motley crew of terrors and sorrows riding shotgun with me in the Maxima, took about a year. The numb unreality of every single *thing* was my buffer zone, so I didn't fall utterly apart, but my body was over-run by a nasty, bug-crawling sensation. And every now and then a sob would break loose and shake me around.

It purely sucked.

At least it wasn't after two a.m. I had one more compromising note to pick up before this night was done.

My guy handed me back my envelope. A trace of curiosity in his eyes.

"Everything okay then?"

If you only knew.

"Peachy. Thanks so much."

I was back in my fabulous Marriott Bed, tucked in with my unauthorized little murder-scene visit and my DIRTY!!! little probable felony, by two a.m. And in spite of the whole new array of guard dog alerts in my head, I was out cold by 2:05. As far as I could tell, Tom had slept the sleep of the just—or the just laid—all the time I'd been gone.

Chapter Seventeen

Thursday, August 20

I was dead right. Tom was worried and mad.

I'd waited to tell him about 1) my unauthorized trip to the projects, 2) the death of Ulysses Grant, and 3) my stealing a piece of paper—until we were having breakfast at David's in the Marriott. I figured he wouldn't yell if there were people around. And I wouldn't cry if there were pancakes and bacon in front of me.

So far it wasn't going too badly on either count. I focused on how handsome he looked. How lean and tan he was. And to ignore how high his color was at the moment. How his sexy smile had gone missing.

"Allie, for God's sake, how could you do something so dangerous?" he hissed. "I mean, at one in the morning on a *good* night—when people don't know you've won a lot of money and there haven't been break-ins and beatings and *killings*, and God knows what all—that is no place to be."

He'd hit "killings" extra hard. The woman with three small children at the next table, shot him a look that was half alarmed, half annoyed. Which was lost on him. I gave her back one that said, *Men. We know how they are.* That put her on hold for the moment.

"Tom." I lowered my voice, hoping he would follow suit. "I know. I know. I'm sorry. Ulysses called and I was shocked he had my cell number. And when I asked him, he said everybody's got my number and yours, too. Because of the Internet. That threw me. And then he also warned me about some man, who was involved with Renata some-how, and who had come around looking for Rune. Claiming he should get custody. Ulysses thought that man was what he called 'big T trouble.' That really tore it. I thought if he had something that could help us…help Rune…help the police…I couldn't just not—"

"Okay. Okay. Why didn't you come get me?"

"You were asleep. I wore you out. You said I was going to kill us both, remember?"

Our neighbor lady must have heard the "kill" word again or maybe the "wore you out" part, and she started rushing her kids through the end of their French toast.

"Besides, Ulysses specifically told me not to bring you."

"Why not?" His face got still and stern, and I had a disorienting jolt of *who is this angry stranger?*

"Why *not?*" he repeated with even more heat. "Because I'm blind? You have to understand one thing right now, Allie. That will never be a good enough reason for you not to tell me what's going on. Not ever."

"No! Tom. That was not the reason. I promise. Ulysses said you looked like 'easy money on a stick.'" I let a grin slip into my voice. "I suppose he could have been referring to your cane—I hadn't thought about that. But now that you mention it—"

After a long couple of steely seconds Tom let his shoulders slump. "Okay. Stop. As long as we understand each other. As long as we have some ground rules. From now on until things calm down, you go absolutely nowhere without telling me.

"I guess all's well that ends—" he paused for a second, reflecting, I presumed, on the inappropriateness of saying "that ends well" under the circumstances, and finished, "with only one dead guy."

The mother next door signed her check, scooped up her young, and departed. As she went by, she muttered, "You people should be very careful."

Tom frowned. "What's wrong with her?"

"Too much death and destruction in our conversation for her kids. But she's gone now and I need you to listen to something and not get so mad you can't hear it. Deal?"

I tried to assess his state of mind. On a one-to-ten scale from "peaceful and loving" to "screaming freak-out," I'd have put him at about a six. I reached over and put what I hoped was a calming hand on his arm. It felt tense to me.

"Tom. There's a bigger problem."

"That's hard to fathom."

"I know. And I'm sorry, but you want me to tell you what I'm up to and not go off on my own. It's hard to tell you anything when you're vibrating like that."

He dragged in a breath and huffed it out. Corralling his state of mind.

"I'm sorry. Most of this mess is my fault, not yours. Go ahead. I'll listen."

"Okay. Here. What happened to Ulysses made everything look different to me. I'm about ninety-nine percent sure somebody killed him. Not accidentally. Not in some shootout that was maybe unmitigated dumb-assed-ness. Killed. Him. On. Purpose. In a clever way that would make it look like he simply died. Ulysses was murdered, Tom. Maybe murdered because he called me. Almost certainly murdered because of something he knew about Felix and those guys not really killing each other in some argument. He was murdered because of whatever that miserable little scrap of paper meant to him. And to us.

"Us."

"The cops don't see this. They've got their hands full. Plus, Valerio and Bob may be mixed up somehow in what's been going on. They may not want to look too hard. And I can't give them the paper now, not just because it's wrong for me to have it, but because it says "dirty" and dirty could mean a lot of people, including cops."

"Allie. Do you mean that?"

"I do. I don't like it, but I do. Hang in here with me. Here's another reason we're on our own: The EMTs looked at Ulysses and saw an old, unhealthy amputee with no bullet holes in him. There'll be an autopsy, but I can tell you—because I heard it from the lips of the Medical Examiner himself once upon a time—it could take weeks for something obvious to show up, and if it's something subtle, they may not run the tests for that at all. Nobody's looking at this as a homicide. Except me."

"And you think we're next?"

"Not exactly. I was scared out of my mind last night, but I'm better this morning. I can't think of any rational reason for somebody to kill us today.

They couldn't use the ticket. Surely nobody could be stupid enough to think about that at this point. We don't have it anymore, anyway, and we don't have the cash yet. Somebody smart enough to murder Ulysses in a way that mimicked his health profile will be looking forward to the moment the jackpot is paid out. So far, I've got no plan for addressing any of this. But rocking along like nothing's happened would not be on my agenda."

Well, I hadn't made him happy, and my stock hadn't gone up much. His face was no longer flushed and angry. Pale now, and troubled. Not an improvement. He smiled, though. It was weak, but welcome. He freed his arm from my iron grip and put his hand over mine. Big sigh.

"If I could dismiss all this, I'd be a happy man. But I can't. Night before last, the moment I heard those numbers and realized what they were—what they meant—everything changed. Fact of life, Allie. The world is full of greed and ruthlessness. It's around us all the time. If we're lucky it doesn't touch us. But guess what? I got so extra-ultra-lucky that it's unlucky. I woke up the greed and ruthlessness. I turned its attention toward Rune, toward me. And you.

"Renata. Margo. My house. Your house. Because of my big bad Mondo, three people were dead before the sun came up yesterday morning.

And now Ulysses. This is my problem. I made it. But it belongs to both of us now. Everybody we care about. Everything we touch—I've got to stop pretending I can make it all go away by not liking it and wishing it had never happened."

He stopped and sat there, silent. Calming down. Pulling himself together. Coming out of his nightmare of regret and disaster. Coming back to me.

"We'll decide how to proceed, Allie. We'll be smart. And careful. But we'll also do what we can to find out for ourselves what's going on. We'll put our skills together. My blind man's sixth sense. Your…" An almost smile of forgiveness. "Your irrepressible you-ness. I'm on board, I swear. But for now, I promised to take Rune to see his mom. And you're going to keep your part of our deal. Yes?"

"Yes. Two Musketeers. That's us, babe. I'm with you."

Chapter Eighteen

A moderately disconcerting thing happened after we left the restaurant but before we made it to the elevator. Tom's cell phone rang. And it didn't simply go *ring, ring* like a plain old phone. No, it had a ringtone like a cool phone. Like mine, as far as that goes. And the ringtone was—wait for it—a few bars from the piano intro of Diana Krall's cover of "A Case of You." The moody, hot, triple-sexy version. Talk about coincidence. And talk about accessibility. There was nothing even slightly disabled about that phone.

It was obvious to me that this was not Tom's special ring for the anonymous credit-card-offer caller. Two notes, and his face shut down into careful-and-contained mode. He stopped and pulled the phone out of his pocket, but before he answered it, he turned to me.

"Allie. I have to take this call. Can you wait for me upstairs, and then we'll see about Rune?"

"Sure." I said the word as if I were. Of myself. Of him. Sure of anything in this world. I walked away, trying to make my footsteps sound confident and nonchalant at the same time.

While waiting for the elevator I looked back down the hall and saw him standing stock-still in the middle of the lobby, his head bent to a serious conversation. A tall, handsome blind man, holding his white cane, not needing any arm of mine to help him traverse his world. A stranger I'd barely met and hardly knew, whose touch was burned deep into my skin.

I was in big trouble now.

The elevator binged and I walked through the open door, closed my eyes, and listened to it hush itself shut behind me.

I was up in the room for maybe ten minutes, arranging and rearranging my state of mind before he and his phone showed up. I knew he couldn't see my face, but I figured he'd probably be able to hear it. So I smiled and said—light as a feather, I certainly hoped—"Your phone is cool. It's got ringtones and everything."

He was pale except for a patch of bright color on each of his excellently sculpted cheekbones. "Too cool for a blind man?" His tone was pinched. Even I, a sighted person, had access to his state of mind. The man was flustered. I wasn't the only one. This settled me down. I found a small, chilly spot—like a bar-sized refrigerator—in the center of my chest and moved into it.

"I'm sorry." I worked on keeping my voice cool and crisp. "I didn't mean to disrespect your phone."

He sighed. "You didn't. Sorry. It—I'm a little fried, is all. It's just a phone. Why don't we use it to call about Rune now?"

There was a long pause, and then he said, a harsh note in his voice, "Allie, come here."

My feet responded to the command in his words and my chest thawed a couple of degrees when I saw the look on his face. He was standing by our Marriott Bed, which had been tautly made up in our absence. I tried hard not to get distracted by the memory of the current of laughter that had surged through us both while he held me in his arms on that exact bed and told me I was the woman he wanted.

I moved closer. He reached for me and found me. I leaned against him, not terribly relaxed. He laid his palms on both sides of my face and pressed his forehead to mine. I wasn't going to fall for that ploy again.

"Allie," he said again, "I need you to trust me. I need to trust you. Everything's moving too fast for us right now. Two days ago, we were…we hadn't… It was an entirely different world for both of us.

Everything's torn up now. There's been no time to fill in all our blanks. I need you to stick with me, until I can explain…things. And you probably have things to tell me, too?"

I heard the question in his voice. We were rushing headlong toward the part of the relationship where it goes deeper or goes away. Away was not my game plan. I was falling for the ploy. I could feel it. I relaxed my forehead against his and let my heart out of the fridge.

"Deal," I said. "Why don't you kiss me now and we'll talk some other time? And trust each other until the blanks get filled in?"

"Deal. Double deal."

I had questions. Now I realized he had questions, too. But as far as I was concerned right then we could wait and pay that piper on down the road. I wanted last night back. I wanted now.

His lips brushed mine and there we were again. The woman and the man who couldn't get close to a Marriott Bed without falling right back in.

• • ● • •

When we called Social Services, we found out that Rune had been placed with a temporary foster family in South Euclid. There was some back and forth about the rules and regs, but we were able to get in touch with Officer Bob's wife, Marie. She cleared the way for us and got us the address and phone number.

Then we called the hospital on McCauley Road, where the EMS ambulance had taken Renata, to see how she was doing. They told us you had to be immediate family to find out anything specific—big surprise—but at least she was alive and still there. I called Marie back and she hung up to call the hospital and do more way-clearing. After a few minutes my phone played "Bat Out of Hell" which was my standard tone for not-totally-anonymous callers. Like "Social Serv." It was her, all right. Sounding professional and stern.

"Renata is alive and awake, but they're telling me she's non-responsive. I'd suspect they're keeping her pretty drugged up. From what I could understand, she's a wreck. Are you sure you want to take Rune there?"

"We promised him, Marie." I was afraid she'd mess us up with Social Services if she thought we were bad for Rune. "We'll take him out to lunch and for a drive and let him spend a minute or two. See her. Tom will be there. He trusts Tom."

She was silent. "Marie," I pleaded, "he's a tough, smart kid. He's seen a lot and been through a lot. From what I've observed, Tom is the main source of stability in his life now. Rune's up to seeing his mother not feeling too well. I suspect this isn't the first time. And it'll do him good to be with people he knows. Please."

"All right. Be careful with him, Allie. Don't make me sorry."

● ● ● ● ●

We were on our way, then, with our new relationship almost intact, happy to be seeing Rune, happy to reunite him with his mom.

"Leave well enough alone" was not my strong suit. I had to ask.

"Do you have one of those ringtones in mind for me?"

He wrinkled his brow in a way that suggested "not threatened, merely giving this important choice serious consideration."

"I believe so. Do you?"

"I do. I've been saving one…for…for you. As it turns out. But you go first. What's mine?"

"'White Rabbit.' Jefferson Airplane."

"What? Oh. The part about Alice? Geez. I do so adore that name. Anyway, that song is all about drugs. What does that say about me?"

He took my face in both his sentient hands, paying no heed to the fact that we were standing in the hall outside our room. "You're my drug, Alice."

"Your drug of choice?"

Always fishing, girl. Keep it up and he'll run away.

His mouth was all mine. My body moved until it was pressed as close to his as the laws of physics would permit. I willed myself closer, trying to pierce the barrier of our clothes, our skin, into the deep, dark soul of us together.

"My only rational choice," he whispered. "Now, tell me mine."

"'Blind Love,' Bon Jovi. It's not about…your being blind. That's just a coincidence. The first winter down here, I was so wild and scared of everything—I'd open up the top of the VW and go out and drive all night. In December, exactly like the girl in the song. Mr. Jovi released it only a couple of weeks ago. I listened to it. Over and over. On my bus rides. And I promised myself that a 'Blind Love' guy was still coming for me, trying to find me. That I wouldn't always be nobody and… alone—"

My voice broke.

He intercepted a tear with his thumb. "Shhh. Alice. Shhh"

He kissed me again. Gently. Easing us back into our separate selves. Time to go.

"I think we both did well with the tones."

"Me, too."

Chapter Nineteen

The house in South Euclid was an Arts & Crafts bungalow, with deep, overhanging eaves and a stacked-stone porch. Everything about it, from the well-tended front yard to the substantial wooden front door, hollered reliability.

Rune was waiting for us on the front porch swing. He was still wearing the red-and-white striped shirt and jeans, but they had been laundered. He was happy to see Tom, and okay with me being along. In a hurry to go.

The foster mother came to the door. She was exactly what you'd think. A little round, a little tired, a lot kind. She told us to be careful and Rune to be good. She watched us go down the steps to the street, buckle the boy into the backseat, and drive away. She was shielding her eyes from the sun and clutching a dish towel in her other hand, like a mom in a storybook.

From there we headed on up to Target, where

to Rune's delight, we rode the famous shopping cart escalator and then bought some new small shirts and jeans, plain underwear "with no action figures, okay?" and "Train Your Dragon" pajamas, plus a suitcase to carry that stuff in.

"For when you can go home with your mom," Tom said.

Then we went to the toy area and picked the kid up a hand-held video game player and games to go in it. Next, we loaded up on notebooks, regular books, sketch pads, and pencils to counterbalance the ill-effects of too much of the video stuff. Which, in turn, led to the purchase of a backpack to put those things in.

I saw how Rune stood close to Tom, leaning in toward him, whenever he had the chance. How Tom would squat down and run his sensitive hands over things like games and sneakers, touching buttons and Velcro fasteners, asking serious, interested questions in his calm, quiet, reassuring Tom way. How Rune looked at Tom. How Tom loved Rune. How I was learning to love them both. I thought about how lucky Rune was to have Tom in his life.

Me, too, I thought. I'm lucky, too.

It was three o'clock before we stopped shopping and dropped into a Wendy's for burgers and fries.

I could tell Rune was dying to ask Tom a lot

of questions about the Mondo, but he knew it might be a sore subject. Finally, the need to know overpowered his fear of another lecture about the evils of gambling.

"I guess we picked good numbers," he ventured.

Tom smiled. I gave him credit for that. "We picked very good numbers. Lots of people are wishing they had our numbers." I heard the irony, but it was well-cloaked.

The boy hesitated and then plunged ahead, "How much did you win?"

Tom's face clouded at the question, but he bore up bravely, and his answer was systematic and Tom-like. "Well, the jackpot was supposed to be five hundred million. But, apparently, people tend to buy more tickets when the pot is that large."

I suppressed a grin. *Apparentleee!* For a second, I remembered my very-small-dollars-an-hour part-time librarian job and decided to call in rich, at least for a couple of weeks. On the basis of the at least ten million I had coming to me since Tom had taken rather liberal advantage of my BOGO coupon offer.

Tom continued. "So when the drawing closed, the final amount was 550 million. And there was only one winning number. The one you and I picked. Now, most people take their winnings in what is called a 'lump sum' and that's usually a little more than half of the jackpot. For this one, the lump sum is around two hundred-ninety million. And then taxes take a good bit to pay for things people need like schools. Let's say our part would be one hundred-ninety million."

"Wow," Rune's skinny shoulders slumped. "That's not so much."

"Rune," Tom's expression was serious. I could see that he didn't want to oversell the size of the winnings, since that was the exact opposite of his original plan. "Rune, that's plenty of money. It's enough money that, if your mother thinks it's a good idea, you and she might be able to move to a house like Mrs. Robbins'. It's enough that you can go to college when the time comes. No problem."

I knew that, for Tom, this was shaky ground. I was beginning to comprehend what troubled him so much. Setting aside our recent experiences with violence, money in huge quantities is still a trouble magnet if you're not prepared to handle it. For Rune's mother it could be a snare that would bind her to unscrupulous men. For Rune it might be a spiral into a too-easy, wasted life. I was getting to be a small cautionary tale myself. I'd already decided to at least temporarily ditch my library career. My life had not yet gotten easy enough to be seriously dissolute. But I had to admit there were issues.

Tom forged on. "You helped pick the numbers.

You're entitled to at least that much. Your mother can help you decide."

Rune looked downcast and I knew Tom, even with his spidey sense, might miss this one. "Rune," I asked, "is something bothering you?"

He bobbed his head, glancing away from me and up to Tom who appeared baffled by my question. "Yeah. My number. The one I picked. The Mondo Ball. It wasn't a true number."

Tom shook his head, "'Not a true number?' What do you mean?"

The boy hung his head low over the table and, with one small brown finger, drew a furrow through a dollop of ketchup that had splashed down in front of him. "It's not my true age. Eight. I wanted it to be eight. But I'm only seven. And a quarter."

Holy cow. I don't know much about luck or odds, but after all the talk about this number and that number, that one piece of information blew me away. Tom's Mondo really was an act of God. The hairs on the back of my neck stood right up.

But the kid looked like he was about to bawl.

"Rune," I jumped in, "eight is the best number you could possibly have chosen. And it's okay to pretend to be older than you are sometimes. I know lots of ladies who pretend to be younger than they are."

His face wrinkled in disbelief. "Why would

anyone want to do that? What good would that do?"

Tom laughed out loud. He found his cane and rose to his feet. "Good question. Enough about money. There's plenty to go around. Let's go visit your mom."

Chapter Twenty

I don't know what it was about that week in August, but after the big storm in the early morning hours of Wednesday—the memory of which I shall always treasure—there was a storm every afternoon for five straight days. I was driving into the Thursday one.

The McCauley Road Hospital was an ancient building, big and gray, its stone façade darkened by decades of industrial grime. It would have been intimidating under the sunniest of circumstances. Now, overhung by the approaching storm, it looked like a prison or a haunted fortress. I peeked into the rearview mirror and saw that Rune's eyes were wide. Clearly he didn't want to go in there. And he certainly didn't want his mother to be in there.

"Rune…" I made my voice as calm and cheery as I could and hoped he couldn't hear the dread I myself was feeling about this grim place. "Have you ever been inside a hospital?"

He shook his head. Mute.

"This one doesn't look so good. We're having a spooky storm and it makes things…maybe a little scary. But hospitals are full of wonderful doctors and nurses. They're very smart and very nice."

Usually, I amended to myself, remembering some very cranky-pants doctors and nurses I had encountered from time to time.

"If you're sick or injured, a hospital is the best, safest place in the world to be." I mentally crossed my fingers. Rune didn't need to hear about inevitable exceptions and deadly infections. "It makes me feel better to know that all the people in this hospital want your mom to get better."

That last may have been a little over the top, but Rune seemed mollified. At least he nodded like he believed me and the fear on his face receded ever so slightly.

The woman behind the information desk, Ms. Ivy Martin, by her name tag, had obviously been hired for her ability to look friendly and act authoritarian. She smiled at us with her mouth but her eye corners didn't crinkle at all. Her smooth brown face was unmarred by empathy or human concern. Her general demeanor was wary as hell.

Of course, she'd have noticed that the three of us weren't exactly a matched set. We told her who we were here to see and explained it was Runako's mom. She softened somewhat. I didn't think she could miss how frightened his eyes were and how he had latched on to Tom's hand like it was the last lifeboat off the *Titanic*.

"Well," she said, consulting her computer screen. "Well. Let me call up to the nurses' station on her floor and check on how she's doing and whether or not now would be a good time."

I gritted my teeth. *Come on, lady.* I cast my attention right on down to the tips of my Nikes so she couldn't read my mind. So I'd appear meek and highly cooperative. I didn't want my bad attitude to hurt Rune's chances.

She picked up a phone and there was a brief conversation. Then she said, "Oh." In a way that made me jerk my head up again. Her expression was grave for an instant and then she composed herself, as if she'd realized all three of us were showing her the same worried face.

She had a grip on herself. I'll give her that. She said, "Thank you very much" quite calmly to the person on the other end of the line and turned to me. "It's going to be a moment, Miss—?"

I filled in the blank.

"Ms. Harper, why don't you have your friend and Runako wait in the chairs over there? I'd like a word with you."

She propelled me into an anteroom with a

door and pulled the door closed behind us. The room was gray and dim, but she didn't switch on the light. Outside, the wind was raving, the lightning and thunder almost continuous. Rain blasted the windows. She faced me, and her pleasant mouth was a thin line. This was going to be bad.

"Ms. Harper, I'm sorry to inform you that Renata Davis passed away about an hour ago. The floor nurse said she had been doing better, had eaten most of her lunch, was fairly responsive, and then, when the aide went in to take away Ms. Davis' tray, she was gone. They called a code blue, but nothing could be done."

"Oh. No." Sorrow rolled over me with anger right on its heels. Natural causes again. This time the blame would be on the beaters, and the beaters would be too dead to be prosecuted. This time, however, I had my act together. "Had she had any visitors today?"

Ms. Martin's face closed up a little tighter. "I wouldn't know. No one has asked me to see her today. Except you. You're likely the first visitor she's had since she's been here. If you have questions, there'll be an autopsy. Then we'll know more."

She gazed at me, wavering between annoyance and worry, and then brought her full attention back online with a little shake of her head.

"In the meantime, I don't know how you

want to handle it with that poor little boy." Her guard slipped, and I glimpsed the compassion her position had taught her to hide. I forgave her for doing her job.

Here's how I was planning to handle it with that poor little boy: I was going to lie like a house on fire.

I did, too. I walked out of that anteroom and I didn't look back. I gave Tom's shoulder a hard "just wait" squeeze, and then I sat down in the chair next to Rune and faced him with my brightest, kindest, most grown-up smile.

"Rune," I began, "we're not going to be able to see your mother this afternoon. She's not doing quite as well." Understatement. "She's going to need more—a special procedure." Autopsy always qualifies as a special procedure in my book. "We'll have to call tomorrow and see if we can come back."

No. This first pure and absolute lie was the one bright spot. We would never, ever have to come back to this horrible place.

Rune stared back at me. His eyes were old and sad. Sadder, maybe, than any eyes I'd ever let myself see into.

"She's dead, isn't she?" he said in a flat, thin voice. "She died before we even got here. Didn't she?"

Ah, hell. No help for it. Truth. "I'm so sorry,

Rune. I didn't want you to find out like this. Here. I thought it would be easier for you if Tom told you."

He shrugged. "It's okay, Allie. I knew as soon as the lady said 'Oh.' Can we go now?"

We went. Tom sat in the backseat with Rune on the way to the Robbins' house, talking softly. Rune answered him in a small, sad voice. What with the car engine, the sound of the rain, and the windshield wipers, I didn't hear much of what they said. Rune never cried that I saw. Not then. Not later. He sat and stared at his knees or out the window.

I cried, though, and did my best to hide it and not drive off the road. I cried for Rune and the family he'd never had and the anguish he'd bottled up inside. I cried for Renata and the mess she'd made of her life, merely by wanting love and security. And I cried for Tom, knowing that he'd blame himself for setting fate into motion and being the unwitting cause of Rune's mother's death, simply by trying to help. Rune would never blame Tom, I was sure. But Tom would never stop blaming himself.

We walked Rune to Mrs. Robbins' door and told her the news. I liked the way she stooped down and put her arms around him and said she was very, very sorry, the way she would have to an adult. Rune hugged her back. I thought that was a good sign. We promised to call and come for him as soon as we knew more about his mom. We told him not to think even for a minute he was going to be all on his own.

Tom and I left him there in her warm, bright doorway. A small, lost kid, hanging onto a new backpack as though it could transport him back to the happy, hopeful moment before the lady said "Oh." We made our way to the car in the rain. Leaning on each other. Not talking at all.

Chapter Twenty-one

"Murder?

"Murder."

It was after eleven that night and Tom and I were lying, very chaste, in each other's arms in our big Marriott Bed. We were tired. We were sad. We were scared. I was predicting to myself that it would be at least two full days before our libidos recovered. In the meantime, it was comforting to snuggle together, cozy as hibernating bears, listening to the rain, reviewing our situation, and considering our options. Maybe this would be the way we would cuddle up when we were ninety and ninety-four. I'd like that.

It was Thursday night. Since Tuesday, we'd been fairly innocent bystanders to one simple breaking-and-entering, two breaking-and-entering/assault-and-battery combos, one triple-fatality shootout, and two—possibly health-related, but to our minds, mysterious and most likely premeditated—demises.

Five dead. That was a lot to deal with by anybody's standards. Tom's early-on comment about tsunamis and earthquakes? No joke. Anybody who thinks winning the lottery would be a cakewalk could learn a thing or two from our forty-eight hours of mayhem. Here we were, barely twelve hours out from breakfast, talking murder again.

My phone went off.

I was getting way too many late-night "Who Are You?"s for my taste. I looked at the screen. "Unknown." As advertised. Forewarned, I was, but not forearmed. Tom rolled into the staring-at-the-ceiling position, even though of course he wasn't. His face was one hundred percent *What next?*

I couldn't resist. I picked up.

"Ms. Harper?"

"Yes."

"This is Officer Anthony Valerio."

"Officer Valerio. Hi. How are you?"

"I'm good, thanks. I hope I'm not calling too late."

"No. No. That's okay."

"There was something...last night. Up on Lake Shore. Did you notice anything unusual? Anything the decedent, Mr. Grant, might have had in his possession at the time of death? Might even have dropped? When he talked to you, did he say he had something to show you?"

"No. He said he had something to tell me."

"And he didn't give you any clues as to what?"

"Uh. I'm trying to remember what he said, Officer. He talked about the three dead men. He found the circumstances of that shooting to be… concerning."

Right then, inside my head, I was conjuring my own video of that last moment. Felix, Muff, and Frank in deep conversation, maybe plotting something I wouldn't have approved of. Then, how about this? How about Officer Dirty Valerio, storming in? Killing them all before they could move. Stunned faces. Jerking bodies. Blood. And then what? Valerio doling out smoking guns, making sure that everybody got one. That part of my head movie wasn't working. What—?

Officer Valerio stepped out of my bloody crime scene, his face dreadful and threatening, and spoke into my ear.

"Ms. Harper? Are you still there?"

"Oh. Yes! I'm sorry. He—Ulysses—caught me off guard. I don't have it word for word. He said it wasn't right. That Mr. Reposado and the others were stupid 'but not that stupid.' That was what he wanted to talk to me about. I suppose. But when I got there it was too late."

"Too late."

"Yes."

"When you found him, there was nothing in his environs or on his person that seemed unusual. I've been led to believe that he had some kind of message or note. You didn't see anything like that?"

"No. Nothing like that. At all."

"Ms. Harper, I'm sure you understand that disturbing a crime scene—tampering with evidence—is a serious matter."

"Of course. But I didn't see anything like that."

"Or pick anything up?"

"Look. I just said I didn't see it. How could I pick it up if I didn't see it? Are you suggesting I'm lying about this? What is this paper you're looking for, anyway?"

"No, No. I'm not suggesting anything. And no doubt there was no paper at all. Good night, Ms Harper. I'll be back in touch if there's anything else."

"Sure thing, Officer Valerio. Good night."

We hung up.

Tom was still not-staring at the ceiling. When he spoke, he spoke to it and not to me, his tone located midway on the continuum between concern and accusation. "He knows there was a note. And he's convinced you picked it up."

Oh, yes. Indeed. Why don't we just save some of this shit for tomorrow so that we're sure we won't run out?

"Yes. But he can't prove it, and he can't do

anything about it tonight. Let's not worry now. Get some sleep."

Ha. Like that was going to work. Twenty minutes later I couldn't tell if Tom was out or not, but I was back circling around in guard-dog country with two pieces of evidence now: one plaid, one a felony....

Oh, maybe I was unnecessarily worked up about the felony thing. If I'd still been married to D.B., sheltered by his money and his natural gift for manipulating felonies into misdemeanors when it suited his purposes, I'd have been braver. But I'd seen how being stripped of your familiar bank account and your place in society made you vulnerable to authority. And not in a good way.

However, I was in complete agreement with that Eagles song, "Lying Eyes," about the high price of selling out. If I were still hiding behind D.B.'s dubious talents, I wouldn't be here in this great bed with Dr. Right, PhD. I decided to give the calming shower another try. Maybe it would work this evening. For a change.

As I came out of the bathroom, squeaky clean if not perfectly calm, I snuck a peek at myself in the full-length mirror. My hair was curling up all over the place—no help for that—but it was not a complete disaster, if you weren't going for elegantly smooth. My eyes were wide and dark with a hint of bluish circles in the no-rest-for-the-wicked zone.

I was wearing one of Tom's delicious white tees and I have to say that, although I wasn't quite as fetching in it as he would have been, I looked okay. It was cut fairly short for sleepwear, of course. Adequate, but not overabundant in the length department. Putting my hands up at the request of an outlaw, for example, would have been awkward.

Too bad Tom wasn't in a frame of mind or in possession of the visual acuity to appreciate the mild provocativeness of my appearance. And too asleep to know I was even in the room. I'd spritzed on my Wild Fig & Cassis, however, to remind him that although we were abstaining by unspoken agreement, we'd live to love another day.

I'd underestimated both of us. When I slid under the down comforter and took up my spot again, he ran a hand lightly over me. "Hmmm," he queried. "Isn't that my shirt?"

"I'm sorry. I forgot to pack anything to sleep in. I didn't think you'd mind."

His hand had found its way down to the top of my thigh, where the shirtage ran out. His fingers searched around as he assessed the situation. "But you didn't borrow my boxers? Did you?"

"No." I was running short on breathable air. "I felt that would be—overstepping."

"I see."

"Nope. You don't."

"I feel. That's for sure."

"Not my problem." Trying to keep my voice steady.

"Well, it's your problem now." His hand had found its way up to the semi-safe area around my belly-button and it rested warmly there, radiating a radioactive force field that made my heart and some other stuff really throb. "Because I'm afraid I'm going to have to ask for my shirt back. It's about to become a favorite of mine. Smells like Jo."

"If you can take it away from me, you can keep it. But then what will I wear?"

"I suggest that you wear nothing at all. For as long as we both shall live."

And then he kissed me. And I kissed him back. And our libidos returned home, safe and sound once again.

Chapter Twenty-two

Friday, August 21

"How did we end up back here?"

"Can't say. You're driving. I'm the blind one."

Ten a.m. Friday. In spite of the promise I'd made to myself yesterday, Tom and I were back at the McCauley Road Hospital. I'd parked the Maxima in the far reaches of the lot with a view down over a short, rubble-covered incline, a ragged assembly of stunted trees, and a steep drop. I was glad for the guard rail.

Yesterday's storm hadn't cleared the air. The morning was hot, muggy, and gray with an ugly drizzle. So far I wasn't enjoying anything about this day.

"You can change your mind, Allie. You'd have my full support."

"I'll be fine. It's a public place. This is Visitors' Parking and I'm a bona fide visitor."

"What does that make me? A lurker?"

"You're merely waiting in the car while I drop in on my Aunt Martha."

"I can't stand her?"

"Thus the waiting in the car. No way we'd ever get both of us past Ivy Martin."

So there we were. Trapped by our vow to follow up on any suspicious deaths related to the Mondo. We hadn't changed our suspicions about Renata since last night, but it's never too late for a few last-minute doubts.

"Allie, she could have just died. People die unexpectedly all the time."

"Definitely. We can testify to that."

"Embolisms happen."

"Bumper sticker?"

"Not funny."

"Sorry. I'm nervous."

"I know. Don't go, then. We don't even know what you're looking for."

"True. But if we believe Renata was murdered, and we do, this is the scene of the crime. And it's getting colder by the minute. I may not even find the room she was in or anything, but this is the place and right now is the only chance I'll get to ask anybody anything.

"They're busy, Tom. They see tons of patients every day. They'll forget Renata, if they haven't already. I'm going. The worst that can happen is I'll get kicked out of McCauley Road Hospital and told never to come back. That would be an ideal outcome."

I kissed his cheek. "You. Stay in the car. That's an order."

He made a clever move and it wasn't a cheek kiss anymore.

"Tell Aunt Martha her pound cake sucks."

· ● ● ● ·

When I stepped into the massive revolving door that could have accommodated me, four or five other folks, and a wheelchair, I was conspicuously all alone. But things went okay. Sweaty, but luckier than I would have hoped.

I walked myself briskly by the desk where Ivy Martin appeared to be embroiled in a discussion with about a dozen family members who wanted to go sit on the bed of someone who'd just had his appendix out. Balloons. Flowers. A Bundt cake. The works. Ivy's full attention was required for that one. At least I hoped so.

In the elevator bay, I was searching the directory for a logical place to start my reconnoiter, and here was luck again. A young guy outfitted with scrubs, a stethoscope, and a cute smile came up and stood right next to me.

Carpe doctor, Allie.

"Hi. Excuse me? My Aunt Martha is a patient here. She fell down a flight of stairs? Hit her head? Came to your ER? And they admitted her. What floor would she be on, do you think? "

He frowned. "The lady in reception could give you her room number. She knows everything that goes on around here."

"Oh. Ms. Martin? She's busy telling about a hundred people not to go bounce on somebody's bed."

I shot him my most knowing *aren't-visitors-a-pain?* look and he grinned.

"Somebody post-surgical, I presume."

"Naturally."

"I'd check the eighth floor. That's Trauma. Ask at the nurses' station."

The elevator binged and we both got on. Having exhausted our one area of common interest, we had nothing more to say and a few remaining seconds of awkward silence to kill. He examined the ceiling panels. I cleared my throat. As he stepped off on five, he held the door and faced me. Smiling. Helpful. "I was in the ER last night. When was your aunt admitted?"

Busted. Think fast, Allie.

I shrugged. "Not sure. I got a call this morning

from my cousin, Kathy. Last couple of days? Maybe?"

The door wanted to close and he let it. I breathed out. Still lucky.

On the eighth floor, though, my momentum died. I realized I had no clue about how to start. To my right, at the nurses' station, two nurses were peering at a monitor and not noticing me. I turned left. Halfway down a long hall was one of those pill-delivery carts.

I headed toward it, making note of the queasy feeling I always get in hospitals—even when I'm not there as a ridiculously amateur detective trying to investigate a probable cold-blooded murder that maybe happened on this exact floor.

A nurse hurried out of the room closest to the cart. Young. Brisk. Friendly. "Can I help you?"

Showtime.

"Hi. A friend of mine. Renata Davis? She was…she had a head injury. I think she's here. On this floor."

The nurse's expression switched from pleasant inquiry to troubled shock. I'd seen this selfsame look happen to Ivy Martin only yesterday.

"Oh. I see. Let's—" She glanced back up the hall. "Let's go in here and sit down for a minute. Didn't you stop at the main desk?"

I recalibrated my face for alarm. "No. It was very backed up. Is something wrong?"

She kept walking. "In here."

An unoccupied room. Two beds, two dressers, two chairs. She gestured for me to take the handiest chair and leaned against, but did not sit on, its impeccably made-up bed. "Please. Sit down. Ms.—?"

"Harper. Allie Harper. What's wrong? Where's Renata?"

"I'm so sorry. If only you'd asked—" She puffed out a tiny, worried breath. "Ms. Harper, Renata Davis passed away yesterday afternoon. It's terrible you have to find out this way."

Déjà vu. I heard Ivy Martin telling me that Renata was gone. Saw Rune's stoic grief. The tears that choked me now were the most natural thing in the world. "What happened to her?"

"We don't know yet. It's not terribly unusual for a patient to come up from ER and not survive. All kinds of injuries. Even comparatively mild concussions like hers, when the MRI doesn't show anything particularly serious. It's sad. I'm so sorry this happened to Renata and that you hadn't been more prepared for the news."

I went into my purse and pawed around for a long second or two, trying to decide what would be reasonable for me to ask. I pulled out a tissue and took my time, wiping my eyes, blowing my nose.

"Was this her room?"

If it was, no way I was going to find any evidence here. Every trace of every thing that had ever happened here in the history of McCauley Road Hospital had been scrubbed clean. It was fresh and tidy. Ready for the next customers.

"Yes. I'm so—I thought you should be sitting down. Have some privacy. I should have realized—"

"No. No. Thank you so much. You've been very kind. I'm fine. We were not super close. Was she alone when—? Did she have a roommate?"

"Yes. No. She was the only one in this room when she…at the time."

I'd run out of questions. I'd learned next to nothing. Tom was waiting. I needed to make my exit before I said or did something stupid. Or before something stupid I'd already said or done caught up with me.

"I should go. You're busy. Thank you so much. Again. For telling me. This is my fault. I should have stopped at the desk."

"No." She gave me an encouraging smile. "I completely understand. It gets chaotic down there."

In the hall I thanked her again and made my way back to the elevator.

Outta here.

Chapter Twenty-three

Not so fast.

Ivy Martin was waiting outside my elevator. I got on. She got on behind me and reached out to press three. Silent. In command. When we got there she held the door open for me. I got off. There was a little conference room across the hall. She held that door, too. I went in. She followed. We sat down.

"Ms. Harper. What are you doing here?

I could see "Visiting my mean old Aunt Martha of The Sucky Pound Cake" was not going to fly.

Let's try the truth again.

"Ms. Martin, I apologize. I know this is irregular. But Dr. Bennington and I, we're hoping to be able to adopt Rune. He doesn't have anyone now and he and Tom have been friends."

"Dr. Bennington. Did he by any chance recently win 550 million dollars?"

But of course.

"Yes. And Rune is the reason." I filled her in. When I arrived at the end, I added, "So everything that's happened, including Renata's death, is because of that. You can see how personally Tom takes this. Someday Rune is going to want to know what happened to his mom. He's not asking questions right now, but he's a smart kid. He'll ask."

Ivy was standing down. Little by little. But every little bit was helping my case. I decided on a bold move.

"You said there'd be an autopsy. Will someone share the results with us? Will it be here or the ME's office—Ms. Martin?"

Her face was telegraphing the *UhOh* reflex. Glazed-over eyes. Pinched brow. A minimal tightening around the mouth. She swept it all away in a microsecond. Too late. I'd seen it. She knew it. Now she had to decide whether to lie to me. I waited.

Once again I was seeing the alternate universe of Ivy Martin, maybe the true one. I was starting to believe that if I'd met her outside her official capacity I'd have liked her a lot.

"Ms. Harper. I'm putting my employment at risk right now. I want to be sure you understand that, at least." We locked eyes and I nodded.

"I understand."

"I saw you and Mr. Bennington. Dr. Bennington. With the boy. Rune. Together. I'm an excellent judge of character. It's an asset in my job. I agree that someday you'll want to tell Rune everything you can about his mother's death. So I'm about to tell you something that would reflect badly on this hospital. You'll do with the information whatever you have to, but I hope you'll be discreet."

I nodded. What was this?

"There's been some temporary confusion."

Confusion? What kind of confusion could there be? Renata was dead. She was no longer in her room. They'd scheduled an autopsy. Ivy had said that yesterday.

So? Here? Or downtown?

Or.

"You've lost her body."

A sigh. "Temporarily. But yes."

"How?"

"Not sure. She was taken to…downstairs. The ME's office sent a van. Somewhere along the line, though, the body…stopped being where it was supposed to be."

"What does that mean?

"For now, I hope you'll share our belief that it's a paperwork error between us and the ME. These things happen, though not frequently. At all. Everybody's rushed. We rely on digital data to track…things. If there's a glitch—"

"A glitch."

"We'll find her. I promise you."

"And when you do, you'll let us know?"

"I will. And in exchange will you keep this to yourselves until we have time to sort things out?"

"I have nobody to report it to. Except Tom. We don't want to cause you any problems. We'll wait until we hear from you."

"Thank you."

"You, too."

I gave her my contact information.

"Oh, one more thing, Ms. Martin. How did you know I was up there?

"Dr. DeRoss checked you out. No Aunt Martha."

• • ● • •

I couldn't get back to Tom fast enough. When the revolving door propelled me onto the sidewalk, I had to restrain the urge to take off running. How many dangerous people were watching me right now?

Don't turn around, Allie. Walk like a normal person, even if you aren't one.

I walked, trying to reconstruct what it had been like to be a normal woman walking and just wondering where she'd parked. I found Tom sitting on the guardrail, hanging his feet over mostly open space.

"You were supposed to wait in the car."

"Taste of your own medicine. I figured I could go off on my own for once."

"You could have gone way, way off from where you're sitting."

"You mean down the berm made of asphalt. Through the smallish trees over the hill. And then off the cliff?"

"How do you know that?"

"Smell of tar. Rustle of weak trees with only a few sad, dry leaves. And the echo from way down there. Pretty far down there. What did you find out?"

"Well, I found out Ivy Martin is nicer than you'd think and a Dr. DeRoss is as suspicious as he is cute. But I only got two pieces of information for us. First, Renata's MRI came back normal. And second, they've lost her body."

After he'd sat silent for a while, no doubt listening to the whisper of sad leaves and the echo of a long drop, he said, "Later this afternoon, but not very much later, I'm going to need a drink."

"Good thinking. I'm with you."

Chapter Twenty-four

I'm going to make a list about all the ways blind guys are better than non-blind guys. I already mentioned the Body Braille thing and the me-waking-up-in-bed-with-a-blind-guy-and-not-needing-to-look-good advantage. But there's also the benefit that results from the blind guy's need to pay attention to exactly where he is in time and space right now and also to where he's headed right after this. This would be Number Three on my new list.

What brought this to mind was the sight of my erstwhile spouse making his way along East Fourth toward the table on the patio outside the Zocalo Mexican Grill and Tequilería, where Tom and I had been, until that very millisecond, working hard to forget the troubling misadventures of the morning, having the drinks that the Universe owed us because of those misadventures, and soaking up the vibe of the trendiest avenue in downtown Cleveland.

I observed D.B. Harper focusing his considerable intellect on whatever overwhelmingly snotty thing he was about to say to me, as he walked into and nearly crushed a smallish woman who was standing in his way. She wasn't killed or even seriously injured, so he mumbled a quick "Oh, sorry, ma'am." And kept on ruining my Friday evening one step at a time.

The mere fact that a guy is 6'4", darkly good-looking, with arrestingly beautiful ice blue eyes, doesn't necessarily make him worth a second look. God. I wish someone had explained that to me freshman year. But incontrovertibly, here he was. Young ladies on both sides of East Fourth were looking. And looking again.

Ironic coincidence: Tom and I had just been talking about the lawyer we were hiring to handle the blind trust and here was one of the city's most successful and well-known. Trampling ladies to get to us.

I needed to get rid of this guy. Meet. Greet. Retreat. I put my fingers on Tom's arm and my lips close to his ear and muttered, "Ex-husband at twelve o'clock. Apologies in advance."

He nodded, aiming an encouraging smile in my general direction. "I heard you grind your teeth all the way over here."

Being married to one man for five and half

years gives an observant woman the ability to read his mind by looking at his big, handsome, evil face. Here—in order—was the progression of D.B.'s thoughts from the moment I came into his view:

"*Wow. There's Allie. I'm amazed she looks even that good. Who's she with? Some loser. Oh, man. Is that a blind person cane? A blind loser? Allie's now scraping the bottom of the ADA barrel. Too bad. Heh, heh. That's too good. Too—*

"Uh! Oh, sorry, ma'am."

"*Stupid women, standing around with their heads up their—Waaaait a sec. Hold on. What was that thing Jack said? He heard a blind guy in Cleveland won the Mondo. Five hundred-fifty million. Nah. That's a rumor. And surely it's not—that blind guy's not—shit. The look on her face—Alice's hooked herself up with 550 million dollars? Shit. Shit. Shit!*"

So there, at the big finish, he'd read my mind, too. For my part, I got to play the alien who blows up people's brains from the inside. All I'd had to do was smile.

The D.B. was speechless?

I sat back and visualized an official of the Olympic Games hanging the gold medal around my neck. I listened to a few measures of the Star Spangled Banner before I said, "Hey, D.B. How's it…going?"

To his credit, he squeezed off a reasonable

facsimile of his usual arrogant smile. "Good. Alice. Great, actually." He paused, waiting for an introduction to the man he was staring at as if he were the white, blind LeBron.

There was awe, sure. Curiosity. But the expression around his eyes was pure dread. I knew he was playing a mental preview of the conversations that would be going down next week in the coffee room at GG&B.

"Tom," I led off, nice as pie, "I'd like you to meet my former husband, D.B. Harper. D.B. This is Dr. Tom Bennington the Third. He teaches at CWRU. Tom, D.B. is a senior partner at Gallagher, Gallagher & Barnes." That was all he was getting from me. I snapped shut like a self-satisfied clam and savored the moment.

D.B. was at a horrible disadvantage. Key information was missing and he had not the foggiest idea how to get at it. He shuffled his feet. "May I pull up a chair?"

I gazed at him. "I'm so sorry, D.B. Tom and I were just leaving."

Silly me. This was a trial lawyer I was talking to.

"No, no. Alice." He hit the Alice exceptionally hard. D.B. was master of the small, disarming irritation, delivered in a killer one-two combo with a put-down designed to leave the addressee staggering. Or maybe crying. Or at least pleading guilty as charged.

Brace yourself, Alice.

"I'm so glad to see you out in public again. Not brooding. Or sulking. That's so great. After all. It's been, what? Two years? Time flies. Let me buy you and your friend a drink. I want to hear all about it. How did you guys meet? Blind date? Oh, hey. Sorry, man. My bad."

I glanced at Tom. He was sitting, quiet and contained, letting the D.B. run off him. My hero.

"No, not at all, D.B." Assurance fairly dripped from that juicy Southern drawl. "Allie and I have been friends for what seems like quite a while. That blind date would surely have been with you."

It was a pleasure to watch D.B. get, shall we say, blindsided for the second time that evening. I made a mental note to sit down with Tom and draw up a list of ways to use a disability against your enemies.

However, I'd forgotten how persistent D.B. could be in the face of rejection. After a moment during which he closed his mouth and returned an expression of not-poleaxed to his face, he went right ahead and pulled up a chair, arranging his long muscular legs and his wide muscular torso all over it. Then he leaned in and planted his elbows on our table in such a way that our end of the street was now dominated by the sprawling presence of Duane Bradford Harper. I caught the wave of his ultra-expensive, signature cologne. I was already getting a headache.

"So. What's new? Tell me all about—everything."

"Oh, there's so much, Duane. So much. And truly, no time at all to talk about it now. We've been very…busy the last couple of days." I smiled in what I hoped was a meaningful way.

Tom mirrored my satisfied smile. "Yes," he drawled, laying his hand on my bare arm with that unerring skin radar of his, "Very. Busy." He picked up my hand and planted the extremely potent kiss I remembered from our first…ah…date in the center of my palm. Everybody at our end of East Fourth got second-degree burns.

D.B. blinked.

I signaled our waiter, a lovely young man named Sean, who had been lurking against the front wall of the tequilería, watching this scene unfold with amused empathy. I believed he'd correctly identified all the players and had witnessed my victory, but he did not, I could tell, know about Tom's Mondo ticket.

He had brought us our Margaritas Fantasticas and extra free snacks and given us flawless, friendly attention in spite of our ordinary, not at all wealthy, demeanor. At my nod, he swooped in with the check, which came to about twenty-five dollars.

In a secret compartment of my wallet, I had a hundred-dollar bill that I'd kept in there for the past two years, to remind myself that I was fine on my own and bound for better things. Or to pacify a mugger, should that be required. There would never be a more propitious moment for me to spend my Ben. Sean put the check down and I dropped the hundred on it. I winked at him. "Keep the change, Sean. Awesome service. Bye, D.B."

I stood up. Tom stood up. He took my arm. We walked.

I couldn't resist a backward glance.

Behind us stood two men with their mouths hanging open.

One ecstatic. One not.

Chapter Twenty-five

Monday, August 24

That was Friday night. Here's some good news. I looked up on the Internet and found out that, numerically speaking, between Friday night and Monday morning of the final week in August, approximately three hundred thousand people on Planet Earth died. That, of course, is not the good news. That's the preamble to the good news. Which is here: I am pleased to report that on that Saturday and Sunday, as far as I know, not one of those three hundred thousand people died because Tom won the Mondo.

That weekend might have been a romantic interlude for us, happily shacked up on those hot summer days and stormy summer nights in our luxurious room. But the glow was diminished by all the accumulated death and destruction we had to fret about, and a lot of other stuff that needed to be handled. Like calling in rich on my library job. Speculating about our murder investigations. Avoiding murderers. Many small details such as that.

Neither of us had the guts to go back to our houses yet, so we had to stock up on some suitable attire for our lawyer appointment. I figured my jeans, shirt, flip-flop ensemble wouldn't cut it in my new role as a woman of gold-digging motivation. Dress for success, I say.

Another anti-interlude factor was my compulsion to keep looking over my shoulder. The creepy, crawly, everybody's-watching sensation that I thought of as "Creepy Eye" was everywhere. Every car that slowed as it passed us. Every shadowy doorway. Every sideways glance. To counteract this, I spent a considerable amount of time online, searching for articles about how to tell if you were being followed, or hacked, or whatever.

Experts thought that if you made four right turns, one after another, and somebody was *still* behind you, this somebody was likely a tail. Or if you thought your phone was being used to track you, you could stop it by doing a total reboot on the phone. That would be time-consuming, but if my phone started lighting up all by itself or popping out some kind of strange code, I'd definitely try it.

I didn't mention any of this to Tom. He felt bad enough about things as it was.

For all these reasons, just about anywhere on Earth would have been very Creepy Eye for me that weekend. Except maybe the hot spot under the down comforter of a Marriott Bed.

Vigilance wears you out.

• • ● •• •

All interludes, by definition, have to end. Even cluttered, distracting, and semi-exhausting ones. Monday morning, we got dressed up in our new clothes and showed up, holding hands and smiling, at the well-appointed offices of GG&B—D.B.'s firm.

D.B.'s lair, more like it.

A sensible person might well inquire why we chose Gallagher, Gallagher & Barnes from among all the big names now available to us. Well, for one it was also the firm of the lawyer I trusted most in all the world. And for two? Spite. One hundred percent pure. This was going to even up an old, festering score for me. With 550 million dollars to spare. So here we were.

When I said "well-appointed," I was not joking. Gallagher, Gallagher & Barnes is referred to around town—and probably all over the known world—as "the venerable Cleveland law firm." Its history extends back to the second quarter of the twentieth century. Its billings are in the stratosphere. If there were a law firm located inside Monticello—Jefferson, Jefferson & Hemings, if there is any justice in this world—its reception room would be the mirror image of GG&B's.

The firm's location at the very pinnacle of the Arco Building, one of the city's tallest, is, I'm sure, an intentional metaphor for its extreme exclusivity. Only the best attorneys. Only the most affluent clients. Everything rarified. Every detail totally under control. Control is a big deal at GG&B. They like everything buttoned up and bolted down. Spouses, as well, I found to my rue, when D.B. and I were a couple.

Nan, the receptionist, was seated behind that imposing desk and beneath a veritable benediction of light that streamed down from the skylight situated above it. As far as I knew, she'd been sitting there forever. I wasn't sure they even gave her bathroom breaks.

She was probably a nice, friendly lady, but it was hard to tell. Like Ivy Martin, Nan was a gatekeeping pro. Part of her job was to impress by intimidation and she needed to have her wits about her. The GG&B client is not to be trifled with and the GG&B attorney is one very busy, don't-interrupt-me-unless-you-absolutely-have-to human being. That's a lot for one woman in a suit and faux pearls to cope with.

"Good morning, Dr. Bennington. And Mrs.—Uh. Alice. It's very nice to see you. Again."

Whoa. Was Nan twinkling? Her small fumble of the Official GG&B Greeting reminded me of good old Mary at the lottery. She obviously appreciated the nuances and ramifications of our visit.

"Good to see you too, Nan," I twinkled back. And I meant it. I knew that Nan had been dealing with D.B. for years. As a matter of fact, we were sisters-in-D.B. One could assume he'd been the son of a bitch to her that he is to everyone he considers below his rank.

I was also sure Nan'd heard many of the details of our shabby "lawyer takes spouse to the cleaners" divorce. GG&B is tight-lipped with outsiders, but a coffee room is a coffee room. People talk. Nan had plenty of personal and general anecdotes to establish what a jerk my former spouse was prone to be. Of that I was sure. And now word had it that the former Mrs. D.B. had hooked herself a sexy, blind, 550 million-dollar buckaroo. Money old D.B. would never see a dime of. How much payback was that?

"I'll let Mr. Castillo know you're here. And, Allie?" She hesitated at the brink of humanity.

"That's a very pretty dress. You look really lovely today."

I did, too. I was dressed up in a flowery pink sundress with a modest jacket and a pair of new shoes of a name and a price tag I'd always coveted

"And—" she hesitated again, "it's very, very nice to meet you, Dr. Bennington. Very nice."

Seeing Tom through Nan's eyes refreshed my own appreciation. His crispy new white shirt was setting off his delectable tan and my handsome-man alert. One might have worried about the sprinkler system.

In so many ways, it was a gratifying moment. To make matters even juicier, my lawyer of choice was one of D.B.'s younger, somewhat subordinate partners. He was going to handle the blind trust and other legal considerations. Right under D.B.'s nose.

Skip Castillo is cute as a bug and ex-football big & tall. Caramel skin, flashing brown eyes, dazzling smile. He's forever been super good to me. Where D.B. is uptight and snobby, Skip is down-to-earth and egalitarian. He's ultra-smart but not a brat about it. His specialty is a giant, happy bear hug that makes you feel like you're the one making his day.

He loped out to the reception area to claim us, booming, "Allie! Wonderful to see you!" and enveloped me in that XXL squeeze. Next, he managed an unembarrassed and skillful handshake with Tom. After that he hustled us into the office proper and down a long corridor, tactfully guiding Tom and sheltering me, dodging gawkers and well-wishers. At last he shooed us into an elegant, comfortably appointed conference room and closed the door. "Boy, oh boy." He was beaming. "This is so cool. Tell me all about it."

We gave him the short version, which was getting longer every day. The rationale for the ticket purchase. Tom's prophetic dismay about possible tidal wave/earthquake-size complications. Enumeration of the subsequent incidents of disaster. I didn't mention the part about my tampering with evidence. The Skipper is an officer of the court, after all. I was pretty sure he wouldn't turn me in. But if he were ever under oath, this man wouldn't lie. I approved of that, even though it might not always work in my favor.

He had called the lottery people and had also made contact with some legal folks who had the rare experience of handling a situation like ours. He thought it would be at least a couple of weeks or so before we'd receive the check. He assured us it would not be the size of a tablecloth, nor would it be presented to us on Public Square. I loved him for saying to Tom, "Wow, I bet everybody freaked when they had to break it to you about the blind trust thing."

He also pointed out that Tom's trust didn't need to be all that blind or all that locked in.

"Given that quite a few folks already know you won, it's not worth all the restrictions. We can set it up so you have more access to the funds. More control." Neither of those observations made Tom all that happy, but we were on a roll of optimism so he smiled and nodded.

After we'd spent an hour or so with Skip, working our way through the details, I felt like I had the big picture. The money would come to Tom in a format he'd never even have to hold. The transfer would be electronic. The money would be secure and maintained in a manner that would cause it to generate an obscene amount of income for Tom. For me, too, of course, because I was still figuring to continue cashing in on his ten-million-dollar offer at least once a day for thirty or forty years. Minimum. Even with a generous distribution of coupons, a lot of prosperity was in my future.

I planned to remind Tom of this as soon as we got back out into the unstuffy world. I was grinning a secret grin, on the inside of my lips, as we made our way down the hall and hugged farewell to Skip. I'd seen nothing of D.B. but I felt a disturbance in The Force that suggested to me he was in hiding, somewhere close by. Fuming wrathfully. We said goodbye to Nan, and she talked to us again.

"I hope everything went well, Allie," she beamed.

"Oh, it was terrific, Nan. I mean, how could you go wrong with Ski—uh, Mr. Castillo?"

She nodded. "He's very competent. Everybody here thinks very highly of Mr. Castillo. And, Allie," she leaned toward me, confidentially, over the polished surface of her presidential desk, "he's just such a hunk."

"Nan," I responded with as much gravity as I could muster, "you are a connoisseur of quality."

Nan blushed up to the roots of her professionally highlighted, honey-blond hair and stole a quick glance at Tom who was waiting, patient and handsome, for me to get on with our day. She twinkled her approval. "You, too, Allie."

Chapter Twenty-six

Okay. When we came out, all the elevator doors were closed except one and that one had a uniformed guy vacuuming its rug. We were proceeding at a leisurely pace because I was murmuring a once-in-a-lifetime, bonanza, double-coupon, top value offer in Tom's ear and he was grinning and saying, "Well, that's a very attractive savings opportunity, Miss. I'd be interested in hearing more. In, say, about a half hour?"

As we reached the open elevator, the maintenance guy popped out, unplugged the sweeper from an outlet by the door, zapped in its cord, rolled it toward the back of the elevator, held the doors open for us, and—in a welcoming "I-take-great-pride-in-my-work-however-menial" way—said, "All nice and ready for you, folks."

Whaddya going to do?

I shelved my plans for whispering even sweeter sweet nothings to Tom on our way down, and said thank you to the guy.

We got on.

The doors whisked shut.

The guy pulled a gun.

I could tell it was a spidey moment for Tom, if a second on the too-late side. Maybe it was the way I startled when our friendly maintenance man produced his chunky black weapon. Maybe it was because I hollered, "Shit!" in my best Margo. Or possibly it was that the guy then moved close to Tom and shoved the barrel of the weapon into his ribs.

He snarled at me, "If anybody gets on and you make a fuss, I'll kill him. And you, too. And them, too, if I get a chance. I got nothing to lose and twenty million dollars to gain. So shut up and push the garage button."

I shut up and pushed it.

I stood as near as I could to Tom, sucking in deep breaths, trying to calm down enough not to cry or scream, wanting to comfort him and myself for this last five seconds of our journey together.

The elevator did not stop even one time.

I didn't believe the guy was intending to hurt Tom. He'd take me away and let Tom figure out how to pay the ransom. Tom hadn't seen him, after all. However, this man who had a nondescript but unlikable appearance—rat brown hair, rat-small brown eyes, squinchy nose and mean mouth, five foot-eight, medium build—had taken no pains to hide himself from me. I knew what that meant. I hoped Tom would figure it out. He could find another use for that twenty million. Which I had planned to earn in the best possible way. In two installments. I blinked back tears, remembering Margo's parting words.

"You just found happiness, Al. This is no time to die!"

The doors slid open to reveal a dank and murky basement vestibule. I stared through misty glass at the ramp leading up and the ramp leading out. Cars passing through had tracked in water from yesterday's afternoon storm. I made note of the gleam of meager illumination on wet surfaces and the red signs that kept on blinking Park and Exit, as if this were any ordinary day when a person could park or exit and not die.

The kidnapper yanked me away from Tom, and shoved me out into the gloom. He stepped back onto the elevator, pushed a button, waited for the door to slide back shut and stepped off. At the last moment I heard Tom call out. "Allie!" in a voice so desperate I almost couldn't recognize it.

"All you have to do now, young lady," the guy said, taking my arm and shoving the gun up under my new pink jacket so that only a delicate layer of fabric lay between me and what I assumed had to be a very big slug, "is everything I say. Exactly how I say to do it. And everything will go fine."

He favored me with a creepy smile. " I think maybe you and me could get along good."

I was torn between making a scene that would probably cause me to get shot right here in the empty garage—where Tom might at least find me and say goodbye before I died—and going along, hoping for a better chance. Make no mistake. I'd read the "What To Do If You Get Grabbed in a Parking Garage" articles and I knew the common wisdom was: *Allie, for godsake, don't go along.* But I was sure if I put up a fight, I'd die right here and now. Almost anything looked like a better chance than that.

"Look," I said to the gun guy, "please. You don't have to—"

In spite of having a long list of things I hoped he didn't have to do, I couldn't come up with a single helpful way to explain them to him. Which was good because that mere "Look" and "Please" caused him to mutter, "Shut your mouth!" and slam the barrel of the gun into my new dress so hard that I could feel the inevitability of a small circular bruise forming on my back. "Perimortem," as those TV coroners love to say while peering at the victim on the tray. I was realizing right then how much about that word I had so completely not understood.

My perimortem world had telescoped into a dark, suffocating cavern where the only sounds were my own ragged breathing, the swish of tires on wet concrete, and some slow, heavy footsteps approaching from the dim reaches of way too late.

The guy I was coming to think of as Rat Man hustled me out of the vestibule and paused to let a black SUV and a red Miata pass us by without even the slightest sideward glance from their drivers.

I was so dead.

In my slow-motion moment of glazed desperation, I heard the approaching footsteps getting louder. Closer. Rat Man, distracted, loosened his bony grip on my arm as a big, wide, black security guard came around the corner, walking through his daily routine, checking things out.

Right after that, in quick succession:

The guard paused to give Rat Man and me a gently inquiring glance.

The alarm from the elevator went off, very loud.

I tore my arm all the way loose, whipped around, and kneed the guy as hard as ever I could, right in the crotch.

He doubled over, screaming bloody murder

and aimed his gun, which was now out in the open and hugely obvious, at me.

And the security guy shot Rat Man.

Can everybody say, "Halleluiah?"

Chapter Twenty-seven

I plopped down hard on a wet curb, giving my rubber knees the reward they'd earned by not dropping me before.

Maybe twenty seconds later, Tom came flying, cane-first, out of the elevator, calling my name in a gratifyingly panicked way.

The guard used his crackling walkie-talkie to summon authority, both internal and external, and collapsed onto the curb beside me, clutching his chest.

Tom located me by the sound of my quavering answer. He groped around until he could put his hands on top of my head. "Allie, thank God," he breathed and slid down to join us on our curb.

I leaned against him, osmosis-ing warmth from his closeness, and whispered a heartfelt, "That alarm, Tom. Perfect timing."

My kidnapper continued to lie very still on the garage floor. It looked for all the world like Tom's

Mondo had now claimed Number Six. It was hard for me to stir up much sympathy, though. Any sympathy.

All that, including a shaking fit I couldn't control and some loud sobbing I'm not ashamed of, was Phase I of the aftermath of my kidnapping and the righteous shooting of the Rat Man whose real name turned out to be Dan.

Phase II followed with the appearance of three Cleveland police cars, rippling a kaleidoscope of red and blue all around us. Back-up guards from the Arco Building spilled out of the stairwells. There was the arrival and containment of a lot of obstreperous spectators, a number of whom simply wanted to retrieve their cars. And the summoning of an ambulance for Arco Security Officer Otis Johnson.

As a member of the Cleveland Police Force for twenty-five years, Otis had never fired his gun in the line of duty. "Not once," he insisted as he rocked back and forth on the pavement. "Not even one goddamn time."

Now in his retirement job with Arco Security, he'd walked around a corner and brought Dan all the way down with a single instinctive shot. He wasn't sorry, not at all. But he was having a reaction that exhibited all the earmarks of a heart attack. I had aspirin in my purse, so I shook one loose and gave it to him. He sucked on it and waited, scared and patient, murmuring, "Not even one damn time" until the huge, square, chartreuse EMS vehicle backed in, in all of its earsplitting, beeping glory. They bundled him onto a stretcher, noted that he'd had his aspirin, loaded him up, and drove him away.

Otis Johnson saved my life. I'd told him so and thanked him from the bottom of my heart for doing his duty and being wonderful. I'd shushed him when he'd looked at me, wide-eyed, and said, "That was so—I coulda shot *you*." Now I was praying he wouldn't turn out to be more collateral damage from the earthquake ticket.

Phase III started when Skip rushed out of the elevator, big, healthy, and worried in a reassuring way. He hoisted me in a modified Skip hug, pulled Tom to his feet, and scooped us in like baby ducks or something. I was so glad to see him I cried. Skip, my Momma Duck. Upon further reflection, I was so glad to find myself alive enough to be hugged by Skip and reunited with Tom that I cried some more.

Skip was, by turns, gentle and soothing to us and outraged at the turn of events. I'd almost stopped noticing that my ratty guy was lying there, bloody, uncovered, and as far as I could tell, unalive. It's possible to ignore a lot of stuff when you're in semi-shock.

But then the elevator doors opened again and

Nan burst out, her face twisted with sorrow and fear. I was about to comment to myself, "Wow, I had no idea Nan cared so much," when she stumbled past me and over to the silent corpse on the parking lot floor. She fell to her knees, oblivious to the effects of a puddle of oily water on her nice suit and stockings, and cried, "Dan. Oh, Dan." That's when I learned Dan's name. And started to understand how we got on his radar in the first place.

The story came out, amid stern questioning from the police, Skip, and—after a short while— some of his partners, not including D.B. Almost all the answers I needed were sobbed out by an inconsolable Nan.

Dan was Nan's brother. In my humble opinion, Nan and Dan's parents had not been thinking it forward when they named their kids. And it might have cheered me, earlier on, if I'd known a lot of stuff that came out now.

Dan had been, to be blunt about it, a most awesome fuck-up.

In his thirty-one short, tedious, and dim-witted years, he'd almost never held a job for more than six weeks. What's more, he'd never been out of juvie or prison for more than eighteen months at a stretch since he was fourteen. When he'd told us he had nothing to lose, he was speaking as accurately as he ever had or ever would. Dan was already a Grade A loser.

The parents were dead, and Nan had been charged with the chore of looking after Dan whenever he wasn't a guest of the state. He'd moved in with her about six weeks prior, and she'd jiggled the system a small amount to get him a job as a custodian in the Arco.

It further evolved that the evening after I'd scheduled our Monday-morning Skip appointment, Nan had chatted on the phone with her best friend in the firm who was somebody's admin. They'd dished it up about me and the blind Mondo guy and the money. How pissed D.B. was bound to be. How I deserved the best. How D.B. deserved the worst. And so on.

Poor Nan. To me, that sounded like a damn fine conversation. C'mon. Life is hard. I reminisced for a half-second about Margo and me sitting around in her garden with our shoes off and our feet up, knocking back white wine and dishing the dirt like it was our job. What are girlfriends for?

But on Friday night, sneaky old Rat Man Dan must have been listening in. He'd focused on the part about millions of dollars and hatched about five minutes' worth of a plan to kidnap me and get ransom money from Tom. There hadn't been much time. And there hadn't been much thought.

Or much of a thinker either. For example, Dan hadn't an inkling that Tom didn't have the money in his possession yet. I shivered, thinking about what it might have been like spending a couple of very long weeks with Dan.

He'd shown up on Monday morning, about a half hour after our appointment was scheduled. He lurked around vacuuming—which to his credit was the job he was supposed to be doing—until we came out. Then he herded us into the elevator, covered us with his big gun, transported us down, sent Tom back up, and dragged me out. That was the sum of his success.

Unlucky, lucky, and shot. That was Dan. In the space of five minutes: He was a loser. He was a winner. He was dead. A synopsis of his entire sorry life, as far as I could tell.

Poor, poor Nan. She stood up to the interrogation while her brother, whom I assumed she loved or at least felt some familial responsibility for, lay bloody and lifeless on the cold, wet, concrete floor. She took her part of the blame like a trooper, sparing herself not at all, but adamantly refusing to share the name of her friend. Which I assumed everyone upstairs could figure out anyhow.

The cops weren't unsympathetic, but it was their job not to unbend much. My Nan was no way an accessory to Dan's sorry plan. I had not a shred of doubt. But the cops didn't know her like I did. They explained she was a material witness and she'd need to come with them and give her statement.

As she went, she turned to the guy who seemed most in charge. With her dirty, oily outfit, her ravaged face and disordered hair, she was a caricature of the immaculate, gracious person I'd twinkled goodbye to maybe a grand total of forty-five minutes before.

"Officer," she said, proud as a condemned queen, "would you please see that someone covers my brother up?"

Poor Nan. If I hadn't already been crying, I'd have started up right there.

Chapter Twenty-eight

Monday night everything was different. For starters, Monday afternoon was the first afternoon since the day we met that it hadn't stormed like a bloody maniac. The wind had changed, the humidity was down, the temperature had dropped, the sun was out, the sky was crystalline.

The honeymoon was over.

Not in a bad way. Not like we weren't still falling in love. I had begun to meld myself into Tom's world where it was always midnight, and I like to think he was finding his way more into the crystal blue afternoons of mine. Now that he had me around to ask about how something was looking, I thought his worldview was expanding. At least that's what he said.

But the delectable, ignorant, us-against-the-world bliss? That had ended Monday morning when one or both of us could have gotten killed.

Here's a bitter truth.

Human beings don't often take someone else's death or threatened death quite as personally as their own. And the death or threatened death of someone you love comes in a photo-finish second on that one. Then your friends. And your acquaintances. The rest of the population of the planet you're only sorry to hear about. Some of those are bound to become part of today's regulation one hundred-fifty thousand. You can get over most of them. But you yourself? And your loved one? That takes the wind out of your sails.

Even our talks about needing to solve some murders and prevent our own had been semi-hypothetical until this morning. Now every bad thing was personal. When Dan pressed that cold muzzle up against my skin, my sassy, girl P.I. illusions evaporated, and I understood I'd squandered my last scrap of beginner's luck. By Monday night I'd become profoundly more realistic about my private eye skills.

Tom and I addressed the dread that came with this shared knowledge of mortality and vulnerability by taking ourselves off to visit Margo. I'll give Margo this. In spite of the way death and destruction were following us around like a lost beagle, she sounded delighted to hear my voice. And she insisted we come down for dinner.

In her words, "Screw those idiots. I'm not

afraid. And you all have to be brave about the things that count. If you can't eat spaghetti and drink some good red wine with your friends, what's the point of being a supergazillioniare?"

Too true.

I drove out the Shoreway, my fingers clutching the wheel again, and my shoulders hiked up around my ears. I made a mental note of every vehicle I saw that didn't pass me up before I took the Lake Shore exit. When I got off the ramp, I pulled over for a minute so I could watch the traffic that came down with us. There was one car. It was full of teenagers.

Even then I didn't go straight to Margo's. I drove around through the neighborhood. Making four right turns in a row may help you flush out somebody who's on your tail, but it made me nearly drive into a phone pole. If Tom noticed, he didn't feel compelled to comment.

After that, I called Margo on my cell, shoving down the tracker paranoia that popped up every time I touched it these days.

"It's us, Margo. Open your garage door and put it down as soon as we drive in. I don't want—"

"Shhh, girl. I've got this. Get yourselves in here. I've been so worried about you."

I drove in and parked next to the Volvo. The door ground down behind us, and there was Margo in the doorway, a halo of warm light from her kitchen behind her. Margo, my beacon. I exhaled and part of my fear and sorrow escaped with the breath I'd been holding onto for what seemed like hours.

Safe home.

In Margo's kitchen a stockpot of something tomato-and-herbal-smelling was simmering on the back of her antique Magic Chef stove and something meaty was making a delicious sizzling sound in one of Mable's ovens. Margo called her stove Mable. Mable was a work of art and a first-class instrument of food. I thought to myself that if I ever had a stove that deserved a name I'd call it Margo. Or maybe Margo-rita. She'd like that.

When everything was ready, Margo led us out to her garden. My favorite hideaway. A table was set in the sheltering arbor. The vine-covered walls gathered us in. A sweet breeze off the lake stirred the trees. Shadows danced.

Those damn dancing shadows were my problem. Everywhere, in all this peace and quiet, I saw stalkers and slayers. Every rustling bush shrouded the gun-wielding ghost of Rat Man Dan. I practiced sitting meditatively, breathing calmingly, repeating silently, *Relax, Alice Jane, you're safe here. It's okay.*

I might have gotten away with it, if something about the way I was jiggling around in my lovely wrought-iron garden chair hadn't alerted The Blind Spidey.

"I don't know what's going on with you, Allie. But it's catching. You're about to make me jump around, too."

"Oh, you don't have to worry tonight, Tom," Margo began. "Because—"

"Margo." I broke into her soothing explanation. I was now seeing an actual someone... something. Lurking. Beneath the long swaying dreadlocks of a weeping mulberry tree. A dark-hooded shape. The gleam of eyes...

I gripped Margot's arm. "Margo, there's someone—there *is*—back there, under that—"

"It's a dog, Allie."

"What—"

"A dog. Her AKC name is Barkly's Princess Vespa. But we can just call her Princess."

At the sound of its name, the dark shape unfolded itself under the mulberry and rose up. Slowly. The shape poked a vast dark head through the cascading leaves and shook it, an action that caused the skin of its face, including its big rubbery lips, to swing freely from side to side.

"What the—?"

"She's a mastiff, Allie. Big. Loud. Mean-looking. Thousands of years of guard dog roots.

Castles and moats. She's an old sweetheart with a killer bark."

A big toothy dog. Margo had been talking toothy dogs for us from the day Felix and those guys got shot. Had she been conjuring the Princess Vespa even then?

"Where'd you get her?"

"I borrowed her. But I like her. The people think she's too much work. I'm not taking her back."

Princess lumbered up, checked me out, and then leaned her big heavy head against Tom's hand. He obliged her by tenderly rubbing her bony skull, and she rewarded him by plunking her whole head like a ton of bricks onto his arm.

He grinned. "Thanks, Margo. I feel much... safer now."

Chapter Twenty-nine

Margo served up the spaghetti in big shallow bowls with homemade sauce from real August tomatoes, many torn leaves of fresh basil, and hefty meatballs that had been roasted to crusty brown perfection. She'd made us a fine salad and there was a loaf of ciabatta and a bottle of robust Italian red. While we ate, the Princess Vespa guarded us and our table, coveting everything on it but the wine.

Strangely enough, with Her Doggy Highness stationed between Tom and me, panting and generating many degrees of body heat, I could let myself feel the terror of the day. Look at it straight on, without screaming, crying, or running away. I soaked up the warmth and kindness of Margo's little table, unclenched my hands, and let my shoulder muscles go. I was beginning to believe I could survive being scared to death.

We ate in reverent silence, mostly, taking a moment here and there for chatting about easy stuff. Like, for example, my beautiful, awesome, expensive Jimmy Choo sandals. Margo allowed how she'd expect nothing less if a person were willing to put out for a babe supergazillionaire. We could laugh now as the tension eased. The wine didn't hurt either.

But the respite couldn't last forever.

"I'd feel better if you guys had a gun," Margo said after we'd skirted around the elephant on the table several times.

That cracked me up. "Margo, give me a break. First of all, you've always been the Goddess of Gun Control. Second, I don't have any idea how to shoot. And last but not least, Tom's blind. His aim would have to be crappy. Things aren't that bad."

Tom cleared his throat. "I take exception to that, Miz Harper." He let the syrup of the South thicken his drawl. "At one time, I was acknowledged by my peers to be a crack marksman. And although I may have lost a step or two in the deadeye aim department, I feel that one's ability to shoot is like one's ability to ride a bicycle. I expect, with a little practice, I could hit anything that, say, beeped."

I giggled. "Remind me never to beep at you when you're armed. Is that what they mean when they talk about a duck blind? If you were shooting I would want to duck. A lot."

Margo refused to be diverted. "Stop that, you

two. Don't laugh! I'm going to take the wine away.
If things aren't 'that bad,' then tell me how things
are. Do not lie to me. I know Felix and those other
two guys got shot. I get the strong feeling there've
been others. And I know there was an attempted
kidnapping and a shooting in the parking garage
of the Arco Building, not some 'upsetting incident'
or whatever the fu—what*ever* you said when you
called. I know you were going there this morning.

"Don't keep me in the dark about this. Sorry,
Tom—oh, never mind. The stuff I know you're
not telling me makes me jumpy and being jumpy
makes me mean. So tell me."

We told her. We told her the good news which
was that we'd got rid of the ticket and that the one
hundred-ninety million dollars was going to be
doing its thing now without any help or handling
by us. We told her about Renata and Ulysses. We
lied and said their deaths were rather suspicious,
but that we were pretty sure Ulysses had died of
natural causes and that even Renata's death could
be considered a probably unintended consequence
of the criminal assault.

I left out the part about finding the DIRTY!!!
note. Bad enough that I'd involved Tom in my
felony. No need to drag Margo into that mess. As
far as I was concerned, the fewer people who knew
about DIRTY!!! the more safe people there'd be.

The sun was low in the sky now, orange and purple. It was falling into a thick mist above the horizon, so that it was something you could stare at and not burn your retinas. If that was anything you worried about. Which one of us didn't need to.

"Do you remember mauve?" I asked Tom, and he nodded. Something about that made Margo tear up, but she hid it well.

Wave music was playing on the rocks beneath the cliff. Gulls were sailing out over the water the way they do at end of day. Morning in the basement of the Arco Building was a lifetime away from here. But that didn't change what had happened. Or what hadn't, that could have.

I could be in a cooler at the ME's office. Me. The once-in-a-lifetime Allie Harper.

I shivered and attempted to pass it off as a shrug. "We were lucky, Margo. This guy, Dan, who—now, don't get all screechy and start swearing—just listen. This guy, Dan, who held us at gunpoint in the elevator and tried to kidnap me, was dumber than Felix Reposado, when it comes right down to it. I don't know how much real danger we were in."

Yeah, I do. I'm lying, can you tell?

"It was over in five minutes. Less. And it's totally over now. Dan is dead."

The word "dead" dropped like a rock into

my soothing monologue, and Margo didn't look at all soothed. I couldn't blame her. I wasn't giving my pep talk very high marks either. It was hard to take any comfort from this morning's train wreck. "Dead" was not the bright spot.

In the silence that followed my summation, I remembered Otis and made a mental note to call about him when we got back to the hotel and to say a prayer for him when I wasn't lying to Margo. I thought *God bless you, Otis*, and then I moved my worries right on over to Nan and the turmoil she must be facing tonight.

Nan would be grieving for Dan and no doubt furious with Dan and then back to grieving again. And in the midst of that was the certain knowledge that her job was toast. GG&B gave no quarter to indiscretion. As much as Nan was an unwitting accomplice to Dan's stupidity, she'd be out. I needed have a talk with Skip about Nan....

Wake up, Allie.

Margo was staring at me. Quiet. Very quiet for Margo. Then she left the table, went into the house for a minute or two. and came back carrying a lantern with a lighted candle in it and a plate of cookies. She set the lantern and the cookies on the table, touched Tom's shoulder, muttered "cookies" to him, and directed her attention back to me.

"I agree with a lot you've said except that

nonsense about no real danger this morning. But it's over so I'll let it pass. 'Sufficient unto the day is the evil thereof.' You got plenty of trouble without getting all mired up in the bad stuff that's happened up to now and is already over. Like this Dan. Like Felix, and those two guys. Muff and Frank?"

I nodded, trying to keep my mind on its toes.

"But in the middle of your sorry-ass story? Where Ulysses and Renata maybe died of 'natural causes'? I don't believe that for a minute. And neither do you."

The lantern cast its flickering shadows on her face. She looked like a Voodoo priestess with malediction on her mind. "The person who was on the scene when those two died is one very smart, very slippery person. A clever, capable, determined murderer."

I opened my mouth and she glared at me to squelch whatever I might be about to interject. I closed it back.

"I mean it. There's a killer out there tonight you both should be very afraid of. Maybe more than one.

"In about another fifteen minutes, even the stupid people will comprehend that they can't steal your ticket. And the smart people will understand that you don't have the money yet. They'll leave you alone. For now.

"But once you get the money—Look at me, Al. Eye contact—they'll be after you again. And it's kidnapping that's your biggest problem. Allie, they'll hone in on the one person that it's getting pretty obvious Tom will pay a lot of money to protect. That's you, girlfriend. And you know it."

I reached around and over the mountain of dog and touched Tom's knee. I wasn't about to agree with Margo. Not tonight. But the three of us were on the same page. Margo—who was no slouch when it came to figuring stuff out—believed the murdering was probably on the back burner for now. And, clearly, the kidnapping phase was well underway. Not that it wouldn't turn back into murder once a ransom was paid. I didn't like it, but how could I not accept it? The events of the morning were speaking for themselves. And I could tell Tom felt it, too, by the way he put his hand over mine.

I also agreed we'd maybe be safe until the money transferred. Except from dolts like Dan. We'd need to be alert to the possibility of dangerous goofballs until we got the money, and after that we'd need to figure out how the rich people stay alive and well—and not kidnapped—without looking over their shoulders all the time. It was going to be a major pain in the patooti. Earthquakes and tsunamis without end, Amen. I was ready to give back the Jimmy Choos.

Tom was silent now, but I knew what he was thinking. "Tom," I began, "I know you wish you'd never—"

"Allie, stop that." Margo's voice was harsh. "And Tom, you too. You guys stepped into a nest of 550 million vipers on Tuesday night. Nothing can change that. Pandora's little jackpot is wide open. No help for it now.

"But if you keep walking around wishing you didn't have it, you'll attract the attention of even more predators who are wishing they did. Respect what fortune has dealt you. Both of you. Be responsible for it. And stay awake."

Damn. She was probably right.

• • ● • •

Dinner was over. We thanked Margo for the food, the fun, and the sound counsel. We told her to lock her doors for a change and that if she felt the least bit threatened, we'd bring her up to the top of the Marriott with us. That made her smile her self-satisfied Margo smile.

"I don't think so. I bet nobody at the Marriott is getting any sleep with you two going at it all the time up on that concierge floor. Besides, I have Princess to guard me now."

I glanced at Princess, who'd wedged herself as close to Tom as she could get and was gazing up at him. Adoringly. I knew how she felt.

"Oh, Princess. I wish you could come with us to the Marriott." I laid my hand on her colossal brow and scratched fondly. This caused the Princess to close her eyes, let her capacious mouth gawp open, and her prodigious tongue loll out. A shimmering strand of drool cascaded all the way down to the ground.

"Then again, probably not."

Time to go. We made a pact to stay safe, one and all. As I hugged Margo goodbye, I grabbed one of her hands in both of mine. "Margo, do you know that thing the kids say? 'BFF?'"

She shook her head. "I try not to hear anything the kids say. They'll corrupt you into wanting to be young again if you give them half a chance."

"BFF. Best Friends Forever. Margo. You and me. Regardless of the current situation. Whatever that may be. Best Friends Forever."

"Well." She cleared her throat, and made a funny scrunched up face. "Well, if you insist. I would have settled for…ah…Current Best Friend, if I had to. But if BFF sounds better to you. Let's go for that." I hugged her again, my own tears too close for speaking.

I drove away from Margo's, past my little

cottage and up my beautiful, ragtag street. Back to Lake Shore, the Shoreway and downtown, checking the rearview mirror, inspecting every car that passed us, without letting them know I was looking.

As we went, I thought to myself, *We need a different rental car. Different make, different model, different color, totally different. First thing tomorrow.*

Tom was quiet with his own thoughts until we pulled up to the valet.

"Did you by any chance just make four right turns in a row?"

Chapter Thirty

The Marriott Grand Ballroom was vast. And mostly empty. A small crew of hotel staff had begun to set up for a banquet. Round tables. Rows of stacked up chairs. The chandeliers were amped down to a romantic, electric-bill-saving glow. The sound system was playing "Tequila Talking."

The workers were moving slow. Folks with no urgent deadline and no bosses around, late in the evening, getting out ahead of tomorrow's game plan, listening to a little country on this quiet night in the big hotel, just to ease the time. The mood of the room, its dreamlike, unhurried pulse, called out to me like the longing for peace.

Tom and I had taken a late evening stroll through the quiet, public spaces. It was after ten p.m. on a Monday night. Not rush hour at the Marriott. Our aimless feet had brought us here to a beautiful tall-windowed corridor that buffered the entrance to the ballroom. I guided Tom through the open doors, taking in the grand space through my newfound experience of what it's like to let all your senses that aren't sight tell you everything you need to know.

I closed my eyes. The room was cool, the air still. Our steps were hushed by carpet. There was the fragrance of Murphy's and well-buffed wax from the dance floor. The papery perfume of wilting flowers from the last party they'd had. Lonestar was winding down about the guy being so drunk he'd accidentally told his ex-girl he still loved her. The way the sound echoed in the emptiness was telling me that the room was bigger than life.

"Where are we, Allie?" Tom's voice was low. "A large space—Ballroom? It smells romantic."

"You're right," I whispered back, opening my eyes, seeing it for Tom. "It's the ballroom. There are a few people here, setting up for a party of some kind. The lights are low. The air conditioning is on. That romantic smell, though…that's all me."

The tequila had stopped talking and a few slow chords signaled the intro of the Trisha Yearwood version of "How Do I Live."

The longing in the music, the heartbreak of a cello in there, drew me to Tom. I took his hand and led him out into the middle of the big dance floor and put both my arms around his neck. "Let's dance," I said. "There's no one to run into. We can both close our eyes."

"Sounds good to me."

How do I,
Get through one night without you?
If I had to live without you,
What kind of life would that be?

It was all there in the song. The sweet attraction, the elemental passion, the bonds we'd been forging between our bodies and our minds. Knowing, learning, discovering each other. I felt the sorrow of comprehending, too late, that I'd put my own heart into someone else's body. And that person now had the power to take me away from me. He was a good dancer, too. For a man who always danced in the dark, he knew how to lead.

Trisha was telling somebody that without him her whole life would be trashed.

No love = No world.

Without you,
There would be no sun in my sky,
There would be no love in my life,
There'd be no world left for me.

Too darned bad, Allie girl. Too darned late.

And I,
Baby, I don't know what I would do,
I'd be lost if I lost you.

As if he'd read my mind in the words, Tom

said, "We're cooked, Alice. We were both doing fine on our own. You were your own free spirit. I was satisfied with having everything in my life all worked out. It wasn't just the Mondo that blew up our worlds, honey. It's us. Us together.

"Us is what we have to lose now. Everything we're counting on. You telling me about the sunsets over the lake, and me getting you to slow down and listen to the world and breathe the world and make love to me about ten thousand more times. If it doesn't work out like that, neither one of us will ever get over it. That purely sucks."

"You're right." I agreed, adoring the warmth of his neck under my fingers, the rhythm of our bodies, moving to the hungry sadness of the song. "We are so screwed."

But he kissed me anyway. And I kissed him back. The music ended and the set-up crew applauded. We took a bow and went upstairs and got started counting on down from ten thousand.

Chapter Thirty-one

Tuesday, August 25

You would think that such an idyllic moment of romance and sweet-talking would have satisfied my restless mind. It did. It did. Then it didn't. The more idyllic things got between Tom and me, the more the watchdog of my mind paced and growled about the danger. My dog wasn't half as unflappable as Princess, probably because my dog wasn't a giant slobbering hulk.

I addressed the onset of this agitation by handling the rental car swap. It was a piece of Mondo cake. Silver Maxima got picked up by one rental outfit. Black RAV 4 got dropped off by another. Slick.

I had to admit I wasn't as enchanted by rental-cars-on-demand as I might have been a week back when my ride was a bus. I knew better now. Money simplifies things. But it costs you. Now a simple, smelly old bus ride—just Tom and me, headed to my house for chili, for example—was beyond our reach. Lost in the money.

Respect the Mondo, Allie. Remember what Margo said. Shut up. Be responsible. Move on.

Okay. I was reassured by the new car. Truly. But after I breathed my sigh of relief, I checked inside my head, and there was Ms. Restless Librarian, still wringing her hands. Here's what she was worried about now: our credit cards; the Internet; the Cloud; the phones, slow, unmarked vans with tinted windows; CCTV; possible corruptibility among the valets….A low-voltage electrical charge fizzed around under my skin. I couldn't handle every single thing I was worried about.

I had to pick one.

How about my scrap of plaid? It was still nagging at me.

Here was a detail I could manage. The scrap had everything. It was easy. It was on my own dear kitchen windowsill. In my own dear house. A place I was aching to escape to.

No kidding. It made sense to protect the plaid. It could still turn out to be important evidence. I mean, what if we found the killer? And there he/she was, wearing a plaid something with a uniquely shaped piece hacked out of it? And—ta da!—here was me stepping smartly up with the perfect match.

How Sherlock Holmes and Miss Jane Marple would that be?

And if I then whipped out that other fragment, the DIRTY!!! one that every now and again whispered "jail time" in my anxious little ear? Who, then, would throw Miss Alice Jane Harper Holmes Marple in the slammer after such a triumph? Another teeny voice at the back of Restless Librarian Mind chirped, "Valerio."

I told her to butt out. I had to have that scrap.

Okay. That was part of it, but maybe not the truest part. Something even worse than my vision of me in an orange jumpsuit was taunting me. Everything Tom had said about our Us Together dream? That was a coin toss. Heads, you win your heart's desire. Tails, you lose it all.

My own irreplaceable coin was up there. For grabs. Threatened by forces I couldn't see. Was I woman enough, brave enough, *detective* enough to go after it now?

Well, first I had sneak by Tom.

I braced myself for an altercation.

"What if I just wanted to run down to my house to check it out and grab some more clothes and stuff. I miss my favorite jeans. Okay?"

Simple plaid pick-up. A nice anonymous black RAV 4 ride. Gone for a minute. Back before dark.

"Allie, wait until tomorrow. I'll come with you.

I have to get these forms for next semester e-mailed back to the dean. I don't want to get Mondo-fired on top of everything else."

"Tom. Stay here. Do your work. I'll be careful. I'll have my phone. Margo will be right across the street. Princess will be there, too."

I went over to where he sat with his school things laid out like soldiers on the large desk the hotel provided for high-powered, executive guests such as ourselves. I put both my arms around his shoulders, touched my lips against the back of his neck, leaned in, inhaling the soapy goodness, and whispered into his ear, "Tempting as it is for me to spend every single moment of the rest of my life with you, Thomas Bennington, PhD, you know that's not going to work. I'm a grown-up. I have to go somewhere, sometime."

I'm scared. And way out of my league. I want to go home.

"What if it were me, wanting to grab a cab and go down to my place by myself?"

"That's different."

He pulled back. "Different why? Because I'm blind. Because that somehow makes me not a grown-up?"

"No." *Think fast, Allie.* "Because you are The Blind Mondo and everybody knows it. I'm still merely me when I'm not all plastered up against you. Like I am right now. Mmm. Danger by association…"

I moved in again, wondering to myself why I wanted to go anywhere. His back was so deliciously…Tom. I could feel the taut muscles of his shoulder through the fabric of his shirt.

But he swiveled his chair around and slipped away. "This is serious, Allie. I've had almost ten years to get capable of doing whatever I put my mind to. On my own. I have no intention of taking you everywhere I go."

"Okay. Okay. Is there somewhere you'd like to go alone right now? Because that's up to you."

Bluff. Bluff. Don't call my bluff.

"No! Right now I want to get this e-mail out but I can't because you—you're distracting me."

My hands snuck back. To his lovely chest this time. So warm. So Tom.

"I am, aren't I?" I kissed him then and he kissed me back, but I could tell his heart wasn't in it.

"See? You're busy. I'm going."

He puffed out a sigh. "Go ahead, then. You're right. I can't stop you. But Allie. Be careful." He turned back to the desk, and I got that weird punched-in-the-gut feeling like when you're in a tug of war with your ten-year-old buddies. You're pulling and straining and then some joker lets go.

But I went anyway and walked right into

another security debate. Trust the valet? Or take my chances poking around in another dimly lit parking garage?

Oh. No contest.

The girl at the valet stand remembered the car change-out and where they'd put the car. Was that exceptional service or sly surveillance?

Chill, Allie.

I hid in the lobby until I saw the car.

• • ● • •

The intense late afternoon sun had bleached the color out of the day and left it blank and strange. I had that eyes-on-the-back-of-the-neck feeling, except in my stomach. It had been hardly twenty-four hours since the Arco garage incident, and a part of me was never going to be the same. That part wanted me to turn around, return the vehicle, and go back inside. I could feel Tom wanting that, too. From all the way down here.

The part of me that needed to muster up some guts had to go.

I drove my pristine RAV 4 up Chester to East 105th. My fellow drivers were unremarkable. Rush hour was tapering off. I was part of a congenial stream of folks gliding along Martin Luther King Jr. Drive, heading for the Shoreway, going home.

Home. I was going to dash in, grab my piece

of key evidence off the windowsill, take a deep breath, and get my equilibrium back. What's more, I'd pick up a new flavor of Jo Malone. Jo has always made me feel invincible. My scary new world was screaming for about a gallon of invincibility.

It was cool and wonderful down among the trees. MLK traverses Rockefeller Park, where manicured cultural gardens fly the flags of many nations. I slowed as I passed my favorite. The one Clevelanders from India had made. There was Mr. Gandhi, my special friend, his tall statue striding along, staff in hand, calling forth his *Satyagraha*, which he said meant, "truth force." Seeing him makes me feel better about us people. I gave Gandhi a little wave as I drove by. *You go, Gandhiji. And if you've got some of that truth force to spare, I could use me a splash of that right now.*

I was smiling as I sped off MLK and into the Village of Bratenahl. The splendid estates along the lake were marinating in golden light. The sun was lower in the sky than I expected. August is where fall thinks it can start sneaking up on you.

Almost home, I'd drifted away from my heightened state of DEFCON 3, so when the big, black Cleveland Police cruiser swam up behind me, my heart jumped and I hit the brakes, but I didn't freak all the way out. I wasn't speeding. I swallowed hard and kept driving like a solid citizen. When I rolled out of Bratenahl and back into Cleveland, however, he lit up and pulled me over.

It disappoints me to say that I still didn't realize who I was dealing with. I was rifling through the glove box for the rental paperwork and preparing my "I have no idea why…" speech, when there was a tap on the glass and I found myself face-to-face with Officer Tony Valerio. All by himself.

Me, too. Alone. Alone. Alone.

Chapter Thirty-two

"Officer Valerio? What—?"

He cut me off. "Ms. Harper. We need to talk. Come sit in my car for a minute."

I had calculated that should I be accosted on this outing, I could always run into traffic screaming for help and any evildoers would be sufficiently put off by my fuss to abandon the attempt. But I'd been pulled over by a policeman. Any running performed by me would be fugitive behavior. If he wanted to haul me out of my front seat, cuff me, throw me into his backseat, and drive me straight into landfill, who would even notice?

I got out of the RAV. Fortunately there was no cuffing. He walked me around and opened the passenger door. Not the trunk. Not even the backseat behind the wire grid. I scooted in, trying to look as innocent and compliant as possible. He got in on his side, slammed the door, and faced me with the stony expression I'd learned to associate with interrogations.

Too much crime TV, Alice.

I needed to change my viewing habits. Assuming I lived long enough.

I waited for him to lead off. My felony and his inquiries into the putative disturbed crime-scene evidence were foremost in my fevered brain, but who knew what he might be thinking? Sure enough, he came right out of left field.

"You got kidnapped yesterday."

Was it only yesterday?

"Sort of."

"And a guy got killed."

"Yes."

"How many does that make? How many people have died who are in some way related to you and Dr. Bennington and his jackpot? By your count."

Counting carefully now. In order of their expiration. "Well, Mr. Reposado and his associates Muff and Frank. That's three. And then Ulysses Grant. Four. And five: Renata Davis. And now Dan. Randall, I think it was. Six. Altogether."

So far.

Please, God, let me not have said that out loud.

"So far."

He said it. Not me.

I decided to pretend for a minute that he was on my side. "What do you make of that? A pattern?

Besides the high-rise housing being a health hazard? We can leave Dan out. He was a wild card."

He shook his head and muttered something that sounded like "*We?*" Then he hesitated as if he were the one editing his comments for me now. Maybe he was.

Anthony Valerio was a stocky guy, mid-forties, handsome once-upon-a-time but not aging all that gracefully. Florid. Tired-looking, with pouches of darkened flesh under weary eyes and the monobrow like a brushy cliff hanging over them. I wondered if he ever thought about retiring and becoming a security guard like Otis. Walking the same route through a damp, dusky parking garage, day in, day out. Unless he found some other way to make money.

His face hardened, almost as if he'd tracked my thoughts around to his motive for maybe killing some guys. What he said was, "That kind of money is a curse."

I nodded. "That's what Ulysses said, too. Did you know him?"

"Some. Not much. We—Officer Clark and I—spend a decent amount of time up there. Lot of petty stuff. Drugs. Domestic. Stealing. People get cut sometimes. Five deaths in less than a week is atypical, though."

"Where is Bo—Officer Clark? I thought you guys were partners."

He scowled at me for almost being over-familiar with an officer of the Cleveland Police Department.

"There aren't so many traditional partners anymore. Clark's young, about two days up from rookie. I look after him when I can, and we ride together on some shifts. Not always. It depends on who's available. We get split up sometimes. Staffing is getting thin."

How reassuring. Back to the five deaths we were talking about.

"Are you counting Ulysses and Renata as murders now?"

Because I sure am.

I wondered if Valerio knew about Renata being MIA somewhere between the hospital base-ment and the ME's slab, and I saw Margo with candlelight playing over her face. *There's a killer out there tonight you both should be very afraid of.*

Was I talking to him right now?

But I knew for a fact Valerio didn't kill Ulysses.

Unless I'd miscalculated somehow. Or. Unless it was poison.

He lowered the brow at me. "What do you think? I don't know about the immediate cause of Renata's death. But getting beat up and dying two days later is murder of some kind, that's for sure. We're still waiting on the autopsy report on both her and Ulysses. But the others—"

Okay. He didn't know Renata was not where she was supposed to be. Or maybe he knew exactly where she was. I was having this schizophrenic moment in which I could see Valerio as both an adversary and a fellow traveler. A guy who had the exact same questions I did.

Someone to trust.

Or not to trust.

I needed to be very careful here.

"Ulysses told me on the phone the night he died that you should check the ballistics on the shootout," I volunteered.

"Yeah. So you said. He was right. To all appearances Felix Tequila shot Muff and Frank, and Frank somehow lived long enough to shoot Felix. It's possible, I suppose. Everybody down there has a gun or two, even the little old ladies, and about one in every twenty-seven is registered. There had to be ample weapons at the scene. Could have been a couple right on the table for all I know. Muff and Frank were both shot with one with Felix's prints on it.

"But here's where it falls apart some. Frank had two. The one that killed Felix—the one with Frank's prints on it—was on the floor next to his chair. Right side. Under his right hand. And another one—little—strapped to his left ankle. Unfired. Unnoticed, I assume."

"You're telling me Frank was left-handed and the person who set him up as the one who shot Felix didn't know that."

If Valerio was the shooter, why was he telling me all this? *Stay awake, Alice.*

"Looks that way to me."

"So maybe Felix didn't shoot Frank and Muff either."

I fell back in. Dismissing the possibility, for the moment, that Officer Valerio might be describing his own crime, trying to draw me out. "I feel better about that interpretation."

"Feel better how?"

Oops.

I remembered again. Reminded myself that the further I backed away from this whole sorry affair, the safer, maybe alive-r, I'd be. But I was committed now. I plunged ahead.

"It's—" I faltered. "Felix shooting Frank and Muff? That doesn't add up from what I've heard. You called him 'Felix Tequila?' That's the perfect nickname for a guy Tom and I met in the elevator on Mondo Night. You did know him."

"Yeah. Sure. Everybody knew Felix. And everybody made fun of his name. About how he had to be under the influence when he changed it. He got around. Petty stuff. Sold crack and meth here and there when he could round some up. I'm sure there was heroin in there, too. It's everywhere around here now. He gambled. Stole what he could. He was a loser, Felix. It was tough to pin anything worthwhile on him because he was so incredibly small-time."

"But he wasn't a killer." There I went again. "That's what Margo said. That he thought about killing her, but didn't. Even though she could have identified him. Lucky for her. But stupid on his part. I'd guess Muff and Frank were about all the friends he had."

"So…" He was gazing at me. Appraising. "What do you think happened to those guys?"

I could see it, but I didn't want to tell Valerio. Especially since at this moment, I'd at least temporarily cast him in the starring role. So not yet. Probably not ever. I stalled. "Where did it happen?"

"They were in a small room on the first floor, down the hall from the common area where you found Ulysses' body."

That long, dim corridor. The door crime-scene-taped shut.

"Felix and those two used to play cards. Gin rummy. For pennies. All night sometimes. Ulysses, too. Maybe he'd been playing with them then.

There was an empty space at the table. We even checked Ulysses for GSR. That's gunshot—"

"Residue. I know. I watched the CSIs like everybody else."

He winced. "Pain in the ass. Wannabees."

"Yeah." I could see his point. "But you didn't find any. GSR."

"No. And he denied ever having been there. But of course he would. His prints were there, of course, like two hundred other guys'. So what do you think?"

I closed my eyes and pictured the small room. Muff and Felix in folding chairs. Frank and Ulysses rolled up to the table. Ulysses leaves. Maybe a bathroom break. Muff, Felix, and Frank are sitting around, waiting, idly shuffling the cards, drinking some beers. Frank, just coasting his way through another endless night. Muff. Who'd ever know what he'd been up to? Felix. Something of a player, who earlier in the evening had probably helped Muff beat up Renata and then terrorized Margo in her house.

Maybe someone—I think I'll call him, oh, say, Anthony Valerio—comes to the game room early Wednesday morning for the information—or the ticket—that Muff and Felix had gone to Renata's and Tom's—and Felix had headed on down to Margo's by himself—to get. Maybe that person is already thinking he's made a big mistake involving anyone else in his plans. Or maybe hadn't authorized any of it. Maybe just said, "Check around and let me know."

Or maybe he's there to see what they're up to and realizes he's tipped his interest in Tom's money by walking into that room. Or he's said the wrong thing to the wrong, stupid, untrustworthy guys with their big flapping mouths. Maybe, right there, on the fly, he decides he needs to do some tidying up.

The person maybe has a gun but he doesn't have to use it because there's an abundance of weaponry handy right here.

He gets his answers, which are something like, "Hey, man. No luck. But we're partners, right?" Or, "Hey, man, what you doing here? Still looking for that ticket guy? Heh, heh."

Cold. Deadly. He picks up a spare gun, walks around behind Frank, and shoots Felix, and then—while the other two watch, frozen—Mutt, heavy and slow, Frank, stuck in his chair. Both unable to process, in the second or two of living they have left, what's about to happen. He walks around behind Felix and grabs the gun Felix maybe used to terrorize Margo and shoots them both. He wipes his prints off, presses the appropriate prints on. Places both guns in their reasonable positions. And walks away. Fast. In case someone who's awake at three a.m. hears the shots and comes running.

But maybe one of them wasn't quite dead yet. I'm thinking Frank. Frank was a good friend to Ulysses. No matter that Ulysses had expressed doubt about Frank's trading in his wheelchair for angel wings. Maybe Frank had used his last moments to scrawl a note warning DIRTY!!! For Ulysses to wheel back in and find.

The note on a lined pad. For scorekeeping? The note with brown smudges everywhere. I shivered. That crumpled note which at this very moment was in the inside zipper pocket of my purse. Which I'd brought with me and had put on the floor of the squad car. Here. At my feet.

My phone rang. "Blind Love." Tom. Calling my heart. I switched it off.

I hurried back to my mental construction of the killer. DIRTY!!! I empathized with the overuse of exclamation points. I would have forgiven Frank for at least six or seven more.

I'd been staring down at the worn seat cover, rubbing my fingers over it as if it were the scene of the crime. In a couple of seconds I was going to have to come back up and meet Valerio's eyes. Did I suspect him? Sure. Why not? I tried one last time to connect with the part of my brain that kept saying NO!!! against all logic, but I couldn't. Quite. I looked up. Shook my head.

"Sorry," I shrugged. "I don't know what to think. It seems very—complicated. I have absolutely no idea."

Wannabees. What do we know anyway?

He shrugged right back, the look in his eyes an accusation. Or maybe a threat. I scooched back against the side door. Waiting for him to pull out his regulation police weapon and shoot me.

He shrugged again.

"Okay. But here's my advice to you, girlie. Watch yourself. Maybe this thing has played itself out. Now that you've turned in the ticket and this kidnapper has been killed and made the news. Maybe not. Good luck, is all I have to say. You'll need it."

That was it. Valerio told me to go on back to my car.

I went.

Chapter Thirty-three

Doggone. I'd taken a very big risk and paid a steep price to comfort the little girl inside me who kept whining, "But I want to go *home*." And to get my puzzle-piece of plaid, of course. The one scrap of evidence I had a legitimate, non-felony, claim to. No way was I giving up, even though the lucid, non-obsessed section of my brain said what I ought to do was hang a U-ey and beat it straight back to the Marriott.

Tom would be expecting me by now. Before now. And worrying some. Make that a lot. This worried me, too. A lot. He'd called. But I didn't want to call him back and have an argument long-distance. I could be much more persuasive if I could put my hands on him. Anyway, the rental car turned left all by itself.

I checked the rearview to see if Valerio followed me down my street, but he passed by the intersection. Slow. But going. Did that mean I was safe?

Or vulnerable and on my own?

Margo had never mastered the "leave a light on" strategy of burglary prevention. A glance told me nobody was home.

Way to go, Margo. And you told me I should "brain up."

Princess was lying sprawled out on the driveway. When I got out of the car and said, "Hey, Princess." she heaved her head up, blinked a dim recognition, yawned, and slapped out hello on the pavement with her tail a couple of times. Barkly's Princess Vespa was steadfastly—or maybe lazily—maintaining her post.

In the fading daylight, my cottage looked drab and neglected. A week of monsoon had given the grass and weeds a fantastic boost. Shrubs by the house had bulked up and were rustling ominously in the breeze coming off the lake.

I let myself in. The lamps we left on were shining, but I didn't feel welcomed. They cast an unflattering glare on my cherished things. The kitchen smelled mustier than I remembered. I could tell Margo had come back to remedy some of the effects of my ransacking, but still.

Everything felt different. Hollow and strange. Lonely.

Dammit, Allie.

I had missed the point on the most embarrassingly clichéd of all platitudes. This wasn't my heart's home anymore. Tom had changed its address.

I picked up my now insignificant, what-was-I-thinking? plaid puzzle piece from its lonely sill. Rushed upstairs, grabbed a large-size bottle of Jo's Pomegranate Noir and one of Lavender & Amber, headed back down and out through the kitchen, locked the door, didn't look back.

But then, hearing the splash and play of waves, I hesitated. Gulls keened. My soul was attuned to gull keening. My lake was calling to me. I stood still, giving it its due for a long second, gazing out at sun dissolving in water. Chiding myself that no matter where my true heart resided, I should never ignore the coming of twilight into a glorious world.

That's when he grabbed me.

"You," he rumbled, low and angry. "You miserable bitch."

Panic froze my body while my mind shrieked, "No! No-no-no-no-no-no-*no!*"

This was a large man, tall and bulky, with a substantial belly. Big. Strong. Close behind me, pinning my arms down at my sides with his meaty hands. He smelled funky—a smoker and none too over-bathed. He gripped tight and shook me. The bottle of Pomegranate Noir slipped from my fingers and smashed on the stones of the walk, enveloping us in a lush, overpowering wave of sensual fruit and spice. This didn't faze my attacker. He gave me another shake and shouted again, "You bitch! You stole my money!"

That tore it. The adrenaline I'd been producing for a good, old-fashioned scream got diverted straight on into rage. I'd been scared way too many damn times in the last forty-eight hours. I didn't care if this idiot killed me, as long as I got to hurt him a lot first.

"What? *What? What money?* What the fuck are you talking about? Let *go.*" I thrashed as much as I could given the iron grip, but he had size and strength on me so I went still again, casting a hopeless look at Margo's house.

Even darker and more obviously empty than before.

Another dizzying shake. This time something in my left shoulder let go, unleashing a stab of agony and a flash of white light behind my eyes. I yelped like a puppy. He ignored me and kept shaking.

"My 550 million dollars, is what. My lottery ticket. That I bought with my dollar. He stole it. That blind Mondo bastard. I want it back."

Okay, there was my answer. *Big fat lying* idiot.

A huge, dangerous, fucking, lying dumb-ass was bruising my upper arms with his filthy hands and breaking my shoulder away from the rest of my body like a chicken wing.

No fucking way.

I focused all the energy from my entire weak, trembling, furious body into my right elbow and drove it into this guy's jiggly solar plexus as hard as I could. My right hand sprang open. The bottle of Jo Malone Lavender & Amber hit the rocks. We were in tear gas territory now.

The guy howled, "Aaaag!" Released his grip long enough to cuff me smartly on the side of the head and then grabbed hold of me again.

I wasn't having any of that. I kicked back at his shin as hard as I could, stomped on both his feet, and screamed, "Stop it, you filthy creep. Get your disgusting paws off of me."

Paws?

Oh, yeah. Now there was a magic invocation. Because…

Out of the gathering darkness, trailing the ghosts of thousands of her ancestor dogs, and emitting the mighty bell-like, gut-wrenching roar that is the battle cry of her breed, The Princess Vespa came forth to kill my dumb-ass.

And, really, her roar got the job done. The guy dropped his hold on me and stumbled every which way, sounding the loser bellow of his own kind as he ran.

Amazing. I was alive. Shaking. Drenched in a blend of fragrance in a quantity neither Nature nor Jo Malone ever intended. My head spinning. My shoulder on fire…

But alive. I fell to my knees in front of Princess, sobbing with gratitude and residual terror. I meant to hug her but she swayed her jowls at me and backed up. I got it. I let her go.

And then, to cap it all off, my heroine and I were engulfed in a wash of headlights. Margo. She pulled to a stop outside my gate and gazed at her dog and me for a long, speechless few seconds.

"Allie? Princess? Where's Tom? Who was that guy? And what the fuck is that smell?"

Chapter Thirty-four

Margo called the police. But did we get "the police"? Oh, no. Of course not. That would have been too easy. We got Valerio.

In the time it took him to show up, the big lying doofus had vanished. All he'd left us was a trail of trampled underbrush and a cloud of fragrance. And my sore shoulder, of course. It wasn't so bad, unless I moved too quickly. Or breathed too deeply. I sat very still. Valerio stared at me. Made no comment in a manner that was itself an extremely unkind comment. Took my statement. By the book. Sniffed his disapproval. And left.

As he was going, though, he gazed at me for a moment, thinking his Valerio thoughts, and favored me with one parting question.

"Seriously?"

● ● ● ● ●

I gave up and called Tom. On the one hand, I couldn't wait to hear his voice. On the other, I was scared of what he would say. It didn't help that I'd forgotten I'd turned my phone all the way off. When I turned it back on, I'd missed seven calls from him.

His "Hello?" was ragged with fear. His first "Allie!" was ecstatic with relief. His second "Allie" was one degree down from white hot rage. After that, he said a few things about what he thought of me.

"Tom." I kept saying "Tom…"

All my tried and true, smart and sassy defenses were trashed. Whatever this was going to be, I had it coming, but I needed it face-to-face. If he was planning to kick me out of his life for demolishing the ground rules, I wanted him to kick me out in person. If this it was going to be goodbye, I was going to be present for it.

"Tom," I broke through at last, "stop. I get it. Listen for one second, will you? Please?

"I'm listening. Go ahead."

"I'm coming ho—back to the Marriott. I screwed up tonight. I don't have any excuse. Nothing. You can say whatever you want. Do whatever you need to. But, Tom…" My voice shattered. "I need to see you."

"Fine." His tone was cold. "I'll be in the bar."

We'd been sitting in Margo's kitchen while I made the call and Margo hadn't budged through any of it, watching me with troubled eyes.

"It'll be okay, Al. Mad is the top layer of scared. He'll get over it. You'll see." She paused and sniffed a couple of times. "Would you like to maybe use my shower before you go? He relies on his senses a great deal...."

"No. I'm going. If I wait, I'll lose my nerve. And if I take more time, it'll only make things worse.

• • ● • •

I paused for a long moment outside of Jake's Lounge, remembering the night of my first big off-the-rails adventure. Ulysses Night. I was checking for threats this time, too. I figured that there had to be at least one: Tom. I had never felt more vulnerable, more out of excuses and bright ideas. More alone.

Show some guts, Allie. Whatever this is going to be, you earned it all by yourself.

Jake's was lively with drinkers and socializers. Quite a few of them took note of my bedraggled appearance as I passed among them and several of those gave me a second, raised-eyebrow glance based on the change in the air. I inspected them right back. I wasn't trusting anybody anymore. Not even effete, upscale barflies.

Tom was sitting at the glowing bar with his back to me, a glass of something brown with melting ice in front of him. I couldn't tell whether he recognized my step or was startled by the smell, but his back tensed as I walked up.

I tensed, too. He wasn't alone.

"Allie."

This "Allie" was serene and distant. I had an inkling of what he was feeling. His face said he'd already laid my memory to rest. It would be a long hike back from that cemetery.

It seemed premature for him to have found a new girl so soon after my demise, however. And a gorgeous one, at that. She'd been whispering to him as I walked up, a low purr of seduction. Weaving a pheromone web of attraction between them.

My arrival didn't break the connection.

"Allie," Tom repeated, his tone formal. "This is Diana. Diana Wiles. She's a colleague of mine at the university."

O.M.G. Jake's Lounge was so destined to be my "Case of You" bar. Diana. *Diana?* But of course. The mystery ringtone. Things were adding up.

I was shocked it wasn't playing.

"Nice to meet you, Diana." I started to extend a hand and then rethought when she drew back. Kind of like Princess, only better-groomed.

"Sorry. I had an incident with some fragrance earlier this evening."

Tom made a sound I was unable to interpret.

I gave this Diana Wiles the onceover. She was everything I always wanted to be—more, even, than blond, sleek, and professional, like Officer Bob Clark's impeccable Marie.

Diana: Dark. Mysterious. Dangerous. Sophisticated. Sickeningly beautiful. *Augh*. As a younger, less-enlightened woman, I had secretly longed to make other women queasy with my beauty. Diana was payback for that uncharitable wish. I wanted to throw up.

I knew Tom could not be moved by the vision of raven hair falling straight down over an ivory cheek, but the silky would translate fine for him. The creamy complexion, glistening lips, flawless manicure—my fingers curled themselves self-protectively into my palms—gorgeous figure gift-wrapped in fluid black charmeuse. The smooth of her, the flawless touch, the tactile of Diana Wiles was a formidable rival.

Yeah, she was nauseating.

She laid a well-lotioned hand on Tom's arm and kept it there, stroking. A caress. Possessive. She turned to me as if unpleasantly surprised to discover me still there, and gleamed at me through slightly narrowed big, dark, lustrous, brown eyes.

Right there, right then, I had a lightning strike of what Tom's supernatural sixth sense must be like. I could sense the tension in the air. Feel it. The pulse of desire.

My brand new spidey sense pinged. *"Spider!"*

Diana's voice had Tom's honeyed echo of the South. "Allie, it is a pleasure to meet you. At last."

Then she leaned into him, locking me the rest of the way out of their private encounter, and murmured, her perfect lips almost touching his ear, "I'm going now. Think about what I said. It could be good, Tom—very good. It could be everything we always wanted. From the beginning. All of it. So think about what that could be like."

"I already have."

Three little words.

My heart took a direct hit.

Diana picked up Jake's sparkly martini glass off the bar in front of her, drained its quicksilver liquid, and set it back down with a force that severed its base from the stem with a crisp chink. She held up the glass at eye level and tipped it in my direction, a toast, and said, "Oh my, how very careless of me. Or perhaps I should say—" She turned it upside down and set it on the polished surface "how very fragile of it."

She slid off the leather-upholstered barstool in a hiss of charmeuse that made me think of static electricity and snakes, and left the bar to the tune of a lot of admiring glances from the guys around there. She wobbled somewhat at the end of her runway, but I guess Manolos will do that to you.

Geez.

I was done. Defeated. Whatever was going to happen would happen. I had not a Manolo to stand on. I was plain. I was badly dressed. I smelled like a busload of hookers—high-priced hookers, let me say. It was Jo, after all.

I needed a shower. I needed to sleep. I had screwed up like there was no tomorrow. Now there wasn't going to be one for Tom and me. I wanted to die. Maybe cry myself to death. I touched Tom on the shoulder.

"I'm going up. I need a shower. We…. Maybe we can talk…in the morning. I…I can't tonight." The tears were on the move again.

"Fine."

Cold, cold, cold.

Let this day be over now, Lord. And make me a better girl. Amen.

And that was it for Tuesday.

Chapter Thirty-five

Wednesday, August 26

That was not it, however, for very, very early Wednesday morning.

It was a little after eleven when I got back to the room. I started to cry as soon as the door clunked shut behind me, and I didn't even bother to try and stop myself. I figured I didn't deserve much but I did have the right to cry as hard and as long as I liked.

So I did. I sobbed and blubbered my way into the shower, stood under the hot spray, leaned my head against the tile, and didn't even bother to wipe my nose. I let it all out. Every time I moved wrong and jarred my damaged shoulder, I let go and cried more. It was as if my one possession in the world was the permission I'd given myself to shed all these tears and not feel ashamed.

Oh, I did feel plenty ashamed about how

stupid and thoughtless I'd been. Everything I'd put Tom through tonight.

Just not about bawling my eyes out.

And then, of course, here was Diana. I now knew for sure that Tom was in a relationship with another woman. A woman far more sophisticated and attractive…and sexier, no doubt…than me. I cried about that. A lot. And for how all my pretty dreams could be snapped apart as easily as a sparkly glass.

After a while the tempest died down, and I concentrated on scrubbing every perfumed inch of me about six times. I washed my hair, the full shampoo, rinse and repeat, twice.

When I gave up and shut off the water, I was a mere husk. As hollow as a chocolate Easter bunny. I toweled off as dry as I could and eased my sore self, naked, under the smooth, white Marriott sheet, a body at peace in its shroud. I figured I was as safe as a dead girl could be. I closed my eyes.

They opened back up again all by themselves. I looked at the clock. 11:45. Breathe, Allie, let this night pass. Breathe.

That went on for a while and I got a small amount calmer. No Tom appeared at all. Would he get another room? Come in the morning and pick up his beautiful blind-associate-professor things and his fabulous white tee-shirts? And move out?

To another hotel? Another city? Would I ever see Rune again? My calm faded. I peeked at the clock. 12:05 a.m. Praise the Lord. Tuesday was over.

Breathe.

I heard the card key slip into the lock.

I lay very still.

Click.

The door opened. The door closed.

Tom said, "Allie. Come here."

I got up as ordered, regretting now that I hadn't bothered to dig up something, anything, to wear. I didn't have a leg to stand on, but I would have appreciated some dignity.

"Tom?"

"Allie." Tense. Harsh. Not in any way good.

He put his hands out and found my arms. I gritted my teeth against the spike of pain from my shoulder.

"You…you're…you aren't…you don't have anything on."

"I didn't think I should borrow your stuff when you're so angry with me."

It crossed my mind that perhaps that had been a small, somewhat unconscious, last-ditch deviousness on my part. *I'll get even with you, Tom Bennington III, PhD, I'm not good enough to wear your shirt but I'm good enough to be irresistibly naked.*

Not irresistible it appeared.

"Angry? Angry doesn't begin to cover how I feel. How I felt when you didn't come back. You didn't call. And you'd turned off your *phone*?"

"I know. Tom, I'm sorry. You were busy. Working. I figured you wouldn't miss me—"

"Sorry? *Sorry*? You're sorry. Really."

A voice hard and cold as iron. My new spidey sense was on full alert now. He was radiating rage. The vibration of it was on my bare skin.

"You assume because I'm busy, or maybe just because I'm *blind* and can't see the sun setting, that I don't know what fucking *time* it is? I measure my life in time, Allie, I orient myself by it. I touch my fucking *watch* and it tells me what time it is.

"On August twenty-fifth in Cleveland the sun sets at 8:10 p.m. You should have been gone an hour and a half. That was six hours ago. You think I didn't know you were somewhere—I couldn't imagine where—in the goddamn *dark*? Lost? Kidnapped? *Dead*?

"So if you think being all sad and sorry will fix this, You are…just…so *fucking* wrong."

He shook me and his hands were on the same tender, bruised spots where the scary, disgusting guy had grabbed me, and the shaking wrenched my shoulder all over again. That did it. I was naked. I was wrong. I was sorry and now I was sobbing again. Dignity was clearly not going to be mine tonight.

"Okay. O*kay!* Tom. Stop! *Ow! Stop*! I was wrong. I screwed up. I…broke my promise. I scared you. It's…unforgiveable. I can't ever make it right. You're done. I get it. Let me go. Just let me go. I'm scared. You're hurting me."

"Good. I was scared, too, dammit. I thought I'd never…see you again. Do you know what that meant to me? The way I'd trusted myself to you. Letting you in. Letting myself see you—know you—the way I did?"

He gripped my bruised flesh harder. My shoulder screamed and reminded me of how terrified I'd been. How alone. How the things he'd worried about were the things I thought were about to happen to me. I cried out and tried again to pull free but he spun me around and pinned me up against the door.

Then something unexpected happened.

He kissed me.

This was not a tender, loving kiss. Until that moment I had no idea that there was such a thing as a furious kiss. Or how that would work.

It was furious, all right. Furiously hot. Hungry. Punishing. The taste of whiskey on my tongue. His chin was rough, his hands running all over me now. Possessive. Angry. And, yes. Exceedingly hot.

I stopped trying to resist. I returned the kiss—hungry, punishing, possessive, angry—in equal measure. I pulled away long enough to hiss, "I was lost and you were with that *Diana*!"

"Shut up. You don't know anything about that."

"And whose fault would that be?"

"Shut up. Just shut up. Don't try to divert me. I'm still mad at you. I'll still be mad at you tomorrow and probably next week. So shut up now. And prove to me you're alive."

He was still going to be mad at me next week?

This was terrific news. I set it aside to enjoy later. I had now been dragged into the heat of his rage. My hurt and dismay about finding him in the bar with a tactile-ly appealing woman while I had been missing and presumed dead, was fueling my own emotional instability.

We were a human torch.

I gave my throbbing shoulder a silent order to butt out and pulled him back across the room to the bed. I lent him a hand stripping off his shirt and pants. The playing field was more even now. I laid my naked self all along the naked heat of him. He rolled me onto my back, kissing me hard, moving into me like some wild, dark storm. I wrapped my legs around him.

I could see that the up-against-the-door part was all the foreplay there was going to be.

Fine.

By.

Me.

In the breathless moments after the fire had finally burned through all the accelerant, he murmured against my ear, "Alice Jane. If you ever scare me that badly again, I swear I'll kill you."

I dug my fingers into his neck, arched my back and tightened my legs around him and said, "Okay. I promise I'll let you."

An exchange of vows as sacred as any vows can be.

And then we fell asleep, still angry, still in each other's arms.

Chapter Thirty-six

"I know you hate all this."

"Yes."

"And you blame me for the total mess I made of yesterday."

"Yes. No. It's not—okay. Yes. For yesterday. You bet. Yesterday, for damn sure. You promised. You and I agreed that you wouldn't go off on your own looking for…for pieces of plaid."

"Well, technically, I said I was going to pick up some clothes 'and stuff.' The plaid was the stuff."

"I assume the tanker truck of Jo Malone was stuff as well? Whatever. I have to be mad at you for how scared I was."

What he had fully communicated to me in his rage the night before was how much self-ish carelessness I'd jammed into the heart of our relationship. How I'd damaged him in the abso-lutely—*everything*—of himself that he'd given to me, like a gift—and trusted me not to destroy. I didn't know when, if ever, he was going to forgive me for that, but it was going to be a deep, dark hole of regret in the middle of my chest for a long, long time.

The only bright spot for me this morning was that, in addition to being way beyond sorry, I was also a little flattered. He valued me at the level worthy of a first-class freak out. This was nice.

We were having a very careful Scarlett-O'Hara-meets-Rhett-Butler-the-morning-after-for-breakfast-at-David's-in-the-Marriott. I gave my plate of the special a disrespectful poke. Scenes from the aforementioned yesterday were ratcheting around in my head.

I had a lot to process over congealed Eggs Benedict.

At least my shoulder was feeling better. I had filled Tom in on what happened at my house, but I'd downplayed the Big Scary Attack as much as I could. I mentioned the arm bruises but not the shoulder. Ibuprofen was my friend. The specter of Diana Wiles was perched up there on the sorest spot, whispering that I could be replaced. I was casting about for some way to heal the damage I'd caused when Tom said, "Allie."

In that voice.

I injected as much abject remorse as would fit into my feeble little, "Yes?"

He cleared his throat. "Allie. I've been thinking."

Uh oh. Here it comes.

"That first night with you. I felt more alive than I've been in a long time. Remember I said I left Atlanta because my parents couldn't let me be independent?"

"I do." So far this was better than what I was expecting.

"That independence I moved 700 miles to get? That willingness to take a risk for a good reason? As careful as I am to manage everything about my life, that freedom is something I'll never give up, even if sometimes I forget how much I need it. And you. You bring that with you. It's part of the Alice Jane package. Even with everything that's happened, I still feel—"

I liked the "still." I waited, trying not to impede his momentum any more than I already had by just being me.

"I still feel so—"

I smashed my fork into the yolks Benedict and watched them ooze yellow-ly up between the tines. *Patience, Allie. Sit. Stay.* I held my breath.

"I love you, Alice Jane."

I exhaled. "You must, Tom Bennington. Or you'd be long gone by now."

"If I led you to believe I'd ever be gone—

ever—that was wrong. I was mad. Scared to death and mad."

His beautiful hand was lying quiet, palm up, on the tabletop, and I laid my guilty little paw in the cradle he'd made for it. His fingers closed around mine, and I felt something that had been locked up in my chest let go. I could breathe both in and out again.

"Listen. Allie. We're in big trouble here. You and me? We're our own little crime wave. It wasn't you who opened the door to 550 million dollar's worth of train wreck. That was all me."

"I suppose in one way you did. But that was not you, Tom. You did not commit premeditated serial-murder-by-jackpot. You can't blame your intention, which was all good and kind. Winning like you did? That was lightning striking. Although the odds for hitting the Mondo are way worse than lightning. It's a million times more unlikely than being struck twice in one lifetime. Seriously. That's a fact. I checked."

I got the improved smile I was waiting for, not yet entirely happy but welcome all the same. "Ah, so that's the burning sensation in my chest."

"No, that's love, remember? Love for me in spite of—" I sure didn't want to enumerate. "—everything."

"Stop. I forgive you for almost everything.

Just don't do it again. Or, as you recall, I'm sure, I'll have to kill you."

"I know."

Oh, yeah. Our sacred vow. And he was remembering that moment, too. I could tell by the flush of color on his fabulous cheekbones.

That angry embrace, fusing us to each other in spite of everything.

"But you need to not talk like that in David's. We're getting a reputation in here."

My appetite was coming back. I rejected my wrecked eggs and helped myself to a triangle of toast that Tom had abandoned. "I'm taking some toast you left here."

"I know." His smile was warmer. "I may be blind but my hearing is—"

"Acute. Your reflexes are slow, though. It's my toast now."

I gazed at Tom. Seeing how everything I loved about him was filling the empty spaces of my life. How my heart jumped when he came into view. How my skin tingled when it remembered him doing…well, everything he did to it. But that was not the whole story of me and Tom.

He was more than his handsome self and his limitless supply of tingle. The part of me that was most satisfied by Tom Bennington III was the sad, lonely, lost, rejected, screwed up part—the part

Duane Pathologically Cruel Harper, Esquire, had broken.

Tom was healing all that, repairing it, by simply loving me the way I was coming to believe I'd always deserved to be loved. Next to that irreplaceable gift, 550 million dollars was an abstract example of pointless excess.

I blinked away some tears. I needed to keep news of my revelation from Tom. He'd use it as an excuse to donate his millions to a retirement home for seeing eye dogs, and I didn't want him to do that until we got my car fixed.

His expression had shifted as I was considering all that and I could tell whatever he was thinking about was a lot more life-and-death than my toast thievery.

"There's something else we need to talk about. About our case."

Our case. Wow. More progress.

"Okay. And I can fill you in on what I talked to Valerio about last night."

"Valerio?"

Oops.

"I saw him yesterday evening before…um…I got to my house. We talked about what happened with Felix, Muff, and Frank."

"And?"

In for a penny.

"We—Valerio and I—we think they didn't shoot each other."

"I don't think so either."

"You don't."

"No. I don't. There's a pattern and that scenario doesn't fit. I sorted some things out while I was worrying about you yesterday and going over everything that's happened. In order. I think better when I'm terrified. Terror concentrates the mind. I read that somewhere."

"And?"

"The high-rise. It's ground zero. It's the Mondo epicenter. Look at the victims. Renata. Felix. Muff. Frank. Ulysses. Renata, again—"

"Plus, there's her missing…um—"

"Plus, there's that. What happened to Renata's body is a giant mystery. But it still fits. Count 'em, Allie. Every single person we met up with in that building the first night is dead. The only wildcard dead guy in the whole bunch is Dan from GG&B, and we know exactly how he got involved. That case is wrapped."

Whoa there. Wrapped? Tom was getting out ahead of me in the P.I. department.

"Your big guy from last night? We can't put him in the high-rise for certain, and I haven't had time to think about him…."

I'd had plenty. I suppressed the shudder by

biting the inside of my cheek hard enough to cancel out the memory. That wasn't altogether successful. Tom noticed. I saw it on his face, and it stabbed me right in my guilt. Again.

He continued, "We can't be sure he lives there, but, in a pinch, he might be the Renata boyfriend Ulysses told you was after Rune. He fits."

Like a scrap of plaid. I thought, but did not say aloud.

Unaware of my secret hypothesis, he continued. "I bet if you went door to door up there on fourteen…."

"Oh, let's not. I don't plan to ever go back there."

"Good. I'm delighted to hear that." A little sarcasm for my benefit. I accepted it with silent grace.

"Rune might know, but I don't want to ask him anything about any of that. Thank God he's is out of there for good. But look at this, too." He touched an index finger to the table, marking the "X" spot. I had to remind myself that he couldn't see the spot except in his imagination and that, in there, it was very likely the ominous tower that loomed sinister in my own memory.

"Valerio and Bob," he said and tapped the spot again. "They're the exceptions. We met them there that night and neither one of them is dead."

Yet.

"No. Not as far as we know. What are you suggesting?"

"Not sure. Do I suspect them? One or both? I don't know. I can't tell whether I should worry for their safety or—I don't know what."

I sat there, realizing I had possession of a—possibly deadly—can of worms. Debating whether to crack it open or let it go.

Okay.

"There's another guy from the high-rise that night who's still alive."

"What? Allie. Who?"

"He was with Ulysses and Frank the first night. They were watching the TV. Together."

"Do you think he knows anything?"

"I actually hope not. Maybe he doesn't and that's why he's still around. As far as we know."

"Maybe we should try to get in touch with him."

"Are you kidding? What did we just agree? And why am I the smart, sensible one all of a sudden?"

"Aren't you enjoying not being the wacky, irresponsible one?"

I gazed at him, approving the crisp shirt the hotel laundry had done for us and a sliver of white hot tee at the throat. I uncurled my hand and trailed a finger along his life line. "I'm enjoying a lot of stuff."

He grinned wide, and the dimple saw the light

of day for the first time in recent memory. His face was dear and beloved and all mine again. "Stop that," he warned. "We're being detectives right now. This is serious. Don't distract me."

I took my hand away, struggling to arrange my voice for sensibleness. "You're right. Back to this guy—my other guy with Ulysses and Frank. We don't know his name. I probably couldn't pull him out of a lineup. And the ones who were with him that night are both—"

"Dead. I'm painfully aware."

"And Felix and Muff, who could have told us, are also out of the picture."

"Nicely put. Aren't you the sensitive detective? That only leaves two guys who have some working knowledge of who's who in that deathtrap. And are still alive."

"Valerio. And Bob. Which might you trust?"

"Neither. Both. Who knows?" He sighed. "Let's count. The first night, I suppose they might have beaten up Renata, but that's beyond farfetched and, besides, I think we have Felix and Muff for the Tuesday night beatings. Margo's is Felix, for sure."

"Felix, Muff, and Frank. Valerio has evidence they didn't shoot each other."

"Okay. That doesn't surprise me. Valerio and Bob were both last seen—by us…well I suppose, strictly speaking, only by you. But I was right there—walking into the building after they drove us back up to get the car. That was maybe two, three hours before those three were killed. So we can't rule out either or both of them for that. I suppose they could have done it. But they don't compute on the others."

"Ulysses?"

"Hard to get them to him. Yes, they were on duty that night, close enough to answer your 9-1-1 call but far enough away to make them unlikely. Especially since there was no obvious cause of death. In my opinion, natural-looking causes would take more finesse and time. And if both those guys didn't kill Ulysses, then neither one could have."

Finesse and time? Mmm. Mmm.

"My, my. Associate Professor Bennington the Third. You're getting good at this."

"Stop sucking up. I'm capable of recognizing the obvious. A kid could get this far. Renata, next."

I took the ball. "We're hypothesizing that whoever killed Ulysses killed Renata. Someone who is good at natural causes and probably body-snatching. We may never find out what happened to her. Or where she's ended up. I suppose we can't rule out Valerio or Bob but I can't make them fit. Not logically. So where are we?"

"I believe we could, with a reasonable degree

of confidence, inquire of Valerio or Bob whether they know who the third guy might have been."

"Which one?"

"I choose Valerio."

"Rats. I'm afraid of Valerio. He's onto me."

"That's why I choose Valerio.

Chapter Thirty-seven

In the beginning, there were three old guys in wheelchairs. Ulysses, Frank, and an unknown old black guy. That unknown guy in the trio—sitting in the middle between Ulysses and Frank, soaking with them in the glow that had emanated from Jimmy Fallon—was the one we were hoping to hear from. He was the one we were on the phone with Officer Valerio about.

Well, to be precise it wasn't us on the phone. It was Tom. After we'd abandoned the wreckage of my morning meal—Eggs Benedict Arnold, as I was coming to think of it—we retired to our room to try Valerio. After we left a message for him at the district headquarters, it took him about fifteen minutes to get back to us. Hardly enough time for a decent kiss.

Tom put the call on speaker so I could hear, but I was the mouse in the corner. Small. Silent. Scared of Valerio. Afraid he would hear my big felonious lie in the tone of my voice, no matter what cavalierly nonchalant tone I managed to gin up. Quaking little mousie, I was.

It was working. Whether it was the blindness of Tom, his PhD, or maybe the *gravitas* being emitted by his money, Valerio was acting polite. And informative.

"Sammy R."

"I'm sorry? Did you say Sammy Arr?"

Valerio chuckled. A new sound in his repertoire. One I'd never heard in his conversations with me, which featured all those suspicious grunts and snorts.

"Yes. 'R' as in Robinson. That's Sammy's last name. Almost everybody in the place has a nickname of some kind or other. Sammy and Ulysses were buddies. Went way back from before they lived up there. He used to play cards with that bunch. Fill in. And he and Ulysses liked to watch late-night TV together. He must be pretty lonesome these days. Why do you want to know, Dr. Bennington?"

The pitch of this question shifted up into the slightly suspicious.

Tom's reply was calibrated for trust. "Just Tom, please. I'm still uneasy about where Allie and I figure in a lot of the violence that's occurred. Whether there are other threats. To us personally."

"The murders?"

"Yes. And the people who were beaten. Margo Gallucci. And Renata Davis, of course, before—"

"Before somebody maybe finished the job?"

"Yes. Is that what you think?"

"Can't prove it yet. But, however it goes, it's murder on somebody. Outcome of the earlier assault. You put her in the hospital? She dies? The crime is yours."

Tom cleared his throat and Valerio said, "I'm sorry. Tom. That sounded—I was speaking of the perpetrator of the original offense. Not—"

"Not me. But I'm sure you get why I feel responsible for a lot that's happened."

"Sure. I get it. But you should give yourself a pass on that one. From what I heard about the circumstances, you meant nothing but the best for the kid when you bought that ticket. The odds—"

"I know. I know. I've been given to understand it's like a million times more unlikely than being struck by lightning twice in one lifetime."

Valerio snorted. My cover was blown. "I can guess who came up with that number."

Tom smiled in spite of it all. "I bet you can. But I was wondering if you, in an official capacity, could maybe just check with Mr. Robinson. See if he has any insights at all—"

"I could do that. It's good idea, actually. And

I'm assuming that the CSI Wannabee won't be following up. Or mixing in. Or anything."

"Not in any capacity. She would want you to know."

Geez, that was mean all over the place. Whose side was Tom on, anyhow? But I sat tight.

"If I find out anything that could point to problems for you and Ms. Harper, you'll be the first to know."

"Thank you very much."

Tom hung up. I breathed a sigh of relief. I had at least four or five issues with Valerio, including me thinking he was maybe a cold-blooded killer and him thinking I was maybe an evidence tamperer and for sure a royal pain in the ass. Our relationship was chock full of pitfalls.

Chapter Thirty-eight

After that we packed our things and checked out of our Marriott.

Last night's attack was the tipping point. We didn't know exactly where that guy fit into our crimefest, but we were following a trail of suspicion, like bread crumbs, from the infamous tower to my place. It was a short walk. If he lived there, we were almost neighbors. Maybe he'd come back last night, looking for a piece of his shirt.

"Plaid," Tom nodded. "Okay. Maybe. You could be right…."

That was a stretch and we knew it, but Mr. Big & Repulsive kept climbing out of my yard and into my brain. I pictured him prying open my window and heaving his massive, plaid-wrapped torso through, snagging fabric as he went. He was one unknown threat too many, and he was still at large. Not to mention any new or unknown perpetrator or perpetrators we might be annoying with our inexpert-but-improving detective work.

Creepy Eye was on us everywhere.

I described to Tom my recurring suspicion that someone was lurking, stalking, or flying a damn drone over us wherever we went. "At first I thought I was overreacting, but now I know they're there. I feel them, Tom. On the back of my neck."

Tom smiled. "And you think I don't?"

Touché.

Moreover, there had been last night's odoriferous scene in the Marriot bar and the possibility that our neighbors up on the concierge floor might have overheard our altercation. Including the make-love-without-bothering-to-make-up encounter. I was more than ready to move on. I was sure our happy memories of the Marriott would overshadow the troublesome ones after a while, but it was time for us to make ourselves scarcer.

The Wyndham at Playhouse Square is not as big or elaborate as the Marriott. For example, it has a concierge but no concierge floor. I lucked out, however, because Tom had a chat with the desk person and she upgraded us all the way into a corner suite with a king-sized bed and a scenic view of the theater district. It wasn't two rooms but it had a sitting area, which made it a cut above the ordinary.

More good news: that king-sized bed had its own fabulous brand identity. The box spring comes with something called "Shock Abzzorber Plus." I shall not comment on that. I hope no one ever tells Margo.

A harsh judge of my character might very well assume that I was unforgivably callous, focusing on hotel amenities and other selfish pursuits in the midst of chaos and sorrow. That judge would be correct. Calloused was how I felt. You can only get so sad, so worried, so plain terrified before your soul is anesthetized.

My antidote to total soul numbness—and possible constant screaming—was to keep my attention on Tom. The bizarre luck of my having met the love of my life at the exact Act-of-God moment when he became both mind-bogglingly wealthy and blood-freezingly hazardous was not going to bring me down. I didn't care.

At least Tom had, as far as I could tell, forgiven me for Tuesday's debacle. It troubled me to consider that, in spite of my recent attempts to reform, he now suspected I was always going to be unreliable. That I had at least one good-sized flaw and he knew about it.

In exchange, I'd forgiven Tom for not enlightening me any further about the mysterious Diana—even though I suspected he was punishing me with silence for scaring him half to death.

It was an uneasy truce, but what the heck.

The prospect of our lying in each other's arms on our Shock Abzzorber Plus—me bringing light to his darkness and him sharing his rich, seductive darkness with me—pretty much swept my mind clear of every terrible thing. Callous? Absolutely.

Sue me.

I could have been happy at the Wyndham for a long time.

But there were complications.

First of all, we'd barely moved in when I got a "Who Are You?" call from a very unhappy man.

"Miz Harper?"

"Yes."

"I need you to get yourself all the way out of my life. Or I'll tell that cop of yours what I know 'bout you."

"I'm sorry? Who's this?"

"You know already who this is. You know about Sammy R. You sicced that cop on me. What you want to kill me for? I ain't done nothing to you. I need you to leave me alone. Or I'll tell that cop what I seen. What you done. The night somebody killed Ulysses.

"I got your number, girl. I seen you. I seen you pick up that paper. That night. Right out of Ulysses' cold dead hand."

I would have begged to differ if I could have talked at all. I would have said, *He was still warm when I got there, Sammy. His hand was dead, all right, but not all the way cold. And the paper wasn't in his hand…exactly. I just…jiggled his arm and it fell out all by itself.*

I settled for a small, involuntary squawk.

Sammy rolled on. "I seen what I seen."

"Did you mention this to Officer Valerio?"

"Mention it? Are you out of your mind? No. I did not. And you want to know why? Because everybody who mighta ever knew anything about what was in that note—before it was tore or after—is dead. 'Cept me. And you. I'm keeping myself alive by not mentioning about it to anybody. Only reason I'm talking to you right now is to tell you to leave me alone. Whatever happens to you? You probably got it comin'. Don't call me. Don't write me no letters. Don't send me no more police. We're quits, you 'n me. And good luck to you. Forget you ever heard my name."

He hung up before I could voice the one thought in my head.

"After it was tore?"

That meant there had been more to the note. Sammy and Ulysses and at least one more person— I was guessing Frank, the author of DIRTY!!!—had seen the whole thing. I'd seen only part. Maybe that meant I was only a little bit doomed to be dead. Or that the saving grace of the note was on the torn off part I was almost certainly never going find out about now.

Good luck to you, too, Sammy. I won't write. I won't call. I'll forget I ever heard your name.

Chapter Thirty-nine

Thursday, August 27

Here's something I've learned about Time. Big money—Mondo-sized Money—accelerates it. If Einstein never mentioned this, he should have. The formula, which I made up myself, goes something like MM>>>T, with the >>> standing for "triple speeds up." While we were chilling out, putting together our plans to get back together with Rune as soon as possible, Time was approaching the Speed of Mondo. Again.

On our first morning at the Wyndham, which was Thursday, while we were having breakfast and trying to figure out how to spring Rune from foster care, my phone played "Lawyers In Love" and it was our excellent, cute, nice lawyer.

The Skipper, Esquire, was calling from the venerable Cleveland law firm of Gallagher, Gallagher & Barnes with great news: Mondo money can even speed up itself. Tom's was in the bank. Figuratively speaking, of course. The cash was now squirreled away in all the assorted places where it was supposed to lie around accruing interest and earning more of itself, and Skip and Tom now had control of it. Tom was officially über rich.

When I'd realized what the call was about, I'd passed the phone over to Tom so Skip could give him the word about his money. Now they were winding up the conversation, and I saw the opening I'd been waiting for.

I asked for my phone back.

After confirming Skip's jubilation about his victory over Mondo red tape, I oozed on in. "Skip. Can we talk about Nan for a second?"

Nan's job was toast for sure. GG&B was all about discretion. It was engraved on their philosophical wall like "To Boldly Go" on the bridge of the *Starship Enterprise*. Only for them it was "To Discreetly Go." I was sure, however, that they would never have split the infinitive.

Unless I could intervene somehow, Nan's fifteen years of devoted service were down the drain. I'd been able to find out that no one was looking at her for accessory to kidnapping anymore. Nor anything related to her being in the plan that resulted in somebody's—namely Dan's—death. The plan and the death were all Dan's now.

Nonetheless, her having been Dan's sister and accessory to his hiring by the Arco folks was indiscretion aplenty for the firm.

Skip heard where I was headed. "Allie, I'm sorry. I don't think there's a prayer."

"Skip. Her brother is dead because he was a criminal and a stupid man."

"That may be, but—"

I cut him off, "I know, I know. GG&B can't tolerate the slightest hint of…" I didn't want to speak the indiscretion word because of the power of its position in the firm's vision statement. I thought fast. "…un-toward…ity."

Skip couldn't help himself. A chuckle escaped. He stifled it immediately, but the damage was done.

I gathered up all my dignity and poured it into the phone.

"Please remind your partners, Mr. Castillo, that Dr. Bennington III and I now wield a considerable fortune. There'll be tax issues, real estate issues, *estate* estate issues, gifts, bequests, all that. Legal crap. Out the wazoo. In perpetuity. Tell them that, unlike another of their partners who comes to mind in this context, Dr. Bennington III is a compassionate man. And way rich. Remind them about that.

"He and I would take it very badly indeed should Nan become unemployed. I'd say a couple of weeks unpaid leave should satisfy their need for righteous retribution. If not—"

I left the rest to his formidable capacity for filling in the blank.

The chuckle was fighting to get out again. "Ms. Harper. Would you and Dr. Bennington III mind very much if I don't say 'legal crap out the wazoo'?"

I released a grin I hoped he could hear. "Use your discretion, Skip. Use your discretion."

• • ● ● •

"No, Tom. This money is good,"

I could tell that Tom was delighted about my apparent success with the Nan conversation, but not particularly elated about the money.

"Now you're out of limbo. Whatever you want to do, wherever you want to go, the money will make it all easier."

And probably three times faster.

He raised his eyebrows over his sexy dark glasses. Skeptical. But then he put his palms up in a gesture of surrender. "Okay, lady. I give. I'm going to stop being so negative about having 190 million dollars to spend any way I like."

"It's 180 million. You've already contracted to spend ten of those millions for the—ah, shall we say—friendship of a gentlewoman."

"Well, I should have five or ten million left when you get through with me. We ought to at least be able to afford tickets to the Rock Hall."

"See. It's all turning out fine. Let's call Marie Clark right now and get her off the dime."

• • ● • •

In the midst of the ongoing Mondo Turbulence, we'd established what Rune wanted to do the next time we got together. He wanted Tom to take him to the Rock & Roll Hall of Fame and Museum. I could come, too.

I hoped Marie was beginning to see we wanted to be in Rune's life for the long haul. That we wouldn't take the money, wander off, and abandon the kid after everything he'd been through. I was certain she'd been holding us responsible for Renata in some circuitous way. I didn't blame her. I thought so, too, a lot of the time.

Tom volunteered that the jackpot had paid out and told her he hoped that meant we could now maybe rent a house with some security until we decided how we wanted to proceed. His expression had been grave as he reiterated to her our understanding of how vulnerable our situation was.

"Yes." He'd nodded and then shook his head. "No. Of course not, Marie. We understand. We'll be with him all the time. Both of us. I promise

Allie will never take her eyes off him." He nodded again. "Absolutely. And it's a very public place. There'll be lots of people around. We'll be fine. Thank you. Thank you very much."

She'd been diplomatic, for her, Tom reported, about whether our situation had gotten any more "stable." Whatever that meant. Maybe she believed we were a bad influence, drifting from hotel to hotel and brand-name bed to brand-name bed without benefit of matrimony. Degenerate nomads. Marie was wrapped pretty tight. I would bet I could bounce a quarter off her suits.

He'd clicked off, beaming. "She thinks we can count on Sunday. She said if she can work it out she'll bring him here for breakfast. She said, 'Don't make me sorry' like she always does, but I could hear her smiling."

For this and the aforementioned fiscal reason, we were in the mood to almost celebrate. Both of us were inexperienced in the management and enjoyment of very large sums of money, but we felt we'd been responsible about handling it so far. All in all, I was confident the elevation of Tom's FICO score to maybe 850,000 should entitle us to a major splurge. Therefore we went to Morton's The Steakhouse for dinner. My lottery fantasies were starting to come true.

We Ubered. The RAV 4 was history. We'd

ditched it at the Marriott for pickup on October 1. Anybody watching it and waiting for us would be watching and waiting quite a while.

Chapter Forty

Morton's is Splurge Central. Its menu offers a wide variety of "Signature Entrees" and a tempting array of "Legendary Desserts." We snagged a quiet table in a more or less secluded corner. Not that it made any difference to Tom, but I found the subdued lighting romantic. Our waiter, Austin, was efficient and well-versed in the explanations of food and drink, though not as much fun as Sean at Zocalo Mexican Grill and Tequileria.

"What is a 'Spa-tini' anyway?" Tom asked after Austin had delivered my rose-colored concoction and Tom's austere old Jack and ginger.

"Mmm. It's a drink in a shiny glass with fluffy delicious foamy stuff on top and…let's see… mmm…yes. A nice amount of vodka in the middle. For only two hundred calories. Wanna sip?"

"I'm afraid your drink and my drink are one of those twains that should never meet. Enjoy, though. I want you to be happy tonight."

After that 'tini, my evening took on quite the shimmery glow. Everything was luxurious, delicious, and XXL. I had a super time eating large delicious stuff and admiring Tom. He had a super time, he said, caressing my ankle with his ankle. I was almost relaxed.

I messed up the mood some, though, in spite of myself. Looking around that lavish room, everything buffed up glossy and built-to-last—even our fellow diners—the last thing I would have expected would have been a shiver of dread. But surprise. There it was. Black and oily, murky as death. I remembered Margo's malediction. "There's a killer out there." And because my mouth was open from realizing this, my dread/surprise blurted itself out in a tiny, insuppressible "Oh."

And because Tom had fine-honed ears he said, "What?"

And because I didn't want to spoil the evening, I said, "Nothing. Goose walked on my grave, I guess."

And because he still had the de-fib-ulator, he said, "You're lying, aren't you?"

And because my heart was Tom-putty, I told him the truth. "I guess I just realized, we're never going to be safe again. I must have been in denial until right now."

He reached out his hand, palm up, the gesture

that was becoming our secret symbol of everything, the wonderful and the terrible, that we'd shared. I fit my hand in there, palm down. He curled us closed and sighed.

"Alice Jane. I've been able to see that from the night we met." He gave my hand a small, encouraging squeeze. "But, honey, that's always been true, even before we woke up the Mondo Earthquake. It's true for everybody in this world. 'Security is a superstition.' You know who said that?"

"No clue. Who?"

"Helen Keller. And if she thought that, I've always figured, who am I...?" He shrugged. "I don't know why it makes me feel better to know that no place is the perfect safe place for anybody. But it does."

"Me, too. It's funny. But me, too."

"The expensive luxury is hanging heavy in here, don't you think?"

"I do. It's unlike me to agree about that. But I do. Let's get the check before they need two guys named Austin to haul it over here."

● ● ● ● ●

Once we'd Ubered on back to the hotel, the evening was still youngish. "Let's stop here in our own bar for a nightcap, Tom," I suggested. "I don't want this evening to end."

"I suppose that depends on what you had in mind for the ending, babe."

He employed the dimple which had its usual inspirational effect.

The Wyndham people called their bar The Blue Bar, and the city light at that time of the night was a definite moody blue. The bar itself curves through the center of the space in an arc of polished inlaid wood. Considering our most recent bar experience, I was delighted to be the only woman sitting with Tom. I was hoping for another Spa-tini, but those turned out to be a signature beverage of Morton's The Steakhouse. I settled for an ordinary but quite serviceable cosmopolitan and sipped it slowly so as to keep the shimmer alive.

We'd been comfortably ensconced with our drinks, our light conversation, and some modest nuzzling for maybe fifteen minutes when I became aware of an exceptionally handsome couple standing in the entranceway, his striking pale blue eyes sweeping the room, her sleek dark head inclined toward him, fall of black hair spilling, her manicured claws sunk into his manly dinner jacket as she leaned into his shoulder.

My shimmer expired.

"Tom," I spoke as calmly as I could over the pandemonium in my head, "why would your Diana be here in the company of my former D.B.?"

Chapter Forty-one

"Money and meanness." I answered my own question. "That would be D.B.'s usual motive. How about hers?"

Tom had vanished into silence, his hands encircling his glass—tight—like it was somebody's neck. My neck? Her neck? D.B.'s? I hadn't a clue, but I would have voted for hers. I'd take care of D.B.'s neck myself.

He drained his glass. Clunked it down on the bar. "Sign the check, Allie. Get us out of here."

He paused. I sat and breathed and waited him out.

"Allie, I swear I'll explain once we're upstairs. Can you tell if they know we're here?"

"The light's not that dim. Anyway, if I know D.B., they're here because we're here. What I don't know is why."

"Let's go."

I signed the check. We went. With alacrity.

D.B and Diana had taken chairs around the curve of the bar. I heard the bartender say, "What can I get you this evening, Mr. Harper? Your usual?"

As Tom and I hustled by, Diana made a small, startled sound and D.B. called out, "Allie!" I ignored them both. We kept walking.

When the elevator door closed, Tom said, in a rush, "She—Diana—she's the woman from when I wasn't blind. My fiancée from Atlanta."

I watched the lights count up the floors: 8. 9. 10. We arrived with a slight jerk. The doors opened onto a little foyer. A demilune console with an opulent arrangement of fresh flowers. A mirror. I saw us. A pale man, a frazzled and flushed-looking woman. We continued on into our corridor and Tom started talking again.

"That first night, I told you the truth, Allie. As far as it went. She broke off the engagement, but she's still entangled with me. In her head. With the past. With what her life was going to be. Some fantasy she had about being a professor's wife. Living in Atlanta. The house. The children. The faculty teas. She doesn't have any idea what life with me would have been like. It's a dream world for her. But, trust me, she's my nightmare."

"She's very beautiful, Tom."

I thought, but didn't say out loud, "so silky and smooth." And, I reminded myself that he must still remember how she looked when she was twenty-one. The complete Diana package. We were well down our long hall now. He stopped and turned to me.

"She's very unstable, Allie. And she drinks. When she drinks, she resents me and how she got frozen in some plans she had ten years ago. When she resents me and drinks, she calls. And when she calls—" He stopped and scrubbed at his cheek with one hand. "She tells me she'll kill herself and it will be all my fault."

"That's—"

"I know what it is. But when it's you and someone you've…known, it's hard not to get caught up. She was working on her PhD back when I was working on mine. She quit when we broke up. She was even hospitalized for a while. Then she got better. Finally finished an MA. She came up to Case about six months ago. Looking for a job."

"Oh."

"Yeah. 'Oh.' There weren't any teaching positions. It's a relatively small department. When I found they'd offered her an admin job, which was an insult to her education, I was sure she'd walk away. She accepted it. I don't know exactly where she lives, but now when she drinks and calls and threatens, she can also stop by."

I used the card key to let us into our room.

Spacious and serene. Cool and quiet. I inhaled the unique scent of a well-manicured hotel suite—eau de fresh linens and careful cleaning, a thousand packets of lovely soap torn open to release their French-milled goodness for a thousand pampered guests—plus, a *soupçon* of bleach thrown in for good luck. I find this fragrance combination very comforting. I bet there's a marketing department somewhere at Hotel Central that put the formula together for the express purpose of entrapping scruffy little human animals like me. It smells like money.

"I'm sorry, Tom. I thought—The ringtone."

He winced. "That. We met for lunch about a month ago. Somewhat safer to be with her in a public place. Fewer scenes. She programmed it into my phone."

"I used to love that song. It's about love. And sex."

"Allie. It's also about drinking."

Well, there was that.

"Why is she with D.B. tonight?"

"The money. You were right. I don't know how, but it's the connection. She's been even more delusional than usual since she found out about the Mondo. She believes I owe her. She feels she's entitled to a share of everything in my life. It's like the way she wanted to be married to me, living in an antebellum mansion, surrounded by well-mannered children and devoted servants. On a teacher's salary. I'd laugh if it weren't so terrible. She wants, she wants. And what she wants is smoke and mirrors, even to her. She's purely the wanting."

"Now I see how this all fits. Good old D.B. is the legal arm of wanting. You want it. He can sue somebody and get it for you. I don't like it. What it means is she's thrashed around enough to wake up a shark. There are worse sharks than D.B. in the waters around here."

I never thought I'd hear myself say that.

Plus, I was thinking, this was perfect for D.B. He might not feel entitled to anything I had, but he'd relish helping somebody snatch it all away—and, no doubt, taking his percentage.

"I don't care about the money. If I thought I could pay her to leave me alone and she'd stay gone, I would. But she wouldn't. She's threatened to make trouble for me at the university. Make me lose my job. Threats and rumors. That's a case of Diana for you." His tone was deep bitterness.

I opened my mouth to console him with "But Tom, you don't need your job. You're rich." when "DOINK!"

I got it.

I clamped my mouth shut, walked over to our magnificent floor-to-ceiling windows, and stared down on Euclid Avenue, barely registering a handful of pedestrians, the twenty-foot chandelier hanging over the street, the theaters spilling jewels of colored light onto the pavement.

I did see one thing clearly as I stood at that window. Me. My reflection. I could see right through myself. I'd been living day-to-day, loving my new independence but hungry for something else, something better. Then Tom stepped into my crosswalk with 550 million dollars in his grocery bag.

I'd assumed that soon he would start appreciating his jackpot as a jackpot, not a curse. So how had that worked out? Break-ins. Kidnapping. Six people dead since last Tuesday. When he'd said, "I don't care about the money," it wasn't ignorance of what that much money could buy. It wasn't even a virtue. It was the God's honest truth about Tom. He plain didn't care very much about money.

I gazed at him, reflected behind me in my window, sitting lost in thought in the warmth of lamplight he'd be able to feel but never see.

In that moment, my Mondo blindness fell the rest of the way off me and I wished, like a silly girl in a fairy tale, that 7-9-16-34-57-8 had been anybody else's number. I wished Tom and I had met in front of Joe's and found life together without riches and bloodshed and the specter of avarice looming.

I could see us. Me guiding him out of the

crosswalk. The two of us eating chili and laughing in the kitchen. Tom kissing me for the first time, at the brink of wild water. That kiss. What if that kiss had never ended? If Ralph had switched off his loud old TV that night and gone to bed and left us alone in the moonlight, not rich, not dangerous. Just…kissing. Our story unfolding as it might have without 550 million dollars's worth of land mines in the way. That was a story I could have loved forever.

I wished. I wished.

And then my eyes came back into focus and I saw what was happening down on the street. A crowd gathered around someone sprawled on the concrete, an EMS ambulance easing up, lights blinking, no siren.

A dark intuition.

A sinking sensation.

A knock at the door.

Chapter Forty-two

An ice-blue eye glared at me through the peephole.

I was learning. I didn't just fling open the door. I pressed my own little brown eye up to the hole and our eyes met. No kidding. It was like the retina scanner thing that identifies the looker. It was D.B. all right. And he knew it was me, too. This was not going to go away.

I still didn't fling open the door. I glanced back at Tom. Comfy chair. Lamplight. He was all attention now.

"Allie. Don't. It might be—"

I didn't think so, but I didn't say it. Not yet.

I put up the safety latch and cracked the door, even as Tom warned again, "Allie, don't—"

"It's okay, Tom. It's only D.B. He's alone. What do you want D.B.?"

"Allie. Let me in. We have to talk. Something's happened. Something bad."

I considered how much I would rather have

D.B. installed somewhere far, far away. North Pole. South Pole. A mere door didn't get the job done for me.

"I like you better out in the hall. Go ahead and say what you have to say."

"It's Diana. Diana Wiles. She—I think she maybe jumped—she's dead. Let me in."

I glanced back at Tom who'd murmured, "Diana?" and half risen from his chair.

No help for it. I opened the door.

Once again, I'd forgotten how entirely D.B. filled up a room. He burst through the door, said, "Hey, Dr. Bennington. It's D.B. Harper—as if Tom were deaf as well as blind—and then pounced on me. "She's—she was a—nutcase. I need to get myself as far away from this as possible."

I went to stand by Tom. Moral support. As much distance as possible from my ex.

"What makes you think she jumped?"

"Because she was talking about killing herself before she left. I thought it was just talk. Drama."

From our long acquaintance, I understood that any time a woman got upset it was "drama" to D.B. but, based on what I'd heard about Diana this evening, I discounted D.B.'s assessment by a meager ten percent.

"She left? You're sure you weren't with her when she 'jumped'?" I made finger quotes to punctuate my point. I didn't figure D.B. for a murderer. He's too smart and way too self-serving. But it was satisfying to imply it. He took it hard.

"God. No! I was in the bar. Ask anybody. She took a call. She got upset. She left. And the next thing I knew there was a ruckus out front. I went out to see."

You went out to see if there was an ambulance worth chasing.

I kept the comment inside my head, but he heard it anyway and scowled at me.

"I don't know where she jumped from. It must have been high. She was—she looked—not good. Sorry, Tom, I know you and she were friends."

"Not friends anymore. Fellow human beings, at least."

Zingo!

That one flew right by D.B., but I approved of it. I gave Tom's shoulder a squeeze and got back a sad smile of solidarity.

Tom focused his attention on D.B. in way that made me think if Tom had a gun and D.B. beeped, it would be "Sayonara, D.B."

"What was your business with Diana?"

"Oh, I couldn't say, Tom. Attorney-client priv—"

I dismissed the motion. "She's dead, D.B. I

expect the court might pry you open if it came down to it."

He shrugged. "Maybe. Maybe not. Anyway, she didn't have much of a case. Diana felt she was entitled to some of the lottery winnings, Allie, and I thought she deserved a respectful discussion. But her claim was thin. I was counseling her to walk away and that's when she started talking about suicide. As I said, I thought it was all hot air. But I guess—"

I was about to let fly with a withering rejoinder when there was yet another knock at the door. I peeked again and this time I saw a guy in a suit and tie. The suit guy had one of those free-range, hand-held badges. I opened the door.

The guy aimed the badge at D.B. "Mr. Harper? Mr. D.B. Harper? Detective Miller. Cleveland P.D."

I saw D.B. consider denying that he was him and then dismiss the idea as unworkable. "Yes. I'm D.B. Harper. Please come in, Detective."

"You were in the bar downstairs with a Ms. Wiles this evening. Before she—"

"I was."

"Could you tell us the nature of that meeting?"

"It was business. I'm her attorney. So…."

The detective moved on, consulting a little notebook. "You'd been there maybe twenty minutes. She'd had two martinis. At about 10:45 she got a call and left the bar. According to witnesses, you waited. Perhaps five, ten minutes later she fell, jumped, or was pushed off the roof. How she got up there—"

"Pushed?"

I couldn't contain my doofus mouth. Now Detective Miller had noticed I was alive.

"And you are?"

"Alice Harper."

"Harper?" He glanced at D.B.

"Yes. Mr. Harper and I were married, but we're not anymore."

I was could see that Detective Miller knew exactly who D.B. Harper was in Cleveland and his estimation of me had gone up slightly on the basis of our severed association alone. That was real irony for me.

"Did you know the deceased?"

"I knew of her. We'd met on one occasion."

The detective was interested in this. He turned to Tom. "And you? Oh, sorry. Sir, you are?"

"Tom Bennington. Ms. Wiles was a long-time friend of mine. We didn't speak this evening, though. Ms. Harper and I were leaving the bar as she and Mr. Harper arrived."

I could see, whatever the detective's agenda was tonight, he couldn't figure Tom to have pushed Ms. Wiles off a roof. However, I could also see Miller had this very second put "Blind" and "Mondo Winner" together. His jaw dropped ever so slightly, but he raised it back into place, almost without missing a beat. He gave his attention to his notebook and wrote for a minute. When he finished, he tucked it into his jacket pocket.

"Thank you for your time, folks. That will be all for now, but I'd appreciate it if you'd make yourself available if we need to get in touch again."

D.B. extended his hand. "Thank you, Detective. This has been hard for all of us. I'll follow you out. Good night, Allie. Tom." His eyes as they met mine said, *I'll be back.*

Mine answered him: *Not tonight, you sorry son of a bitch.*

I double-locked the door.

"Tom?"

He'd collapsed back into the chair again. Collar loosened, glasses off, eyes closed. Destroyed. He spoke to me then in a voice I'd never heard from him before. Dull. Hopeless.

"The detective. Did you hear the way he talked about her? The way he said, 'Fell, jumped, or *pushed*.' He doesn't believe Diana fell or jumped, Allie. He thinks she was pushed. It's murder all over again."

"But why Diana? As far as I know, the only person who had any motive for killing her was me. Where does she fit? She's not like the others. I don't have a clue. Or a plan. Where do we start? And what about how she got to D.B.? And how did they find us? It's such a mess...."

"God, Allie. I just wish I never..." He let the sentence drift away. We both knew where it was heading. Mere minutes ago I'd been wishing the same damn thing.

I went to him and knelt down so I could take his hands in mine. They were cold.

"Tom. Don't go there again. You're blaming yourself for things other people were responsible for. Even Renata. Even Ulysses. Even—maybe especially—Diana."

After about my fifth or sixth word, he'd started shaking his head and now it was a steady rhythm back and forth. I was trying to ignore it, trying to break through. "Tom."

"No, Allie. I'm sorry about Diana but I'm not blaming myself this time. Whether I was ignorant, well-meaning, or whatever, I'm letting that go. It doesn't help and I might as well be regretting I ever met Rune. Or moved to Cleveland. Or was born. I'm not to blame for this...evil. I know that. Even if I don't always feel it.

"But Allie..." He took his hands away from mine and put them on my face. "Where will I be if the next person to die is you?"

Chapter Forty-three

Friday, August 28

Friday morning early, I called the Fifth District and asked to leave a message for Officer Bob Clark. The person who took my information said Officer Clark wasn't there but he'd be in around ten-thirty this evening.

"Would you ask him to call me? Any time? It's important." I gave her my cell number. She said yes, okay.

I had a fond memory of his "You know how to reach me. Dial 9-1-1."

The current situation felt like an emergency to me. I wanted a man with a gun. And a Taser. And a nightstick. And a walkie-talkie so he could call a bunch of other guys for backup. We'd trusted Valerio with the Sammy inquiry and all he'd done was make Sammy mad at me. Now it was Bob's turn.

Call me back, Officer 9-1-1, as fast as you can.

I went into our luxury bathroom to watch Tom shave. He used a regular razor with a blade. I found this worrisome, but his hand danced over his face with unfaltering assurance. "Did you find him?"

"No, I had to leave a message. His shift ended already. He's gone home. They said he'll be back tonight. I don't even know if I should have called him at all. But we have to trust somebody. I admit I like Valerio, but I wouldn't dare rattle his cage again, after how mad he made Sammy. Bob's at least as trustworthy as Valerio. Don't we agree?"

He felt around his face to determine the perfection of the shave. It was flawless. I would like to have helped with that, but the timing was bad.

"Lord, Allie, I'm not a hundred percent positive we know anything. I'm so tired. And confused." He picked up a towel and wiped away the extra shaving cream. "I'm sad about Diana. She was in my life—very unpleasantly, I'll grant you—for a long, long time. She was so unstable, so lost. But I know her folks. They'll be devastated. And when we were kids? When we were twenty-one? Those are good memories. She was a different person. I was, too."

A green tide of jealousy washed me away. I was ashamed of myself. The lady was dead. I was alive. I had the man in my possession. But the idea of Tom and Diana, twenty-one and gorgeous, the both of them. Him not blind yet. Her not lost in some dream world. I plain envied her. I did. I'd willingly be dead for at least three and a half minutes, to have had a moment or two of Tom like that. So our eyes could meet, just one time. I walked out of the bathroom.

But not before he'd read my mind again.

"Allie, come back here. Please."

At least he was saying "please." I went. He drew me in, warm arms, bare chest, nice minty smell.

"Allie, I can see you. I know you don't feel it, but it's true. I've memorized your face, every square inch of you. You're so incredible, so beautiful…."

I made a pitiful sound of disbelief.

"Listen to me. Eyesight is a miraculous gift. I know that better than most, but it's not the only way to see somebody. Lots of people are out there using their perfectly functional eyes to systematically not see a damn thing all day long. They don't need a cane to keep from falling down a manhole, but nothing registers. It's a blur. A busy, thoughtless, wasteful blur."

He held me tighter, "Alice Jane, you're not a blur to me. I know you. My mind, my whole body, is filled up with you. I can't believe I'm lucky enough to have found you. To have you find me. That's why if something happened—"

Oh, no. Tom. Don't go back down that road. I hate that road.

Before I could interrupt him with an encouraging word about me not dying anytime soon, I was rescued by The Who. Officer Bob to save the day.

I picked up. "Bob."

"Miss Harper, it's Anthony Valerio."

"Officer Valerio. Hi. How are you…um…today?"

"I'm okay. I was by the desk and saw you'd left a message for Officer Clark. He's not here now. Is there something I can help you with?" Nice as pie.

I could hear background noises: talking, laughter, footsteps. I could picture Officer Anthony Valerio standing in the Fifth District headquarters, surrounded by our men and women in blue. He'd have to be gutsy to make a criminal move from the heart of a place like that. Or possibly a psychopath. Okay, all right.

"I called Officer Clark because I wanted to ask—last night, a woman named Diana Wiles, jumped or fell off the Wyndham Hotel. She was a friend of Tom's from Atlanta who worked at CWRU. She had been in the Wyndham bar with my former husband, D.B. Harper.

"And you want to know if you're a suspect."

"What? No! Why?"

He paused. "Look, Miss Harper." The ambient noise faded as I heard him seeking somewhere quieter for a more private conversation. A door closed. Was that suspicious? Maybe. But now I absolutely had to hear what he was going to say. "Is it okay if I call you Allie?"

"Sure. I guess. Can I call you Tony?"

That made him smile. I heard it. "Yes, Allie, you can call me Tony. Just not—oh, never mind. You're a piece of work, you know that?"

"I've heard it before, yes."

"Okay, this is so far off the record and so out of line, it doesn't exist, understood?"

"Understood."

"This case belongs to Homicide, obviously, but since it's high profile and D.B. Harper is involved— not as a suspect—"

"Please continue, Tony."

"Everybody's talking about what happened."

"What do they say happened?"

"Off the record?"

"It doesn't exist."

"They say she struggled with somebody after she got a call and left the bar but before she hit the sidewalk. There were specific bruises that were not associated with injuries from the fall. They also found trace. You're a CSI fan, right?"

Don't mock me, Tony.

"I was."

"So you understand when I tell you they found trace evidence under her fingernails?"

Those perfect nails.

"It means she was murdered. It means she fought with somebody, clawed them? They'd be marked. How long will it take for the DNA?"

"Sometime next week. Maybe. They put a rush on it."

Next week? A rush? Well, Toto, we're not on CSI, *that's for sure.*

"And I'm a suspect? I'm not marked."

Other than my Lying Idiot bruises, of course. And a fading stain of purple across my shoulder. No extra charge.

"That's a very good thing. I know Detective Miller reported you didn't look like you'd been in a fight." The smile was back. "Except for your hair. Somebody might want to take a look at you at some point. You should let them. But if they want to question you?"

"Yes?"

"Lawyer up. It's stupid not to. Of the three people at the Wyndham last night who knew Diana Wiles, you're the one who's not blind and didn't stay in the bar."

"And it's almost always someone you know."

"You got it."

"I didn't push Diana Wiles, Tony. I was with Tom and he'd tell you that. He doesn't lie. He and Diana were engaged to be married once. He wouldn't protect me if I'd pushed her off the Wyndham. Because…because if I had, I wouldn't be me."

"If I wasn't sure of that, I wouldn't be talking to you. But Allie, consider this. You and Tom leave the bar and find your way up to the roof. He calls Diana. You wait, she arrives. He steps back. You step up. She's a little drunk from two martinis in ten minutes or whatever. Off she goes."

Wow. As a theory, it worked for me. And I was the off-she-goes-er in this scenario. I could hear iron doors slamming behind me.

"Tony. That works. I could believe it myself. But wait. Do they know who the call was from? Because I know for sure it wasn't Tom. Or me."

"You don't listen much, do you?

"Please, Tony. I don't want specifics. Just… I'm a little…scared. Does the number…point to anybody besides us?"

"Not hardly. It was a burner. That's pay-as-you-go—"

"Yeah, I know what a burner is." No help for me there. "But when the DNA comes in, I'll be off the hook. You can swab my cheek."

He choked on something that sounded like

a laugh. "Don't go overboard trusting the DNA to save you. DNA isn't for sure until it's for sure."

"But for some unknown reason you don't think it was me? Us?"

"No. I'm working another theory."

"Which is?"

"Not for you. Not yet."

"What about Bob Clark?"

"What about him?"

"Does he think I did it?"

"I don't know. He didn't say. He likes you."

"Did anybody check him for scratches?'

"Of course not. What an odd question. He was with me last night. I thought you were friends."

"Sorry. I don't know why, I—sorry. That was rude of me. We were. We are. I'm having a hard time trusting anybody these days. And now I need to dig up another suspect for this murder. Besides me."

"No, Allie. Listen to me. You stay away. Far away. From all this. No digging! When I have an answer, I'll get in touch. But remember, if they bring you in for questioning…"

"What? Oh. Lawyer up."

"Yeah."

Then he sighed so heavily it sounded like a gale was buffeting his phone around. "And, Allie? There's one more thing."

I winced. My sleuth skills were getting honed.

I could tell this wasn't going to be anything I would enjoy. "What? What thing?"

"Sammy R had an accident. Hit-and-run on that red scooter of his. In the crosswalk up by Joe's."

I shivered and my eyes prickled, but my voice was matter-of-fact. "So now Sammy's dead too."

Eight.

"Dead? No. No. He's in the hospital all banged up. Dopey from the painkillers and pretty muddled. Pissed off. Not telling us anything. No surprise. That seems to be his M.O.

"The scooter was trashed, but he'll live. I got somebody watching him. I don't know how whoever it was got onto him. But I should have stayed clear. Or been smarter. No way it's not connected to…everything else. I've replayed it a thousand times, but—Tell Dr. Bennington. This one's on me."

He was gone. No goodbye.

I stood for a minute, pressing the phone to my chest. Blinking. The news that grumpy old Sammy R was alive and still keeping his mouth shut just about knocked me over. All the tears I'd been about to shed for a poor old dead guy went ahead and ran down my face. All happy.

Good news, Sammy R. The Big Bad Mondo is going to buy you a brand new red scooter.

Anonymously, of course.

Chapter Forty-four

Bob Clark never called. Not Friday. Not Saturday. Not Sunday morning. That made me wonder. Had Tony Valerio made sure Bob never got my message? Did Bob not want to talk to me and if not, why not? What was I supposed to believe now?

At least Tony hadn't killed Sammy, and I didn't believe he'd tried. His guilt about the accident sounded authentic. Tom and I decided not to blame him for some possible misstep that might have gotten a guy merely run over—small potatoes, from our current perspective—and to keep both him and Bob on our "maybe trusted" list.

I had never considered "triage" as a word for sorting through the people who were most likely to help you and least likely to grab you, steal your money, and then kill you. But now we were picking our allies based on the direness of our need and the likelihood of their being able to save us. At the moment, we only had the two and we needed them both. We had Margo, of course. And Skip. And each other. But, as far as I knew, none of us had guns and Tasers.

I liked Tony. And surely a stone-cold killer wouldn't make jokes about my bad hair. Unless, of course, it served his purposes. Nefarious purposes. Why did I assume I was the only one who ever played the cute smartass out of pure nefariousness? And, why, exactly, had I thought we should handle some of the crime-solving on our own? I answered my own question. We were desperate. Triage again.

Plus, if all that wasn't enough new and disturbing information for one weekend, on Saturday I did get one call—which I'd answered "Bob?" again and was wrong about again. It was Ivy Martin this time. She sounded neither happy nor relieved. "Ms. Harper. They found her."

"Oh. That's good news." *Or not.*

"Yes. It's good that at least we know where she is."

"Where is she? Where has she been?"

"Her identification was mixed up. And her body was moved."

"From where to where?"

"As far as we've been able to determine, someone took her out of our…temporary storage area and moved her and her paperwork to—I'm sorry to be so blunt, Ms. Harper but I promised to tell you. Although this is nothing you'll ever share with Rune."

"That's okay, Ivy. Can I call you Ivy? And would you please call me Allie? I trust you to tell me the truth. And you can trust me to not go ballistic about whatever the truth turns out to be."

"I know, Allie. Thank you. You've been patient about all this. I'm sorry though and very upset. What happened is irregular and I don't see any way it's not, at the very least, malicious."

She paused, gathering her resolve, I imagined. "And more likely criminal. Her body was moved to an unused janitor's room, Allie. The room is in the lowest level of the building and very…chilly, so no one…noticed until yesterday. She's with the ME now, but the autopsy will be compromised, I'm afraid. The police are involved. At least, when everything is over, you'll have her remains for a service, though, I'd suggest…"

She stopped herself. Ivy Martin was done suggesting. She had kept up her end of the bargain. I thanked her again, hung up, and gave Tom the news. We agreed that our fact-finding mission at McCauley Road Hospital had given us more evidence for something we already knew.

Murder was all over the place.

• • ● • •

If anything could have made me gloomier than our current murder/danger situation, here it was. As Tom and I were trying to figure out how Diana had hooked up with my despicable ex, it hit me that the one person on the planet who might be able to answer that question was my despicable ex.

I groaned. An authentic groan, chock full of pain and despair.

"Allie? What is it? What's wrong?"

"Oh, Tom, dammit. Double dammit. I'm going to have to call D.B."

It was a short, insulting, and ultimately frightening conversation.

"It's me. We have to talk. How about we skip your snotty remarks and my snotty rejoinders. The sooner we can hang up, the sooner we'll both be happier. This is important, so just listen. How did Diana get to be your client? Did you find her? Or did she find you? And how?"

"May I talk now?"

"Oh, just…don't—Yes. Please."

"She found me. What makes you think I know how—?"

"Cut it out, Duane. I get it. You'd still like to squeeze a couple of bucks or some skimpy satisfaction out of all this. Give it up. Protect yourself. You're the expert at that. Diana was murdered. Somebody shoved her off the hotel into Euclid

Avenue. You think the Mondo is good news, you should count the bodies that go with it. Five hundred-fifty million dollars is not even worth a dollar if you're dead, D.B." *And burning in hell,* I added to myself for my own gratification. "Just tell me and I'll go away."

"Oh, all right. I'm surprised you haven't heard, you being a librarian and all. There's this thing called the Internet…."

"We're cutting to the chase, D.B."

"Fine. There's a website. Address is www. MondoSecrets.com. You should go there. You're famous. And I'm there as your 'former spouse, senior partner at—'"

"—'the venerable Cleveland law firm of Gallagher, Gallagher & Barnes.' I bet they were thrilled." *That had to sting. Ha.*

"I've told you what I know, like you asked. Go take a look. You'll love it."

He hung up.

I used my phone to access the site which had not been formatted to look good on a small screen. Or on any screen. "Down and dirty" would be overgenerous. The background was black. The font was mostly comic sans, in garish red and yellow, a random assortment of sizes. Hard to read but much too clear.

Photos of our houses, embedded Google Maps

to pinpoint the locations. Shots of us ducking in and out of the rental cars, the Marriott, the Wyndham. Bios. Lies. A head shot of Diana, including her hope that she and Tom would be able to "mend their differences and rediscover their love."

The stock phrase "my privacy has been violated" came to life and punched me in the gut. Tom and me. Us. On display in this sinister, smelly online rathole. The specter of Ulysses A. Grant was back. *This is the Age of In-fo-mation, baby. Didn' anyone tell you that?*

As I scrolled through, I gave Tom the bare bones of what was there. Read him what Diana had said. I didn't mention the fuzzy shot of us in the Marriott ballroom or the one of us leaving Wendy's with Rune. I could spare him that, but I was sure he interpreted my silence as the choking ball of rage it was.

"Who are these people, Tom? How do they have time for…for this…this garbage?"

He put his arm around me and didn't mention that I was shivering. "Take a breath, Allie. We needed to know. Now we do. I think you should call Valerio back and make sure the police have all that information. It may help them. I'll get in touch with a student of mine who spent more time online than on English 186. She's a genius at all that. Maybe she can find out where it comes from. Maybe even shut it down. Can't hurt."

"If we find them, can I pour Pepsi in their hard drives?"

Chapter Forty-five

Sunday, August 30

My brain was a whirlpool of fear, outrage, and useless speculation. This one. That one. Someone. All? It was Dr. Seuss on meth. Plus now there was the extra-added wretchedness of knowing Creepy Eye was out there with a camera, tracking us all over the World Wide Bleeping Web. It made me dizzy.

I had to ask myself to "step away from the vortex, ma'am." So I did. Today I had somewhere better to go. It was Sunday at last.

Rock Hall Day.

If I wasn't talking with Bob, at least I had Marie on my side. She had actually picked up Rune from Elaine herself and delivered him to us, bright and early, at the Wyndham. I could see that she was bubbling over with a bunch of good Marie-style admonitions that neither Rune nor Tom had the attention span for just then. I dragged her down to the restaurant for breakfast and some girl talk while the boys ordered up room service.

It was Marie's day off and she was attired in the Marie Clark version of casual. It was more like business casual. Serious business. Her jeans looked like they'd maybe been ironed, or at least pulled out of the dryer immediately after the buzzer went off. Neither of those things had ever happened to a pair of jeans of mine. But all in all, Marie looked more relaxed than usual. She even agreed to let me pay for her oatmeal and tea without an undue amount of fuss.

I'd loaded up on pecan waffles and sausage patties, plus fruit compote and juice at the buffet and I was trying to appear less greedy by minimizing the amount of food on my plate as quickly as possible. I let Marie do most of the talking while I chewed like a chipmunk and looked as solemn as I could while doing that.

I figured Marie to be probably five years younger than me, but she had a lot more authority. Maybe it was the clout of all those reservations she had about letting Tom and me take Rune anywhere.

"I can't say I think this is a good idea."

Oh, really. I chewed some more, nodded responsibly, and arranged my face for maximum trustworthiness.

She regarded me with those very professional blue eyes.

"I understand that Tom is competent for a visually impaired person. But I don't see how he could do much to protect Rune in case of something unexpected happening."

I didn't bother to explain about Tom's sixth sense, or his beeping marksmanship, for that matter. I figured none of it would cut much ice with Marie. The responsibility was all on me and I was happy to claim it.

"Marie, Tom is a lot more competent than you might believe. But you can count on me to watch over Rune. Today or any day."

Marie nodded and spooned up some oatmeal. She hadn't used any of the brown sugar that came with it. I was surprised she hadn't picked the raisins out. She still seemed less than convinced but she sighed and twitched her trim shoulders in what passed for a Marie shrug.

"I promised, Allie. Now it's up to you. Stay alert. And don't forget you've been a target yourself. And might be again. Watch out for yourself while you're at it." Another sigh, this one all resignation. "I'm counting on some of the unfortunate attention cooling down."

Well, "unfortunate attention" was one way to describe six murders and an attempted kidnapping.

I returned the sigh with interest, to demonstrate my commitment. "Me, too, Marie. Thanks." I offered a small, comradely grin. "I won't make you sorry."

She nodded but her expression was still troubled. "I know you mean well, Allie. And that Tom does, too. Bob and I have talked about this. One minute, there you were. Fine. Ordinary. Not in a bad way. Normal, I guess you'd say. Then the next moment, the jackpot. All that money put you into the spotlight. Bigger than life. Very, very exposed to dangerous individuals."

I smiled to myself. "Dangerous individuals." That was just so Bob. I pictured the two of them shaking their golden heads over our plight. Bob might be too busy to talk to me, but at least he still cared. I tuned back into the truth Marie was telling me. "You don't have the experience that rich people have to protect themselves."

Margo had said that same thing. About six times.

Pay attention, Allie.

"You weren't prepared. How could you have been? I'm not sure you are now. Even after everything that's happened. Be careful. That's all I'm saying."

She stood up. No preamble. No segue. "Thanks for breakfast. It was nice to see you. Take care."

"Geez, Marie. That wasn't breakfast. You didn't even sprinkle on your brown sugar."

She regarded me over her shoulder without saying anything, as if my parting comment were an unforgivable frivolity which reinforced all her serious, serious doubts about me. Then she left and the clouds rolled back from my sunny day.

Chapter Forty-six

As part of its permanent "Legends of Rock & Roll" collection, the Rock & Roll Hall of Fame and Museum displays a "glove of Michael Jackson." I'm certain Michael had more than the one glove, but the Rock Hall has an authentic one of those. And Rune wanted to see it. Bad.

Among all the awful things that had happened to Rune that summer, his shocking discovery of the death of The King of Pop had definitely made the top three. Renata had every single album Michael ever made, from *Got to Be There* right up through *Invincible*. Rune knew every song by heart, whether he understood what they were about or not. He was steeped in the rhythms of them.

Nobody had bothered to inform him that Michael had been dead since 2009. Somebody's casual acknowledgement of June 25th as the sad anniversary had broken a big chunk off Rune's reality. Now his mother had joined the ranks of the people who'd died when he wasn't looking.

The music was everything to him. It carried him away into a magical world where Michael still danced and sang. Maybe Renata was still alive in that world, too, for all I knew. In any case, Rune was aching to visit Michael's glove.

It was a few minutes shy of ten a.m. when I nudged our new Jeep Wrangler from Avis into a space in the parking garage. Rune was jazzed by the vehicle—its desert-like sandy color and its cowboy-soldier-guy attitude. It wasn't exactly undistinguished, but it had a certain hide-in-plain-sight nonchalance. At that hour, the garage was almost deserted. I was spooked by the chill, shadowy surroundings, but all was calm.

I was more worried about the phones ratting us out now, but I'd stored my life in mine, and I hadn't been able to let it go. Not yet. I'd restored it once and I turned it off whenever I thought of it, but then it would be after me, poking at me to turn it on again. Reminding me that Margo or Elaine or Benedict Cumberbatch might be calling. Addict that I was.

We'd withdrawn money from Tom's account and stopped using the credit cards. Except, of course, we'd used his for the Wyndham. I was plotting another move. And a windfall of hard, cold analog cash. I thought I could get Skip to handle that. I was doing the best I could, striving to make up for my inexperience with my innate hyperactive vigilance.

I herded my small tour group up a flight of stairs and out onto the sweeping plaza where the Cleveland skyline glared down on us as if we could never worship it enough to make it feel good about itself. We emerged into that bright, hot day looking like the family I hoped we were slated to be. Rune vibrating with excitement. Tom, beaming and looking incredibly attractive. Me directing traffic, mom-like. And like a wife, I was thinking. That was how we walked across the sun-splashed plaza and in through the big glass doors. Tom's hand on my elbow. Rune dancing and twirling out in front of us.

OCD Librarian Allie had a sinking second or two of wondering whether I'd neglected to lock the Jeep's doors, but Rune was spinning out, the Rock Hall awaited, and we had nothing of value in the car anyway. I hit the key fob a couple of times, hoping it had a phenomenal reach.

The museum rises off the lakefront like an icon out of *The DaVinci Code*. Designed by I.M. Pei, its glass pyramid is a mountain range of glittering shapes. An aficionado could spend a week and not do justice to half of it. This was Rune's trip, though, and he was doing that kid radar thing. Seeking out what he wanted to see and ignoring the rest.

He held tight to Tom's hand, guided him to

the escalator, and through the chaos of sights and sounds, straight to the case where The Glove of Michael Jackson revolved on its turntable, shimmering under the lights like the religious artifact it had become. Rune's eyes were wide, his mouth slightly ajar. He was drinking it in, storing it up for a rainy day.

The thing made me think of a domesticated falcon tethered to its perch. Its stuffed fingers curled above the pole that was slowly turning it for our viewing pleasure. Trapped and pathetic. I was sure Rune was picturing it on Michael's actual living hand. A placard reported that he had worn it on his Dangerous Tour in 1992—back when our Runako Davis was still years and years out from being born.

After Rune had soaked up the glitter of the glove to his heart's almost content, he moved on to the rest of the display, describing to Tom everything there was to see. Here was the tattered red leather jacket from the "Thriller" video. I pictured the mad entourage of fabulous, choreographed zombies. A wolf mask from the video bared its teeth at us. The mood was magical. Magical and disturbing.

Rune was wearing out from absorbing Michael's beautiful, lost strangeness into his seven-and-a-quarter-year-old brain. I could feel it myself. The swift current of celebrity and sorrow dragging me down. I was trying hard not to remember how

Michael had won his own Mondo. Seized the golden ring of celebrity. And death.

It was the dead of night down here. Shadowy. Glittery. Fey. I was experiencing a lot of jitter and twitch. Creepy Eye was crawling over my spine, trailing cold fingers across the back of my neck. Were we live at www.tomandallietakerunetotherockhall.com? *Yeesh.*

I put my hand on Rune's shoulder, prying him away from the enchantment. Easing him out. "Why don't we get something to eat and then we'll go to the Hall of Fame Movie and see the real Hall of Fame?" He nodded and cast one last, hungry glance at The Glove on its lonely perch, endlessly turning.

Goodbye, Michael.

Then he straightened his shoulders and reached for Tom's hand, leading him along, talking to him nonstop about the things he'd seen. We swept out of the murky rec room of Rock and Roll, moving back toward the light of day.

Chapter Forty-seven

The café on the third floor of the pyramid gave us a high vantage point for the gaudy riot of wonders below and a view of the lake, steaming blue in the midday sun. Rune, oblivious now to the abundance of wonderful things, focused on his food.

He'd opted for nachos and a Coke. I had a small salad and a bottled water to offset the waffles of breakfast. Tom got a big oatmeal cookie and a cup of coffee. I would have frowned at him for being an irresponsible role model if that would have done any good.

He grinned as he bit into the cookie and said, "It doesn't do any good to disapprove of someone who can't see you disapproving. I'm a free man, lady. Unless you talk to me out loud."

"You wouldn't like it if I spoke my mind all the time."

"Try me."

Rune was shifting his gaze from Tom to me and back again. Anxious. "Are you guys arguing?"

Tom shook his head and had another bite of cookie. "Nah. We haven't hung around together long enough to have anything serious to argue about."

What? This was an outrageous lie, and I had the red hot memories to prove it, but Tom's face was bland.

Rune squinted his eyes in a way that reminded me of Margo. "Are you guys going to get married?"

I ducked my head and started examining my salad for flaws, and then I realized that I could search Tom's face and he'd be none the wiser. When I did, he was focused in my direction with his famous quizzical expression. "What do you think, Rune? I can't see her. Does she look like she thinks we're going to get married."

Oops. Back into the salad.

"She's looking at her lettuce and stuff. I can't tell what she's thinking."

Ha!

"So much for setting your seeing eye kid on me. He doesn't read minds."

"Maybe not. But I do. Listen up, Rune. In about another fifteen minutes all this Mondo nonsense is going to blow over." He paused. "Or at least die down a lot, and Alice Jane and I are going to get very married. You're going to be in the wedding.

It'll be terribly mushy. Lots of kissing and hugging. You'll hate that."

Rune was nodding his complete agreement to the last statement. Then he swiveled to me, "Is your name really Alice? Why does everybody call you Allie?" he demanded.

I was all busy processing what Tom had said about married kissing and hugging, but I had to deal with Rune's question.

"Your name is Runako. How come everybody calls you Rune?"

He wrinkled his nose. "Runako is not a fun name. Everybody wants to know what it means and then they tease me."

"Ditto for Alice on the not fun. You may notice that Tom is teasing me about it. Tormenting may be a better word."

"What does tormenting mean?"

"Big teasing. Only over and over."

He was digging around in the nachos container for the last bit of cheese. "I think you were doing that, Tom."

Tom laughed out loud. He had a great laugh. I hadn't heard it anywhere near enough.

I raised my water bottle. "I propose a toast." Tom found his coffee cup and Rune picked up his Coke.

"To more laughing for all of us," I offered,

nudging Tom's cup with my bottle. Rune put in his Coke can, grinning from ear to ear.

"To more laughing for all of us, and to Alice saying yes," Tom added.

"Did she say yes?" Rune came back around to me, his brow crunching up in confusion.

"Yes." I laid my hand lightly on Tom's arm. "I said yes the very first day we met."

Rune hid his face in his hands. "Are you guys going to kiss?"

"I'm afraid so," I answered. "Don't look for a sec." Tom's lips were warm. For Rune's sake, I didn't linger. "That was a very nice proposal, Dr. Bennington III."

"I already told you. We're forever, Alice."

I leaned back in and spoke low into his ear, "I believe the word you used before was 'cooked.' And the word I used was 'screwed.'"

"Those, too. Now, let's go."

"Is it safe to come out now?" Rune's voice was muffled by his hands but he was smiling under his clasped fingers.

"You better. We still need to visit the real, authentic Hall of Fame."

That moment. Right there. If the house of me were burning down, that's the mental picture I'd risk my life to save.

• • ● • •

I made everybody take a bathroom break. Rune went with Tom, and, remembering my promises to Marie, I had a moment of second thoughts about that. We had established over the last few days that Tom, while not sensitive about his blindness, *per se*, was something close to rabid about his hard-won independence. Given the plans we both had for Rune, I didn't dare start suggesting he wasn't able to keep the boy safe. I bit my tongue and let them go.

The ladies room was freaky because the one light over the sink, was fritzing out. Every few seconds it would buzz alarmingly and flicker the room down into darkness. A strobe. How Rock Hall was that?

There were two stalls. One was already occupied. And here's the thing. Once I got settled in my cubicle, I could see that the flickering shoes of the occupant were, shall we say, genderly ambiguous. I know. I know. Guy shoes and girl shoes are very often the same shoes, but these were very big shoes. This lady could have played for the CAVs. The person wearing the CAVs shoes was also exceedingly still. I got this huge waiting vibration. No audible breathing. Only the surreal buzz and the strobing blackness.

Oh, boy. Was I really going to get kidnapped

or killed in a bathroom? I decided I did not have to go as badly as I'd thought. I did a hasty zip-up and stepped out of my stall.

A voice from next door. "Ma'am?" A guy voice.

"Sir?" I was edging toward the door, but my feet were encased in cement.

"Ma'am, I'm so sorry. I came in here to fix the light and I didn't have the yellow folding sign to warn ladies not to come in. I thought I could just jiggle the fixture, but then I heard you coming and—I could be fired for not following procedure."

Geez. Discontinue CPR.

"Okay. I promise I won't say a word, but you'd better come out and find your sign. The next visitor is likely to run away screaming."

Like I am. On the inside.

A sigh. "Thank you, ma'am. Thanks very much. I will. I'll do that."

I went back into the hall and waited for Tom and Rune. After a long minute a tall, nice-looking, young guy in a blue work shirt and pants, sporting some very large feet and carrying a bulky tool box, came out. Sheepish. He gave me a nod. I gave him a nod. Then the boys emerged from the men's room and I forgot all about being scared.

Chapter Forty-eight

After the dazzle captured in the glass façade of the pyramid, the core of the museum—its sacred shrine—is its darkest night, enveloping visitors in the sound and the spirit of the inductees.

The world outside vanishes. The music-makers hold sway.

Rune was awed speechless by the theater soaring up into gloom, its three massive screens projecting non-stop images, performances, and interviews. The presentation was gripping, moving, loud. The Michael parts came soon and went by fast. Michael with the Jackson Five, his fresh round face almost as young as Rune's. Michael grown up, transformed. The camera caressed his sculpted profile, worshipped his compelling, androgynous beauty, showed us his caricature of himself, then let him go.

A splash of music. A flash of light. Done. We were ready to move on.

The Hall of Fame itself is, in fact, a dim,

narrow hallway. Of fame. A promise of musical immortality to the chosen few. The passageway spirals upward from the theater and is drenched in the music that spills out of it. On a wall of black glass the names and autographs of the immortals are etched in starlight.

People moved quietly, reverently. Pointing out names. Murmuring to one another. I put my hand against the glass. Cold. Smooth. I had hoped Tom might be able to at least run his fingers over the names, but no.

We had gotten to The Jackson Five, and Rune was inspecting them with solemn attention. He'd put a tentative finger on Michael's name. I was getting a kick out of the smiley faces that Jermaine Jackson had drawn into his florid, rounded Js, and I'd turned away from the wall and from Rune to describe this cute idiosyncrasy to Tom when Armageddon struck.

The fire alarm went off, whooping and wailing. The lights died. People started screaming. As I whipped around to put my hands on Rune, something came out of the blackness and struck me hard on the back of the head. The blow, the dizzying pain, the smothering darkness, the panicked shriek of the alarm brought me down. My knees buckled. I hit the floor with my palms out. Somebody stepped, full weight, on my hand. From a long distance I could hear Tom's voice through the din, calling, "Allie? Rune!"

From Rune, there was no sound at all.

Chapter Forty-nine

The sun was setting. The Rock Hall had been locked down tight for hours. We were huddled in the café. Tom had his elbows and his glasses on the table and his face buried in his hands. I was watching, without great interest, the police cars beginning to disperse from the parking lot, their headlights coming on in the dusk. There had been a lot of them. Not that it did much good. An Amber Alert had been put out for Rune. I had called Marie and Elaine. Told them he'd been stolen. They were upset. For me. With me. I'd made Maria sorry, I could tell.

Yeah. Me, too.

I was learning now how easily it could have been arranged. I hadn't fooled anybody with my pathetic maneuvers. Somewhere, maybe everywhere, I'd left a loophole, probably more than one. I cursed my naiveté. The kidnappers had known we'd wind up there in that black hall, sooner or later.

Anyone could pass as an ordinary fan of rock & roll, lurk in the gloom of the seats, and observe everyone arriving. Identify the targets. A blind man, a woman, a boy, age seven and a quarter. As we stood together in the entrance, gaping at the big screens, outlined in the muted light from the hall, that person would identify us. They would see where we sat and watch us as we watched the film. They knew the instant we rose to go.

According to the cops, there was a fire alarm box on the wall by the door. After the three of us were well into the corridor, the watcher could pull the alarm. Its shriek was the signal for an accomplice to cut power, and our attacker was assured of a very long moment of pure chaos before the backup generators could kick in. To pounce. To clobber me and grab Rune unseen.

Tom, with his years of honed skills and senses had an advantage the rest of us wouldn't have had in the dark, but he'd been overwhelmed by the running, shoving, and the incessant blare of the alarm.

After that it was subdue the boy—gently, I prayed—and carry him away. No one would hear a child crying out when everybody in the place was hollering. Even if Rune were struggling and begging for help, it would get chalked up to the panic of the moment. They had avoided the cameras or at least there was nothing of the boy in the tapes.

He was gone.

I'd talked with Margo. Tom had called Skip. I kept glancing over at the table where we'd sat—it felt like moments before—and been happy. Tom had stopped short of telling Rune we'd be a family. Now I wished he'd known. That we loved him. That we'd do anything to get him back.

"I want him back, Tom. I just want him back. I can't stand this. I can't be here."

He didn't move from his despairing posture, but he groaned all the misery I felt.

"I'm sorry, Tom. I'm not helping."

"There is no help for this, Allie. I want him back, safe and sound, like you do. I want them to contact us and I want to pay them what they ask. I want—"

I didn't think he was aware he'd stopped talking. I watched him follow his thoughts into the same intractable loop of fear and despair I was trapped in. There was nothing either of us could say that would change any of it. Until the kidnappers made contact, neither of us could do anything. Except wait.

While we sat there, alone, in silence, unable to comfort each other, I had plenty of time to condemn myself. Of the two people who might have saved Rune, I was the one who could see, the one who'd been only a tiny step away when the alarm went off. I kept thinking I should be able to operate time manually. To hit replay. In that beautiful new version—which played and replayed behind my eyes—when the blow came out of the dark, I used my scrap of awareness to throw myself over Rune, covering him with my body. Holding him. Holding him tight.

How could I have failed us all in that moment? Where was Rune?

A guy was there from the FBI. He seemed nice enough, but a little too human for my requirements. I wanted a god. I wanted a guy who could fly and walk through walls and bring Rune back before he even knew he was gone.

This guy, this Agent Steve Bukovnik, seemed competent, but not godlike.

He lectured us on protocol, and I was trying to pay attention but my heart was elsewhere. He explained it all with extreme care. How the kidnapper or kidnappers would contact us. What we should do. What we should not do.

The important thing was for him and his people to be in control. I didn't think his heart was bleeding enough for him to be in control. He could live without Rune. He'd been doing that for his whole life, up to today. He'd manage. We wouldn't.

For a second I was glad when I looked up and saw Officer Anthony Valerio threading his way toward us. At least his was a familiar face. Valerio and Agent Bukovnik traded a small amount of alpha dog posturing, but Bukovnik let him through and then stepped away to a discreet distance.

Valerio pulled up a chair and started in, glowering at me from under the monobrow. "Ms. Harper, Allie, you have something that I have to have access to now. This is not about you having tampered with evidence. I could care less. This is about the boy. I can help you, but I have to see that piece of paper."

Well. If he was a criminal, he was the boldest criminal I'd ever seen. Right under the nose of the FBI. I stared at him through the glaze of pain and sorrow that was distorting everything. He still didn't look like a bad man to me. I hesitated.

Tom made my decision for me. "Give it to him, Allie."

I reached into my purse.

Valerio leaned closer, blocking Bukovnik's line of sight. "Keep this between us. It'll only confuse things. I need some freedom to move. Trust me."

Did I? Trust him? I brought out the note, smoothed and folded. I glanced at the agent. He was gazing out the window. I passed the note to Valerio. He unfolded it and stared at it for a moment. I searched his face for a clue to what he was thinking but except for the slightest tic at the corner of his mouth, his expression was noncommittal. He folded the paper back up and made it disappear. Another pivotal moment going, going, gone.

Valerio leaned toward me. "Allie. Here's what I want you to do. I want you to do exactly what Agent Bukovnik has told you to do. Don't pay these people. Don't go where they tell you. I'm going to leave a phone on this chair in a minute when I leave. It has my number programmed. When you get the call, call me. And tell me where they want you to go. And don't let FBI see you pick up the phone." He gave me a tight smile. "I know you can get away with that."

He left. He had "DIRTY!!!" in his possession. Maybe he'd now tied up the last of his loose ends. Maybe all he needed to do was bide his time. Get the money he was going to demand. Kill us all. And retire without a trace of parking garage guard duty in his future. Or maybe he wanted to fit the piece of the puzzle I'd stolen into a piece of the puzzle he'd been working on all along. Help us. And save Rune. What did I know?

There was a cheap burner cell phone on the seat of his chair. I palmed it and slipped it into my purse, remembering Valerio trying to explain to me what burner meant. I had traded one item of contraband for another, and now I was hiding things from the Federal Bureau of Investigation. Moving up in the world.

"Tom—"

He cut me off. "Allie, listen to me. I know you're blaming yourself. I want you to stop it. This is not your fault. Not even mine, really. Things happened. They can't be undone. The people who've died—and Rune and us. I can't—"

"Tom—"

"I'll do whatever I have to. It probably won't turn out. You should run away now."

"You have got to be kidding. Where could I possibly go?"

"You'd be safe if you weren't with me."

"I'd be nothing if I weren't with you."

I reached across the table. His hand was clenched and cold and it didn't open to my touch. I brushed the hurt of that aside and made my voice as confident as I knew how.

"Sorry, Tom. You said it yourself. We're cooked, we're screwed. For better or worse. This is the worst. Let's hang on and be cooked and screwed together for as long as we can." I hoped he couldn't hear me crying.

His face, drawn and gray, didn't relax, but he nodded. And let his shoulders slump. I couldn't tell if he was relieved or didn't have the energy to argue. I could foretell the trajectory of our relationship if we never got Rune back. I would remind him of everything he regretted, everything he'd lost. It would make him sad. Even how much I loved him would make him sad. It would be over. Slow and agonizing. And then over. Along with my life and any chance I might have for happily ever after. Which had seemed within my grasp. A heartbeat ago.

Agent Bukovnik strolled over to tell us we could leave. Go straight back to the hotel and wait for the kidnappers to call. There was already another agent stationed in our suite at the Wyndham. When we got a call, he'd put everything in motion to get Rune back. "Follow my instructions. Do what our agent says. We'll handle this. Everything will be fine."

Or not.

We went. As we went, I told Tom about Valerio's phone, but, of course, it turned out he already knew because of what he'd overheard.

"Can we trust him, Tom? Do you think?"

"I don't know, Allie. I know we can't do anything to put Rune at risk. We'll have to decide when the time comes."

I couldn't stand walking across the plaza—the two of us—in the sultry twilight with Tom's hand dead weight on my arm. I couldn't stand the steps to the car. I couldn't believe I'd have to drive down the ramp, present my validated ticket, and save two dollars on parking, when my life was over.

Tom went to the passenger door. I got in on my side. Big surprise. I hadn't locked it. Well, at least the car was still here. My negligence hadn't been punished this time. Or—there was another one of those pay-as-you-go phones on the console. I slammed my door so hard the Jeep shuddered.

The phone rang.

Chapter Fifty

I answered.

The voice, if you could call it that, on the other end was filtered through one of those mechanical, distorting devices I'd heard a hundred times on crime shows. It was an inhuman sound. I couldn't tell if it was a man or a woman. I could, however, understand every word.

"I have the boy."

"Let me talk to him."

"That is not possible at this time. I drugged him. He's out. If you want to talk to the boy again, you must do as I say."

"Please. Don't hurt him. What do you want me to do?"

"I want you to give the phone to the man and drive out of the garage. Do not alert the attendant. I am willing to kill the boy."

"Okay. Okay."

"Allie. Who is that? Is that your phone?"

Was the car bugged, too? I didn't care. Tom deserved to know what was happening.

"It was here when we got in. It's a mechanical voice. Distorted. They say they have Rune. They're going to tell us where to go. Here. You talk to them. I'll drive."

It looked like Agent Steve Bukovnik was going to be way disappointed.

I drove. Tom translated. That helped. Coming through him, it didn't sound as terrifying. He listened. Told me where to go. I did what he told me.

It was full dark now. The voice told Tom I should not try to lose the car following us. I looked in the rearview. A junker. Big. Old. Rusted red. With tinted windows that hid the driver. God. It was a regular "Christine, from Master of Horror, Stephen King" of a car, complete with a gaping chrome grin.

The voice told Tom to get rid of our cell phones. To throw them both out the car windows.

"I am watching. I will know."

We rolled down the windows and dropped them out. "White Rabbit" and "Blind Love" crushed in the street.

We were then directed to go to an ATM and draw out the max on both our cards. That was six hundred dollars apiece. I could only access three hundred-sixty of mine because of my non-balance situation. We were instructed not to use a credit card for anything from here on out.

"Good. You are now off the grid. Keep driving."

I drove.

I drove all over the place. I had to stop and get gas. I paid cash with a smile. I gave no indication that we were in trouble. Big trouble. The car had pulled off behind us and waited outside the perimeter of the lights of the gas station. When we came out, it fell in again.

I drove some more. My head was pounding and I was having the out-of-body sensation you get when you've been terrified, clubbed on the back of your skull and stepped on, frantically worried, horribly sad, and then, ultimately, all of the above plus very tired. At last we were ordered to move east up Euclid Avenue. We were off the grid, for sure. Nobody was behind us for as far as I could see, but The Car and The Voice.

Except we weren't off the grid. Not quite. I had Valerio's phone. The wild card. How about that, Voice? And I didn't have a clue about when Tom and I could have a conversation that might help me decide whether or not to trust Valerio.

Was this a Valerio test? It seemed an improbable coincidence that I now had two brand new phones. If I hit speed-dial for Valerio, would the nightmare voice answer? No. Not even if Valerio was back there, guiding us around town. He'd keep that persona separate, but he'd know then whether he could trust us. Maybe he'd punish us. By killing Rune. By killing all of us, by and by, after he had Tom's money. So should I call him when I got a chance?

All our sleuthing, our scrabbling around for suspects and allies, was coming down to this choice? Yes. No. Flip of a coin. Decision deferred.

I could also use Valerio's phone to call or text someone else at some point. But who? Not our trusty FBI guys, who must be going nuts at the Wyndham by now, wondering why we hadn't shown up. Bukovnik was realizing, no doubt, that he should not have sent us stumbling off alone. I almost felt sorry for him. Even with all my vicarious fictional experience, I wouldn't have predicted this wrinkle.

Should I call Bob Clark? He'd proved himself trustworthy and a friend more than once. And whenever I hooked him up in my mind with the crimes, the logistics didn't work out. But surely contacting any of the authorities I might have access to might mess something up and put Rune—and us—at more risk. I knew Tom would vote against it.

So dialing 9-1-1 for Bob? Not practical. At least not yet. Besides, he hadn't been my good old

Officer 9-1-1 the last time I'd tried him. Where had he been? Why hadn't he returned my call?

I wished I could ring up Margo, just to hear her voice hollering obscenities at me. I knew we'd be talking with Skip again soon enough. Bukovnik would be following the money and he'd find his way to Skip. But even then, what could Skip and Bukovnik do without putting Rune in jeopardy? My brain was cardboard.

Tom reached across the console and found my hand on the wheel. Tears stung. I started to say, "I love you." But the phone chattered again and Tom said, "In two blocks, turn left."

We'd passed out of Cleveland and into East Cleveland. I turned left as directed and drove some more. You'd have to be more generous than I was feeling not to say this was one of the nastiest, druggiest, car-jackingest neighborhoods in town. Another left turn brought us onto a street of bars and the kind of churches that rescue people from bars.

The voice spoke again. There was a motel up ahead on the right. The Price Motel. A reservation had been made for us. How thoughtful. Sure enough, up ahead, part of a yellow neon sign was blinking "RICE OT L." And, naturally, "Vac cy." With a fully intact, "$49.99. Ask about weekly/monthly."

It's remarkable the accommodations 190 million dollars can deliver you to.

The motel stretched back away from the street, two grimy stories staring down on an ugly patch of concrete courtyard. An insufficient number of non-burned-out lights struggled to illuminate dank, narrow concrete aisles with their ranks of liver-colored metal doors and railings. A weary-looking woman behind reinforced Plexiglas allowed as how she had our key. Room 19 was ready and waiting for us.

Cool. I could see that I was not going to be able to keep the promise I'd made to myself, somewhere along the way during my college years, never again to stay anyplace where the reception desk had to be bulletproofed.

The woman seemed kind enough in spite of the apparent rigors of her workplace. She called me "hon" in dulcet four-pack-a-day tones and encouraged us to get a good night's rest. Then she blinked at Tom, standing there looking like a worn-out blind man, holding a burner phone to his ear.

"Uh, hey, hon. He's not that guy—?"

The blind guy 'ut won the Mondo?

"Who won the MondoMegaJackpot? Hardly. No offense, ma'am, but do you think he'd be staying here?"

She snorted and shook her head. "None taken.

Have a good night. I see you ain't got no luggage. Would you care to purchase a toothbrush?"

Yes, as a matter of fact. Even if your life is falling apart, you still need to brush your teeth. At least for me that's the bare minimum.

"I'll take two. And toothpaste, if you've got it."

"Twenty bucks."

I handed it over.

She looked askance at us again as if wondering why I hadn't bothered to haggle about the ridiculous price. Well, they called it the Price Motel. I expected nothing less. Then she shrugged. "Have fun."

You bet. I took my dental supplies and the key. As I put the key in the lock at 19, I glanced over my shoulder. The Christine car was idling across the street from the motel. But then Tom's phone spoke for the last time that evening.

"Wait there. You'll get a call."

The car slid away, and we stumbled inside. I locked the door behind us as many times as I could.

Chapter Fifty-one

I peered at myself in the brownish light from the bare bulb that was screwed into the broken fixture over the sink. I could see by a jagged edge peeking out of the socket around the bulb, that it once had a white glass cover, designed to reduce glare and add style. No biggie. The bulb was nicely dimmed by smoke residue anyhow. The Price Motel clearly didn't aspire to a no-smoking policy. And style wasn't happening here either.

Someone had done a presentable job on the mirror and taken a swipe at the tub and the basin, but the pink tile and the popcorn ceiling were filmed with decades of greasy, pungent stains.

I took inventory. There were a couple of small but perfectly utilitarian cakes of pink Camay soap and the regulation shampoo and conditioner set. Thank God for our generic toothbrushes and slightly bigger than single-serve tube of Colgate.

I recognized my state of mind. Everything in

there was terrifying. The idea of Rune, in the control of a ruthless killer, frightened, maybe hurt. Or worse. My dread of the road we'd have to travel to have even a prayer of getting him back. Whether we'd survive. Whether love could.

So here I was. Counting soaps. Tidying up. Gathering in the supplies. Living minute to minute, hanging on to the details as if they could keep me sane. Cave woman, making do. Building a fire. Pushing back the night.

I opened the bathroom door as quietly as I could. Tom was asleep on a bedspread I wouldn't have wanted to check out with that special light the CSIs had to reveal bodily fluids. I bet it would have been a revelation. In 3-D.

We hadn't talked about much of anything when we'd come in. Except whether to prop a chair under the door handle. Answer: Yes.

Everything between us was already out on the table. Everything we knew and didn't want to know. Everything we wanted to know and had no way to find out. The dire desperation of our situation. Our anguish over Rune. The two phones, one for the voice and the other for Valerio, if we decided to call him. Our determination to do whatever it took to get Rune back. All the givens.

The one thing we hadn't talked about out loud was my theory that the reason our lovely room had been reserved for us was so it could be bugged. I might be able to find the electronic ears and/or eyes, but even then, if I disabled them, we'd probably get a call from the mechanical man.

I longed to consult with Tom about whether to contact Valerio, but I couldn't figure out a way. If Voice had provided itself with video as well as audio, we wouldn't be able to even step outside to talk. The car wasn't safe if it was bugged, too. By neglecting to lock it, I'd made it super easy for someone to bug it. I decided to give myself a pass on that one. If somebody could pull off a kidnapping, they'd be able to pop a car door.

I wondered if someone was watching from outside. In person. Or maybe from an adjoining room? The acid green and silver wallpaper on the bed wall was the busiest metallic pattern I'd ever seen. And it had several of what looked like bullet holes. Were they for surveillance? Or fun peeping? Or just from bullets? What if we hadn't been left on our own at all? A ruse within a ruse within a ruse?

I could see I might have to decide for myself about the Valerio phone. But not now. Not tonight. I'd think about that one tomorrow. At Tara.

I stripped off my clothes and folded them up neatly, debating for a long moment about rinsing out my undies. No. I started up the shower and let the rusty water run itself clear before I stepped in.

I scrubbed all over with the Camay and then dried myself with a stingy rough towel. I left the light on and the door ajar enough to keep the dark at bay.

The bedroom was stuffy in spite of an air conditioner sticking out of the wall, toiling away. I had to give it some credit for exhausting its last teensy bit of energy to crank out that horrible screechy racket. I pulled back the bedspread and slid between sheets that were stiff and harsh to my bare skin but actually smelled of laundry detergent. Small favors. This was not the Marriott or the Wyndham, but it would suffice. I wedged myself as close to Tom as I could get, with him on top of the covers and me sandwiched inside.

I closed my eyes and ordered myself, *Alice Jane Harper, do not think about anything at all.*

Sleep dragged me under.

The next thing I knew it was morning.

A phone was ringing.

Chapter Fifty-two

Monday, August 31

The mechanical voice said, "*Today is the day you arrange for the money. Tomorrow you bring it to me and get the boy back.*"

"Let me talk to Rune. Please."

Tom was struggling to sit up on the bed, still completely dressed, still on top of the covers where he had collapsed the night before.

"*The boy is sleeping. You should prefer it that way.*"

"You're drugging him. Don't—You'll kill him if you—He's very small. Please—"

"*The boy is fine. I am monitoring him very carefully. But, think about this. If you do anything at all to interfere, it will be a simple matter to increase the dose and let him go. He's halfway there right now. You decide. It is completely up to you.*"

I'd put the burner on speaker so Tom could

hear everything. Now he answered, "Tell me what you want."

"*I want you to call your lawyer or whoever has access to the money. It will be a conference call. I'll hear every word you say. Do not make the mistake of believing that the call can be traced to your location. It cannot. And any attempt to interfere will hurt the boy. I want you to arrange for the transfer of the entire amount to a numbered bank account. I will give you the necessary information when the time comes.*

"*Today is the day you get the money. Tomorrow you get the boy. The man stays in the room today. The woman may leave to get food because she knows I will kill the boy if she steps out of line. I am watching and listening. Be sure to follow my instructions exactly.*"

The call ended. Tom and I sat for a minute without saying anything. Processing.

Finally, Tom broke the silence. "What did it mean? Watching and listening? And why do you think he—it—refers to us as 'the man' and 'the woman,' not by our names? Surely this person knows who we are."

"He knows. I don't understand that either. It's weird. Maybe they're trying to creep us out. Which is working for me. But we have to assume the room is bugged. Why else would they rent it for us when we have enough cash? It's not like there weren't plenty of vacancies here."

I walked into the bathroom, reconnected with my pathetic stack of clothes and brought them back to put them on. This was Creepy Eye at its dead worst.

"Okay. I put our toothbrushes and paste on the edge of the sink. I cleaned there first. Return them to that spot if you value your health. I'll get the car and find us breakfast. And coffee. We'll feel more human if we have coffee."

I slipped into my clothes. As I left, I stopped where Tom was slumped—silent, dazed—and planted a kiss on his forehead. At least he didn't pull away.

"We're going to be fine," I told him with all the bravado I could muster. "None of this is your fault. None of this is my fault. These are bad people."

"Shhh, Allie."

"Don't worry. I bet even they don't think they're solid citizens. I'm not telling them anything they don't know. We're going to talk about whatever we need to talk about."

Except The Valerio Phone Decision. I cursed how abandoned I might be for that one.

"They'll get their money and go away. We'll have Rune and be happy together. Your house or mine." I forced a grin big enough so he might be able to hear it. "You're going to have to help me clean up my credit report, though."

He wasn't quite smiling. Not at all, really. But the hard, tired lines of his face relaxed some. That would do. I touched his cheek and grabbed the car keys and my purse from the desk. Disengaged the chair from under the door handle. And left the building.

I don't care what the healthy food people say about salt, sugar, and fat. Even a terrible day looks a small amount better after you put away a couple of Egg McMuffins and a large coffee with extra cream. My hands had stopped shaking, at least. I'd got us big OJs, too, and those compacted fried potato things, plus I'd thought to ask for ketchup. I'd wiped off the desk and pulled it over next to the bed so we could both sit down at it. If you didn't count the bedside tables which had been nailed to the wall, the bed, the desk, and its chair were the sum total of furniture in this demoralizing room.

I'd checked around for video. I could stand the listening, but I couldn't help how the idea of the possible watching made my skin crawl. I'd found nothing at all that looked like a camera. Who knew? But I felt better. The spies could be out there or next door, but maybe there was some small vestige of privacy for us here in Room 19.

The phone rang.

I picked it up. Put it on speaker. The Voice told me how to do the conference call. I dialed

Skip's number, which Tom knew by heart. "Blind man's phonebook," he'd said without smiling. Skip picked up on the first ring. I would have bet he wasn't alone. Bukovnik would be there, next to him. He was going to be disappointed. I didn't see any way for him to take control of this situation and/or save the day.

"Allie," Skip was sounding as anxious as I was feeling. That didn't help. I needed his XXL strength and courage. "Are you okay? Where are you? What happened to you last night?"

"Don't forget, woman, that I am here."

I was doing my best to ignore it. As long as I kept the conversation on the straight and narrow, I could take refuge in a moment with Skip.

"Allie? What was that? Does this person have you, too?"

"It's a three-way call, Skip. I can't tell you where we are, but it's Tom and me in this—place. That's the kidnapper, somewhere else on the other phone. He's going to listen to every word we say. He says these phones can't be traced. I assume the FBI is with you. You can tell me."

Skip sighed, but I could feel him collecting himself. *Thanks. I needed that.* "Yes. They're—Agent Bukovnik—is here. I was afraid of something like this. Are you in danger right now? What is that racket?"

"It's an air conditioner. I'll switch it off for a moment. Wait. There. No. I think we're safe enough now. It's—it's very good to hear your voice, Skip." I shoved the tears down. Skip. My Momma Duck. I bucked up and soldiered on. "We need to transfer the assets from Tom's accounts to a numbered account. We'll get that information when we need it. We have to do this with a phone call tomorrow and they'll give us Rune."

"Allie. That's not going to be easy. Some of these things are big-time locked in. They'll lose value. There'll be penalties for early—The…kidnappers?" I could tell he was having a trouble saying the word, knowing the kidnappers in question were on the line. "They're asking for everything?"

"Everything. We demand it all. Or the boy dies."

For one wild, disjointed moment I considered that this had to be a landmark conference call for the professional and experienced conference callers at GG&B. I almost laughed. I almost sobbed. But all I said, my voice calm and controlled, was, "Everything."

Tom had been listening from his seat on the edge of the bed. Now I put the phone into his hand. "Skip. I'm here to authorize you to strip the accounts. Take everything that's liquid and pay whatever penalties you need to on anything that's not. Set it up so I can access it, and then transfer it tomorrow."

He abandoned his businesslike tone for a moment. "Skip, I know that's asking a lot and I'm sorry. But you know I never expected to have this money. Nobody needs money like that. It was always about Rune. Allie and I, we just want him back. Can you do this?"

"I can try."

The Voice barged in. "*Do better than try. Do it. Or the boy dies.*"

Skip would be getting pissed at the repetitiveness of the threats. It was aggravating me, too. But you can't say, "Give me a break, you jerk," to someone who truly is willing to make a kid die.

Skip mastered his annoyance "I'll do what it takes. You need to understand, whoever you are, that I can't get the entire amount back without some very long negotiation. It's not up to me. These financial—entities—are bound by their own regulations. I don't have the authority or the power. But I believe I can get at least eighty percent. The rest will probably go into penalties."

"*And the man and the woman will have nothing left of this money?*"

That was odd. It confused Skip. And me. I could sense him wondering, as I was, while he paused for a long second: Why did they care, when they were getting eighty percent of 190 million dollars? It felt very personal.

"Nothing. Pennies on the dollar at some point. Maybe."

"Pennies."

That seemed to satisfy it.

Tom broke in. He was annoyed, too, now. "You don't get it, do you? Whoever you are. This money has never been important to us. All we care about is the boy."

"I get it. You will give it all to me tomorrow. I will give you your boy."

"Wait. Once I've set this up, Tom could move the money from anywhere on the planet. Why does he need to be with you?" I could hear that Skip was getting worried about us again and ignoring the obvious.

"That's for me," Tom answered for the kidnapper. "I will not give the word until I have my hands on Rune. And this person will not give me Rune until the money is moving. Stalemate."

A satisfied hiss.

"Yesss. Stalemate."

All done. Tom passed the phone over to me and fell back on the bed. The arrangement that Skip and The Voice and I agreed on was that the kidnapper would initiate a conference call like this one, every hour on the hour, until the transactions were handled. It was going to be a long day. We all hung up. I pictured the kidnapper hanging up.

He looked like Darth Vader.

I could see Agent Bukovnik pacing around Skip's office. Skip would stop him in a minute and tell him to go find himself some coffee or something so the work could get done. I imagined Skip's young handsome features troubled by the irrationality of the task, by the danger of our situation, by the indiscretion of the FBI roaming the halls of GG&B. That made me grin. A little bit. Skip would grin, too, after he had that thought, because he'd think of me. We were almost grinning together then.

I switched the air conditioner back on. I was beginning to see a use for it. Besides cooling the room, which it was lousy at, it had to be messing with the bugging device. I could barely hear us over that thing. Ha. And when I needed to consult Tom—and if we decided to call Valerio—it might come in very handy.

I slipped back into create-order/ignore-horrible-situation mode. Tidying up the breakfast stuff. Packing all of the scraps and containers back into the McDonald's bag. I opened the door to let some morning breeze in. I could smell a dumpster out there.

I was counting on the eleven a.m.-ness of the

sunny day to keep the cutthroats and dealers out of the courtyard for a while so I could deliver my bag of trash to the dumpster. Down the way, Doris, the night desk clerk, to whom I had formally introduced myself earlier in the morning, was pushing a cleaning cart. No wonder she looked tired. No wonder the cleaning job was so crappy.

"Hey, Doris." I held up the trash bag in case she was one of the spies I feared. "Tidying up."

She trundled the cart up to where I was standing and took a moment to light a cigarette and ease her back against the filthy wall. "Afraid the cleaning ain't too good. They give me this cheap dollar store spray-on shit an' then go an' water it down so it don't do nothing. Moves the dirt around a little, is all. An' that guy who set up your reservation? He said skip your room anyhow. Not to bother you, cleaning up."

"Well, that was thoughtful." I took a chance. "Who made the reservation? I'd like to...thank them."

She squinted at me. Skeptical. "Don't know how thoughtful. I never got his name. He's some guy from the street. Homeless, maybe. Drinker, you can tell. Fumes. I don't think it was his idea. His money neither, far as that goes. He was nervous-like. Scared. He ran through a little list he had. An' then kinda skittered away."

Doris'd been living and working in the don't-pay-attention-don't-ask-questions zone for too long to wonder much or to ask questions. What happens in the Price Motel stays in the Price Motel. On the bedspread, to be specific. But I could tell we didn't add up for her. Under different circumstances, I might have hoped against hope she'd call the police for us. But that wouldn't help. And it would hurt Rune.

I trudged back to the room, savoring the bright heat of the sun and trying to figure out what to do. Tom wasn't in the bedroom and I could hear the shower going. I walked back out and asked Doris for a couple more bars of Camay and another shampoo. She gave me a handful and didn't ask me to pay for them. For a long moment she looked at me in a worried mom way. "Are you okay in there, hon?"

I almost lost it. If I'd burst into tears right then, I don't know what might have happened. But I pulled myself together and nodded. "We're fine. Just…tough times. You understand."

She nodded back, relieved that her good nature hadn't gotten her dragged into somebody else's jam. Glad for me that I was merely down on my luck. Good people pop up in the most unexpected places.

She gave me a smile of commiseration. "Tell

me about it. Take care." She retrieved her cart and
moved on down the row.

We were so on our own.

Chapter Fifty-three

Monday limped by, broken every hour on the hour by the phone call to check Skip's progress. He was progressing. I used a spare soap to clean up some more around the place. Tom and I agreed that the bedspread was something we could fold and put in the corner.

At lunchtime I got us Wendy's. For dinner, Popeye's Cajun chicken. I was beginning to flash on that *Super Size Me* movie. On the way back from Popeye's I stopped at a gas station and picked us up a six-pack, which I didn't mention to Tom. I knew he'd reject any suggestion of unwinding until everything was in place.

The day would have been tedious beyond description if I had not had the intimation that it would be our last one together. On the eight o'clock call, Skip said we were set and that 152 million dollars could transfer tomorrow.

God bless you, Skip Castillo, I said to myself,

trying not to cry for about the fiftieth time that day. *I hope you live to be really, really old and miss me sometimes if we don't make it.*

We'd have to call him tomorrow when we had Rune with us to get the password and finalize the transfer. That was good. I'd like to hear his voice from wherever we were going. I was learning to take comfort from the meagerest stuff. That was it. The Voice signed off. It would call tomorrow with directions for where we would be going to get Rune.

Over and out.

So there we were. Together for a maybe last night, in this miserable, stifling room with the air conditioner howling. I'd stopped noticing the cigarette smell, almost. Poor Tom. This was no feast for the heightened senses.

He was sitting on the bed. His feet were bare. I admired his ankles and considered that I hadn't yet had ample time in my life to admire his ankles. He'd discarded his presentable Rock Hall trip shirt last night and hadn't bothered to put it back on today. His beautiful white tee-shirt was stained with sweat. Tom's worst fears about the curse of the Mondo had come all the way home to roost. He was down for the count.

Not if I could help it.

"Hey." I went to sit beside him. "I have a plan."

I'd bought a six-pack-size cooler to keep my

secret beer cold. And a couple of those frozen things to go in with it. Cave Woman plans for every contingency.

"Let's take a shower in our luxury bathroom. Together."

He didn't seem all that thrilled with the prospect, but I could follow his logic as he got up, with no comment, to join me. He was hot and sticky. He needed a shower. If I were there, it couldn't hurt. I'd keep him from tripping over things. Rune wouldn't be any more kidnapped than he already was if we got into the shower together. My thoughts exactly.

We scrubbed. We used up most of two bars of Camay. It was companionable in the shower, if not romantic. Yet. I had more plans. We dried ourselves off with the skimpy towels. This was good. I felt chilly. Back in the room, it didn't seem practical or desirable to dress again in our smelly outfits. Save that for tomorrow. Save everything for tomorrow except being here tonight. Time for my plan.

"Look," I said easing down next to him on the bed again, "I got us beers. They're even cold." I popped a top and stuck it under Tom's nose, letting him breathe in the yeasty spray from the can. He almost smiled.

"Alice," he said, "you're a wonder. I should

marry you. That beer smells as good as…what was it? Wild Fig & Cassis? No disrespect for Jo."

"No disrespect for Jo, I'd have to agree. And Jo would understand. She and I have been through a lot together. I'm probably her best customer. Ever."

I popped open a beer for me. I took a sip. It was wondrously cold. We sat for a while, drinking our beers. Making them gone. I let them take effect, ever so slightly, and then opened another two cans for us before I said, "I have a proposition."

His smile faded. "Allie. We can't. Not if they're watching. And not with Rune—"

"Stop." I put my fingers over his mouth. "Forget them. I don't give a damn about them. I don't see how they can hear doodly with that hot air machine cranking. And they're not watching anyway. That was bullshit. Rune is sleeping. He's fine tonight. Tomorrow we'll be with him. No matter what. And wherever we're going tomorrow when we're with him, we're all going there together.

"This is tonight. We have an obligation," I was crying all the pent-up, unshed tears of the day. "A sacred obligation. To live as well as we can, as long as we can. We have tonight, Tom. Think of all the people on Earth who would give anything for one more night with the person they love."

He was crying, too. I put my arms around him and right away we both noticed about the no clothes. We smelled like Camay and that was fine. I kissed him. He tasted like overpriced toothpaste. And beer. I remembered our first kiss. Beer and chili. I willed us back to the cliff at the edge of the lake.

"I love you, Allie," he whispered. "I'm so glad you found me—we found each other—even if—"

I put my fingers on his lips again. "Stop with the 'even ifs,' Tom Bennington. Make me glad you're with me tonight. Like it's your job."

He made a small sound of acquiescence then and pulled me all the way into his arms. We were clammy and only semi-clean, but the terrain was wonderful and familiar. We got ourselves properly into the bed, between the scratchy sheets. Skin to skin, our bodies started to remember everything our minds had been trying to make us forget.

All of it was present for us as we lay together. Every kiss, from the first kiss. Every passionate moment we'd spent since our first stormy night. The heat was flowing through us as it had been from the beginning, but the love was there now, too, infusing every touch with tenderness. All the knowing of each other, the seeking. Two almost strangers who'd been drawn inexorably into a very lucky kind of oneness. If only for a while. If only for one last night.

We fell asleep—almost content, almost happy, almost at peace—in each other's arms.

Chapter Fifty-four

Tuesday, September 1

Morning again. Before we'd drifted away on love and beer last night, Tom had whispered in my ear, "In the morning. Call Valerio."

We had absolutely no Plan B. I was about to use the Valerio phone, and let the chips fall. I'd decided to call, not text. It was maybe riskier to assume that nobody was watching us, but I wanted to know for sure that Valerio got my message, and I wanted to hear him and gauge his intentions while I was putting our lives in his hands. I wished it could have been Tom doing the truth analysis on that one.

The Voice had rung us up at nine a.m. sharp. We were to get in our car and drive to an abandoned warehouse in an industrial section of Collinwood. Part of an old complex built to service the railroad that still ran through there. The address was on

Salter Road. I'd never heard of it, but according to the caller it was accessed off 152nd.

Ten-thirty. Fine. We'd be there.

We showered, separately and in silence, lovers again, eternal, but focused now on what was next. When Tom went into the bathroom, I moved the desk chair over to the air conditioner and eased the contraband phone out of my purse. My gut told me that there was no video, but I was taking as few chances as I could. I climbed up on the chair, as if I were trying to make the laboring box work better. I slapped the machine in pseudo-frustration and jiggled a knob as I pushed the speed dial number. Valerio answered on the second ring.

"It's me. Can you hear me?"

"Yeah. Barely. What's that noise?"

"Air conditioner. This room is bugged. We're meeting the kidnapper at 2370 Salter Road, off 152nd, in Collinwood at ten-thirty." I repeated the address and time, hung up, and said a prayer for my gut to be right about a couple of things. Then I turned the damned air conditioner off. The sound of it not being on was a beautiful thing. Tom liked it, too.

• • ● • •

When we got into the car at ten, I expected to see Christine, but there was no sign of her. Maybe the bad guys were understaffed. They needed to cover the exchange—please, let it be an exchange—and be ready to blow town. I wanted to reassure Tom about Valerio, but if the car were bugged, that would be a fatal error.

I pulled through the rusted-out gate to the parking lot at 2370 Salter at 10:23. The place was a big warehouse facility that had been vacant and trashed for about twenty years. A huge red brick eyesore. The lot could have parked maybe fifty cars in its heyday. It stretched out around us to a chain-link fence full of gaping holes.

I described it all to Tom as we went. "Here's the door. And it's unlocked, like they said. In here it's…an office? Maybe a reception room. The windows are boarded up, but the boards are rotted and some have been pulled off. So there's sun enough—"

Dusty rays of light broke through and fell in bands across the floor which was littered with all kinds of debris. Animal, vegetable, and mineral. Also a dead man in a pool of blood.

This was happening way too often.

"Tom. There's—I'm sorry. There's a body here."

The dead man was a cop. And the cop was Officer Tony Valerio. Here was my answer. Stricken by guilt and regret, I led Tom over to his body and knelt down. "It's Tony."

"Valerio?" Tom knelt down beside me. "Are you sure it's him?" He gingerly touched the inert form.

"Yes. It's him."

"What happened?"

Ah, God.

"I'm afraid he came to help us and met up with the kidnapper…he was our last hope…we're so…"

What is the square root of screwed? I let my voice trail away. Tony's gun was on the floor by his hand. A gun might come in handy.

"Tom. His gun is here and—"

A voice from behind us. "Leave the gun where it is, Allie. This is your fault. You should never have involved Tony. Now you stand up and come in here with me."

I turned.

It was Bob Clark.

All along.

I stood up.

"It's you."

Not an accusation. Statement of fact. Process of elimination. Valerio was dead. Nobody else here but Bob. Bob was DIRTY!!!. I couldn't fill in all the blanks, but I didn't have to. The logic was standing in front of me. Pointing a gigantic black gun at the center of my chest. Smiling.

"You got it."

"Why? Bob?"

"Allie," Tom was getting left behind. He got to his feet and stretched his hands out. "Stay with me."

"That's okay," Bob's voice grated. He was standing where a narrow shaft of light penetrated the dusty little room. The sun glinted on his golden head. His blue uniform fairly bristled with insignia, baton, mace, Taser, what have you. He could never have looked more like a knight in shining armor than he did at that moment. "Come with me, Tom."

Bob grabbed Tom's arm and dragged him, stumbling, through the door into the main room. I followed, having nowhere else on Earth to go.

This room was vast and mostly empty, a rectangle probably three hundred feet long. It was lofty, too, with catwalks running back and forth in the gloom above us. Windows up at the tops of the walls—you could call them clerestories, if they were in a cathedral—let in all the light they could.

The light was streaming down—glorious, as from real cathedral windows—but this was no sanctified space. Some of the windows were broken. Birds fluttered around up there, cooing like pigeons, looking like them, too. There were droppings everywhere. Shadows. More shadows. Shapes in the shadows. Nasty. Spooky.

Directly in front of us about ten yards from

the door was a packing crate. On that packing crate, Rune was lying. Dead still. In one of those lovely, heartbreaking pools of sunlight. I didn't say anything. No reason for Tom to know about this in whatever time we had left.

But Bob needed us to believe Rune was alive.

"Rune's asleep. I gave him something to knock him out. He'll be fine. You need to call and start the transfer. When the money is in my account. I'll tie you two up and leave you here with him. He'll wake up in a little while and untie you."

That was a pretty story. I liked it. It could have made sense. It might even have been true. I didn't believe it for a minute.

Tom didn't either. He shook his head. "No. I need more assurance than that. I need you to let Allie go with Rune. Then I'll call."

"Then you'll die. And she will. And the kid. You don't have much to bargain with here."

"On the contrary. I have 152 million dollars."

The inevitable stalemate.

Not. Bob let go of Tom's arm and strode over to where I was standing. He grabbed my arm and twisted it. Hard. I cried out.

"I'll kill Allie, Tom. And you can listen."

Tom shook his head. "You're going to kill us both as soon as I make the call. Allie, I'm sorry. The most I can do is not give him what he wants.

That's not much revenge for everything. But it's all I can control."

"How about hearing her scream? How's that going to affect your 'control'?" Bob snarled. He stepped away from me and fired his gun into the dimness over our heads. The pigeons went nuts. "I'll shoot her in the leg first, to be nice. And then I'll work my way up."

"Allie," Tom's anguish made his voice harsh. "Allie, talk to me."

"Tom." I answered him, loud and clear, with the force of every emotion in my heart. "I love you. Forever. No matter what."

Right then a most remarkable thing happened. Tom produced a gun from under the tail of his Rock Hall visit shirt, and before Bob could respond in any way at all, Tom shot him three times. In his chest. Bull's-eye. Bob dropped like a rock and lay very still.

"*Tom?*" My world had turned slow and dream-like. I was lost, underwater, with no idea of how or where to swim.

"Tom? How did you do that?"

Tom lowered his arm and let go of the gun. It clattered on the floor. He smiled a thin bit. "You beeped on the left. He beeped on the right. And you said my aim was crappy."

Then he went bleak again. "Check on Rune."

I stumbled to the packing crate and put my hands on the boy. He was warm. And he was breathing, slow and deep. So beautiful. "He's alive, Tom. He really is sleeping. Drugged. We need to get him out of here."

The room kept moving around me in the most disorienting way. My ears were ringing from the shots. I turned slowly back to Tom, but I couldn't resist a glance at Bob Clark. I remembered Margo, at the start of all this, saying "Even seeing someone you barely know shot dead, is worse than I imagined."

It was bad. Knowing the person enough to believe he was a friend made it even harder.

Bob opened his eyes to glare at me.

This was the worst.

His face was a terrible bleached color. A dying color. He looked scared. And young. And enraged. Maybe about dying when he was planning to live it up on Tom's jackpot. He was struggling to speak, choking, but determined to have his last words. What he said was his simple truth. It had confused me yesterday that The Voice sounded as if it wanted revenge for something. Now it got clear.

"That…night, Tom. All that…*money*." He forced the words through clenched teeth that were painted with his blood. "You…you didn't even *want* it…you…*upset* you'd *won*?"

His expression was pure, incredulous exasperation.

"I was…working so *hard*…overtime. Sold my *soul*. For…*pennies*." He spat the word, a bitter taste. His voice rose. "*Pennies!* What the hell did you expect me to do…?"

All the emotion sank out of him then, and he was gone.

That did it. I couldn't move. I stood staring down at Bob. I had been dead like that, too—as good as dead—seconds away from Bob's promise to shoot me slow so Tom could hear me scream. I had absolutely no idea how to be alive again.

"Allie?"

Tom hadn't expected to be alive either. I heard it in his voice and read it on his face. The way his arms dangled at his sides. Slack. Empty. "Allie?"

I came back partway. For him.

"I'm here, Tom. You saved all of us. You shot him. You shot him dead."

"Are you sure?"

"Pretty damn sure."

Bob looked pretty damn dead to me, but I'd proved to be a unreliable judge of deadness, back at the beginning of all this, with Renata. I was taking no chances this morning. I picked up his service revolver and threw it as far from us as I could.

After that, I took aim at Tom's gun….

This one had to be Valerio's gun. I remembered whispering, *"Tom, His gun is here...."*

Bob, behind us, waiting unseen. Then commanding me to come to him.

Tom, left behind, still kneeling by Tony.

Tom, slow to rise...

This gun had been a last gift for us from Valerio. I blessed him as I kicked it safely away.

You saved us, Tony.

"Come on," I urged Tom. "I'll carry Rune. You put your hand on my elbow and we're out of here."

"That is never going to happen."

Marie Clark stepped out of the shadows, walking slow and sure. Bob's widow. Deadly determined. As crisply beautiful and impeccably dressed as always. Her cool composure trained on me like the weapon in her hand. All her rage and turmoil glaring from her eyes.

I could read those eyes. It was easy. She didn't want her Bob Clark back alive. She didn't want her 152 million dollars. She didn't want a private jet with two pilots and an escort to the airport. She wanted to shoot a bunch of very large holes in me and Tom and Rune.

She had an evil little gun to do it with.

Me first.

She pointed the gun, dead on at my heart.

"You made me sorry."

Chapter Fifty-five

I learned something in that moment. It may have been the crowning lesson of my first venture into the world of crime-solving. Somebody raises a gun and points it at you? Ignore everything you've ever seen in popular culture. Almost always in the real world, the next thing that happens after they raise the gun and point it at you, is not an improbable miracle. What happens next is they shoot you. That's what Marie did. She shot me.

It was like being socked with a mean fist. Appalling. Rude. Burning, but not terribly painful. Frightening beyond belief. I looked down and there was a hole in the front of my shirt on the left side, and blood was starting to come out of it. Out of me.

It scared me so bad I fainted. The room got all sparkly, and as the sparkles were turning black, I heard another shot. Tom. I tried to call his name. This wasn't fair. If I was about to die, I wanted him to hold me while I did it. If we were both going to cross over, I wanted to cross over holding hands. Too late. Exactly like in popular culture, everything went dark.

Score one for me. I didn't die. I didn't even stay fainted very long.

I woke up maybe one minute later, and Tom was holding me saying a lot of desperate, wonderful stuff, his mouth warm and alive against my cheek. Two for two. My chest hurt like hell and I was covered in my own blood. Okay. Two for three. But I wasn't dying yet.

God bless Tony Valerio. While Marie was busy shooting me, he'd managed to reclaim the gun Tom snagged from his apparently lifeless body—the exact same gun I'd kicked away from Bob Clark's definitely lifeless body—and fired it to kill Marie with a single shot before he passed out and started looking dead again.

I consider myself fortunate beyond anybody's power to comprehend that I owe my life to accurate shooting by a blind man and a dead cop.

Chapter Fifty-six

I bet it had been decades since the parking lot at 2370 Salter enjoyed the level of traffic that met my eyes when the EMTs, having confirmed that, although I was impressively bloody and at a level of pain I considered considerable, my wound was probably not life-threatening, wheeled me out into the sunlight.

Multitudes of East Cleveland and Cleveland police cruisers. Three boxy chartreuse ambulances. A scattering of intimidating black vehicles for FBI and assorted others. Plus a silver SUV that belonged to Skip. And all around the scraggly chain-link fence, the curious, the awestruck, the neighbors, and their kids. If it weren't for the dead and wounded, it could have been a dynamite block party.

Valerio had alerted Bukovnik and the other FBI guys as he sped to Salter Road. When he'd finally had his hands on my purloined note, it told him "BOB!!!" but not the where or when. The FBI had arrived too late to get in on the action and were royally bent out of shape about that. Skip was right behind them in spite of the fact that Agent Bukovnik had ordered him to stay put. They'd all convened in time to hear the last round of shooting and been baffled but pleased by how well that had gone, given the givens. The concept of blind beeping marksmanship and dead cop firepower was far, far beyond their experience.

The first ambulance took Valerio away. Bob had shot him twice. Once in the arm which might sound minor but a ton of a person's blood supply goes through there. Once in the chest.

Turned out, Valerio had been a stickler for never wearing his vest, so it hadn't occurred to Bob that today might be different. Nonetheless, he'd lost a shocking amount of blood and was unconscious again by the time they got him onto the gurney. The EMS guys were frowning as they slammed their big green doors.

The second ambulance was for me and Rune. I was woozy and trying not to cry anymore. Rune was woozy and absolutely thrilled by all the excitement. He blinked at me.

"Allie? Is that real blood? Are you all right? Are you crying? What happened?" Before I could make any reassuring replies, he continued, "Wowww. There's like a hundred cop cars here. Cool."

If you're a resilient seven-and one-quarter-year-old, an ordeal you have no memory of is hardly any ordeal at all. He told us he'd been surprised to see Marie rescuing him from the fire drill in the Hall of Fame, but not scared a bit. Everything got way dark. And then something stung him and he'd gone to sleep. It sounded to me as if she'd maintained him never more than semi-conscious for all the time they'd had him.

He talked a little about bad dreams, but he wasn't a kid to get freaked out by a nightmare. His life had been way too interesting so far for that to impress him very long. He mentioned, too, that while he had slept, Michael had come to him and sung him the same song, over and over.

"Which song?" I was not one to take issue with anything that he found the least bit comforting.

"'You Are Not Alone,' of course. Like angels."

I saw no reason to dispute that. I could have used Michael singing to me during those days.

All the same, a shiver ran up my back when he added. "My mom was there with him, too."

Agent Bukovnik had helped Tom get Rune outside before he woke up all the way to the mess in the warehouse, so he was oblivious to that. He was delighted by our twin gurneys, with Tom walking in between. The center of our twin universes.

He was bewildered by how emotional we both

were. "Don't cry, you guys, I'm okay and Allie's going to be fine. It's just some blood," he'd insisted. "What's wrong with you?"

After that there was a cool ambulance ride. Rune's day could not have gone any better. Mine was improving too.

They were keeping me and Rune overnight at The Cleveland Clinic downtown, whether we needed it or not. There had been a brief scuffle about insurance cards, but Tom waved that away. There was also some mild resistance to putting Rune and me in the same room until Tom requested one of the Founders' Suites. That greased the skids.

The cash was back.

Once Skip realized I wasn't shot too much, he'd grinned from ear-to-ear, happy to inform us that, what with one financial thing and another, we still had a major chunk of 190 million dollars socked away.

One day it will mean a lot to Rune to know that Tom would have paid 190 million dollars to save him. Laid it on the block without a backward glance. That should make a guy feel pretty good about himself. Plus give him some deep insight into the character of another guy, I'd say.

Now that most of the MondoMegaJackpot was back in place, Tom was discovering that ridiculous amounts of cash were good for something besides getting people killed and buying Legendary Desserts at Morton's. We had this super room with flowers. And carry-in. Skip brought the carry-in from Table 45, The Clinic's fancy restaurant. He assured us this would be even better than whatever fancy food came with our fancy digs.

Rune took in the food, the beautiful view, the lovely furniture, the flowers, and the better-than-average art. "Wow, I can see why they call this a sweet."

Nobody was giving me any of the fancy food, though. Not even obscene amounts of dollars can get you dinner at The Cleveland Clinic if you're on the docket for slug removal. I had that feverish, otherworldly glaze you might get from being shot but not too shot.

A young resident-looking woman in a gleaming white coat explained kindly to me that if a person had to be shot in the chest, my bullet had been "the good, small kind" from what she called a "mouse gun" and had landed in the best possible place.

She drew a little picture of my heart and lungs nestled in behind my ribs and showed how all the important stuff had been spared and how all that got hit was a rib which would hurt but heal fine, and something she referred to, rather unkindly I thought, as "fatty tissue."

She told me I was lucky, but the bullet definitely needed to come out of there. Then a wonderful nurse named Paul injected something into my IV that eased the pain and disconnected me from the fear of death. After a while they came and wheeled me down into unconsciousness.

I awoke a long drowsy time later, pain-free and ever-so-slightly flying. My very bad/very lucky day was done. The sky was navy blue and the moon was a sliver of pure radiance in my window. Tom and Rune were curled up in the next bed, both breathing slow and quiet. Beloved shadows.

I decided this tender little slice of moon was the earthly deputy of God in my world tonight. I thanked it for every single wonderful thing and closed my eyes.

Chapter Fifty-seven

Wednesday, September 2

Valerio was pissed at me as usual.

Tom and Rune were on a tour of the Clinic, which I assumed would lead them past the cookie department at Au Bon Pain. While they were on their own, I'd cajoled a nurse to wheel me around to visit Valerio in his own lovely room.

I gave Tom a lot of credit. In spite of major distractions, he'd had the presence of mind to get someone to prevent the EMTs from delivering our rescuer to McCauley Road.

The wheelchair was silliness, but I wasn't in a mood to mix it up with anybody about anything since my recent discovery of *au bon* painkillers. I was content to roll merrily along. Valerio was very, very pissed, though, and I was trying to keep him from harshing my mellow. That's drug talk. I also was planning to divest him of vital information before he came out from under his own mini-high and got more alert. He was unfortunately alert, however.

"Everything you've asked me since 'how are you feeling?' is off limits," he growled. "You need to butt yourself out of police business, missy, and take you and your blind death-magnet out of town for a while. Jesus."

"I thought we were trusting each other. Calling each other Allie and Tony. Off the record, of course. Tony."

He grimaced in an attempt to crush a smile. Valerio was a hard-edged cop with a sweet nougat center. And he liked me. He kinda liked me. Whether that was going to find me out what I wanted to know was another matter.

"Answer one thing. What was up with Marie?"

Another grimace. This one unalloyed. He groaned and rearranged himself on the pillows. His right arm was wrapped in thick bandages, but I could tell by the way he massaged his chest that the cold betrayal of a bullet, stopped by Kevlar on its way to his heart, hurt the most.

"I tell you what, Allie. Off the record. Everything that happened—Let me count 'em out for you: Felix. Muff. Frank. Ulysses. Renata. Almost Sammy. Tom's Diana. And Bob. Especially Bob. That was all her."

I squelched my *Yeesh!* reaction to Tom's owner-ship of Diana. "She couldn't have killed them all, Tony."

"Not in person, no. I don't see the whole thing, of course. Nobody ever will since key players are dead. But I can piece it together. That night, after we heard about the kid with the ticket, Bob excused himself. I figured he was going to the john.

Now I'm guessing he called Marie and she overreacted. 'Get the ticket away from that kid!'

"Then he maybe sent Felix and Muff off on a impromptu mission. If so, I'm sure he thought the better of it even before we left the tower. After it was too late. In any case, there's plenty of evidence that those guys had beaten up Renata and that they'd gone down to Tom's. Maybe they'd made Renata tell them where he lived. That's lost now. Doesn't matter.

"After Bob fumbled the start, Marie took over. She was the driving force behind all of it. Could be she did the hit-and-run on Sammy, for all I know. She was one tough cookie.

"That scenario you worked out for Felix, Muff, and Frank wasn't just—" I could tell Tony's next word was about to be "bullshit," but he switched gears. "—half bad. You came as close as any of us. My theory is Marie made Bob shut Felix and Muff down, once she saw the liability they were. Frank was collateral damage. Too bad collateral dies dead as target."

I was seeing the real Marie now. Moving through the last couple of weeks. Everything I'd missed. How quickly she got Bob to clean up his mistake. How over his head and sloppy he was at first. The rookie killer…

"She was the brains, Tony. If you can call it that."

"Yeah, I suppose. She did Ulysses. I'd bet on it. Bob must have—When he saw you there with the body that night…"

He shook his head. "Renata, too. With Renata out of the way, Rune was Tom's. The bargaining chip she was looking for. Marie was there when Diana went off the Wyndham. We have the scratches on her and the DNA on Diana to prove that one, at least."

Diana. Her obsession with Tom's money. Her reckless alliance with a ruthless lawyer. I couldn't stop picturing her last moments. Meeting Marie up there, alone, on the precipice of greed. Both of them after Tom's money. Eyes locked on the jackpot—clawing at each other—matching each other, instability for instability, dollar for dollar…

I shook myself loose from the spell of that grim scene and started paying attention to Tony again.

"Bob was…God, I don't know. He could

be this great guy, Allie. But there was something messed up with him. His right/wrong switch was busted. A good woman might have made him a preacher. But Marie took his weakness and turned him into her own deadly weapon."

Valerio paused and touched his bandaged arm. Gingerly. Pensive. I don't think he was aware he did it.

I used the silence to process my epiphany that Bob Clark was in hot pursuit of the Mondo by the time we met him. How, at the exact moment he was warning Tom to sign the ticket, he was realizing that Rune had never had it, that Tom had never taken it to his house. Obsessing, then, about the mistake of deploying his thugs.

What might it have been like for him? To walk into Tom's house with us and Valerio, praying that Muff and Felix had gone, freaking out while Rune was describing those two talking—terrified that the boy might have heard them say "Bob."

Our good old helpful Bob had rushed to my house that first morning because he was panicked that the ticket had been stolen by someone other than him. The "Let's-cash-in-your-ticket-I'll-drive-you-to-the-lottery-place" Bob was already three murders down that morning. Committed to Marie's kidnapping scheme. Did he really plan to kill us all, there at the end?

As I tuned back into what Valerio was saying, I realized I'd been rubbing my sore spot, too.

"Way before that first night when we found you and Tom up on fourteen, Marie was turning him wrong. He was always a little bit on the take. Some little angle. Always shaking somebody down for small change. I wasn't around for that. But I suspected. That's why they called him Dirty Clark around the projects."

Ah, DIRTY....

I tried to fend off the avalanche of blame, crashing down. What if I'd left that balled up scrap on the floor under Ulysses' hand that night to be discovered in the righteous order of things? What if Valerio picked it up? How many of the dead would still be alive? How many of the still alive might now be dead? How much of the Mondo tsunami of blood was on me? Suppose Bob was the one to pick up the note? What then? Who dies then?

Valerio wasn't focused on any of that.

"He was a good cop, Allie, when we were working our shift, or at the precinct. Then, when he was with a guy like Felix Tequila, he'd be someone I was trying not to see. With Marie he was whatever Marie needed him to be. And that was never anything nice."

Valerio hadn't jumped me about the note, so

I resisted the urge to grill him about why he'd kept quiet about Bob. I didn't have to.

"Why didn't I do something? Or say something? You're thinking it. I can see. You civilian CSIs live in a dream world about what it's like for us. I believed he'd make a good cop in the end. He was young. He wanted to be a hero so bad. He did a lot of good. When we rode together he always had my back. Bob was my friend, Allie. Maybe he was my…family. I guess that's why it took me way too long to admit to myself…to believe…"

I tried to pour all my empathy for Valerio and his hopes for Bob into my face without interrupting him. He was oblivious anyhow.

"Whatever Bob was, Marie was uglier. Psycho, maybe. She could have been one of those female serial killers, except I don't believe she got off on the killing. It was all money with her. Marie wanted to be rich. Wealthy. She told me once she wanted to see her house in some fancy architecture magazine. She wanted designer clothes. She wanted to quit her job and lie on the beach and have guys bring her umbrella drinks. Truth was, Marie wanted every single dime Bob Clark could squeeze out of every poor son of a bitch he could get his hands on. And when your 550 million-dollar dime dropped in front of Bob that night, it drove her wild."

Wild Marie. I grappled with the rage that

swept over me every time I remembered all her righteous warnings. How she'd shepherded us and Rune to the Rock Hall. How she'd smiled, nice as pie, over breakfast, while pretending to be the guardian of his wellbeing. How she'd drugged Rune. How she'd said, "You made me sorry." And shot me, not sorry in the least.

Like swatting a fly.

I did not feel bad about feeling good that Marie was dead.

"How did she kill Ulysses and Renata?"

"Don't know for sure. Not going to find out, I don't imagine. They didn't look real hard at Ulysses and they didn't find Renata until it was way too late to see much. The theory is insulin. Marie was a diabetic from the time she was little. Good with a needle."

My memory sparked and I saw the container of brown sugar sitting untouched by her bowl, that morning before she kidnapped Rune.

Valerio picked up the thread again. "And Renata. Maybe insulin. Maybe something else. That's even harder to know now. The autopsy was compromised, of course."

"Diana too?"

"No question on that. Diana and your—that D.B. Harper, got themselves on Marie's radar. Guess is Diana found out about him on that

MondoSecrets.com you called me about. Our techs tracked all three of them through there, though Harper was never in direct communication with Marie.

"It's funny. People think they can do whatever they like online, but a lot of times you can get better evidence than fingerprints off there. Diana used information from the site to find D.B. We shook that out of him, thanks to you. Something Diana did or said there must have made her look like a threat to Marie's plan."

Ah, yes. Here was the Diana I understood now. That Diana would have dressed up her relationship with Tom, their "very long engagement," their plans, their new life together, their newfound riches….Her gorgeous, self-assured photo. Marie would have been all over that.

Valerio continued, unaware of my small "Ah-ha!"

"Marie was batshit about loose ends. Your—that D.B.—is lucky he didn't go off the Wyndham too."

I contemplated this scenario for a second and rejected a comment I'd probably regret.

"Bob was with me the night Diana was killed, but when they cleaned up at the warehouse, they found another body. Unaccounted for. No ID yet, from what I hear. Another of Marie's loose ends,

I bet. Accomplice, looks like. Tall, good-looking white dude. A younger, supersized Bob. Not a mark on him except for the needle in his arm. They're thinking heroin for that one. Shirt off. Don't know how he fits, but he fits."

That might explain Size 14 Shoes in the ladies at the Rock Hall. A janitor with a tool box but no yellow sign. Perhaps a chilly "janitor's closet" at the McCauley for Renata, too. Maybe he'd been a real janitor after all. Maybe he'd had a key for access to the HVAC up on top of the Wyndham. Loose ends.

"I could maybe help you with that one, Tony. In exchange for some information."

"For some—? Are you nuts, Allie? Shit. I already told you…Way more than I meant to. There's something funky in that IV."

"Yeah, ain't it great?"

He grinned. A sad, pained grin. "It is, Allie. It is so great."

"All right. Truly. One more. How did you know I had the note?

"Okay. And this is it. Allie. It. You do comprehend 'it', don't you?"

"Yessir. 'It' is what this is. Now, give."

"Before Ulysses called you that night? He called me."

Chapter Fifty-eight

Later that same day they checked Tom, Rune, and me out of The Cleveland Clinic. I would like to have stayed longer. Maybe forever. The Founders' Suite was great. I felt safe. The Clinic is The Clinic. Oprah goes there. I rest my case. But we couldn't stay. They needed the room.

We had to give Rune back to Elaine. It wasn't her fault, after all, that she'd been a pawn of Marie like pretty much everybody within a fifty-mile radius of Cleveland. She was the same caring mom-person she'd always been. Saying goodbye was hard for us, but Rune went without a fuss. The kid took his home with him wherever he went these days. He was a turtle. A spunky, hard-shelled, smart little turtle. Tom had convinced him that his place in our world was secure. He still hadn't used the "family" word. But we were going to make that happen.

After we dropped Rune off, we went back to the Wyndham. To a different suite this time, for my sake, with no view of the theaters or the sidewalk down on Euclid. Sure, it was all tainted by violent death and other bad memories, but we'd grown us some turtle shells, too. And, honey, it was clean there. The Price Motel had sold Tom—even Tom— on the value of an expensive, clean hotel room. With silent air conditioning. And nothing sticky or smelly on it anywhere. Plus the Shock Abzzorber Plus. Did I mention that was a definite plus?

Also, no wonder Vicodin is a controlled substance. It removes pain and it also tempers bad memories and takes away anxiety without, as far as I could tell, impairing many of the sensations a person would still like to enjoy. Tom had been gentle and considerate with the kissing and touching up until the moment I'd murmured, "Is that all you've got, Dr. Bennington the Third? Because this is lovely, but I'm missing the—" And then I whispered in exact detail what that missing stuff was. Message delivered. I got exactly what I'd asked for.

Did it hurt? Maybe. Did I care? I don't remember.

We were waiting for our hearts to calm down and our bodies to bid goodnight to each other, when the thought hit me.

Like an echo. A *frisson* of uneasiness.

"Unaccounted for."

Valerio had told me nearly everything I wanted

to know. But someone—besides my dead janitor guy in the warehouse—was unaccounted for.

Big Lying Idiot. Mr. Probably-Plaid. Where the hell was he?

Tom was in a unique position to feel the ripple effect of the realization course through me. "What? Allie, you just thought about something. Something bad."

"Yeah. I did. The big guy who grabbed me at my house."

In spite of this unwelcome memory, I yawned.

Thank you, Ms. Hydrocodone. You are my Fairy Godmother.

"But y'know, Tom, he's not here, as far as I can tell. We're okay tonight. Way okay. Let's talk about this at breakfast. Between the drugs and the part where you—" I whispered in his ear again, "I'm feeling too wonderful to mess with him right now."

We gave ourselves a rain check on worry and went off to our dreams like the lucky, happy, satisfied people we were.

Chapter Fifty-nine

Thursday, September 3

We didn't even have to wait for breakfast to start accounting for our guy because we got a call. Our original phones had been crushed under the wheels of countless vehicles in downtown Cleveland, and the FBI had confiscated the burners. I'd asked Skip to order us new ones. We needed some way to take care of business and stay in touch with Rune. My new phone had been waiting for me at the Wyndham, all programed with my number and ready to go.

Bright and early the next morning it rang.

Generic ringtone.

Excellent. I could deal.

It took me a moment to figure out I was talking with Nan Randall.

"Alice, it's Nan. From GG&B."

"Nan. Oh, hey. Hi. How are you?"

"I'm okay. I'm doing better. I was off work for a couple of weeks, but they didn't fire me. That was a miracle. You made it happen. You and Skip Castillo. I'm not supposed to know that, but a receptionist has her sources."

"Well, I'm glad. It didn't seem fair for you to not have your job. After…" I paused in the presence of my thought that Nan's life had maybe been improved by a bullet "everything."

"Alice, I think D.B. is up to something. He's so pi—mad about all that happened. That Diana Wiles episode didn't help his standing here at the firm. You know how they are."

Oh, yes.

"I'm sure, Nan, but—"

She was on a roll, talking fast before her training could overtake her heart. "I think you and Tom should check out this very disgusting man named Lester Grose. He's after your money. All of it. And I think D.B.'s working for him now. Good luck, Allie."

• • ● •• •

"This very disgusting man named Lester Grose."

Well, hey. He sounded very much like my unaccounted-for-disgusting-guy. Mr. You Bitch, You Stole My Money & Likely Plaid Man. Could I prove it? Nope. Did I believe it? Sure worked for me.

Nan's call was our first official alert. But people around and about had already been talking. First there was a whisper, then a nagging whine, and after that a rumble. A rolling rumor, gathering no moss. Somebody new was laying claim to the winning Mondo money.

Imagine that.

Lester Grose had been busy since he'd found an attorney and stopped assaulting me. Once I got a good look at all of him, in his multi-channel local TV interviews, my fuzzy mental pictures came into focus and fit like the last piece of a puzzle.

I had my man. My tall, heavy-set, white man of indeterminate age. Long gray ponytail, bulbous, pocked up, red nose. A penchant for lumberjack-y shirts and broken-down contractor boots. Matching up this guy with the memory of his grubby hands on me and my hypothetical snapshot of him wedging himself through my living room window gave me chills.

I'd guessed right on Lester's address, too: High-Rise of Death. #1419. Same floor. Same time as Renata and Rune. Claimed he and Renata had been a couple. Claimed Runako had been like a son to him. Claimed he'd bought the ticket to please Renata, who liked to play the Mondo and was dead now. They'd won and been so happy. Then someone had beaten Renata up bad and she had later died. Lester dabbed at his eyes with a soiled hanky.

But the boy had taken the ticket. Maybe only for a minute, to show someone. Maybe not knowing how valuable it was. And that someone had got ahold of it. It was someone who'd been—ah—close to the boy. And who could ever know what that relationship had been? That man had cashed in poor old Lester's fortune. Rune's, too, of course.

Lester Grose. Not since Felix Reposado had I gotten such sour amusement from a name.

The officials at MondoMegaJackpot were confident that Tom was all fine. The money had transferred, after all. And, of course, possession, as Bob Clark had told us the fateful first time we'd met, is everything. But the officials were considering allowing Lester to file a claim. Or at least add a statement to the file. So there'd be no confusion— or costly lawsuits—on down the road.

The lottery folks suggested that, as a strategic move, we make an appearance on the occasion of Lester's coming to visit them. In their scenario, Tom would show up as the rightful holder of the ticket and intimidate the daylights out of Lester.

Skip was hacked off enough to want us to file a suit for defamation of character, in particular, the innuendos about the boy. We were worried that any minuscule suspicion of unseemly behavior on

Tom's part would mess up our chances to adopt Rune. The idea that Rune might be questioned by anyone anytime about the ticket or anything else, enraged Tom.

And me. I was even madder.

Turned out, I didn't need to hear from Nan or consult my own ex-wifely intuition to find out that Lester had him a lawyer. It was on the news. According to Lester, speaking with wide-eyed sincerity into the camera, he'd got his lawyer *pro bono*. Lester pronounced the *bono* part like the name of the guy from U-2. Nobody we talked to had seen this lawyer, and Lester hadn't identified him, but the situation had D.B. written all over it.

The smoldering sensation in my chest was not all bullet wound. *Pro bono*, my Aunt Fanny.

I figured D.B. understood there was no real hope for Lester's claim. Except for the harm it could do Tom and me. The man was a snake. I thought it likely that the fury he was stoking about how rich and happy I was about to be and how thwarted he'd been all along the way—from the Zocalo Mexican Grill and Tequilería to the Blue Bar at the Wyndham—was making him a crazy snake.

You should never turn your back on a crazy snake but I guessed that D.B. was banking on our doing that.

"He thinks we'll do what he would do," I

told Tom. "Go into hiding. Someplace secluded and expensive. With a lovely beach and a lovely bar. He'd ignore Lester. Let him thrash around, all wounded and betrayed, until he gets worn out and goes away."

"It's tempting," Tom agreed. "I could consider that."

"But Tom, here's what that would do. It would turn people against us. Stir up all the natural resentment that the good, hardworking people of Cleveland could harbor toward somebody with a lot of unearned, and possibly stolen, good fortune. Five hundred-fifty million dollars is a lot of good fortune.

"We want to live in this town. You want to teach here. We want to raise Rune here. Heck, I might even want to be a part-time librarian here. But D.B. would love to make sure we reap every scrap of misery from the appearance of having swiped the ticket from some big, ugly, poor old guy."

That was my reasoning for wanting us to show up at the lottery with Tom looking like the handsome, refined, educated, dignified, hot, blind guy that he was and put paid to Lester's claim once and for all.

"If we're going to get stabbed, I want it to be in the front. Not in the back. By a crazy snake."

Tom suppressed a smile. "To mix a metaphor?"

"Whatever."

We worked it out with Skip that he'd meet us there on Friday, a few minutes before lottery closing time, and we'd put it to Lester and Mr. Duane Pro Bono U-2 that Lester would be facing serious litigation for making slanderous statements. We thought the odds were good D.B. couldn't show his snake face and his GG&B credentials in the light of day. And that Lester would cave.

It was an excellent plan.

Chapter Sixty

Friday, September 4

We drove up to the headquarters on Friday at a quarter to four. The press was all over the place, and Skip was nowhere. Plus, there was a crowd of fifty or sixty solid citizens, attracted by the excitement generated when the TV crew vans popped up their satellite dishes on those giant telescoping poles.

The reporters had positioned themselves and their camerapersons between us and the door. Once out of the car, we were trapped like bugs. Tom was, of course, beleaguered by the questions coming at him from all directions. He looked distressed, a little scared. It was an expression some people—for example, suspicious, angry, jealous people—could have read as guilt.

I collared one of the reporters and told him, in what I hoped was my most professional part-time librarian speak, "Dr. Bennington will talk to you all after the meeting with Mr. Grose. With his attorney present."

I gave Tom my non-surgical-side arm in as un-gold-digging-slut-like way as I could muster and he followed me back through the jostling crowd to the car. It was hot, though, and I didn't want to run the engine for the AC and thereby appear anti-environmental on top of everything else, so the windows were rolled down.

That meant that every five seconds, some woman or man in a nice outfit would stick a microphone in through the window. In case we'd changed our minds.

I noticed, however, that the woman from Channel 16 had positioned herself well back from the car. Was she was trying to stay out of view? Not SOP for Channel 16 reporters. Piranhas don't opt out of one of those fabulous cow-in-the-Amazon moments. She couldn't hide entirely and when I got a good look I realized why she didn't want me to see her.

Me. She wasn't hiding from Greater Metropolitan Cleveland News Land. She was hiding from me.

"Stay here for one second," I ordered Tom. "I gotta see somebody. I'll be right back. Don't talk to anyone but Skip."

I clambered out of the driver's side, dodging

two more microphones and a camera, and hot-footed it over to the blue, Channel 16! It's News To YOU! van and the woman who was skulking in its shadow.

She was pretty. Very blond, with flawless makeup you could have cracked an egg on. Dressed nice, too. A tailored bronze safari jacket and a spiffy black skirt that showed off her sleek shape and nice knees. I was becoming the connoisseur of so-cool-you-could-get-brain-freeze shoes. She had a pair of those, too. Black, sling-back, open toes, thirty-inch heels.

She had looked a lot less professional and a lot madder the last time I saw her. We were all alone now. Face to face. The other media mavens were circling the car with poor Tom holed up inside. I couldn't take long for this conversation, but I wanted it. Bad.

"You're the woman from the Hummer, aren't you? I knew you looked familiar and I'm not a regular 16 viewer. You're the woman in a huge hurry. You honked at a blind man in a crosswalk. You're her. Aren't you? You're her? And you remember both of us."

It was true. I could read it on her face. Like she would slink off the face of Cleveland if she could.

She folded. "Okay. Yes. I admit it. I do. It wasn't my finest hour. I was on my way to a story about possible pesticides at the farmer's market up in Euclid. I'd borrowed that crappy old Hummer from one of the anchors. I needed to get it back. I'm hanging on by my fingernails at 16.

"I apologize to you, Ms. Harper. To Dr. Bennington. To the Universe. That was really disgusting. I'm an idiot. I'm sorry. I really am. What are you guys going to do? Sue me? Make a fuss? Ruin my career?"

I thought she was going to burst into tears right there, behind the It's News to YOU! van in front of lottery headquarters.

My heart thawed. I smiled as kindly as I knew how and patted her on the well-tailored shoulder of her shiny bronze jacket.

"Heck no, HummerWoman. I've been blessing you every day for the last three weeks. I'm going to send you flowers. I think Tom will, too. You were having a bad day. I expect you weren't yourself. Tom and I met and fell in love because of you. That was luckier than the Mondo. You and me? Girl, we are way beyond even-steven. You can call me Allie."

She looked surprised for a second and then she grinned back and blinked at me, dazed. It was a nice look for her. Freed up that flawless veneer. Then she snapped back into professional mode. The look in her eye went all scary.

"Give me a second here, Allie." She turned

and motioned to her cameraman. "Let me ask this joker a question nobody else had the presence of mind to ask. Get your boyfriend out of the car and bring him over. I've got a good one for him, too."

I hustled to the car, extracted Tom, and led him up behind her as she stepped over to the spot on the sidewalk where Lester was holding court with a gaggle of other news folks. Sometimes you have to go with your gut, and just then mine was saying, *We don't want to miss out on this one, Alice Jane.*

"Sir," she began, "May I have a moment? Lisa Cole,16 News." She flashed him her dazzling reporter smile. The crowd hushed and the other stations' camerapeople panned around to capture Lester's response.

Lester Grose was flattered to be talked to by a very pretty TV news lady and no doubt assumed she was into him because of his chance to get hisself some major cash.

"Yes, Leesa." He returned a broad grimace that revealed a dental situation Lester should always try to hide.

"Sir, your number. The number you say you picked. And I understand from information provided by the Lottery, that the winning number was picked and not an auto-selected number. The number? I wonder if it was meaningful to you. Something you always play?"

The smile faded. Ah, that was a relief. "My number," he repeated after her.

"Yes, sir. Your number. The one you picked."

"Ah. Er. Ha. That's funny. I don't even remember right off. It was just some numbers. I won and then, a'course, my ticket was stolen away from me…." His voice dribbled into awkward silence.

Lisa whirled back to Tom. "And Dr. Bennington, the number you picked?"

Tom donned his most trustworthy, professorial expression and recited, "7-9-16-34-57-8. It's a combination of my birthday, my mother's birthday, and the age a young friend of mine wishes he were."

The sound the crowd made was a satisfying combination of AhHaaa, Ohhhh, and Oooooh in the rush of fifty voices. It was the oooh-aaah of wind whooshing lonely in high branches. Or maybe a dying breeze abandoning the sails of Lester's crummy little boat.

Lester got the message. He deflated. He sank. He edged toward the curb, mumbling words like, "Never mind. I shoulda known. A regular guy can't get a fair shake in this world. What with the media always on the side of rich people." And so on.

"Rich people with good teeth," I could have added if I'd felt less charitable. But Lester was fading clean away. Disappearing from some major trouble he was about to be in. I wondered how his attorney was doing. I glanced around but the multitudes were dissipating and D.B. was still nowhere in view.

And that's exactly the way I like it.

And that was it. Lester had thereby withdrawn not only his claim, but also his person. Lisa and I exchanged glances of gratitude, redemption, and triumph. She climbed back into the van and it vanished, followed in short order by the stragglers and the rest of the media. After about ten minutes of smiles and "no comment," we were standing alone on an empty sidewalk, soaking up the silence and the relief.

Everybody was now as accounted for as they would ever be. Almost.

Two minutes after that, Skip screeched up in his SUV.

He was fuming of course.

Someone at GG&B had gotten into his admin's computer and changed the address of the lottery. When Skip had entered the address into his navigation system, as was his routine, it'd directed him straight to the Nature Center in the Rocky River Reservation of the Cleveland Metro Parks. By the time he'd wakened up from his customary fog of driving and thinking about the law and realized where he was headed, he was way late. And burning mad. And, for some odd reason, blaming D.B.

After I gave him the story of Lisa-from-16 and her assault on Lester The Gross and how it all had worked out aces for us, even without him, he calmed down. He wanted to go after D.B., of course, and see that he was besmirched at GG&B by the suggestion of indiscretion, but I encouraged him to let it ride.

I was bound to be sorry one day, but the idea of D.B. jobless and at loose ends was scarier to me than it was entertaining. I'd gotten more practical with my desires for revenge. Besides, none of us had ever seen him around Lester at all.

Tom agreed, "All's well that ends—" The memory of our first stormy breakfast at the Marriott seized us both, and we blurted, in unison, "with only one dead guy!" Laughing like idiots.

Chapter Sixty-one

Monday, September 7

We showed up at Elaine Robbins's house on Monday morning at nine a.m. on the dot, all full of confidence, to tell Rune he was coming to live with us forever as soon as we could arrange it. We understood that there would be a barrel of red tape to work through, but we were up to the challenge and we could be patient. We knew that the system didn't favor mixing up kids of one race with parents of another, but there was a lot of precedent for overriding that when circumstances called for it.

We knew Rune. He loved Tom. Tom loved him. I loved them both. Tom and I would get married and we'd be a legal, traditional family unit the way the system likes things tidied up. We had the means to raise him and we'd give him the education—and the love—he deserved. That moment at the Rock Hall before everything went south kept coming back to me. The Family Us. Supper around the table. A room with Michael posters and a nice fuzzy bear for a kid who was no doubt way too grown up for it. I needed that damn bear and his boy. They would heal my heart of a raft of tired old sorrows.

It might take some time to finalize it all and make it official, but we expected to walk out of the foster home with our boy in tow. At least for today and after that for always. Tom had a baseball mitt and a ball, although we agreed that if anyone was having a catch with the kid, it would have to be me. It turns out there's, no kidding, a National Beep Baseball Association and I thought Tom was destined to be a natural. But we didn't have the beeping ball today. We were laughing about that. Happy.

There was a Ford Explorer with Pennsylvania plates in the drive. When we came into the living room, Rune was sitting on the couch with a boy who could have been his twin. Their close-cropped dark heads were bent over a comic book they were sharing as if they'd been reading side by side on couches for years. There was a woman there, too. Renata Davis's sister, Iona. Family. Out of touch for years. But authentic. And alerted to the knowledge of Renata's death and Rune's situation by news coverage of the Lester nonsense.

Rune didn't need us to be his family. He had one already. Iona and Damon, the one of her four sons who was Rune's age, had come to take him home.

She was nice enough. Kind to us. And very, very grateful for all we'd done for Rune, but firm. A steady, uncompromising woman who knew what she had the rights to and what she was going to do about it. She saw the mitt and the crushing disappointment we couldn't hide, and she was as sorry as she could be, and gentle about her insistence, but she knew her mind and in her mind her responsibility was clear.

What Tom couldn't see he could feel in my grip on his hand and hear in the introductions. Iona, calm and straightforward. Rune excited to introduce his cousin Damon to his friend Tom, who was way rich and who owed him a hundred bucks.

It was all pleasant, fast, and final. Like being run over by a Good Humor truck. We delivered the mitt and ball. We promised to come to Pittsburgh to visit Rune and meet his Uncle Clarence and his three other cousins.

We said we'd bring his money, and his Aunt Iona could put it in the bank for him. That last part wasn't great news, but Rune was so distracted and jazzed up about going home to stay with

Damon, that it didn't register much. Another five minutes for exchanging phone numbers and e-mail addresses and we were out the door with our composures intact. Almost.

"Wait."

Tom took a deep breath. "Stop. There's something I need to say, Rune."

And Rune, who I guess had been paying more attention than I thought, answered, "What, Tom?"

If I hadn't already been in love with Tom Bennington for nearly three full weeks, that moment would have tipped me over.

I watched him get a grip on himself. I could see his determination to say what he had to say without hurting Rune or making trouble with Iona. He moved toward the boy, navigating the space between them with that magical certainty, and crouched down, close. I knew he would sense the warmth coming off Rune's skin, his little boy sweetness. This son he now knew he wasn't going to have.

But Tom's voice was calm and warm, no trace of the tears I was pushing back. "Rune, I need to make sure you know something about me. I don't have many close friends. Friends I'd do anything for."

Anything.

Kid, you have no idea, I thought, clenching every muscle in my chest to trap a sob that was fighting to get out. I could see Rune lying again on that wooden box, asleep in the light, and Tom standing up to death in the dark. Ready to sacrifice every single thing for one small boy.

"You're someone special to me, Rune. You and I are that kind of friends. I'm so happy for you. You're going to live with Iona and Clarence and Damon and—" He actually managed a smile "three more brothers. A family. Your own family. That's amazing. And lucky."

Rune nodded, a tiny bob of his head. His face was solemn now, his eyes fixed on Tom. I hoped Tom was feeling everything that I could see.

"Rune, you're family to me, too." He laid his hand against his chest. There was the slightest tremor in those beautiful fingers. "You're in here. For good. For always. I will always be listening for you. If you ever need me, for anything. Just to talk. Maybe come for a visit. Anything. At all. Iona has my number. Just call. Anytime. I'd like that. I hope you'll e-mail me, too. Sometimes—" His voice failed him at last.

Rune was staring at Tom now, his own fist pressed hard against the new tee-shirt Iona had brought. "Tom? Are you crying?"

Tom cleared his throat. "Yes, Rune. I sure am. I'm happy for you, but I'm still sad for me and Allie. We'll miss you. Until we see you next time."

With that, Tom reached out and pulled Rune tight against his heart and the sob I'd been hanging onto broke through my last defenses. Behind me, someone—Iona, I thought—blew her nose. Rune clung to Tom for another moment and then rubbed his face against the front of Tom's shirt.

"Okay, Tom. I promise I won't forget. Can I really come to visit you? Will Allie be there, too?"

"Yes. Really. I hope it'll be soon. And about that last thing? God, I sure hope so."

I sobbed some more, feeling a small scrap better.

Another couple of minutes and we were standing by our rented car.

Two again.

The sorrow Tom had been holding in was all over him now. He'd collapsed against the car door, his shoulders slumped, his arms crossed across his heart. I was afraid to touch him. Afraid he might break.

"I'm so sorry, Tom. I'm sorry for both of us."

I was struggling to banish from my memory that moment over lunch at the Rock Hall. All the moments when we were both risking everything to get Rune back. This was not fair. It hurt too much. I took a deep breath, not wanting to let him hear how close I was to losing it all the way down.

"Iona seems like a very good person."

He wiped his hand across his face. "Tell me what she looks like."

"How about you tell me?"

He sighed and cleared his throat. "Okay. Very lovely. Very brown. Like strong coffee. Five-four. About one-fifty, to be polite. Big flowers on her dress, sensible shoes. Hair like your fourth grade teacher. Nice eyes. Nice smile. Smart. Someone you'd trust with a kid you cared a lot about. Loved." His voice cracked again.

"Remarkable," I managed to choke out. "Everything but the dress. How do you do that?" And then because I was desperate to make him smile, "Or have you been faking blindness so you could see me naked?"

I didn't get my smile, but the corner of his mouth twitched a sad little bit. "It worked, didn't it?"

"Don't get too thrilled with yourself. I knew it all along. But Tom…?"

He'd slipped back under the sorrow of everything we'd lost. "What?"

"Look at it this way. If his aunt and uncle are now his mom and dad, Rune will be short one aunt and one uncle.

"You and me, I suppose."

"Iona promised we could visit whenever we wanted. Think about it, Tom. She's got a houseful.

Rune makes five boys. Plus a husband and a career. Once she gets to know us better, she'll be glad to share him. For weeks at a time, I bet. Whole summers maybe. He loves you, Tom. He hasn't forgotten that. You know he'll want to spend time with us. He's already thinking about it. You can help with expenses. For all of them. When Rune comes home from college it'll be you he wants to visit, too. It'll all work out. You'll see."

"Would you stop making painful references to my disability?"

"You're way too sensitive," I kissed his smooth, manly cheek, trying to coax that dimple out of hiding. "I think we need to go practice your Braille."

Chapter Sixty-two

I drove us back to the old neighborhood, taking the long way around but not too paranoid about who was behind us. We picked up Margo and took her out to lunch at The Flying Fig over by West 25th. They've got some tempura green beans there you'd rob your grandma for. Anyway, Margo was sure she would.

We didn't talk about Rune. Margo had taken one look at the two of us and seized command of the conversation. At her insistence, we reviewed our health-and-well-being preservation plan, which consisted for the most part of being heads-up and maybe traveling for a while until things died down some more. After The Lester Episode, Tom had thrown in the towel and taken a one-semester leave from teaching.

On the bright side, there was considerable evidence in recent news coverage that trying to steal Tom's millions got people dead. In quantity.

Or at the very least, discredited and embarrassed, to about the tenth power. So maybe they'd all wise up and leave us alone. I was trying to bank on that.

We had one police guy on our side, at least. More or less.

Valerio and I had another conversation after he got out of the Clinic. The Renata Mystery was most likely unsolvable now, but her earthly remains were available for a service if we wanted one. We would, I knew. Closure for Rune. Closure for everybody. For us, especially, now when we needed to be the Cleveland branch of the Davis family.

Valerio had a good word for me, too. I hardly knew how to deal with that.

"Don't take this as encouragement."

"What? Don't take what?"

"What I'm about to say.

"Oh, Tony, I would never take anything you say as encouragement."

The patented Valerio snort. "I want you to stop blaming yourself for the sh—the stuff that happened. You and Tom. It's a waste of energy. Take my word for it. There's always plenty of blame to go around. You need to be responsible as best you can and then forgive yourself for whatever's left over. You were an idiot. No doubt. But not as bad as I would have figured.

"Here's your last CSI lesson, girl. In the real

world, when all's said and done—or not done—
there are almost never any high fives. You did okay.
For a wannabee. Quit while you're ahead."

On a more comforting note from law
enforcement, I'd had a call from Otis Johnson,
my parking garage hero. In spite of getting feeble
prayer assistance from me, he was recovering from
his quadruple bypass. I assured him he could always
count on Tom for whatever he needed.

After the pleasantries, he had a question for
me. "Ms. Harper, you and the mister—the doctor.
You all are going to need a bodyguard, right?"

"Allie. Call me Allie, Otis. A bodyguard? We
hadn't given that any serious thought. I suppose
we might. Maybe."

"No maybes. You all are going to need a
bodyguard. And I was wondering if I could be it?
They say I'm going to be fine. Good as new. Better.
As soon as I recover from the surgery. I'm already
workin' out a little.

"I don't want to go back to the Arco. For a lot
of reasons. But I'd make you an excellent bodyguard. Didn't I already save your life once?"

He had me there. "Yes, indeed, Otis, you
already did. Let me talk to Tom. We'll figure this
out. Keep getting better and I'll talk to you soon."

A bodyguard sounded awful. A bodyguard
who was Otis didn't sound half bad.

We were on the move again. It was too soon for either of us to go home. There was still considerable straightening up to be done at my house. Ditto for his house. The Marriott and the Wyndham had been fine. The Price Motel had been serviceable. But now that our ship had docked at last, we deserved the priciest. At least once.

Chapter Sixty-three

After we dropped Margo off, I drove us straight on downtown to The Ritz-Carlton, Cleveland, where they checked us, very deferentially, into the actual Presidential Suite in spite of our obvious lack of luggage and our casual attire. They've come a long way at that hotel since they refused to serve Tom Hanks because he was wearing jeans. I didn't even have to reassure them that we didn't plan to be wearing any of our current attire very long anyhow.

I'd never had full access to over-the-top extreme luxury before, so I was impressed by the Jacuzzi, the champagne, the floating rose petals. However, I had had considerable access to extreme Tom, so the suite's formidable amenities were not the most anticipated or impressive aspect of my evening. All in all, The Ritz-Carlton, Cleveland, did not disappoint.

Later, much later, after we'd had another rose petal bath—being careful not to wet my small bandage or drown anybody—and the whole bottle of champagne with a boatload of lovely room service food, we were sprawled on the king-sized bed—which didn't seem to have its own special name—wearing our fluffy complementary robes and talking about our future. I told Tom how I'd had my little epiphany that terrible Diana night at the Wyndham. How I'd seen that his work meshed with what he wanted in his life.

But then I got quiet and asked myself what it was that I, Alice-Jane-Allie-Harper, wanted in my life. Besides more Tom and as much Rune as we could get.

There it was. My question again.

I was embedded in the cushiness of R. Carlton, The Mattress, as I'd decided to refer to it, lying so still I could hear my heart, bumping away. *Alive. Alive. Alive.* My little heart. I'd scared its pants off about one hundred times in the past three weeks. Overdosed it on pure adrenalin, utter stupidity, and the threat of extinction. So why did it feel all bright and bouncy?

Because, Allie, I explained to myself, *you're not the lost girl you were. You got your self-respect back. Your guts and your brains. You survived. You're entitled to feel good about it.*

I grinned, visualizing myself jamming an elbow into Lester's fat belly, dousing us both in

Eau de Too Much. *And another thing, Allie girl,* I said to me, *you were never cut out to be a part-time librarian. That was your lick-your-wounds-and-hide interlude. That crap is over.* "No disrespect, Library."

Tom stirred. "Huh?"

I realized I'd spoken that "No disrespect" bit out loud.

"Nothing. I was thinking."

He'd been quiet for so long, eyes closed, I'd thought the champagne might have waylaid him. But it hadn't.

"Me, too. I'm thinking I'm not the same guy, Allie. The guy who had made himself a nice, safe path through the world. That narrow path was all the independence he could imagine. He was naïve. He'd never spent his last night on Earth with the woman he loved." A sly smile. "A far as that goes, he'd never spent his first night of being incredibly wealthy with a sexy young thing he picked up in a crosswalk."

I rolled over and placed my hand on his chest, "That was me. I was attracted by the smell of money. Or maybe it was the soap."

He curled his hand over mine, serious again. "That poor, stupid guy. He had everything figured out. He was getting along okay, Allie. But I think he may be gone now. He might even be dead. This guy…" he tapped our joined hands on his chest.

"This guy here is prepared to explore all kinds of different options. With the woman he loves."

"Me again."

"You again." He sighed. "The money still isn't a big deal to me, Allie. If it were gone tomorrow, I'd be fine. We'd be fine. Except for your credit rating, of course. And the bill to get us out of here. But in some ways, Bob was justified in being angry. The money is an extraordinary gift. I was wrong to turn my back on the good it could do."

Carpe this opening, Allie.

"Well, you know what could be interesting? A way we could do some good? Help some people? I've been thinking. Maybe you and I could be the—um—T&A Detective Agency."

He looked slightly nonplussed. "I'm not sure what that would be, but may I suggest we put your initial first? In any case."

"That's thoughtful of you. Thanks…"

Oh! Right.

"But seriously. I always thought I'd make a very good P.I. Not all by myself. At least at first. But with both of us, Tom & Allie—or Allie & Tom—solving mysteries, fighting crime, but mostly helping people find things and answer their questions." I didn't want to press my luck too far. "From a safe distance and using your money. Judiciously, of course. And having Otis on the payroll for bodyguarding and professional expertise. And Valerio around to yell at me, of course. With maybe Margo for…swearing and pasta. With your secret sixth sense and my 20/20 vision and sex appeal? We'd make a great duo. Trio. Team. Could we do that, do you think? Someday?"

He pulled me closer and nuzzled the very rose-petally spot behind my ear. "Alice Jane. Honey." He murmured in his best, sexiest, Southern drawl, "We're crazy rich. We can do anything we want."

"Perfect," I murmured back, "that's what I like to hear. Let's try some of that anything. Right now. Before your coupon expires."

To see more Poisoned Pen Press titles:

Visit our website: poisonedpenpress.com/

Request a digital catalog:
info@poisonedpenpress.com

CPSIA information can be obtained
at www.ICGtesting.com
Printed in the USA
BVOW03s2303070417
480706BV00002B/3/P

9 781464 207877